# VILLAGE BOOKS

## BY CRAIG MCLAY

Editorial Assistance: Jennifer Harris (www.lucidpulp.com)
Cover Design: Carl Graves (extendedimagery.com)
Layout and Back Design: Cheryl Perez (yourepublished.com)

Edition: January 2014

ISBN: 978-0-9879478-4-0 (Trade Paperback Edition)

*FOR CHRISTINE, SAM AND BEN*

# -1-

I love bookstores. I suppose that's part of the reason I've worked as an assistant manager in one for three years.

First of all, they're quiet. I'm not sure why a proximity to books makes people whisper, but it does. Second, you have almost all the knowledge and art ever created in the history of human existence packed in there with you. Walk down the aisles and you can hear it calling down through the centuries: Homer, Shakespeare, Cervantes, Proust, Dickens, Orwell, Nabokov, Mailer, Wallace. They're all here. Reach out your hand and you can grab the sum total of their life's accomplishments in a single motion. Third, you aren't accosted by five salespeople within 30 seconds of stepping in the door the way you are in an electronics store. Most retailers completely fail to understand that no one wants to be mobbed like that. It's the reason so many people go to car dealerships on Sunday.

Village Books is about 3,000 square feet on two floors. I'm the Zone 1 manager, which means my domain covers fiction, history, science, art, architecture, travel and drama – pretty much the entire ground floor. Upstairs you'll find Zone 2, which is made up of lifestyles, business, self-help and kid's books.

Lifestyles and business may seem like odd shelf-fellows, but both are completely guru-driven. Whether it's dieting or investing, people display an almost religious reverence for the ramblings of almost any idiot with a daytime talk show, even if said idiot is fat or broke (or both). It's human nature. Many of us don't like to do our own thinking when someone else is willing to do it for us. Whether we want to admit it or not, most of us would much rather fail as part of a large group than be separated from the crowd, even if the rest of the crowd think Enron stock looks like a good buy.

Kid's books is more like what the army euphemistically calls a "forward action area." Every day, parents drop their kids off (in direct violation of the sign advising them not to leave their offspring unattended, I might add) in the storytime nook, where they immediately set to work destroying the craft area, ripping books off shelves and attacking the miniature wooden railway set like an F5 tornado with a thousand opposable thumbs.

I am extremely glad to not be permanently responsible for those areas, although I have been unofficially looking after them for the last few months since the regular manager, Mischa, went on indefinite mat leave.

Mischa recently gave birth to a five-and-a-half-pound baby girl she named Natasha. It should be noted that Natasha bears absolutely no resemblance to Mischa's German husband, Helmut, and quite a lot of resemblance to the sales rep for Hakamoto Books, a short Nigerian fellow by the name of Simon, who dropped by the store to check on sales far more often than was necessary given our limited inventory of Japanese erotica. It's common knowledge that Mischa has left Helmut, taken her daughter back to Estonia and has no plans to return. Simon's whereabouts are currently unknown. He hasn't checked on sales for almost a year.

That's the other thing about bookstores: things may appear quiet on the surface, but passions run high. When you're surrounded by the innermost thoughts of some of the world's greatest minds and greatest perverts (often one and the same), it can have a tangible effect on the brain. Squeeze twenty or so full- and part-time neurotics into a space like this over time and strange things happen.

Take Mischa, for example. She and Helmut met through an online service designed to hook ugly, middle-aged North American male citizens up with young, attractive women from former Warsaw Pact nations who were just a few points shy of qualifying for landed immigrant status. Helmut was also an active participant in a swinger's club, and so in addition to becoming a citizen, Mischa was also signed up for membership in Erotique, a dumpy grey block building with no windows out near the airport. I suppose you could consider it a fitness club for genitals. We found out about this when Mischa had one slivovitz too many at last year's Christmas party and "accidentally" let it slip that some of the meetings were podcast.

Tracking this down to watch it for reasons that had absolutely nothing to do with an interest in film, we learned that Mischa has a tattoo of the northern hemisphere on her left breast and the southern one on her right. My friend Sebastian wryly observed that Scott would not have gotten lost on the way to the pole, particularly in cold weather. I was happy when I heard that Mischa had left, not because we didn't get along, but because I couldn't see her after that without hearing the old Sunday school song "He's Got The Whole World In His Hands."

The store manager is Dante Andolini. He's in his mid-thirties and completely under the thumb of his mother, an enormous woman from Calabria named Lucretia, whom he refers to as Beelzebub. Dante lost his right eyebrow and has only partial use of his right hand after a fireworks accident when he was twelve. He is self-conscious about this and tends to angle himself to the left when talking to people. This takes some getting used to. The first few times we talked, I thought he was talking to an invisible person standing next to me.

Dante is a hypochondriac. Actually, he's a hypochondriac because of his mother. Well, to be completely accurate, he's a hypochondriac because he's terrified his mother will find out that he's gay. Lucretia, being a staunch papist, stubbornly refuses to acknowledge even the possibility of her son's orientation and clings to the notion that he simply hasn't met the right woman yet as firmly as gravity clings to physics. Since she believes he's too incompetent to be entrusted with choosing the mother of her grandchildren on his own, Lucretia has taken this responsibility on herself, going so far as to set up profiles for him on several online dating sites. She insisted on using a pencil to fill in the missing eyebrow and provided a description that, despite its grammatical shortcomings, makes her son sound like the most powerful, charismatic and potent Italian male since Silvio Berlusconi.

Lucretia sifts the candidates and handles all communication to the point of arranging the first meeting, at which point she will advise her hapless son of where and when to show up. In order to get out of these encounters, Dante has been forced to invent a series of horrible-sounding, but, in reality, innocuous diseases that have supposedly struck him down only hours before his face-to-face with Angelica or Natalia or Cristina or whomever it is this week.

In the beginning, these conditions were easy to come up with – a flu would suffice – but as time has marched on, it has forced Dante to become more creative with his diagnostic abilities. This has compelled him to turn to professional resources like Web MD and the Mayo Clinic online. Reading so many descriptions of all the horrible, incapacitating things that can befall the average human body has understandably warped his mind, and he has started to believe that he really has some of these diseases.

I have been bugging Dante to hurry up and hire a new Zone 2 manager for ages now. It's October, which means we're starting to ramp up our inventory for the holidays. Traffic is increasing and I'm tired of being one of only three people with a key, Dante and our head cashier, Mina, being the others. Being a keyholder means I have to either open or close at least every other day and the hours are starting to get to me.

This is exacerbated by the fact that Mina is frequently sick, which means I get called in a lot at the last minute, often when I've been up late after closing the night before. I especially don't appreciate this if I spent much of the previous night at Falstaff's for a well-earned pint or three after kicking the last of the browsing laggards back out onto the sidewalk. It's time Dante stopped stalling and got a replacement. If he doesn't, I will ask his mother to do it for him.

I am on my way back to the tiny manager's office to broach this subject when I almost trip over Ebeneezer Chipping kneeling in front of the Coles Notes. Ebeneezer is a retired school teacher and widower who works part-time evenings. He is crotchety in the extreme, but has more of what we in the business call "product knowledge" than the rest of the store put together. Everyone else in the store is terrified of him and refers to him as "sir." Being, at least nominally, his boss, I call him "Mr C."

The only person who does not refer to him with deference is Fermina Marquez, the Spanish émigré who runs Café Olé, the coffee shop next door. She calls him "Ebby." I think he has a minor crush on her, but he would never in a million years admit to such a thing and I would never in a million years ask.

His hatred for Coles Notes, however, is undisguised and legendary. More than a few times, I've caught him trying to return the entire section or shrink the shelf space down to non-existence.

"Evening Mr. C. Reorganizing the Coles Notes, are you?"

He acknowledges me with barely a grunt. "Worst thing to happen to literature since the television. Damn you, Logie Baird."

A voice pipes up from behind me. "But sir, what about Zworykin?"

I turn around to see the dreadlocked girth of Aldous Swinghammer. Aldous is a 20-something philosophy dropout who also works part-time evenings and some days. Despite the fact that he is as white as Dracula and comes from a distinguished family of Swiss industrialists, Aldous actively cultivates the look of a Jamaican surf bum: dreads, tie-dyed shirt and open-toed sandals. His look is based on the assumption that people frequently mistake eccentricity for genius. Aldous desperately wants to be thought of as a genius. It is his stated intent to write the first great philosophical treatise of the 21$^{st}$ century.

"A plague on both their houses," Ebeneezer mutters. "Now away with you and your Bolshevik demagoguery."

Aldous, however, can rarely be dismissed that easily. He is incapable of resisting the urge to take any subject of which he believes he has expansive knowledge (which is all of them) and then somehow relating it back to himself.

"Television is central to my thesis," he says. This is despite the fact that since he was asked to leave university in the middle of first year under mysterious circumstances, he didn't actually get to *write* a thesis. "I believe that all human endeavour springs from the realization that seven billion people have no idea you exist. Television and the internet only amplify this realization. I call it Swinghammer's Axiom."

Ebeneezer finishes reducing the linear footage of the study guides by half and gets to his feet. "Swinghammer, you dolt. An axiom is a principle that requires no proof. Surely you don't think you're going to stun what's left of the thinking world with this doggerel when you yourself cannot tell the difference between an axiom and an aphorism?"

Aldous smiles in a way that he thinks is condescending. It's a way he employs frequently and that is meant to imply "you simply don't understand what I'm talking about." In reality, he just looks vacant. I will not be at all surprised to one day read that he has been clubbed to death during a peasant uprising in some dirtbowl banana republic.

"You see, sir, you understand what I'm trying to say!" he says. Having once again failed to intellectually shock and awe, he will settle for isolationist camaraderie. "You understand the challenge implicit in trying to make the common man understand. That's why I'm here. I want to understand him so he can understand me."

Ebeneezer also smiles, but his is much more withering. "My boy, the only reason you are here is because you spent more time in school ingesting proscribed substances than Kant. Allow me to save you some time. All you will learn of the common man here is that he is ignorant, lazy, petty, dull-minded and easily led. I'm sure that when you do get around to publishing your magnum opus that this latest generation of buffoons will no doubt hail you as the greatest thinker and intellectual since Dr. Phil, but I'm afraid that your theory, no matter how penetratingly trenchant it may be in its understanding of the human condition, will be forced on to the back pages by glossy photos of Paris Hilton's vagina and Bradley Pitt's teeth."

Aldous shrugs and asks me what I'd like him to do. I tell him to start clearing out the back category fiction to make room for the new holiday stock that is approaching us as silently and implacably as a tsunami. If we don't make space for it, we will literally be drowning in books in a matter of weeks. Aldous nods and wanders off to get started. I wouldn't dare tell Ebeneezer what to do. He's been here longer than I have and will no doubt spend another fruitless evening trying to talk middle class urban professional moms into buying Hemingway or Mencken instead of Dan Brown, Janet Evanovich, some courageous story of survival in the face of genital mutilation, or whatever the hell else Oprah has told them to buy this month. It is a lonely and unglamorous crusade, but he wages it with pride.

I know how he feels. Yesterday I was dismayed to see that almost all of Harlan Ellison's work had been classified BACKE. Our stock is divided into "FRONT" and "BACK", with the front being the new books and the back being the old ones. These are in turn subclassified from A to E, with A being the newer or more in-demand titles and the Es less so. The next stop after BACKE is OP, which means out of print. OP means we can no longer return it to the publisher.

As a matter of policy, we're supposed to return a title as soon as it flips to BACKE. I have refused to do this for many titles just as a matter of principle, but it does create a space issue as new books are coming in all the time and there's only so much shelf space. I don't care. I will return a million FRONTA Danielle Steeles or Nicholas Sparks before I send back a single Patrick O'Brian or Richard Ford.

I don't want to sound like a snob, because I'm not. Not everything can be *Ulysses* (a book I only got 100 pages into before packing it in *twice*) nor should it be. I have nothing against chicklit. Publishers love it because women are, by and large, the only people who read anymore. Most of the men I know, including some of the ones who work here, don't read anything more in a week than the cooking instructions on a microwave lasagne. Women are surpassing us in university admissions and will, I hope, shortly be doing likewise in executive roles and compensation. Patriarchy is dying and, unlike those who want to beat each other senseless in basements or bang drums in the forest, I say good riddance. If putting more women in charge reduces our chances of blowing ourselves up or cooking the planet, then count me in favour, Margaret Thatcher notwithstanding.

This is exactly what is running through my mind when I round the corner and encounter, all hyperbole aside, the most remarkable woman I've ever met.

She's standing in front of the drama section and turns towards me in a swirl of red hair, smiles and asks: "Is this all the Mamet you have?"

I am so stunned that I blurt the first thing that comes into my mind: "Marry me!"

She laughs and holds up her left hand. On the third finger is, the angry caveman part of me must grudgingly admit, a ring with a diamond large enough to cap a city-destroying laser in a 1960s spy movie.

"Sorry," she says. "Somebody else beat you to it." She gestures towards the shelf. "I see *Oleanna*, but where's *Speed The Plow*? Or *Sexual Perversity in Chicago*? My drama group was looking to do one of them."

"You're an actress?"

She strikes a pseudo pose. "What, you don't recognize me?"

I realize that I am grinning like a moron, but can't seem to stop myself. This happens to me when I encounter beautiful, charming women. The last time it happened was when I interviewed a former model for a part-time cashier position a year ago. She actually turned out to be good at the job, but I'll be the first to admit that it was not the reason she was hired. We men really are shallow bastards.

"Clearly, I need to get out to the theatre a lot more than I do," I say, sticking out my hand and introducing myself.

"Leah," she says, shaking my hand with exaggerated firmness, a way designed to communicate that this is all extremely formal and not awkward in the least, *ha ha*. "It's an all-women's group, so *Oleanna* would be interesting, but we need something with more speaking parts." She slides the thin volume back onto the shelf. "Maybe something in the public domain. We don't have a lot of money. Any suggestions?"

I purse my lips and try to look thoughtful, but the truth is, I don't know much about theatre and consider myself lucky if I can tell Beckett from Brecht. "Ummm…"

"The director's pretty pretentious. She's talking about doing the *Oresteia*, but I can't say Clytemnestra without laughing." She snorts. "See? So I'm looking for something else." She makes a face and checks her watch, which I notice she keeps on the underside of her wrist. I've tried wearing mine that way so that I don't keep scratching the face when shelving books, but I just can't seem to get into the habit of strapping it on like that. It must be genetic. "And that being the time, I have to go. Thanks for your help, though. I'm sure we'll be seeing each other again soon."

She says this last part like she actually means it. This gives me a tiny and entirely unfounded sense of hope until I remember that she's an actress. If being an actress is about making people like you, then she can count me as a fan, but now she's gone and I'll most likely never see her again. Ah well. One of the great truths of being male, and the trickiest one to come to terms with, is that you will encounter far more attractive women in a day than you will ever be able to date, even if you're Hugh Hefner in his prime and it's sort of a job requirement.

This is different, though. I've never been hit by a thunderbolt like that before. Mild electric shocks, yes. The kind you get from trying to get a better grip on a plug when pulling it out at an awkward angle. But never the tree-splintering explosion that leaves you sniffing ozone and charred hair before you fall on your face with a confused and oddly serene expression.

I want to run after her, but what's the point? She's already engaged. Plus she'd think I was some weirdo stalker creep, and if the engagement ever does fall through and I do happen to run into her again, I want her to remember me as the charming and slightly befuddled bookstore guy who proposed marriage and not, say, Travis Bickle. That way, I'd be able to use my social incompetence as an ice breaker, engage her in my best version of witty banter, talk her into coming out for coffee, then the movies, then dinner, and finally propose marriage properly. Possibly all on the same evening.

Not that this is ever going to happen. I will, of course, likely never see this woman again.

Feeling both brighter and sadder at the same time, I turn around and head for the manager's office, which at the moment contains the only man in the store actively looking for ways to avoid dates.

"Hey Dante. How you feeling?"

Dante is, as usual, parked in front of the computer. "Hey, which do you think sounds worse? Compartmental Hydrodysphasia or Tenticular Gangrenospermaphore?"

I wince. "Ugh, the second one. By a wide margin. What is it? Actually, you know what? Don't tell me. I'd rather not know."

One of the most irritating things about Dante aside from the hypochondria is that, missing eyebrow aside, he is an inordinately handsome man. He looks like a Latin version of George Clooney. Like a true Italian, he also dresses in a way that makes the rest of us look like a

Nascar pit crew. Women routinely throw themselves at him with a vigour that would embarrass a recently paroled felon. It's one of the reasons that he rarely leaves the office.

"So when are you gonna drag yourself away from the Mayo Clinic for long enough to hire us a Zone 2 manager?"

"I did," he says, nodding proudly.

My relief is guarded. Dante has a habit of saying he has already done things that he plans to get around to before he dies. Maybe.

"You did?"

"She just left."

I'm confused. "What, today?"

"No, like two minutes ago. Her name's Leah. Leah Dashwood. She starts Monday. You'll be doing her training."

I admit that it takes my brain longer than it should to make the connection. "Huh?"

"Yeah, she's trying to be an actress or something, but she's worked in a bookstore before. Shouldn't take her long to figure out how we operate."

Oh dear.

Everyone should work in retail at least once in their lives. Consider it a form of national service.

Being a relatively small operation, we don't have a policy of allowing customers to get away with whatever they want for problems that cost less than $50. For example, you can't call our head cashier a lying whore because your special order of Michael Bublé-inspired cross stitch patterns has been discontinued and is no longer available (happened). You can't try to return a year-old edition of *Vogue* magazine from which you have cut out every photo of a woman in a dress because a small voice in your head tells you these images are blasphemous (happened). And you can't spread out the *International Herald Tribune*, your coffee, your egg and cheese bagel and your overcoat on the cash desk because it happens to be the only flat surface available (happened).

We don't have a national brand identity or unlimited HR budget, so we don't force our staff to take soul-destroying customer-appreciation courses. If you come into the store and are deliberately rude to the staff, threaten to call the Better Business Bureau or the cops, or are destructive to the merchandise, I am going to respond based mostly on how I feel at the time.

And mostly that's tired.

I am tired of watching the daily parade of humanity regularly sink to meet my lowest expectations. The flipside of requiring everyone to work in retail is that there is a limit to how long you can work here before you start to view every human encounter as an irritation.

I've been here for three years now and I believe I have reached that point. If I stay here much longer, I will develop a pathological and possibly irreversible hatred of all humanity. I will turn into Ebeneezer. The alternative is to turn into somebody like "Mother" Teresa Barker, who has been working in kid's books practically since the store first opened its doors almost thirty years ago. She's nice, but it's a vaguely glassy-eyed and vacant sort of niceness. It's like she's been coated in a thick shellac that's shiny and keeps the cranky thoughts from penetrating, but also cuts off all oxygen to her brain.

She's a member of a fringe sect called the "Assembly of the Chosen." They go door-to-door, believe that they should sign over all their worldly possessions to the church and that they will all one day move to a divinely-selected hilltop somewhere in the Muskokas where they will prepare for the great vacuuming up of the preferenti. Trying to make her angry is like trying to find a corner on a bowling ball. The closest to mad I've ever seen her was in my second week, when she found out I was an atheist and we got into an argument about irreducible complexity. Her smile never vanished, but her jaw muscles bulged like the biceps on an ultimate fighter.

"But creation requires a creator!" she said in a shrill voice. "Like that shelf! It didn't just organize itself that way!"

"Not if they're created by natural forces," I pointed out. "Like the Grand Canyon. Or the universe. God didn't re-alphabetize the books on that shelf. Aldous did. God, if he existed, probably wouldn't have made as many mistakes between N and T."

She told me that she was very sorry that I thought that way and would pray for me anyway. We have maintained a professional détente since then, although I have caught her on a few occasions trying to hide some of the more risqué art and photography books in receiving. One of the reasons that

I can't get excited about the concept of an afterlife is the knowledge that I would have to spend it with people like Mother Teresa.

The only reason I mention difficult customers is because I have one in front of me now. It's Saturday night and the store is busy. We get a fair amount of walk-in traffic courtesy of the Prestige, which is the small rep theatre down the street. It usually shows limited-release stuff, which tends to generate a younger, artsy crowd made up mostly of students and hipster 30-somethings with no kids. Tonight, however, it's recycling the summer's big 3D animation hit involving talking animals, which I assume they have to do sometimes to make up revenue not generated by Belgian documentaries about dung beetles. As a result, we have more of what you might call a general audience milling about. It consists mostly of those too cheap to fork over the extra four bucks at the big theatre or too technologically impaired to download the thing illegally.

At first glance, this complainer doesn't look like the usual species of card-carrying jerk. They tend to be middle-aged men, most often single or newly-divorced. Some work menial jobs and others are arrogant, high-level professionals. The former look for every opportunity to exercise what power they don't have over someone they perceive as being in a subservient role and the latter just automatically view everyone as lessers.

I would guess she's in her early 20s. She's thin, with stringy blonde hair tied in a ponytail that shoots straight up from the top of her head like a pineapple. I notice she has one hand on the counter, which is not a good sign. People often do that to give themselves a physical anchor from which to spout off, like a priest at a pulpit or a politician at a lectern. There's a guy standing slightly off on her right. Based on the embarrassed look on his face and the physical distance he's trying to put between them, I'm guessing he's a boyfriend who has been dragged into this consumer showdown against his will and will therefore not be a factor in whatever's about to happen.

I have been called up here by my best friend, Sebastian Donleavy. Sebastian and I started on the same day, me as a full-time fill-in manager and Sebastian as a part-timer in the evenings while he ostensibly finished his English degree during the day. Sebastian, however, enjoys university life far too much to ever want to do anything quite as silly as graduate, and has been chugging along at the rate of one course per semester for some time now. He's a part-time everything: writer, painter, musician, actor, student. The only things he pursues on a full-time basis are women and drinking. His parents divorced two years ago and his mother has been loathe to throw him out of the house despite his procrastinations in order to avoid further destabilising life for his younger brothers, who are nine and seven.

We bonded fairly early over a mad fascination with two different women who both worked at the store. I was enamoured of a tall blonde who was eventually impregnated by a travelling oil lobbyist and moved to Edmonton; Sebastian with a brunette who was fired for falsifying return vouchers. Although the women didn't work out, we learned that we have very similar outlooks on film, politics and literature. And pubs, for which we had developed a complex rating system that is largely based on proximity.

Sebastian has come up to work on our spare cash register since Mina has once again disappeared. Whether she is on break, in the bathroom, or hiding in the manager's office crying next to the safe, I have no idea, but any of the above are possibilities.

Sebastian gives me a wide-eyed look that tells me all I really need to know. I do my best to smile and be casual. Like going to a Hollywood movie, I have to pretend that I don't already have a pretty good idea how this is going to end. "Hi! What can I do?"

The stringy-haired blonde spins around and fixes me with her beady eyes. "Are you the manager?" Her voice, like the rest of her, is thin and reedy. She sounds like she just barely avoided strangulation. I continue to smile, still trying to pretend that this might be an easy, even friendly encounter – simply a misunderstanding that can be brought to a speedy, mutually satisfying conclusion – even though I know in my heart of hearts that it will not.

I nod. "That I am."

She points back over her shoulder at Sebastian. "This dipshit just told me I can't return this," she says, waving a large cookbook in my face.

I glance towards the line of people waiting at cash – a line that includes several kids under the age of ten – and try to motion her towards the alcove where our discussion will not be so easily overheard, but she's having none of it.

"Uh uh," she says, sticking out her chin and waving at the line. "These people need to hear this."

I sigh. Calling my best friend a dipshit is not a shortcut to my good side, and doing it front of kids has made me decide, before she says another word, that she is not going to leave here happy.

I take the cookbook and look at it. I recognize it as an out-of-print edition that may have been sold out of the non-returnable bargain bin. It's a 3-ring binder style that would have come shrink-wrapped. When I open it, I see that the binders have come loose from the spine. I try to make my next question sound innocuous.

"Do you have your receipt?"

Now that I am holding the book, she is free to gesture with both hands, which she does, throwing them up like she's conducting an orchestra of spastics. "Tell me, whatever the hell your name is…" She leans towards me looking for a nametag, but our staff don't wear them. "Do you keep all your fuckin' receipts?"

A couple of the parents in line shuffle their feet and murmur to their children to ignore the shrieking woman. I would like to say that it amazes me that someone can get this worked up over four bucks, but I can't. I've seen too much of it.

I maintain a calm, reasonable voice. I do this mostly because it usually drives the rageaholics nuts that they can't get a rise out of me. "So you'd like to return a damaged, out-of-print book with no proof that you even bought it here."

Now she knows, from my tone if not my words, that she has not reached a sympathetic ear. Before she can say anything, I hold up a hand.

"Tell you what," I say. "I'll give you back the four bucks this cost on one condition."

Her mouth purses up tightly. "What?"

"Promise me you'll put it towards an e-reader so that you can do all of your book shopping online from now on."

She yanks the book out of my hand and stuffs it back in her bag. "Forget it. Let's get the hell out of here, Rodney. Assholes." The last part is tossed over her shoulder as an aside, but not the sotto-voiced kind.

"Ah! A line used in eighty-eight per cent of action movies, without the 'Rodney' part of course," observes Sebastian as they leave. "No screenwriter would ever get a green light with an action hero named 'Rodney'."

I hop on Mina's till to help Sebastian deal with the rest of the line. Arbitrarily, I give them all a 10 per cent discount for proximate rudeness. When they're gone, I ask Sebastian about his online date from the previous night.

"A Brontë, unfortunately," he says.

A Brontë is code for a 'Withering Sight', or extremely unattractive woman. A "Fellini" is an attractive woman requiring far too much work. Remember Mastroianni wading into the Trevi fountain after Anita Ekberg and getting nothing but wet pants for his trouble? A "Scorsese" is code for a psycho (imagine Robert DeNiro dressed up like the maid in *Cape Fear*). A "Polanski" is one that should be avoided for legal reasons (underage/married/boss). A "Kubrick" is cold, detached, mechanical, unattainable and yet strangely compelling. A "Spielberg" tries too hard to please. Auteurs rarely collaborate.

"She just had something injected into her lips," Sebastian says. "I can't remember what she said it was. I don't think it was botox. In truth, it was rather difficult to make out a word she said."

"Plastic surgery? How old was she?"

Sebastian shrugs and pulls a small canteen out of his hip pocket. He offers me a sip, which I politely decline. I wonder if his drinking may be crossing the line between funny and *Lost Weekend* funny. "According to her profile, she was 25. She would have been normal, but her lips pushed her into the uncanny valley. Imagine Mick Jagger's mouth on someone other than Mick Jagger. It was a good thing it was just drinks. She had to take everything through a straw. I don't know what she would have done with food."

"Well, maybe give it a week or so for the swelling to go down and then call her back."

"Can't do it." He looks around to make sure no one is listening and drops his voice a couple of notches. "So we went back to her place..."

"You did what? She has camel lips and you went home with her?"

"I had no idea what she was saying, but whatever I was saying must have worked, so there we are, on her couch and the next thing you know my pants are open and she's working away."

I let out a laugh like a gunshot. I am trying hard not to picture this scene in my mind.

"The problem is, she's using this special cream on her lips. It's like this topical anaesthetic. For the pain, the swelling, I don't know. All I do know is that after a minute or two I become aware of the fact that I can't feel a damn thing. My dick is completely numb."

I have almost my entire hand crammed into my mouth. A customer comes up with an atlas and wants ten percent off because the cover is slightly torn. I agree without even looking and Sebastian rings him through.

"What happened?"

Sebastian takes another sip from his flask. "I was able to cover pretty well in terms of pretending. Then I felt guilty, you know. So we had sex. Because of this stuff I was able to last, like, an hour before the numbing wore off. It was incredible. Now I'm starting to wonder if she may have done it deliberately. It's a strange culture we inhabit, my friend."

"So are you going to see this woman again?"

Sebastian shakes his head. "I don't think so. She's probably stopped using the ointment and the problem is, she'll expect me to live up to the initial standard, which is just not possible. I can't really ask for it again. Besides, the whole thing was a bit surreal for my taste. And she had horrible taste in music. It may not have been all the drugs. It may have also been the Jefferson Starship."

I have nothing to compete with this tale of lust and pharmacology, so I change the subject. "Where's Mina?"

"Went home. Said she wasn't feeling well. She looked okay. No idea what's wrong with her."

Unfortunately, I think I do.

# -3-

Looking at history, I'm struck by the realization that most of what humans believe has turned out to be completely wrong.

Whether it's the idea that the earth is flat, that bleeding will cure an infection, that *Avatar* was a great movie and not just a shameless ripoff of *Pocahontas*, or that there was no end to the subprime derivative market, we're pretty good at getting things wrong as a species. I'm no exception. I would be the first to admit that dating Mina Bovary was not a good idea.

There are exceptions to that statement, of course. It wasn't technically my idea and "dating" is really too chipper and wholesome a word for it, but it would seem trivial to raise such objections now. Like McNamara and Vietnam, I didn't resist the idea strongly enough when one regime moved out and a new one moved in.

It was wrong for many reasons. She was (and still is) married. She was (and still is, only barely) an employee and I was (and still am, in theory) a manager, which makes me nominally her boss. This is a grey area as Dante is, technically, directly responsible for cash and receiving, but I doubt such a distinction would stand up in court. She is also a clinical depressive currently on her third cocktail of antidepressants, but I didn't know that at the time.

The whole thing started a few months ago when she attacked me one night long after the store had closed. As the head cashier, she was helping me to complete the quarterly cash audit when she pushed me onto the safe and climbed on top. I am not regularly assaulted by women who are unable to keep their libidos in check and, in my confusion and surprise, didn't put up as much of a fight as I probably should. I know now that it was probably only a side effect of the new medication she was on. If, as originally planned, it had been Dante in that room instead of me, the same thing would probably have happened although I'm sure that the outcome would have been very different.

I didn't really know her all that well before then. She wasn't one of the regular group who hung out at Falstaff's after work or went out to movies or anything like that. I knew she was married, but was under the impression that she and her husband were separated. It turned out that they were separated by his 15-month tour of duty in Afghanistan, where he was working as a sniper in some sort of secret special operations unit. I must admit that a cold shiver went down my spine when I found out that little tidbit of information. Not only was I a disreputable letch, I was an unpatriotic one as well. What I was doing most certainly did not qualify as 'supporting the troops' (a phrase I don't like because it's too easily employed by crass politicians aware of the fact that support for the troops is equivalent to support for the military action, but I digress). I had nightmares of waking up in a coffin and being unable to yell for help because my testicles were stuffed in my mouth.

I tried to break it off, but she made veiled threats about telling Dante or even telling her husband. Some of what she might say might not make it past the military censor, but I'm sure he'd glean enough to get the gist. I saw her a few more times after that, but was always careful to make it a well-lit public place. If she suggested going anywhere else, like a movie or back to her apartment, I always demurred. She showed up at my apartment a few times late at night and left long, tearful messages on my voicemail, but I didn't budge.

She said that she was planning to leave her husband because he was violent and abusive. I told her to go to the police and get counselling but she always rebuffed that idea, claiming that her husband's top secret military connections would never let him go to jail and were secretly plotting to have her locked up in an institution. She believed that her mail was being intercepted and that her phone was tapped. She also believed that there were tracking devices sewn into some of her clothes and that CSIS was monitoring every movie she rented and every book she checked out of the library.

Things seemed to get better when she started a new medication. She stopped sending me cryptic emails and leaving messages and showing up in the middle of the night. Her work improved, too. She stopped missing shifts and got back into the habit of balancing her till without having to call in a team of forensic accountants. She seemed close to being on the verge of happy. When Sebastian told me that she had gone home sick, I was worried that she'd slipped back into her old habits again, which is why I agreed to meet her after work.

This is just a chain coffee shop eight blocks from the store, which pretty much guarantees that we're unlikely to be observed by any of our fellow employees, most of whom are probably now holed up in the regular booth at Falstaff's. Mina is 20 minutes late and I'm starting to think about leaving the cold dregs of my tea (I've never liked coffee) on the table and heading over to the pub when I see the door open and she walks in.

She's smiling, so hopefully that means good news and not bad. A cold claw grabs my guts. What if she's pregnant? She could think that was good news. She said everything was fine, but she also said that her landlord had trained his cat to spy on her. Oh man, what was I thinking?

She sits down without ordering anything. "Thanks for meeting me."

No apology for being late, of course. She notices my almost empty cup and glances towards the counter. "What are you having?"

"Oh I'm done," I say, waving my hand over the rim of my cup in the same way I would signal to a dealer that I don't want another card. A universal gesture for "no more, thanks."

"I'm not staying long, so I think I'll pass too," she says. I feel a dangerous optimism. It's the same feeling that characters in horror movies must have when they reach the front door of the house only to find out that it's locked and the maniac vivisectionist is, despite having been nowhere in sight for the last ten minutes, now standing directly behind them with a cranial saw.

"So what can I do for you?" I ask.

"Well…" she says, looking around as if what she's about to say is written on the wall somewhere. "I wanted you to be the first to know that I've met someone."

I pause for a moment just to make sure that the *someone* in this case doesn't turn out to be me. Mina talks that way. The day after the night in the office, she casually mentioned that she thought she might be in love with one of the managers. Since Dante's orientation is public knowledge to all but his mother and our other manager was in Estonia, it wasn't too hard to play the process of elimination game.

No. She seems to be serious. Can it be possible? The door is in front of me…the handle is turning…am I going to be the lone survivor who goes running off into the daylight as the credits roll?

"That's great!" I say, trying to sound happy and not relieved. "Anyone I know?"

She smiles and looks at the floor. Oh no. It is someone I know. Who could it be? Sebastian? No, he just spent half an hour talking about his marathon bonkfest with Botox the Clown. Aldous? He's tubby and pretentious, but he can be funny and does actually have some interesting ideas. Plus, because of his lack of experience with women, he probably wouldn't recognize a train wreck until he was already on board (although I got my ticket punched too, so I'm not exactly in the realm of the ethereal).

Not Dante. Not Ebeneezer. There's Willard Kurtz, our head of shipping and receiving, but he's currently cohabiting with an unregistered massage therapist and has a 2-year-old daughter. He also has a green mohawk, several tattoos and more piercings than a stop sign in rural Alabama. Mina is an introverted arts grad who writes spectacularly bad nature poetry (sample: "your fall is my sunset of hearts / when we kiss I feel stirrings in parts"), so I can't see the two of them together. Miroslav Defoknik, aka the village idiot of Village Books, wouldn't be a prime candidate, either. The guy dropped a brick on his head not once but three times while trying to build a firepit in his parents' backyard and the general consensus is that it didn't make him any smarter. Plus, Mina hates him because of his gross, sexist sense of humour, which many of the rest of us consider his sole redeeming feature.

It could also be a woman, of course. Mina has told me of a few previous dabblings in that direction. Before I can run through any of the possible candidates, she starts talking again.

"I don't want to say too much about that," she says quietly. "It's still in the early going, but I've got a really good feeling about it."

I smile. Poor bastard. He (or she) probably has no idea what they're in for. But, it is no longer me, and that's all that really concerns me at the moment. It's not that I don't care about Mina, it's just that I realize no possible good can come from my involvement here and it's time for me to gracefully step aside and out of the picture. This is the reason I don't mention her husband. When sneaking past a sleeping bear, it benefits one little to poke it in the eye with a stick.

"Well that's great," I say. I'm such a phoney. What I really mean is that it's great for *me*.

"You sure you're okay with it?"

Don't laugh you bastard, you're almost home free! The door is open. The music is starting to rise…

"I'm fine."

She lets out a big breath. "Well, that was easier than I thought it was gonna be!"

What is she talking about? For her or me? It was pretty damn easy for me. Some breakups are like the ejection scene from Top Gun in that you both realize that it's a good idea to leave, but only one person makes it out intact. Some are like the assassination of Moe Green from *The Godfather* in that one minute you're half naked and being rubbed by a woman and the next you've lost a perfectly good pair of glasses and a sizable portion of your mind. And then there are the ones that are easier than dropping off a book at the library. It was interesting, but it wasn't yours and now the time is up.

This one feels more like the end of a hostage-taking in a bank. Was she expecting me to put up a fight? To beg or plead or manifest some form of Stockholm Syndrome? This would be difficult to do when I'm using all of my willpower to suppress the urge to bounce out of my chair, throw open the door and dance down the street. Which is more or less what I'm planning to do when she leaves, minus a high kick or two.

"Well...that's good."

We get up. She gives me a hug and I notice she's wearing the same perfume she had on from the night on the safe. Before leaving, she asks if she should be worried about me. I tell her no. My only worry is that I may celebrate so hard that I will forget this happened.

# -4-

Falstaff's is a genuine Irish pub in the sense that it's owned by a genuine Irishman. Mickey Lee O'Malley was born in Donegal on the day Brendan Behan died. There's a picture of Behan arm-in-arm with Jackie Gleason on the men's room door. Women get a picture of James Joyce in a Photoshopped red dress.

No one knows what Mickey did before he bought this place because he never gives the same answer twice. He may have worked as Pierce Brosnan's stand-in on three of the Bond movies. He may have been hired to keep Adam Clayton away from hookers and hash on the Elevation tour. He may have secretly looted millions of dollars worth of royal knickknacks while working as a tour guide at Buckingham Palace. He may have won the 1988 New York marathon if he hadn't been disqualified for using the subway. He may have been relocated by British intelligence after years of undercover spying on the IRA. Or he may simply have inherited a small fortune when his bauxite mine-owning father died and decided to open a pub.

He's a big guy with jet black hair that clings unevenly to his skull like moss and a nose that looks like it's been set a couple of times by someone who probably wasn't a doctor, so no one has yet challenged him on the veracity of any of his accounts.

There's only one television in the place, which I like. Most sports bars seem to think that the last thing you want to do is talk to the people you came with and cram giant plasma screens in every corner like a gallery running out of space. Mickey refuses to show hockey, soccer, basketball or any of what he calls our "sissy sports" and instead broadcasts only that bizarre variant of all three called hurling, which is beloved by the Irish and understood about as well outside of that country as cricket is outside of England.

Unlike most of what passes for pubs these days, Falstaff's hasn't been shoehorned into a strip mall and "atmosphered" with franchise décor straight out of a business plan. The property is actually a 154-year-old mansion that used to belong to a local brewery owner who was reputedly murdered by gangsters during prohibition and his body hidden in a barrel in the basement. This has given rise to the rumour that the place is haunted and provided a name for one of the house beers (Dead Joe's Cask Ale). Because it's an old house, it's full of lots of oddly-sized rooms, narrow hallways that meet at unexpected angles, creaky floors, uneven stairs, small, draughty bathrooms and lots of exposed wiring and plumbing.

It also has the best pub food and the best selection of beers in town. Weekends usually feature a live band. They must have at least one Irish member or one member who can prove Irish descent to play. Most of the time, however, the music is whatever Mickey feels like playing. Based on his mood, this can range from Van Morrison to Therapy? to U2. When I push open the door and walk in, I'm greeted by the glorious caterwauling of Shane McGowan cursing and slurring his way through "Bottle of Smoke". It matches my mood so perfectly that I'd sing along if only I knew what the hell he was saying.

Mickey is standing in his usual spot behind the bar gesturing towards an open copy of the *Donegal Daily News* and debating something, undoubtedly hurling-related, with a couple of older regulars. Falstaff's is popular with students who know better and expats eager for a taste of home. Tonight the place is packed and buzzing with conversation.

I wander up to the bar and order a pint of what Mickey insists I refer to as "the liquid gold," and indeed, I have no cause to argue with him on this point, because the two match up well in terms of their colour, rarity and price. Falstaff's is the only pub I'm aware of on the continent that serves Scrumpy Jack, which may not sound like much from its name, but is in actual fact the most delectable cider ever to pass through human throats. It's not cheap – it costs almost twice as much as an average import. Mickey doesn't list it on the draft boards, so only the regulars even know about it.

If someone else does get wind of it and tries to order a pint, they have to pass a test that's probably very similar to the one the Irish Culture Ministry would give to new immigrants to make sure they will fit in. Knowing that I was a bookstore manager, Mickey asked me to name the wife of Stephen Deadalus, which I was able to do only because it also happens to be the name of a pub in my hometown.

"Howeyeh then?" Mickey asks as he fills my glass. "See thon fellah got a pitcher o' yer Loch Ness monster t'other day?"

I forgot to mention that Mickey is also a supernatural and conspiracy nut. He believes, amongst other things, that NASA faked the moon landing, that JFK shot himself, that erectile dysfunction ads are secretly broadcasting subliminal messages to Freemasons and that Sarah Palin is actually a robot built by the Democrats to make Republicans look like idiots (we agree on the last one). He calls it "my" Loch Ness monster because my family is of Scottish extraction and therefore indirectly responsible for everything that tiny nation foists on the world, which includes bagpipes, haggis and Gerard Butler romantic comedies.

This is a test. I once told Mickey that there was no Loch Ness monster. I explained that the lake itself is only about 10,000 years old and does not connect to the sea, which would make it difficult for a dinosaur that went extinct 70 million years ago to get in there. Also, unless we were dealing with the oldest living thing in the universe, there would be a lot of them. And they would spend most of their time at the surface, so sightings would not be quite so infrequent. I think I had had a few pints by then, so I even went on about thermoclimes and water density and blah blah blah.

After my rant, I couldn't get another pint of Scrumpy for two months. Mickey told me that the keg was out and that he was still waiting for the next shipment to arrive. Plenty of the regulars were still drinking the stuff right in front of me, of course, but there was no point in bringing that up and turning my probation into a custodial sentence.

"That's interesting," I say, raising the glass to my lips. "Cheers."

Mickey winks and wanders down to help a woman who is leaning over the bar to ask if the television can be changed so that she and her friends can watch a hockey game. Mickey will shake his head sadly and inform her that the television only gets one channel and, as improbable as it may sound, the Gaelic Athletic Association's Hurling On Demand network happens to be that channel. If she has any sense, she will abandon her quest there.

I take my pint and wander into the back room to find a small contingent from the store in our usual booth. There's Aldous, pontificating about something that I thankfully cannot hear. Next to him is our Croatian sex-bomb magazine lead, Invanka Urfe. Sebastian was once delayed for 15 minutes in the break room because he was watching her eat a banana. She is studying criminology at U of T and has a black belt in some form of obscenely violent Brazilian wrestling. Dante is there with his latest boyfriend, an unemployed painter named Doug. Doug's thing is taking a mouthful of paint and spraying it out on the canvas, so his smile is often colourfully off-putting.

Dante can come here and relax because it's absolutely the last place on earth his mother would enter, other than Trentino's Deli, of course, which she refuses to patronize for reasons upon which she refuses to elaborate. Next to Dante is Miroslav, trying to figure out why the coasters are resisting his attempts to stack them into houses (they're round) and –

Oh.

Leah Dashwood.

I consider turning around and running out of the room, but Dante has already spotted me and waves me over. I smile and, gripping my pint glass hard so as not to drop it, stumble across the floor like a recently reanimated corpse. What is she doing here? How does she know about this place? What on earth am I going to say to her? There are not a lot of options left after you propose marriage, after all.

I pull up a chair and end up sitting next to Leah, who smiles and eyes my glass. "Is that Scrumpy?"

I nod. Huh?

"What the hell!" she says. "I heard this was the only place in town that serves the stuff and then I get here and the guy tells me that they're out, but more should be arriving in six weeks or so. I was so disappointed!"

"Well, we can't have that," I say, getting back up. What I am about to do may get me excommunicated, but there is no turning back now. I am a man with a mission.

I sidle up to the bar and give Mickey a hopeful look. He wanders down looking confused and suspicious. "Now what is it ye might be wantin'?"

"Er, another pint of the liquid gold, my good man."

His eyebrows crease. "Wha? Surely ye haven't put it away already?"

We both know that this is not possible. If I had swallowed an entire pint of Scrumpy in the minute-and-a-half since I got it, I would not be back at the bar asking for a second because I would have been donated for medical research. On a sliding scale, Scrumpy's alcohol content is somewhere between rubbing alcohol and pure alcohol. It's the kind of drink that's best enjoyed slowly. Allowing it to fall into the hands of a fraternity house would be like giving enriched uranium to terrorists.

"Uh, no…" I mumble. "It's, uh, for a friend."

Mickey gives me a penetrating look. "Ah think we're all out again. Won't get any more in fer a couple o'months."

I collapse pathetically against the bar. "I know! I know! But I'm helpless to say no! It's for a woman."

"Ah, well, in tha' case, we won't be getting' any in fer a year, ye know."

"No, Mickey, it's not like that." What is it, though? She's engaged. Do I seriously think I can win her away from her fiancé with a pint of hard cider? Well, it wouldn't be a bad place to start. "She's dying to try the stuff and she heard this was one of the only places in the country she could get it. Then when she got here and you said you were out of stock, she was heartbroken."

"An' where did she hear a thing like that, then?"

I shake my head. The first rule of Scrumpy is that you don't talk about Scrumpy. "Oh not from me. I just met her today."

"This'un isn't married an all, is she?" he asks.

How does he know these things? I never came in here with Mina, at least not just the two of us. "Engaged."

"Jaysus boyo, yer a fookin' disaster. I should cut off yer dick as well as yer Scrumpy before ye kill again."

"I know. I'm totally irredeemable."

"Is it the redhead?"

"Yes."

He pulls the pint and hands it over. When I try to pay, he waves his hand. "Ye'll pay fer this with yer immortal soul, ye degenerate little bastard."

I genuflect with my free hand. "Thank you, father." I take the pint and head back to the table, where I notice that my seat has been taken by a pudgy guy with a crewcut who is busy sucking every last fibre of meat off an enormous plate of wings. There is red sauce slathered over his flabby cheeks and his T shirt, which reads "Wholesaler of Death" and features an elaborate graphic of a large-breasted woman holding a minigun in one hand and multi-barrelled grenade launcher in the other. There is a small pile of bones stacked on the table next to his plate. I feel like I just walked in on a bear in the process of eating poor, deluded Timothy Treadwell.

Leah's eyes light up. "Oh my God, you got it!" she says as I hand over the pint. The lump does not look up from his plate and shows no sign of moving over to make room, so I'm forced to go looking for a chair. Fortunately, a group of club-bound students are getting up to leave and I snag one of theirs. Aldous makes room and I shoehorn my way into the table, reaching over to move my own pint away from the beast before it's devoured like everything else within his reach.

Leah takes a deep chug and blinks her eyes in surprise. "Wow!"

"I should have warned you to take it easy," I say.

"I've had it before," grunts the beast. "It's not that good."

"I forgot to introduce my fiancé," Leah says, gesturing towards the Rancor Monster. "This is Grover Whetstone. He used to work for Google."

He looks up slightly and nods. At least I think it's a nod. He may have just gotten momentarily caught on a tendon. I'm glad that he shows no interest in shaking hands.

"Google, huh?" I say, taking a larger than usual gulp from my own pint, which I feel like I need. "So you were good at finding stuff?"

He drops another bone on the table. "That's funny," he says without laughing.

There's a pause while the rest of the table silently makes up its mind about whether or not to simply go on and pretend that Grover isn't here. Being the most recent arrival, I press on.

"So if you used to work for Google, what do you do now?"

"Started a new company with a friend," he says between mouthfuls. "Can't really say too much about it, but we're gonna make Google look like fuckin' Pets.com by the time we're done. We've got two point four in VC and another six lined up behind that. So even if Julia Roberts here doesn't make the A-list, we'll still be able to live like she did."

I take another drink. It surprises me that I'm still at a loss as to how to deal with obnoxious people outside of a work setting. It's not like I don't get enough practice.

"Did you know that five per cent of the Screen Actor's Guild makes 95 per cent of the money?" Grover continues. I'm not sure what he expects us to make of this nugget. "Waste of time." He shakes his head and grins smugly, his cheeks shaking like jell-o. I sneak a glance at Leah, who just rolls her eyes. What the hell is she doing with this guy?

"I'm sorry," I say. "What's a waste of time?"

He shrugs. "I'm just saying why would you bother with something if there's like no chance you're going to make any real money at it?"

I laugh. "Well, it's a good thing Van Gogh didn't think that way. Or Mozart. Or Frank Lloyd Wright. Or Bergman. If they did, then the whole world would look like East Berlin before the wall came down." I know I'm wasting my breath, but I don't care. Guys like this are impervious to art. I could strap him into a chair like Malcolm McDowell and force him to listen to Beethoven's 9th or clamp his eyes open to watch *Wild Strawberries*, but his first response the next time he encounters them would still be to vomit. His clockwork is already orange.

"Come on," Grover says. "The only reason anyone cares about any of that stuff now is because it's worth a lot of money."

I'm getting angry. I shouldn't be. "Oh really? What kind of a dollar value would you put on *The Seventh Seal*? Or *Hamlet*? Or *Love in the Time of Cholera*? Or the Ninth Symphony? How would you monetize their contribution to the culture?"

Grover waves a dismissive hand, inadvertently getting hot sauce on the boobs and mini gun. "I'm talkin' today, not like a hundred years ago. You artsy types always think what you do is so important. You know what's important? Bridges. Tunnels. Like, electricity. Bandwith. Without them, society doesn't run. Can it run without fuckin' Beethoven? Uh yeah. It's been running without him for, like, 800 years."

I turn to Leah. "Wow, Leah. Why don't you tell us all how you ended up betrothed to such a renaissance man."

She sighs and puts down her pint – the pint that I feel like I went to Mordor and back for only to see it dropped on the floor. "We met in university. Believe it or not, I started in computer programming."

"And she sucked at it," Grover mutters.

"I did," she says. "I would have probably failed first semester if Grover hadn't helped me out. I was good at math and my parents kept telling me to just go, so I did. It was a dumb idea. Waste of a year."

I pick up my pint. The more I see of this Whetstone guy, the more I think that, although there almost certainly is no God, if there is, he's a nasty, petty, evil, sadistic little son of a bitch. At least the Scrumpy is good. "And then what did you do?"

"I dropped out. Tried improv. Sucked at that. I like knowing what I'm going to say and preparing for it and getting it right. Improv was like wandering into a mental ward where they randomly electrocute the patients. I got into a couple of small theatre groups, though, and that I liked. We only just got back into town a little while ago, so I'm still kinda feeling out the scene. I've got an audition for a commercial, though!"

Grover snorts. "Yeah, for sandwich bags."

I want to punch the guy, but settle for pretending that my stare is enough to melt the skin off his face. I raise my glass. "Good for you! Here's to your audition!"

The rest of the table shout hearty agreement and do likewise. She smiles shyly and returns my toast.

Oh dear. I fear that I am falling into extremely deep trouble.

# -5-

Dante is covering Sunday, so I have the day to myself. Large chunks of unbooked time can be intimidating when you're single. Mealtimes are the worst. I hate eating by myself. I'm not sure why, but the thought of preparing a meal for one and sitting quietly in my tiny dining area while I mechanically shovel it in depresses me.

On the spur of the moment, I decide not to stay home and clean the apartment. Instead, I head out for the AGO, where I spend an enjoyable but back-stiffening afternoon wandering through the permanent exhibits and paying extra for a featured presentation of the photography of Robert Doisneau. Art galleries and museums are like bookstores in that they are quiet, contemplative spaces where you can stand around with a lot of people without feeling compelled to make conversation. In that sense, they are the opposite of parties and clubs. I don't mind parties if I know a large proportion of the invitees, but I hate clubs. I can't dance. I don't like yelling in people's ears and I have pretty much zero skill at approaching women I don't know.

After the gallery, I get takeout from Enrico's. It's my favourite Italian place to take dates, but not a place that I would eat alone. To sit there at a table by myself while surrounded by couples would be a corruption of the atmosphere, like wearing a bathing suit at the dentist's office. On the way home, I pick up a Valpolicella Ripasso to compliment my Chicken

Parmigiana, both of which I intend to consume while sitting on the couch and watching either *Hot Fuzz* or *Scott Pilgrim vs. The World*. I figure I've done my time in the high culture trenches. The rest of the evening is mine.

I don't mind being by myself. I like being able to come and go more or less when I want. I like being able to sit down and spend an entire day reading (which I did when the last Harry Potter came out), only breaking for the bathroom and food. I like the quiet of my apartment. It's a 750-square-foot, one-bedroom, rent-controlled space on the third floor of what used to be an old Masonic temple. The electricity and plumbing need an overhaul, but it's got a lot more character than the steel and glass erections shooting out of the ground closer to downtown.

Solitude is an acquired skill. Many people that I know are pathologically terrified of it. Sebastian, for example, is active on no fewer than five online dating sites and uses a spreadsheet to keep track of the many women he has working their way through his relationship pipeline. He tracks where they live, where they work, which jokes and lies he's told, their level of physical attractiveness, whether or not he has seen them naked, whether or not he has shown them *The Man Who Would Be King* (his favourite movie) and a million other details. All told, he probably spends more time in Excel than he does in the women he catalogues there.

Sebastian keeps trying to talk me into joining up with one of the many online hookup sites to which he subscribes, but I'm something of a luddite where technology is concerned. I do have a computer, but it's old. I bought it six years ago, so it qualifies as Palaeolithic by processing standards. I use it for writing and checking email, which no one seems to be using anymore because they're all logged on to social networking sites. I only broke down and got a cell phone six months ago because I was having trouble with my land line. The phone company said that the problem with reception was related to the line coming into the building and wanted to charge $500 just to investigate the issue, so I told them to stick it. It's just a phone. It doesn't surf the internet or take pictures and it cannot be used to tell which coffee shops I go to or how many government secrets I may have uploaded to Wikileaks.

It's not that I'm anti-tech. It's just that it moves so fast these days that everyone's turned into an early adopter. My strategy was to wait until something appeared to have a useful purpose as opposed to being just an expensive novelty accessory. Most of my music is still on CD. I don't watch movies on my computer, but that's mostly because I have a basic connection and by the time the movie had downloaded I would be in a retirement home. All of my books are still on paper.

There's been a lot of nervous rumbling that e-readers are about to put places like Village Books out of business, but there haven't been any concrete signs of it yet. Our business is actually up in sales this year over last. It saddens me to think of a place like Village Books no longer being around in ten years. On the flipside, of course, we may have run out of oil and the ice caps may have melted, so the parts of the planet that aren't under water will probably be under the control of barbarian tribes bombing around in solar-powered dune buggies, fighting for gas.

I am just sitting down to eat when the buzzer rings. I open the door to admit Sebastian, who is looking out of breath and more dishevelled than usual. I offer him a glass of wine, which he gulps, and part of my dinner, which he fortunately declines.

"Frightfully sorry to intrude, old bean," he says. "But circumstances demanded."

I pour him another glass of wine. "Not at all, my good man. What can I do for you?"

We sit down at my kitchen table where I begin working on my dinner.

"Well," he says, "I feel I should preface any further discussion with the admission that I slept with Mina."

I spit out my mouthful of angel hair pasta and marinara. Fortunately, it lands right back on my plate and not in my lap. "What?"

"I know, I know. I didn't entirely mean for it to happen, but there you go."

"When?"

"Well, yesterday. And the day before that. It all started a few weeks ago."

A few weeks ago? "What about the woman with the novocaine camel lips?"

"Nah, I just made that up. You looked like you could use a laugh."

Sebastian does not know that Mina and I had an, er, interregnum. I'm not sure why I didn't tell him. Embarrassment, probably. Mina's mood disorders are no secret to the rest of the staff.

"Why didn't you say something sooner?"

"As I recall, you also failed to admit that you had boffed said fair damsel, mi amichi."

Mina must have told him. "Touché."

"That's not the problem, though," he says. "The problem is her husband."

"What about him?" I ask. "She said he was in Afghanistan or something."

Sebastian nods. "Yes. *Was*. He *was* in Afghanistan."

The fork freezes halfway to my mouth. "He's back?"

Sebastian gets up and walks to the window, where he hides behind the curtain and peers nervously out onto the street. "Nobody knows. He's gone AWOL. Or UA. Or whatever the hell they call it. The point is, he's gone off the deep end. Off the fucking reservation. She told him she'd met somebody else. Apparently, he freaked out and disappeared. Took several weapons and fragmentary explosive devices with him."

"Uh oh. When did you find out about this?"

He comes back from the window. "Last night after work. I spent last night hiding under the mattress of the Hotel Duluth where I'd checked in under the name Juan Espanol."

"But he doesn't know it's you, right?"

Sebastian rightly intuits that I am not asking this question solely out of concern for *his* personal safety. "Who knows what she said? It's Mina. She could have faxed him a copy of my driver's licence for all I know. Or yours. Or Academy Award-winning director Sam Mendes. Sanity is clearly not the rock upon which they have built their church. The best part is she tells me this right in the midst of our nocturnal activities. I lost the initiative faster than the U.S. in Somalia. Lemme tell ya something." He pulls at his shirt. "These colours do cut and run. I was outta there faster than a jihadist at a military tribunal. Adios, motherfucker! Flying, like a bird."

I hold up a hand. "Relax! The guy's off his rocker! They'll find him in the latrine with a back issue of *Guns & Ammo* and an inflatable Pee Wee Herman doll. He'll never get off the base, let alone back into the country."

Sebastian shakes his head. "Prudence dictates that I point out he's not just crazy. He's *special forces* crazy. He specializes in sneaking weapons into the country and assassinations and all that covert shit! He could be anywhere! He could be you for all I know. I could be him! He could be both of us! It could be like the end of *The Thing* where I'm Kurt Russell and you're the other guy and we're both just sitting there staring at each other after the base explodes."

I pour him more wine and order him to drink it. I hope he walked here. "The important thing is not to panic."

"Why? Why is no one ever allowed to panic? Finding out that there's a psychopathic universal soldier coming to kill you has a way of preoccupying the mind."

"Keep in mind that it's Mina, so she may have been making that up. Maybe he's not a black ops spook in a war zone. For all we know, he could be one of those guys who vacuums dog turds off people's lawns in the spring. He may not even exist."

Sebastian thinks about it for a moment. "You may have something there. There weren't any pictures of him up around the apartment. She said it was because he doesn't like to have his picture taken."

"Nothing? Not even a wedding picture?"

"Well, keep in mind that I did go there for the express purpose of removing her clothes and performing various connubial acts. Asking to see wedding pictures prior to such defilement could be considered perverse in the extreme, not to mention something of a mood killer."

"Good point. So what are you going to do now? Break it off?"

"If I don't, her husband will, I'm sure. But how do I do it without making her upset? The last time I checked, she'd left me, like, 294 messages. My mailbox was actually full."

"You're kidding. How many?"

"Okay, one was from my dentist to remind me I had an appointment which I missed because I was hiding under the bed in a strange hotel room. But it was a lot. If I make her angry, who knows what she'll tell this guy? She could say that I locked her in receiving and forced her to do terrible things on the returns table."

"Look, just tell her that you don't think it's a good idea for the two of you to spend time together while her husband is, well, for want of a better expression, on the loose."

Sebastian purses his lips thoughtfully. "Yes, go on."

"Tell her you think it would be better if you spent some time apart to figure things out, let the situation calm down. You don't call. After a while, she gets the idea or hooks up with someone else. Either way, you're out of the picture. You need an alibi, well, that's why I'm here."

The two of us have often joked about opening our own professional witness service. Need an alibi? Or someone who can swear that the other driver ran through the red and not you? Or that you can't possibly be cheating on your wife because you were at a very important company team-building event at that hotel and not actually sneaking into room 425 with two former adult movie actors and a suitcase full of inflatable novelty items? That's where we would come in.

Or rather, that's where *We Saw The Whole Thing* would come in. For as little as fifty bucks, you get a credible witness willing to swear on whatever ancient text you'd like that you are absolutely devoid of blame. Sure it's technically illegal and undermines the pillars of our legal system and even democracy, but it's also an easy way to make fifty bucks.

"Ah, see, I knew there was a reason I came here!" Sebastian says. "Truly you are endowed with great wisdom." His expression momentarily darkens again. "Mina didn't say anything about me, did she?"

I look at him suspiciously. "About what?"

He fidgets awkwardly. "Well, there was one point…and in my defence I must say that I'd had an entire bottle of Tattinger all to myself because she took one sip and then remembered she didn't drink the stuff. Tattinger! Where I may have suggested we try something that is only legal in enlightened states such as our own but that in execution proved to be slightly less than the rousing spectacle one might have expected based on all those epic poems and grand sonatas and the like…"

"No she never mentioned anything like that."

"Good, good. Sorry to interrupt your dinner, by the way." He points to the TV, where the DVD screensaver is bouncing around like a ping pong ball. "What were you going to watch?"

"Hot Fuzz or Scott Pilgrim."

"Fucking A!" He jumps up. "I'll go get a suitable supply of beer and be right back."

He disappears through the door. Well, I figure, at least I won't be eating by myself.

# -6-

It turns out that Leah has already worked as a bookstore manager. She spent a year and a half as an assistant manager for one of the big chain bookstores in the states while her IT slug fiancé was still toiling for the search engine, so there isn't a lot I need to do except introduce her to people.

We start at cash, where I have the unfortunate duty of introducing her to Lolita Havisham. Lolita is an obsessive compulsive germaphobe. It takes her twenty minutes to sign on to a till because she has to clean it three times, open every coin roll, count every coin four times and then disinfect everything within a two metre radius with her own antibacterial spray. Dante puts up with this because her till has never been out once by even a penny. She is, however, less beloved by her fellow cashiers, who nicknamed her L-O-L behind her back. It's not just the delays caused by her compulsiveness that drive the other staff up the wall. She also has an abrupt manner and tendency to complain about them while they're within earshot.

She has an unusually tinny voice that makes her sound like everything she says is coming through a subway PA system. She cuts her own hair in an uneven but spiky blonde brush cut and her eyes bulge like they're threatening to jump out of her head and attack you.

Leah says hello and offers to shake her hand, a gesture from which Lolita recoils. I feel stupid for not warning Leah about this, but it's not like I'm in the habit of making introductions for Lolita.

"I don't shake hands," Lolita says flatly. No hello. No nice to meet you. "Do you have any idea how many germs the average person has under their right index fingernail alone? I might as well follow them home and stick my hand in their toilet."

"Oh, sorry," Leah says, dropping her hand and looking slightly deflated. I give her a pained grin and a quick eye roll to let her know that I will try my best to explain this later. I want Leah to have a good first day.

Handshakes are funny things. Some people – primarily jocks and old guys who don't realize that bow ties look ridiculous with anything other than a tuxedo – treat them more like contests of strength or will than simple social gestures. I hate breaking off a handshake early with someone who continues to squeeze and pump away, refusing to relinquish my hand because they're trying to prove something. I have never figured out what that something is. That they are not wimps? That life was better under Eisenhower? It's a mystery.

"Mina left the cash office in a horrible state last night," Lolita informs me. "Two of the coin rolls were in the wrong tubs and I found a paperclip in one of the cash envelopes."

Oh my, I think. Truly, this is a reason to bring in the special investigations unit. "Thanks, Lol – ita." I almost slip and use her nickname. I've done this dozens of times. Fortunately it's an easy save. Good thing they didn't tag her with something like "Shrek", whom she would more closely resemble if she were green.

Leah has already met Aldous, so we head upstairs where I introduce her to Mother Teresa.

"What a lovely young woman!" Mother Teresa says, shaking hands with as much enthusiasm as Lolita lacked. "Why, you look familiar. You look just like a girl who used to attend my church. Are you a member of the Assembly of the Chosen?"

Mother Teresa does this often. It's her version of subtlety. She can't just come right out and ask if someone is a catholic or a muslim or a member of a weirdo fringe splinter group, so she sneaks it in the back door by pretending to have seen them before.

Leah shakes her head. "No. My parents worshipped Poseidon. Once a month we used to take a boat out onto the lake and sacrifice a goat. But it turned out that there was a law against killing a goat on a boat, so in the end we just ended up taking out a couple of expired pork chops and tossing them over the side. Seemed to work just as well."

Mother Teresa looks confused for a moment before bursting out in laughter. "Ha! Poseidon! Honestly."

Yeah, I think. As if Poseidon is any more bizarre than the stuff *she* believes. Here's a simple experiment: any time a politician says something like "God is on our side", mentally replace "God" with "Thor" or "Zeus" or "Amun Ra". If you think it sounds ridiculous, you're right. They *all* sound ridiculous.

Leah mentions that she's done a linear footage analysis of the department over the weekend with data provided by Dante and looks forward to working with Mother T on some changes.

"We're going to have to shrink Children's Religion by about eighty per cent," Leah says quietly as we make our way down the stairs. "It's selling about a dollar fifty per foot while she's got Teen Series, which sells a hundred times as much, crammed into about half the space."

"Good luck with that," I say. "She'll fight you like an Alabama school district."

Our last stop is receiving, where our head receiver, Willard Kurtz, is having an argument with Ivanka over whether or not Green Lantern could beat Superman in a fight. Actually, arguing is the wrong word. He's just giving his opinion while she fills out magazine return forms, sips her coffee and tries, as always in vain, to pretend he isn't there.

"Whaddayou think?" he asks, pointing at Leah as soon as we step inside.

Leah shrugs. "Well, I guess if Green Lantern lost his ring, he'd be fucked. But otherwise, I think he could take him."

Willard's love of Superman is deep, broad, perverse and totally immune to logic. I've seen his apartment. He has Superman bed sheets and shower curtains. He has a complete set of Superman mugs that were only briefly available through a now-extinct fried chicken outlet in Australia. He uses a Superman toothbrush and a Superman comb. He even has a Superman brand of pomade that probably expired in 1942 and makes his hair smell like a diesel engine full of dead rats. There is much speculation that this is what is keeping his mohawk in place, since not a single hair on his head appears to have moved or grown in two years. It may also be responsible for his hair's nuclear green colour and the kind of neurological damage that seems to allow him to watch 24 hours of violently pornographic animé without a break.

I think Willard's attachment to Superman stems from the fact that they were both adopted. Willard was taken away from his mother when he was two and bounced around in foster homes for a couple of years before ending up with a solidly upper middle class family in the 'burbs. Despite their normalcy, his inner superstoner could not be contained, and he started going off the rails shortly after he started high school.

Willard has a 2-year-old daughter named Raven, so called because she came out with black hair which has since turned yellow-blonde. He works a second job in the kitchen of a Serbian restaurant. Raven's mom is as an exotic dancer/masseuse at a club out near the airport but is trying to get her high school equivalency so that she can go back to school to become a legal secretary or something like that. Listening to Willard talk about his life always makes me very happy that my parents insisted I get some sort of post-secondary education.

Willard originally started work on the floor, but too many customers found his overwhelming enthusiasm for certain fantasy and sci fi series books and appearance a bit much to take, so Dante moved him into receiving, where he has settled in nicely.

In between his two jobs, Willard is also trying to make a go of things as a musician. He fronts a band called Death in Van Nuys that plays a variant of SoCal ska punk crossed with a Voidoid sort of space metal freakiness. Their average song runs around eight minutes, which, considering most of them move at 164 beats per minute or higher, is actually quite insanely long. They lost five drummers to ligament damage before settling on a drum machine. Willard claims that they have a small but devoted following. Having been to one of their shows, I can report that this following appears to consist of their sound guy and whichever one of their friends couldn't come up with a better excuse to be somewhere else that night.

"See?" Willard says. "Superman melts the ring with his heat vision and kicks Green Lantern's sorry little leprechaun ass!" He holds up a hand for Leah to give him a high five, which she does. "Hey, I hear you're an actress."

"Yeah," Leah nods. "Well, I'm trying."

"I tried that once," Willard says. This is Willard's answer to most things and substances. "I did this indie movie a few years back where I played the head of a zombie biker gang. Called *Harley Hellriders*. Twist was, we're actually still kinda human. We ride around trying to find the cure for a virus being spread by this evil corporation that's actually a front for an alien invasion. Well, I wasn't the head of the gang at the start. I became the head when the original leader got eaten by this giant plant."

"Hey wait," Leah says. "I think I saw that! Didn't it play at the Sacramento film festival?"

Willard's eyes light up. "We showed, like, 15 minutes of it there to try to raise some money to make the rest!"

"I thought I recognized you," Leah says. "You were the one with the rod sticking out of your face, right?"

Willard nods like his head's on a gimbal. Leah may not know it, but she has just made a friend for life. "My guy's backstory was that he's a nuclear scientist who gets caught in a reactor explosion when the invasion happens, so he's got this big fuckin' radioactive rod sticking out of his cheek. It's cool 'cause he can yank it out and use it as a weapon. We storyboarded out this awesome scene at the end where I break into the complex to get the cure that's gonna save mankind and I have to battle, like, 200 aliens to get at it. I was even learning all these martial arts moves for it."

Ivanka snorts. "You twisted your ankle trying a simple spin kick. I finally gave up trying to show you or you'd have broken something."

"She's just pissed 'cause I was getting' so good at it," Willard whispers.

Ivanka stands up. "Oh yeah? How about we try again?"

"Relax, I was just kidding!" Willard says, backing down faster than a senator caught soliciting an undercover cop. Ivanka smiles and sits back down. Willard may be the nominal head of receiving, but there's no question that the magazine department holds the balance of power back here.

"Did you get the money to finish it?" Leah asks.

"Nah," Willard says. "But I did get to shoot one cool fight scene where I light my arm on fire. They put all this goo on there to make sure I didn't burn, but I guess the guy didn't mix it right and there were these, like, flaming gooey meteorites flying off as I was punching dudes. It looked awesome, but I got a pretty bad second degree burn that trashed one of my tattoos. Plus I melted this other guy's glasses."

"Willard doesn't just suffer for his art," I say. "He makes other people suffer, too."

I spend the rest of the morning showing Leah how our restocking and ordering system works. It's not as sophisticated as the one she used to use, but the volumes are also a lot lower, so there's less chance of making a catastrophic error.

"I once hit zero instead of return and accidentally ordered three hundred copies of a computer manual instead of 30," Leah says. "Fortunately, it turned out to be the new edition and not the old one, which would have been non-returnable."

"Don't call it luck," I say. "Take credit for being ahead of the curve. The publisher once sent us a thousand copies of Kim Kardashian's autobiography. Took up a whole skid. It was a mistake on their end, or so they said. I think they were just looking to get rid of it. I'd never heard Dante swear so loud."

"Why? He hates the Kardashians?"

"That and Willard accidentally dropped the skid on his foot. It was the first time in years that Dante had a legitimate reason not to go on a date arranged by his mother."

"His mother arranges his dates?"

"It's a long story."

"Does she not know that he's gay?"

"She's from a tiny village in Calabria where they stone you if you don't wear black for the rest of your life after your husband dies."

No sooner have I said this than Dante steps into the office.

"How goes the training?" he asks.

"Good," Leah says. I see her consider saying something about Dante's mother and decide against it. She has only just started and doesn't know how Dante might react, even to sympathy.

Dante takes off his coat and tosses it over his usual chair. "Great. Now we can actually have a manager's meeting with all the managers. Except for Mina. She's still sick, but she's hoping to be feeling okay enough to cover her shift tonight."

The head cashier usually attends the manager's meetings, but it's been so long since we actually had one that I had almost forgotten about them. Dante grabs himself a piece of gum from his desk drawer and sits down, jaw muscles working away like he's warming them up to climb a mountain.

"The first item on the agenda is that Umex has increased their offer for the building."

I sag in my chair and swear under my breath. Leah looks confused.

"Sorry, who?"

"Umex is a ginormous holding company," I explain. "One of the companies they hold is our national competition, Iterations. They want to buy up this block so they can knock everything down and build another shitty retail monolith on top of it that will include said giant bookstore."

"That's right," Dante says. "This building is owned by Cynthia and Marty Ackerman, who started Village Books more than 30 years ago."

"Are they thinking about selling?" Leah asks nervously. It's never good news to find out you may just be about to lose a job you have barely started doing.

"That's not the issue," Dante says. "The problem is, Marty had a stroke a few years back and believes that every day is June 7, 1976. He's in a palliative care centre that he thinks is the member's lounge of the Optimist's Club where every night is poker and ribs night. Cynthia would never sell in a million years no matter what they offered, but her health isn't the best, either. She broke her hip last year and has been talking more about moving down to Orlando where it doesn't ice up so much in winter."

"If that happens," I continue, "it'll mean turning control of the business over to their kids, who have no romantic notions about it and would sell the whole thing in five minutes flat for a new iPhone and a case of beer."

The Ackermans have two kids: Walter and Maude. Walter has been tossed out of two universities. He was kicked out of the first for repeatedly showing up for classes drunk and the second for never showing up for anything ever. He went to India to "find himself" last year, but evidently he wasn't there, and he came back empty-handed. He is currently living in his mother's basement, where he spends most of his time waiting for her to die. Maude is a soulless Bay Street lawyer who works 150 hours a week and thinks her parents' attachment to their life's work is "quaint." Having met her, I can safely say she's not the kind of person who would have any compunction about getting her mother declared legally incompetent to turn this site into condominiums.

"Don't worry about it," Dante says. "Cynthia's tough. She's gonna live forever."

He doesn't really believe this and neither do I, but it's all we've got. Poor Leah is having a rough first day: a germaphobe, a zealot, a zombie punk, and now looming unemployment.

"On a brighter note, we need to start organizing the Christmas party," Dante says.

Because seasonal shopping starts the day after Halloween, those of us in the retail ghetto can only afford to take time away for a party either in the last two weeks of November or the beginning of February, when the extended boxing day sales are finally over. We always have ours in November. We need to get our drinking in early or we'd never make it through the season.

"Falstaff's?" I ask, although I don't need to. We always have the party at Falstaff's.

Dante nods. "I already talked to Mickey about getting the private room upstairs, so we just need to organize a few details and make sure Willard doesn't smuggle in any pot this time. Can I leave that up to you two?"

"We will make it our primary action item," I say, giving Leah a nod. The party doesn't need any actual planning, per se, so I'm going to have to work hard to invent some. Any operation that involves me working more directly with Leah is going to get my fullest attention.

# -7-

I'm on my way in to Café Olé when I bump into Ebeneezer on his way out. He's carrying a large and wonderful-smelling coffee in one hand. Although I don't really care for the taste of the stuff, it smells great. He also has the distinct look of a man caught sneaking out of his neighbour's house while the husband is away on business.

"Oh, er, hello, my boy," he says, clearly flustered. "Just finishing for the day?"

I nod. "Just starting?"

He nods rather a lot. "Oh, indeed, indeed. Ah…" He looks around like a new topic of conversation might be flapping around in the air like a loose parrot. "The new manager seems like a very, uh, capable young woman. What's her name again?"

"Leah." Ebeneezer has never forgotten a single thing for as long as I've known him.

"Yes, yes, indeed," he says, distracted. "Tell me, my boy, did you ever hear anything back from that publisher who expressed an interest in your book?"

"I did. They were scaling back production and couldn't fit it into their slate after all."

"They are buffoons who will rue the day," he says, shaking his head. "The important thing is that you not become discouraged. I absolutely forbid it."

I smile. "That's very kind of you."

"Oh tosh. You know, Joyce self-published his first novel and a bookstore was the only one willing to publish Ulysses."

"Joyce didn't write about a psychopathic religious monomaniac obsessed with an 11th century military religious order who stalks a college campus."

"And without doubt he would have sold far more copies had he done so," Ebeneezer says. "I found it gripping."

"Thank you, Mr. C, that means a lot."

He checks his watch and says he must run, so I hold the door open and allow him to pass. There's a distinct chill in the air and I've come in for one of the café's signature Spanish hot chocolates before heading home.

Fermina Marquez, who has been the owner of Café Olé ever since she came to the country about 25 years ago, is behind the counter. I would say she's in her late 50s or early 60s, but with her dark, Latin features could easily pass for twenty years younger. She's from a small town on Spain's Mediterranean coast called Luceno del Sol. Every winter she complains a little more about the cold and the snow and talks about moving back, but she hasn't done it just yet.

There's a rumour that she had a torrid affair with Pablo Picasso and was actually one of the subjects for the great painter's "Female Nude and Smoker" (the other being Pablo himself), but this is unconfirmed. Rumours are Fermina's stock-in-trade. Rare is the piece of gossip that escapes her electronically amplified hearing or bifocally corrected gaze.

The only thing she appears to be completely unaware of is the fact that Ebeneezer is besotted with her and has been for some time. Her husband Miguel died in a construction accident about five years ago. Apparently one of the workers on a demo crew lost his balance when trying to shoo away a pesky crow that had been trying to steal their lunches and fell on Miguel's car from twelve stories up. While Miguel was still in it. Miguel wasn't actually injured, but the shock caused a heart attack that in turn caused him to drive through the barricades and into an abandoned subway tunnel that was being excavated by a city works crew. I'm not sure what the coroner wrote on the report under "cause of death", but whatever it was, it was probably a gross oversimplification.

According to Dante, Ebeneezer has been a regular ever since the place opened. The only time he doesn't make a café stop part of his day is during the three weeks in February that Fermina makes her annual pilgrimage home, leaving the store in the custody of her small army of regular part-timers. I try to schedule Ebeneezer for as little time as possible during that period because he is even more crotchety than usual.

Fermina lost some of the hearing in her left ear to a virus when she was young and wears a hearing aid that makes it a lot easier for her to eavesdrop on the many secret conversations that take place in her café. This is the prime reason that she's the best source for the latest gossip. She's better at eavesdropping on other people's conversations than Harry Caul.

I amble up to the counter and order a *churros con chocolate* to go. It's a pudding-thick hot chocolate that comes with finger-shaped doughnuts that are used for dipping. The doughnuts are made fresh in the back every morning and are absolutely delicious.

"My Ebby seems almost as infatuated with this new manager as you are," Fermina says as she begins scooping the *churros* into a small brown paper bag. "I have seen her betrothed. It will not last."

"I appreciate your confidence, Fermina," I say. There's no point pretending otherwise. Fermina probably knew about my Machiavellian desires even before I did.

"Is not an opinion," she says. "Is fact. I saw them in here just the other night. They were fighting at that table right there." She points to a corner table at the far side of the café, next to the door.

My curiosity is piqued. "Fighting?" I ask, leaning forward and dropping my voice. "Really? What about?"

Fermina smiles enigmatically. She's not about to give up the goods that easily. Information is her currency. "But how can you pursue this woman when you are already dating the cashier? The one whose husband has deserted his army post?"

"I'm not," I say, keen to set the record straight. "She's going out with S...omebody else now." Best not to use Sebastian's name. "Besides, we were never really dating. So what were they fighting about?"

"Well, of course I did not hear everything," she says, which is not true, but we'll let that go for the time being. "He does not want her to join some group of actors. He said it would interfere with his business plans or some such thing."

She must be talking about the theatre group, which I'm sure Grover thinks is a great big waste of time. "And what did she say?"

Fermina drops the *churros* on the counter and turns to get the hot chocolate. "She say she has joined and will not quit. It seem she do this already once before. She even threaten to give him back his ring."

I am not aware of it, but I have actually stopped breathing. "And what happened then?"

What happens then is that the door opens and Leah strolls in.

"There you are!" she says in a way that suggests I have been hiding out under an assumed name because of a fatwa. "Are you around Friday? Anything going on?"

I was supposed to be going to see a movie with Sebastian, but those plans are now tossed in the can. "Nothing that I know of."

"A friend of mine's working backstage at a production of *Rosencrantz & Guildenstern are Dead* and got me tickets to the opening. You wanna go? Grover's outta town on a business meeting."

Do I wanna go? Is the pope a sexually repressed white man? "Sure! That sounds great."

"Awesome. It's an early show, so maybe we can grab a bite at Falstaff's after. I'll call you tomorrow at work."

And then, just like that, she's gone again. Somebody could have thrown a grenade through the window and I would not have been more stunned. Fermina hands me my chocolate with a knowing look.

I feel so good about this that the next day I allow Sebastian to talk me into pulling the ISBN scam on Miroslav for what must be the hundredth time.

It works like this: we find an old, unused, out of print entry in the system and give it a new title, a new classification, and a large enough quantity that it should be relatively easy to find. One of us then calls the store pretending to be a customer, provides the ISBN number, and then diligently waits while our target goes searching in vain until either the penny drops or they admit that they can't locate it and ask for a phone number so they can call back after a more extensive search.

Because new staff are taught that whatever is in the computer is gospel, a surprising number of them fail to realize that there is no science fiction book called *Prince Dink's Voluptuous Testicle Battle on Uranus*, no children's religious self-help book entitled *Why Does God Hate Us, Mommy?*, no *Pedophile's Guide To Southwestern Ontario* in travel guides and no tween series called *Barbie's Vampire Fraternity Gang Bang*.

I usually come up with the titles and Sebastian makes the phone call. As an aspiring actor (amongst many other aspirations), he's much better at disguising his voice, which he usually does by adopting an outrageous accent. He has so far been a Transylvanian count, an Australian bush pilot, a disgraced Italian former cabinet secretary and a world champion banjo player from Kentucky. Today's special guest is a KGB defector named Vladimir who is desperate to get his hands on a copy of *50 Ways To Love Your Lever – An Onanist's Guide* by P. Niles Troker.

Miroslav is the only staff member who has fallen for this ruse more than once. While I freely admit that it is wrong in a corporate HR sense to subject an employee to this kind of exploitative harassment, it is also fun. When a small shipment of commencement bibles was partially burned as a result of an accident in receiving (Willard tossed a joint in the wrong direction), instead of throwing them out, we convinced Miroslav to set them up on a small display table with a sign reading: "Signed by the Author". For safety reasons, we made sure to do this on Mother Teresa's day off.

While Sebastian waits for Miroslav to find his whack guide, I inform him of my pending social engagement with Leah.

"No shit? Zat's terrific! Do you zink you can wheedle zis Whetstone lump out of ze picture?"

"I don't know, comrade. It wouldn't be a very *perestroika* thing to do."

"Screw *perestroika*," Sebastian says. "All it do is drive up price of wodka."

I don't tell Sebastian that Leah and her fiancé were fighting as this will only egg him on and I don't need any encouragement. "Speaking of other men's wives, how are things going with Mina?"

Sebastian is about to answer when we are interrupted by a knock at the door. We always make these calls from the manager's office as the phones on the floor would be entirely too conspicuous. Miroslav sticks his head in.

"Guy on phone look for tug book," he says, gesturing in a way that would be enough to end most political careers. "I no find. You see?"

I pretend to think, which is really just a cover to try and screw my expression into something other than a laugh. "I think I remember seeing Lolita putting them in the dump bins up at cash. Why don't you ask her?"

Miroslav nods and disappears.

Sebastian shakes his head and smiles. "You are evil bastard."

He's right. I am an evil bastard. I send halfwits off in search of imaginary masturbation guides. I don't take my job very seriously. I screw other men's wives. I try to steal other men's fiancées. I once accidentally shoplifted a CD and didn't take it back. I don't volunteer and haven't given any money to charity since buying a box of chocolate almonds from a little kid in front of a grocery store two years ago. I think most people are a pain in the ass – particularly my downstairs neighbour, who likes to have sex to George Thorogood songs. Or he did until I snuck into his apartment while he was out and replaced *Ride Till I Die* with a burned copy of *Trout Mask Replica*. Things have been quiet since then.

"She came over last night," Sebastian says, looking sheepish.

"Say what?"

"What can I say? She's very insistent and I don't have your monk-like superpowers of resistance."

"What about her husband? Sergeant Section 8? Aren't you worried that he's gonna walk in on you changing the oil and skullfuck you to death with your own amputated leg?"

Before Sebastian can answer, Miroslav comes back on the phone to say that he can't find the nonexistent book. Sebastian says thank you in his best Vladimir Putin voice, provides the phone number of the local conservative member of parliament for callbacks (the last time we used the number of a local adult novelty supply shop) and then hangs up.

"Sure, it crosses my mind every once in a while," he says. "But I have bigger things to worry about."

"I'm afraid you have me at a loss. Is she pregnant?"

"No. Christ! I hope not. No, my problem is that the pope has found out about it."

By "the pope", he means his mother. Sebastian's mother is the principal of a Catholic girl's high school. She is a former nun and takes a dim view of many of her offspring's extracurricular activities.

"Oh. And does she know…?"

"She knows everything," Sebastian sighs. "Mina's mother called the house one night looking for her. You ever meet Mina's mother?"

"Nope."

"Ugh. She's a monster. All she does is smoke, play online poker and complain about her knees, which apparently swell up like melons if it rains. Anyway, she gave my mother the full lowdown."

"Uh oh."

"Fucking *uh oh* is right. Now there's a papal decree requiring that I break the whole thing off. If I don't, then I'll be excommunicated."

"As in…"

"As in fucking kicked out on the street as in. I'll be fighting for space with that crazy guy who stands on the corner with a coffee cup full of Colt 45 screaming at taxi cabs."

"Well there you go. Now you have both a financial incentive and a survival incentive to shut the whole thing down."

Sebastian gets up and starts to pace. "Unfortunately, I'm afraid the whole thing isn't quite as straightforward as that, old bean."

"What? Why?"

"Well, it seems that, as a side effect of all this wanton fornication, I have rather, well, developed genuine feelings in the process."

"Seriously?" I feel bad about saying it that way, but, I mean, come on. Seriously? *Mina*? The possibility never even occurred to me. Which, I suppose, is one more reason why I'm an evil bastard. "Wow. So whatcha gonna do?"

"I don't know," he mutters. "I'm rather attached to domesticity. By which I mean, not living in a box beneath an underpass."

With anyone else, I would float the possibility that it was just a bluff, but I know that's not the case. I've had an audience with the pope. Her edicts are not bull. "You can't exactly move in with Mina. Shtupping a guy's wife is one thing, but taking over his garage is completely offside."

"Thanks for the sympathetic ear."

"Sorry. You can always crash on my couch if you need to."

"Thanks. I wish I'd paid more attention during that fraud seminar Dante made us sit through last year. Pulling off an identity theft would be extremely helpful to the cause right about now."

# -8-

Celebrity biographies is one area of the store I can do without.

They come in several varieties. First, there's the latest star of some canned TV comedy who is handed a book contract by a desperate publisher (which is all of them, these days) and now has to scramble to fill 150 pages or so with something other than one liners. These books tend to contain a lot of lists, silly graphics, personal revelations that have been carefully vetted by the star's legal and public relations staff, and banal anecdotes about what a dork they were back in high school. Like the shows they come from, they usually have a couple of good jokes and the rest is filler.

The next category is rock stars you thought were dead already. These ones are bought for lurid descriptions of drug-fuelled groupie sex and sticking it to the man by destroying a hotel room that costs more per night than the average person makes in a year. They often climax with the sobering death of some nameless session musician or roadie that inspires the wastrel subject to get back on the righteous path of his artistic muse.

Actor biographies are the worst. If they've been at it for a long time, their bios read like a long list of ego-boosting, name-dropping, backhanded compliments designed to enforce the fiction that despite becoming one of the richest and most famous people on the planet, they're still just the same old dreamy small town kid they always were. This even if they were arrested twice for throwing a potted palm tree at a concierge. Or breaking

Lily Tomlin's nose with a tennis racket. Or stealing the pillow Lincoln's head rested on after he was shot.

The final group is the non-famous famous people. This includes business executives, movie producers and software pioneers. Nobody reads those. They ship us 20 copies and then ninety days later we ship 20 copies right back. So you took a cheesy British reality show and repackaged it for American audiences with great success? Good for you. Got the Stone Roses out of their 25-year contract with Silvertone? Hey, pat yourself on the back. Now sail off over the horizon on your yacht and stop cluttering my shelves with your memories of the time you rear-ended Tom Clancy's limousine on the Rickenbacker Causeway and he shot out your windows with an unlicensed MP-5.

I only bring this up because I just realized that I've been talking a lot about other people, but have said very little about myself. Fair enough. Some detail is in order, but I'll keep it to a minimum.

I was born in Scotland and moved to Canada when I was two. My parents considered moving back when I was nine and we spent the summer there looking at relocation options. The only thing I remember was that the first questions kids my age asked on the street or in the park was whether I was a "p" or a "c." I had a hard enough time understanding them as it was. In this case, I knew what they were saying, I just didn't have any idea what they were talking about. They were, of course, asking if I was a protestant or a catholic. That didn't help much, though, because I didn't know the difference. The difference, it turned out, was spending a pleasant afternoon kicking around a soccer ball or *being* the soccer ball.

The word *cunt* was also incredibly popular. Scottish schoolkids threw it around the way my Canadian friends might say *knob* or *doofus*. Not knowing what it meant, I made the mistake of calling my uncle William a silly cunt when he dropped his knife on the floor during dinner and I spent the rest of the evening in my room. My parents decided shortly thereafter that Scotland was not for them and we returned to the familiar sprawl of the great Canadian suburb.

I was a quiet kid. I was generally a good student in everything except for math. Numbers made less sense to me than hieroglyphs, which at least had some sort of interpretive symbolic meaning. I wasn't terribly social. High school was the closest thing to a penitentiary that I ever care to experience.

Other details. I'm a decent pool player. I like wine and beer, but liquor makes me barf after even limited exposure. One part of my heritage did survive in that I love soccer and think hockey is a sport dominated by toothless goons. In Scotland, the toothless goons are usually in the crowd. I keep track of the hapless Toronto FC by geographical default, but think that watching FC Barcelona move the ball around the field like the other team isn't even there is as close to athletic perfection as a sport can get.

I took journalism because I wanted to write and realized during my internship that I didn't want to work for a newspaper. I came to this realization at 7:15 a.m. on the second Saturday I had to work when one of the editors mentioned that a 7-year-old kid had been hit by a car the night before. All they had was the last name. They wanted me to call every single one of those names in the phonebook until I got the right one and ask if she was dead or just badly injured. I got lucky. It was the first number I tried and it was just a broken leg. She'd be fine in a few weeks. My career aspirations, however, were significantly damaged.

Even if I had wanted to work for a newspaper after that, they were being closed down faster than speakeasies. I got a job working for a small electronic publishing company that specialized in lifting (although "stealing" would be an equally valid description) government contracting information off the web and repackaging it for subscribers. I was one of the people who lifted and repackaged. It was mostly data entry work and was every bit as exciting as it sounds.

After two years, the owner had to sell because his wife was suing for divorce. Apparently, he also ran a spray-on tanning business in Orlando and had been caught using the application wand with three of his staff, one of whom posted video of their escapades online. He said not to worry as his various lawsuits would have no impact on day-to-day operations, but the next day everything had been cleared out, including some of the leftover food in the staffroom fridge.

With job prospects thin on the ground, I went back to school and took film. I spent my days trying to shoot a properly-timed exposure of a grey card and my evenings working at the campus bookstore, which paid me just enough to cover utilities or groceries, but rarely both. I was in a permanent state of debt. At the end of first year, I made a spectacularly awful 28-minute short about a newspaper reporter who discovers that all the news is invented by a little old man in a tiny office on the eighth floor. He follows the old man home and accidentally ends up running him over with his car. The next day, he gets to work and discovers that he's been assigned a new office on the eighth floor. I called it *Late Edition*. I don't know what the hell I was thinking.

First year ended and I didn't have the money I'd need to go on to second, where I would be expected to come up with the financing to produce an even bigger cinematic affront than the existential farrago I had created in the first. Since I was no longer a student, I was disqualified from working at the bookstore, and so in one fell swoop was divested of both direction and occupation. I did manage one small piece of luck, however: a former classmate named Lucia Andolini, an economics major who had taken the same Film Theory course I did as an elective, mentioned that her brother Dante ran a bookstore downtown and needed somebody with experience in a hurry.

So began my association with Village Books.

I did a modest amount of dating in that time. In journalism school, I dated a girl named June who lived on a farm that was 45 minutes outside of town. I know it's shallow to admit it, but the length of the drive and the barn smell that pervaded the place really kiboshed the enterprise. Her older brother Maynard played competitive banjo, which required him to practice constantly. I don't know about you, but I personally find it difficult to develop any sexual momentum whilst images of Ned Beatty getting sodomized by toothless yokels are replayed in my head. Maynard was a weird guy. He was 35 years old and spent his entire day playing banjo, eating microwaved Cheezeroos (a bar app of his own invention consisting of a slice of processed cheese melted overtop a bowl of Cap'n Crunch) and watching Doctor Who reruns on TV.

In any event, June failed first semester and went to work for the dairy council as some sort of administrative assistant. Maynard won a major banjo competition in Kentucky and was a guest musician on Steve Martin's last album.

I stayed away from dating for a while after that In film school, I hooked up briefly with a leather-clad bisexual named Noomi. Noomi looked like a biker chick with tattoos and piercings all over her body, but in reality had just completed a postgraduate degree in economics as a Rhodes Scholar at Oxford. Instead of going to work for a think tank or a bank, she decided to become the exact opposite of everything she'd just spent the last twenty-plus years preparing for and dove headlong into the counterculture with the same ferocious determination she had displayed in academia.

To this end, she fronted a performance punk band named SlutWok and made experimental short films using a cell phone camera. Most of the videos consisted of close-ups of her inserting and removing things from various bodily cavities intercut with train derailments from Thomas the Tank Engine videos. I'm not sure what she was trying to say, but I don't think she did, either. The films were only two minutes long, but I never managed to watch one all the way through.

I think she liked me because I had a certain amount of knowledge about film and music and culture in general. Once she had extracted that knowledge, she moved on. She also had an incredibly annoying tendency to act like she'd known about something forever and that everyone else who liked it was just a parasitic cultural tourist. Her tendency to high dive into her own shallow pool of pop cultural knowledge led to more than a few social injuries. She got into many arguments that turned nasty when it became apparent that not only did she not know what she was talking about (no one in their right mind would argue that *My Best Friend's Birthday* is Tarantino's best film) but that she didn't even know enough to realize how terribly out of her depth she was.

Sex was the same way. Her parents had only ever approved of one boyfriend throughout her university years: a sallow, dry martini lie-back-and-think-of-England type she referred to sarcastically as Sir Tristan Limpdick of Lesser Fuckington. She attacked her lack of sexual experience the way a pack of starving hyenas might pounce on a Kenyan mail carrier. She started with toys (handcuffs, dildos, vibrators, saddles), most of which she ordered online. After those had been tested, she moved on to swinger's parties and clubs, but those didn't last long because she found most of the members were old, fat, hairy and gross, so she started her own club called Noomi's Sex Dungeon. This gave her the ability to vet the members, so to speak.

I watched all of this with a certain bemusement. I didn't mind if she was seeing other people, but I drew the line at also being in the room with them when they were naked. As Jerry Seinfeld once said, I'm not an orgy guy. She laughed at what she called my bourgeois inhibitions and stopped calling. I was fine with that. Certain piercings, as anyone knows who has tried to negotiate them under poor lighting conditions, can be something of a logistical nightmare.

Her real name was not Noomi, by the way. It was Cicely. The last I heard, she was working for the IMF and about to marry a Tory cabinet secretary.

After that, I dated an Italian girl whose father owned 22 shotguns. I know this because he insisted on showing them to me the first time I came over to the house. He didn't do this in an overtly threatening way. He had been collecting them his whole life and showed them to every male who set foot in the place, including meter readers and repairmen. Despite the fact that he was an anti-government, pro-gun right winger and I'm a left wing socialist nanny-stater, we got along immediately. I spent more time at the house talking to him than I did to his daughter and in fact we still keep in touch. Every year he gets a permit to hunt a moose in Newfoundland and this year one of his party dropped out, so he asked if I wanted to come along instead because they need at least eight people to lift the thing. Unfortunately, Dante was taking his vacation the same week and I couldn't get the time off.

His daughter was a culinary student at George Brown that I met when she came into the store looking for a cookbook that had been turned into a dull piece of lifestyle porn that was playing at the theatre down the street. You know, the kind of movie that says everything will be all right if you just move to the south of France or Tuscany, eat whatever the hell you want and have sex with the token Local Hot Single Person, who, despite being the only hot person for 200 miles, is mysteriously still single.

We got talking and ended up going to see the movie a few nights later. I thought it was formulaic and dull, but she liked it. I kept my opinion mostly to myself because she was the only hot single person who had wandered into my orbit in a while and I didn't want to screw things up.

We managed fairly well for a while despite the fact that we had almost nothing in common. Still being a student, her idea of an enjoyable Saturday night was to get liquored up at the campus bar and then head down to stand in line in front of whichever nightclub was new and hot that week. I went along a few times, but it really wasn't my scene. On other nights, we'd go to restaurants or the movies or even the theatre, which I always pronounced *thee-ah-taaah* to try to make it sound more fun and less pretentious, but it never really worked. She was a book that I was only reading to find out how it ended.

She graduated and got a job in the kitchen of a large and plonky Niagara winery that catered to packaged tours for seniors and downmarket honeymooners who couldn't afford Europe. I went to visit her there shortly after she started. It was like *Dirty Dancing*. Every night the hotel put on a vaudeville comedian and a "musical spectacular" for a well-lubricated dinner crowd, most of whom wouldn't know the difference between *Il Trovatore* and *Starlight Express*.

I could tell that something was up as soon as I had arrived for the weekend to find that she had not booked the day off as planned and was in fact working the whole time. I hadn't even opened my suitcase when she dropped the big one: she'd met somebody else. His name was Gary and he was training to be a sommelier. They were going to work at the winery for a couple of years and then open their own restaurant, where she would do the cooking and he would suggest expensive wines to go along with the food. They were going to call it *NemaTode* because they thought it sounded funny.

I should have accepted this news with equanimity and dignity, wished them luck, and been on my way, but I had just spent three frustrating hours stuck in hellish traffic on the 403 and was in a mood to unload. I pointed out that a nematode was a microscopic worm that eats bug larvae, which was a perfect metaphor for the two of them. I don't know how, exactly, but it sounded better at the time when I yelled it across the lobby. I told her that she could have told me she was screwing this Gary guy sooner and saved me a three-hour drive. I told her that she was lousy in bed and had a vagina that was like a small bag full of partially-melted ice cubes. I would have said more, but I was escorted from the building by security, at which point I threw my suitcase back in the car and peeled out of the parking lot so fast that I almost ran over half the contingent from the Sleepy Valley Retirement Lifestyle Community.

In retrospect, I'm surprised I reacted the way that I did. I never really thought things were going to work out and was actually kind of glad to see her go. Her father took my side in the whole thing. He didn't like Gary. I could tell this from the glee in his voice when he informed me that Gary had been fired after he was caught having sex with one of the pour girls (the ones who pour the wine into tiny free plastic cups at the tasting bar) in the climate-controlled storage cabinet. If NemaTode was going to happen, it would be without Gary's questionable expertise. His daughter, meanwhile, had given up on the restaurant trade and was going to night school to get her real estate licence.

And that, aside from one minor indiscretion in the cash office, is that.

# -9-

I got my first clue that my night out with Leah wasn't a date when she showed up with four other people. I got my second when I saw that one of the four was Aldous.

The other three attendees consisted of women from Leah's theatre troupe: Girta the pretentious director, Ribika (yes, that is how it's spelled) the coke-snorting lighting director, and Penelope, who I at first thought was a deaf mute because she never said a word but was later informed was in fact conducting an acting exercise in "the power of silence." Penelope was Aldous's nominal date. I told him as an aside to spare no energy or expense in pursuing her as I couldn't imagine a better match in the history of human relationships.

The second piece of bad news was that the courtesy block of tickets for the Stoppard play had somehow failed to materialize and that we were going to see something called *The Origin of Speciousness* instead. It was playing at a hole-in-the-wall theatre in the East end with bench seating where we constituted 75 per cent of the audience. The other two members of the crowd were a couple of homeless guys who wandered in at the halfway point to get out of the rain and sat in the back row making unintelligible catcalls before wandering back out at the start of the second intermission. I guess even pneumonia was preferable to sitting through five more minutes of what was happening on stage. I can sympathize with that, as I considered bolting myself.

The play opened on two women standing back-to-back at centre stage, one wearing only a bra and the other wearing only yoga pants. Standing far off to the right was another woman who I at first thought was a stage hand as she was wearing a construction helmet and overalls, but it became evident when she failed to shuffle out of sight that she was somehow a part of the proceedings. What that part was, I'm not sure. She seemed to spend most of her time trying to impersonate a flowering geranium.

The two women on stage began reciting a litany of advertising slogans from the last forty years while images of supermodels, playboy centerfolds and stills from Russ Meyer movies projected on a large white screen behind them. I didn't think it was possible for something like that to go on for half an hour, but somehow they managed it. I also used to think it was not possible to become bored by the sight of breasts, but I lost that illusion years ago when I saw *Showgirls*.

When we got up for the first intermission and wandered into the lobby to gaze uncomfortably at pre-poured glasses of tap water and some very suspicious looking baked goods arrayed on a table (ambitiously priced at $10 for a combo – *all proceeds to our productions!*), I was at a loss to answer when Leah asked me for my opinion.

"Well…" I venture, "at least they didn't have as many accidents as *Spider-man* the musical." This was not counting the time that the woman at the side of the stage leaned over too far and her construction helmet fell off with a loud thud. That may have been intentional. It was hard to tell.

Girta takes a large mouthful of what may be a Danish and laughs. I don't see her put any money in the payment jar. "They're trying so hard! Poor things. They obviously saw my production of *Cymbeline* from two years ago."

"I saw that!" Aldous says enthusiastically. "It was bold."

I happen to know that the only reason Aldous saw this is because it was widely publicized as an all-female topless rendition of the play, not because he happens to be a fan of late-period Shakespeare. I also happen to know that what little critical attention it drew was not overwhelmingly positive, even from Aldous. He claimed that the staging was awkward, by which he meant the boobs were small and saggy.

Ribika returns from the bathroom for the sixth time, not-so-subtly wiping the white powdery flecks away from her upper lip. I didn't realize that people still did cocaine. I guess the recession is making people cheap and nostalgic. I have been reading lately about how cocaine is making a comeback, particularly in the boho arty sector where it's being cut with Prozac. I guess the mood enhancer helps the user to feel better about being a drug addict.

She too grabs a pastry and crams it in like an anaconda. "Their lighting totally sucks," she says, jaws mulching furiously. Her eyes are so bloodshot that she looks like she has double 8-ball haemorrhages. "The only kind of theatre they should work in is an operating theatre. Ha!"

Penelope uses her fingers to draw invisible lines of expression on her cheeks and then arches her eyebrows in a manner that is entirely mysterious, like the villain in a silent movie. I look at Aldous, not for interpretation but to see how he's making out with all this. He's clearly as lost as the rest of us, but, being Aldous, would never admit it.

"I find it almost Dadaist in its portrayal of fascist female archetypes," he says. "I can't wait to see what's coming in the next act."

I can. This is not the evening I was expecting and the disappointment has put me in a sour mood. Things don't improve when the so-called entertainment portion of the evening ends and it's time to eat. Girta insists we go to a newly-opened Kenyan place called Ghali. The gimmick here is that they have no menus. You place your order from your table using a downloadable smartphone app that costs as much as a bottle of the house red. Not having a smartphone, I have to piggyback my order with Aldous, who hits the wrong button and ends up selecting a bowl of live and writhing bug larvae that I have to pick up with a small silver tool that looks like a pair of dental pliers. The maggots are then cooked by holding them over a Bunsen burner placed in the middle of the table.

Keen to show off for Penelope, Aldous swaps dishes with me and offers to eat the maggots himself. Under normal circumstances, I would refuse such offers (especially since what Aldous ordered doesn't look much better), but I just sat through 90 minutes of godawful theatre and am starving, so I happily accept. I don't know what it is that Aldous ordered, but it actually turns out to be pretty good.

Aldous, meanwhile, makes a game stab at holding the larvae over the flame. The first time he does it, he accidentally holds on too long and burns his tongue on the pliers, dropping the braised pupae in his lap. After a couple more tries, he seems to get the hang of it and offers one to Penelope, who politely refuses by making a gesture that we interpret to mean she's vegetarian. Or it could mean she has no stomach. Or that she would need to be drunk first. Or that she's from a small planet in the vicinity of Betelguese. The power of her silent expression has not overwhelmed us.

"Oh look!" says Girta, pointing at a bald man near the bar. "There's Rod Spacek! He directed that low-budget horror flick that should have won the audience award at TIFF last year! *I Regurgitate Your Mother*. Such a unique visual style! I heard the Weinsteins are producing his next film! I think I'll pop over and say hello."

She gets up and crosses the room with the deliberation of a marine negotiating an obstacle course. I'm surprised that it took her this long to move. Every time the doors opened, she would spin her head around to see who was coming in. It was like eating with the witness in a RICO case. At least we now know why she picked the place. Ribika has, once again, excused herself to use the ladies' room.

Leah leans over and whispers in my ear: "Sorry about this."

"That's okay," I say, poking my plate. "I'm actually enjoying this, whatever it is."

She leans over again. I am compelled to report that she smells wonderful, and that the feeling of her breath against my ear means that I will not be able to get up myself for some time without causing social awkwardness. "This wasn't exactly the evening I had planned."

I shrug to indicate that this isn't exactly the kind of night I had been anticipating either. "What happened to the *Rosencrantz* tickets?"

Leah waves a hand. "Girta said she knew one of the assistant stage managers, but there was some kind of mix up and blah blah blah. I think she was full of it. She just wanted to drag us out to some crappy production she could feel superior to and then come here to suck up to bottom-feeder industry types."

"Why do you bother with them?"

"Believe it or not, they're not as bad as some of the theatre groups I've worked with, and they didn't demand a ton of acting experience or a membership fee, so there's that. And some of their productions are actually pretty good."

Aldous looks up from his larvae. "Ribika's been gone for a long time," he observes.

I look at my watch, trying to remember what time we arrived. Ribika's sea bass curry has been sitting in front of an empty chair for quite a while. "That's true. Maybe one of us should go back there to make sure she isn't dancing facedown on the tile with melted brain matter leaking out of her nostrils."

I start to get up. I don't know why I do this because:

a) she's in the women's bathroom, where I can't go; and

b) I can already hear the sound of approaching sirens.

I'm suddenly overcome with a strange feeling of inevitability. I know the sirens are coming here. There are at least two distinct wails and they seem to be coming from different directions, but they're both getting louder at about the same rate. Where else could they be going? The feeling reminds me of a time that my father told me my uncle couldn't move to Canada because he'd been in jail in Scotland for mail fraud. Don't ask me how, but I knew that was what he was going to say before he told me. Call it a sixth punitive sense.

That's why I'm not really surprised when the ambulance and not one but three police cars screeches to a halt in front of the restaurant. All conversation in the room crashes to a halt. On the sound system, Ali Farka Touré continues to bop along like none of this is happening.

The ambulance crew make it through the door first, weaving between the tables in their dark blue jackets, their bulky red supply bags swinging wildly as patrons lurch out of the way. The cops are right behind them, radios squawking.

"Wow," says Aldous. "What do you suppose is going on?"

The paramedics make their way immediately to the women's washroom where, it later emerges, Ribika has passed out on the toilet and fallen on the floor where she is mistaken for Taylor Swift – I suppose there is a vague resemblance – who happens to be in town for a concert at the ACC. The mistaken identity comes courtesy of a slightly nearsighted 13-year-old bulimic fan who went in to the bathroom to purge and instead found what she thought was her idol passed out on the floor in a puddle of puke. Said fan then took several photos and uploaded them to her Facebook page ("OMG T SWIFT DEAD IN MY TOILET!!!!") before her mother came back to see what was taking so long, grabbed the phone and called 911. The story gets a large photo and three paragraphs under the official concert review on page two of the entertainment section of the *Sun* and no mention whatsoever in the *Star* or *Globe*. Ribika is not named and is simply referred to as a "local veterinary school dropout."

Blood tests later reveal that Ribika has enough cocaine in her system to keep Charlie Sheen awake, but not enough in her purse to be charged with trafficking. Girta clears out of the building in the confusion, leaving the rest of us to answer the questions and pay for her half-eaten *wildebeest a la cornichon*. Penelope comes within a hair of an obstruction charge before grudgingly giving up her mime routine to provide a statement to the police, who are not the least bit interested in the integrity of nonverbal communication.

I finally get back to my apartment at just before midnight and am in the process of relaxing on the couch with a glass of Chablis, some reheated chicken wings and *I'm Your Man* on the stereo when the buzzer goes.

"Sorry for barging in so late," Leah says, stepping tentatively into the hallway. "You weren't heading off to bed, were you?"

"Oh no." *Unless you want to, of course...*

"I just wanted to apologize again for dragging you out for such a lousy evening."

She's smiling in a way that makes me wonder – is she flirting with me or is it just my imagination? Why is she here at midnight? She could have said this tomorrow at work. Or by email. Or on the phone. Or not at all. It's not like the whole thing was her fault. I would very much like to kiss her right now.

Stop it, man. Get a grip on yourself. You've already had a full glass of wine. It's late. These things are affecting your judgment. Stay the course. Firm hand on the tiller. Restraint, dignity and respect.

"Hey, how often do you get to see two half-naked women scream at no one in particular and follow it up with maggots and an overdose?" I say. That's right. Keep it jocular.

"Are those chicken wings?" she asks, looking at my plate with predatory hunger.

"Did you want some?"

"Would you mind? I didn't really get a chance to eat at the restaurant. My food arrived right when the cops got there and I'm not even really sure what it was that I ordered."

"Not at all," I say, waving her into the small dining area next to my galley kitchen. I hand over the entire plate and turn on the oven to prepare some more. "Help yourself."

She sits down at the small circular table and begins to chomp away with a gusto that I find alarming and cute at the same time. "I don't want to eat them all!" she says, although she is well on her way to doing exactly that.

"Relax. They take ten minutes to cook and I have plenty. Eat!"

She gestures to the stereo. "I saw this guy at the Sony Centre."

"Me too!" I say excitedly. "Maybe we were at the same concert."

"Thank God his manager robbed him blind or he'd probably never have toured again. I cried when he sang *Hallelujah*."

"For me it was *Everybody Knows*. And *First We Take Manhattan*. That song has the best opening lines in the history of music."

She drops the bones of her third chicken wing on the plate and lets out a burp that makes us both laugh.

"Sorry!" she says, embarrassed. "Christ, I'm so uncouth."

"Did you want some wine?"

"Please!"

I consider pulling one of my crystal glasses out of the cupboard. I got them from my grandparents. I only have four and save them for special occasions. Although this definitely qualifies, it won't match the one I'm drinking from and will look like I'm trying too hard. Ah, fuck it. What am I saving them for? It's not like Monica Bellucci is gonna get a flat tire right outside my front door and come looking for some help and possibly a dish of pancetta pasta served up with a budget-breaking and nudity-inspiring bottle of Brunello.

"Ooh, nice glass," she says, taking a sip, followed by a gulp. "Nice wine, too."

"Thanks. I got them from my grandparents. The wine came from France via the liquor store around the corner."

"I've been dieting for this audition, so I've been hungry and stressed pretty much all the time."

"Dieting?" I say, giving the word the proper amount of scornful disbelief. "Pardon me for saying so, my dear, but you most certainly do *not* need to diet."

"Thanks, but you should see the women who go in for these things. They look like they're auditioning for World Vision commercials. You know how the camera adds ten pounds? Well that makes them look almost normal."

I can sympathize with the female fixation on weight. We men really are the most incredibly shallow bastards imaginable. That said, I do not care for women you would not want to approach let alone insert something into for fear of stubbing a valuable appendage.

I am trying to think of something to say when she drops the bomb:

"Grover isn't away on business. I broke up with him."

I am aware of the fact that I am standing looking at her and possibly holding something in my hand. Yes. It's a wine glass. Blinking suddenly requires conscious effort.

"Oh. Wow."

"I'm surprised that Fermina didn't tell you."

Fermina? Fermina who? What am I doing standing next to the stove? "Sorry?"

"At the coffee shop. You guys were talking about it before I came in."

Instructions are coming in from my brain, but the receiver has fallen on the ground and no one is picking it up. "Well...that's...too bad."

I look at her hand and see that the ring is in fact gone. How could I have missed that earlier?

"I'm just at a point now where I really want to focus on getting my career off the ground and he wasn't helping. He'd be out working all these crazy hours and then just show up and ask me why the place was such a mess because he had potential investors coming over in like, two minutes.

And why weren't his favourite awful frozen meatloaf dinners all stocked up in the freezer? I told him that if he wanted a maid he could just hire one like he does everything else. You know he went to a massage parlour?"

I shake my head because there really is no way that I could know this unless I was at the same place at the same time. Which, I hasten to add, I was not.

"I couldn't believe it. Of course, he tells me like it's no big deal." She adopts an exaggeration of a manly voice, which is not what Grover possesses: "'*Oh yeah, me and the G&C guys went to this grimy hole in the wall called The Black Rose where these hot eastern European sex slaves gave us $500 hand jobs.*' These wings are excellent, by the way."

I admit that I am having trouble keeping pace with this conversation. "Oh. Thanks."

"I was going to end it anyway. The rub 'n' tug episode was just a handy excuse. Ha! Pardon the pun."

"So where are you living?"

"Oh I got the apartment. He's gone back to California. I may not have it for long, but for now it's nice to have the space. Your place is great."

Is she asking to move in? Something's burning. Why can I smell burning? Do I have some sort of brain tumour? Like that woman in the commercial who tells Dr. Penfield that she can smell burned toast? I think that commercial showed electrodes being applied to an actual brain, the sight of which traumatized me when I was five. It still bothers me, to be honest. What is it that neurosurgeons say? *Once the air hits the brain, you ain't never the same.* You'd think neurosurgeons would be able to come up with something better than just a near-rhyme, what with their god complexes and fancy diplomas.

"Thanks. It's a heritage building, which means I'm legally required to get permission from the historical society before I can hang a picture or open a window, but it makes up for that with bad plumbing and electrical. For example, every time I flush the toilet, the TV changes channels."

She laughs. "That must make channel hopping difficult."

"That's only half of it. When people came over for my World Cup party, I told them to piss out the window during the match."

"That must make it – oh hey, I think your wings are burning there, Icarus."

Huh? Did we start speaking in metaphors? Does it seem like I'm hitting on her or something? It actually takes the smoke detector going off to make me realize that she's talking about my midnight snack. I look down and realize that I put the oven on broil instead of bake. I pull open the door, causing a cloud of smoke to hit me in the face, and yank out the tray, which is now the resting place of a dozen small black carbonized chunks of what was, only minutes ago, edible food. It looks like an aerial photo of a firebombing.

I turn on the range fan and Leah waves a towel under the alarm until it finally stops going off.

"Sorry," she says. "That was my fault for distracting you."

"No, it was my fault." *Besides, you're a wonderful distraction.* No, that wouldn't sound right.

The smoke alarm has broken the mood as effectively as somebody turning on the lights at a party. Leah apologizes for barging in at such a late hour and says she really should get going as we both have to be up to go to work tomorrow, where she is opening and I am closing.

"But we should do this again," she says on her way out the door.

"Absolutely," I agree. "Except have it be completely different."

She laughs. I could listen to that sound all day. Well, maybe not all day. Laughter that lasted all day would sound a little insane. "Good idea. We should definitely do something simpler. How about we go to a movie at The Prestige and then I cook something at my place?"

Did she just suggest that we go on a date? I think that's what she said, but the smoke alarm is still buzzing in my head and there's a lot of smoke in the air. Perhaps it's just the fog of war. "That sounds great."

"Awesome. I'll talk to you tomorrow." And with that, she leans over, pecks me on the cheek, and is out the door. I am still trying to figure out if what I think just happened really happened when the smoke detector starts bleeping again. I climb up on a chair and pull out the battery, then go open a window. It has finally stopped raining and the night air is sharply cooler. We're supposed to get snow tomorrow.

Not that I'm thinking about any of that.

# -10-

Dante has a problem.

Lucretia has just been diagnosed with a rare blood cancer and has an indeterminate amount of time left to live. She could last another ten years or she could go tomorrow. Well, not tomorrow, but soon. She has announced that it is her solemn dying wish that her only son marry before she goes.

Not being one to waste time, she has already arranged a date with the recently-divorced daughter of a family friend, who has apparently had a crush on Dante since they were kids. There is absolutely no way that Dante is going to be able to get out of this one as it is going to take place at his mother's house tomorrow night. Both families are going to be there. Formal introductions will be made, small presents will be exchanged, and nothing will be left to chance. In my mind, I am already picturing the courtship and marriage sequence from *The Godfather* where Michael is exiled in Sicily after shooting Sollozzo and McCluskey. As all self-respecting cinephiles know, that marriage did not end so well.

"What are you going to do?" I ask.

Dante wrings his hands. "I don't know. I may have to go through with it. It may not be so bad, right? People did it all the time in the fifties."

"Are you kidding? Who are you? Douglas Sirk?"

"You have no idea what it's like to be gay and Italian," Dante says. "I might as well be in the army or on a professional sports team. You just don't talk about it. The prime minister admits that he may be a corrupt letch who screws 13-year-olds and gives them cabinet posts, but at least he's not gay and the whole country nods its head and just keeps electing him."

"Come on. Italy has a long and proud tradition of gays. Look at Michelangelo. His women were just naked men with tits."

"You'll never get a wop to admit it," Dante says, shaking his head. Being Italian, I guess he's free to refer to himself and his countrymen in extremely un-PC terms and frequently does. "They'll say he was just a lifelong bachelor who used male models because he was too pious to look at a naked woman."

"What about Doug?"

"Oh we broke up," Dante says. "He used the wrong kind of paint by accident and his jaw stuck shut when it hardened. He had to go to the hospital. They removed all his teeth."

"Ouch. That's awful."

"It's not so bad. He has false teeth that he can take out now when he's working. He's got an exhibit coming up at the Heissen Gallery next week called *Spittychs*. We're still friends. I'll probably go. He was just a little too artsy fartsy for me. Sooner or later, a man needs to get a job, dammit."

Although his orientation requires him to be socially liberal, in fiscal terms, Dante has the political outlook of a Hollywood action star.

"How is your sister handling the news?" Dante's sister is the only one in his family who knows Dante's big secret. After she graduated, she moved out to Vancouver and took a job with an NGO that organized microfinancing in Africa.

"Lucy's in Botswana. She'll be back at the end of the month. She and my mother were never what you would call close. Especially when Lucy got pregnant at 17 and then got an abortion and went off to school instead of marrying the guy."

"So Lucy's probably not on board with the whole fake marriage idea."

Dante chuckles grimly. "She thinks I should just tell her. She thinks the news alone might be enough to kill the old bag."

"You're not actually considering this, are you? 'Cause I kinda get the impression that you are."

Dante rubs his chin. "Ugh. This whole thing is giving me fibromyalgia."

"I don't think you can catch that."

"Then maybe it's gout. Or lupus."

"Do you even know what that is? Wait a minute, who am I talking to? Of course you do. Far be it for me to tell you how to live your life, but I'm going to anyway. You can't marry this woman just because you're afraid of your mother."

"I wanna make her happy at least once," he says defensively. "You know she wanted me to be a priest? Maybe I'll just go along with it for a little while like I did with the seminary."

"Seminary? How'd you get out of that?"

"I faked pneumonia. It was a really cold, draughty old building."

"So what happens if your mother holds on for another ten years or so? I don't think pneumonia is legitimate grounds for a divorce in this province. You may have to take it one step further and fake your own death."

"I know people who can do that. My cousin Marty fakes car accidents to rip off insurance companies."

"Dante, you're hopeless."

"My mother's had a hard life. My father ran off with the cleaning woman when I was seven. She told everyone he died in a coal mine collapse."

"I didn't realize that Scarborough was such big mining country."

"She put on black and never even looked at another man. Well, she might have had a thing for our local city councillor. He got a zoning ordinance drafted that forced a Planned Parenthood office to move to another neighbourhood. He used to drive us to mass in the winter. But she broke it off when she found out that one of his parents was Algerian."

"As John Sayles once said, it's always heartening to see one prejudice defeated by a deeper prejudice."

"She's old school, man. My father only moved 20 minutes away in Newmarket, but as far as she was concerned, he was dead. She never even signed the divorce papers. That was a sin, she said. They'd probably still be married if he hadn't gotten drunk and climbed into the polar bear enclosure at the zoo."

"He got eaten?"

Dante shakes his head. "Not totally. They found one of his shoes, which still had his foot in it. And his left arm, which was full of steel pins from the time he tried to manually signal a turn and accidentally swatted a motorcyclist. I guess the bears couldn't bite through those."

"Yeesh." I hope he did this at night when the place was closed and no one was around to watch.

"He was cremated and they sent the ashes to my mother. She dumped them over the head of the cleaning woman, who was having dinner with her sister at Trentino's Deli at the time. She was sure to include the steel pins."

"Seriously?"

"'*You wanted him, you can have him*' she said. '*I'm sure it's not the first time you couldn't get him out of your hair.*' I wasn't there, but I heard about it later."

"I take it back. Maybe you should get married."

"Maybe I could have her committed somewhere," Dante muses. "How many doctors' signatures do you think you need for that? Not anyplace with real dangerous crazies or anything, just someplace with nice high walls and guards to make sure she can't get out. At least not until I've left the country."

"Or you could join the army."

"That's true. At least they would give me a gun I could use to defend myself. The problem is my trigger finger doesn't work. That might be an issue."

"I'm not sure what else to suggest. Either you tell her the truth, or you become part of a long and ignominious tradition of closeted gays in sham marriages. Hey, it worked for Rock Hudson, right? For a while, anyway."

Dante groans. "She wants me to start going to church again so I'll be able to take the wedding prep courses. You know, when the time comes."

"You Catholics. No wonder you invented the Inquisition and set science back 500 years. We'd probably have light sabres and flying cars now if it wasn't for you fuckers. On the plus side, your high school girls do have cool uniforms."

"I'm glad that I don't have daughters who live in your neighbourhood."

"Hey, you keep this up, maybe you will."

Dante picks up the sports section and pretends to study the headline. "I see the Leafs lost again."

"Those guys couldn't beat a handful of cock."

"That's very descriptive."

"You wanna work on some hetero banter? Stuff you can say around her brothers and father so they won't suspect anything?"

"Don't you have any work to do?"

"I thought my work consisted of trying to talk my good friend Dante out of ruining his life, but as he seems hellbent on pursuing that course, I'll head back out onto the floor and try and help Sebastian find space for the approximately one million copies of the new Dan Brown novel we just received."

"Oh yeah, I saw the boxes piled up in receiving. What's it called?"

"*The Puccini Engorgement.* His main guy – you know, the one Tom Hanks is using to buy another private island – he finds out that L. Ron Hubbard's dick is buried under the Washington monument and the church of scientology is keeping it a secret because they're trying to raise the money to make a *Battlefield Earth* sequel."

"You're pulling my leg."

"You should say '*Yanking my chain.*' It sounds more macho."

I get up and am about to head out onto the floor when Dante remembers something.

"Oh hey, you don't know of a reliable cleaning service, do you?"

"Mine isn't bad, but she doesn't always clean the bedroom when I'm in there naked. Why? What's wrong with Esmerelda?"

Esmerelda is a tiny, middle-aged woman from Kingston, Jamaica who cleans the store at nights after we've locked up and everyone else has gone home. I've met her only a couple of times since I've been working at Village Books. She always picks one particular book to read and then hides it in some other section to reduce the chances that someone will buy it and she won't get to find out what happens next. She says she doesn't have the money to waste on books and is lacking the photo ID necessary to get a library card, so she does all of her reading here on breaks between dusting the shelves and vacuuming the floors.

She prefers the kind of romantic series books that are received and returned on a monthly basis like magazines. These books are colour-coded from pink (safe for Victorian ladies to read without incurring brain fevers) to purple (which would make a Penthouse subscriber blush). She favours the *Black Lace* series, which is erotica specifically targeted at middle-aged women of African descent. I know this because I keep finding them stuffed in the Philosophy section. Last week it was something called *Tickling Ebony*.

"She said she can't keep cleaning the store," Dante says. "She claims it's haunted by evil spirits."

"What?"

"She says she hears strange noises coming from receiving. She also says that things are moving around on their own."

"Moving? As in, right in front of her eyes?"

"No. As in, she'll lift something down to clean a shelf and then she'll come back two minutes later and it'll be back where it was. She's refusing to come back unless we have a *bokor* perform a protection ritual."

"A what?"

"Apparently it's some sort of voodoo priest."

"Well I'm sure they're listed in the yellow pages under V. Want me to call and get some estimates?"

"It's weird. She's a good cleaner. She's never struck me as the hysterical type. Maybe we are haunted. This building did used to be part of an old institute for the criminally insane."

"One might argue that it still is."

"You haven't seen or heard anything weird, have you?"

"Since I started or since I walked in the room?"

"Never mind."

"I haven't seen or experienced anything supernatural, if that's what you mean."

Dante waggles his shoulders and looks around nervously. "I don't know. Sometimes I get the feeling that there's this evil…presence hanging around."

"There is. Her name's Lucretia. You always get that feeling when your mother comes in."

Dante gives me a tired look. "True. Thanks for your thoughts on the matter. I'll take them under advisement."

"You always say that and then you never do. Remember the time you asked me if I thought you would look good with permed hair?"

"I do not recall that."

"Remember what I said? I said no one looks good with permed hair. You spent almost a month looking like the teacher from *Welcome Back, Kotter*. Gabe whatever his name was. Kaplan. Then you burned your fingers so badly trying to iron it out that you had to go to hospital. You couldn't dial a phone for a week. You're the only person I know who still has a rotary dial telephone. You really should donate that thing to the Museum of Natural History."

"As I said, I have no memory of any such incident."

"All I'm saying is don't get the perm, Dante." I open the door and head out onto the floor. Unfortunately, I think Dante's only real hope is that his mother kicks the bucket before he ends up walking down the aisle. And, knowing Lucretia, even that might not be enough to stop her.

# -11-

The weekends leading up to Christmas are not unlike the start of a military campaign. No matter how carefully we plan, we know that some of our tanks will run out of gas 50 yards short of a fuel dump. Good personnel will be lost. Defences will be overrun. Blood and coffee will be spilled. Tempers will be short. Erotica will be found on the floor in the men's washroom. And no one will buy any of the 25 copies of *Catelaine* out of the bargain dump bin no matter how steeply Dante discounts them.

For those unfamiliar with it – and that's just about everybody – *Catelaine* is a parody of the monthly women's magazine that has, with a stunning absence of creativity, extended a feline pun over 216 painfully unfunny and at times disturbing pages (one section provides advice on tongue-grooming the kids). They came from a local boutique publisher that went out of business two days after we received them. We tried giving them away as part of a buy-one-get-one-free promotion last year, but even then nobody wanted them. It was a total bust.

Over a three-month period, our inventory will swell from under a half-million dollars to three or four times as much. The store doesn't actually get any bigger, of course, so books are stacked on every single flat surface we can find, which includes the floor. We have even hung them from the ceiling using a fake hammock as part of a promotion for a literary travel book about the South Pacific islands. This lasted until a 300-pound customer in search of a place to sit decided that it looked like a perfect spot to park his substantial mass and brought down part of the ceiling.

It's Saturday afternoon and the store is buzzing. Sebastian, Aldous and Ebeneezer are working the first floor while Mother Teresa and Ivanka do their best to contain the chaos upstairs. Mina and Lolita are working cash, which has had a steady lineup almost since the doors opened. The first real snow of the season is still three inches thick on the ground and it has definitely put everyone in a more seasonal mood. It's so busy that you could go from the front door to the manager's office without touching the floor.

I've been trying to get some of the giant backlog of new releases out of receiving and onto the floor, dealing with the usual cash and customer issues, helping with the phones (we only have two lines, but they are either ringing or on hold at all times), and trying to find someone to cover Miroslav's evening shift since he drilled a hole through his left hand trying to hang a picture.

I've been so busy, in fact, that I've had hardly any time to think about the fact that tonight's my first real date with Leah. At least, I'm pretty sure it is. Her fiancé is out of the picture and we're going to dinner and a movie. That's a date, right? It all happened so fast.

I duck into the manager's office to grab a bite of lunch and am surprised to see Aldous sitting next to the phone. The 3-digit security code to open the office door is common knowledge and Dante can't remember how to change it, but it's an unwritten rule that staff aren't supposed to just wander in of their own volition when there is no manager present, so this is a minor but surprising transgression.

"Oh, sorry," Aldous says, jumping out of his chair like he's just been caught doing something he shouldn't. Which he has.

"Hi Aldous," I say, looking confused and slightly stern. I sense something is out of whack here. I've never caught Aldous breaking into the office before. Sebastian and Willard, yes. Sebastian sneaks in to take the occasional sip from his hip flask when it's too busy to do it inconspicuously on the floor and Willard sometimes sneaks in to look at pictures of albino boa constrictors online. I think they look like giant tapeworms, but he really wants one as a pet. His live-in girlfriend is not sold on the idea.

Wait, I think. What if this is a genuine HR situation? What if he just found out a family member died? What if he's going to tell me that his parents beat him with sticks? The human resources side of the job is not my strong suit. I hate doing employee evaluations and dealing with their personal crises. I've had employees break down in tears in the office because their cat just died or they just got dumped or they were about to be thrown out of their apartment. I never really know what to do except awkwardly wait for them to stop. Mischa was always better at that stuff.

"What brings you in here, Aldous?"

Aldous looks awkward and embarrassed. What was he doing in here? I look around for an issue of *Maxim* or a loose volume of the *Black Lace* series and am relieved to see neither.

"Sorry," he mutters. "I just needed to use the phone and it was so crazy out there on the floor."

I close the door and sit down. I have, technically, caught him doing something against the rules, which allows me to exercise my authority by indulging my curiosity. "Who did you need to call?"

Aldous chews on his lip. Maybe I am going too far, here. It really is none of my business.

"Oh, it's that girl. You remember. She came out for dinner with us a while back. Penelope. The one who never said anything?"

"I remember." Not that I would be likely to forget. "You two going out again?"

Aldous shifts in his seat, drums his fingers and looks at the floor. "Well, I was thinking about it."

The penny drops. I really am quite incredibly dim sometimes. "Ah, so you were going to call her up and ask her out again."

Aldous nods. "Well, technically, I didn't ask her out the first time. She just came out as part of the group and I thought that we seemed to get along well."

How he could come to that conclusion when dealing with a woman who was socially catatonic for almost the entire evening is a mystery. Maybe he's better at experimentations with silence than I am.

"My hat's off to you, my boy," I say. "I don't care if it's landing on the moon, storming Juno, or running into a burning building, nothing requires more testicular fortitude than picking up the phone cold and asking a woman out. I'll leave you to it. Let me know when you're done."

I get up and move towards the door, but Aldous raises a hand to stop me. "No, that's okay. I already did it."

"Oh." I sit down. His overall vibe is not positive. "And?"

"She said she was busy with rehearsals."

"Shit. Sorry to hear that, man. Well, maybe she really is. Or she might already have a boyfriend. Anything's possible. Don't take it personally."

This is, of course, total bullshit. No human in the history of dating has ever not taken *I'm busy* personally with the possible exception of Larry Flynt, who is not, I think, actually human.

Aldous does not look like he's going to bounce back so easily. "I suppose," he says. "This has happened a few times, though."

"What? Where you've asked a woman out and she said no? That happens to everyone. All the time. You get used to it. Unless you're a rock star or a Rohypnol dealer. Actually, that's a lie. You never really get used to it. It's a kick in the balls every time."

Aldous sighs. "Well, the thing is, I don't really...date. If you want to call it that."

Oh dear. I fear we may be entering into sticky territory here. The wise thing would be to withdraw and allow Aldous to be alone with his thoughts, but I think he's probably spent too much time with them already.

"Have you ever been on what one might call a date? Not counting that, uh, expedition to the theatre?"

"I became quite violently ill after that," Aldous says. "I think it's entirely possible that I didn't sufficiently braise one of those larvae. I also ate one of those pastries during the second intermission. I suspect that was what really did it. I've been out with groups that have included women before, but in terms of semantics, I suppose none of them could really be defined as a, well…you know."

As I recall from Aldous's personnel file, he's 23 or 24 years old. I had better do something to help get this boy laid before he goes Unabomber on us.

"You know things about women," Aldous says. "What should I be doing differently?"

This makes me laugh out loud. "Aldous, what I know about women could just about be squeezed onto the space bar of a Blackberry and is mostly cribbed from other sources."

"Please don't be modest," Aldous says. "I thought about asking Sebastian, but he's loud and I find him slightly intimidating."

How did I get myself into this? All I wanted was a quiet place to eat my lunch. "I can't really tell you anything about women. They're all different. All I can do is give you some general advice."

Aldous leans forward. I really do have his full attention. I'm going to have to tread carefully here. Aldous pays little attention to his personal appearance. It's part of the air of eccentricity he is so careful to cultivate. Unfortunately, this also generates an aura of genuine olfactory unpleasantness and creates the impression that you could cultivate real crops in his grimier crevices.

Often, he'll come into work wearing the same shirt he had on the day before. Because his hair is up in dreads, he washes it rarely, if ever. In winter, he carries a black walking stick with a white ivory handle and wears a heavy wool overcoat that makes him look like a Victorian detective. None of these things exactly scream "babe magnet."

"Keep in mind, this is just general stuff. This could apply to anybody."

Aldous nods eagerly and motions for me to continue. I take a deep breath. What the hell.

"Okay, basics. Hygiene. Everything starts there. I don't care if you look like Brad Pitt, no woman is going to come anywhere near you if you smell like a pig farm. Well, some might, but if you don't look like Brad Pitt then let's just round that number back down to zero. Shower every day. Do it twice if necessary. Use deodorant. Trim nails and errant hairs. Brush your teeth. Carry gum or mints. Wear cologne if you want, but don't put it on like you've got a special attachment for your shower nozzle. With me so far?"

Aldous nods. Nothing to do now but plough ahead.

"Second, hair. Wash it every day. Have it professionally cut. That means not by you and not by some 70-year-old guy who could suffer a stroke at any moment and take your ear off with the clippers. No barber shops. Go to a real salon. Golden rule: have your hair cut by the kind of person you want to date. If you want to date a 70-year-old guy, then more power to you. If you want to date attractive women, then have one of them cut your hair. This is doubly advantageous. One: she'll know what styles are in and hopefully cut your hair accordingly. Two: it'll force you to engage in conversation with her for the 20 minutes or whatever it takes to do the cut. Keep the conversation going. Don't fall back on the weather unless everything else fails. Try to make her laugh. It's good practice. That way, when you do approach an attractive woman on the street, she might not seem so intimidating. It'll help you learn that women are just people and not unattainable objects that sit up on plinths in museums. Follow?"

Aldous nods again. I'm not sure if any of this is sinking in, but at least he hasn't stormed out.

"Third, clothes. Do the laundry. Never ever EVER wear something that's dirty or stained. Women will think – correctly – that you're a lazy slob who'll never do a load of laundry when you'd much rather sit on the sofa and scratch yourself. If a stain won't come out in the laundry, send it to the dry cleaners. If it still won't come out, toss it or use it for painting. When you shop for clothes, don't be afraid to spend. Buy clothes that fit. Buy real shirts and dress pants. Have at least one suit. Buy a good pair of shoes. Look at Dante. Women are throwing themselves at that guy every day. Part of that is he's handsome, but he also dresses well. Granted, it's all moot in his case, but the message is the same. Women notice how you're dressed, so try not to look like a tour guide at Disney."

"This seems like a lot of work," Aldous observes.

"Oh yeah? Think about how much work a woman has to do before she goes out the door in the morning. Hair. That can be an hour right there. Makeup. I'm going to go out on a limb and guess that you don't shave your legs every few days. They're a lot more self-conscious than we are, so they will notice those same details right away when you get them wrong. If your aim is to attract their interest, then bitching about the workload is going to get you nowhere."

"Right, sorry. What else?"

I take a deep breath. "Well, that, basically, is it. After that all you can do is be yourself and hope that the rest falls into place. If that doesn't work, then become a musician or a movie star. Even a monkey could learn to play drums or bass. And as for acting, you don't need to be Brando to read three lines off a cue card. A certain type of woman will naturally gravitate towards either of those options."

"What about a philosopher?"

The historical record is not rife with stories of Wittgenstein, Schopenhauer or Derrida engaging in the kind of orgiastic bacchanalia enjoyed by Errol Flynn or Gene Simmons, but I think I've already given Aldous enough to chew on for one day.

"Or a philosopher, sure. Just keep in mind that not many of them get their name up in lights at Madison Square Garden."

Aldous thinks for a while before getting to his feet and heading for the door. He's an enigmatic fellow, so it's tough to gage his mood. "I should get back out there before Ebeneezer decides to come looking for me. Thanks for the suggestions."

"Anytime."

He looks like he's about to say something else, but instead opens the door and steps back into the chaos. If he comes back with a gun and shoots everybody, it's probably my fault.

It's suddenly very quiet and I have the sinking feeling that I may have set something terrible in motion.

I'm always at a loss whenever anyone asks me to name my favourite book.

I don't really have one, which I suppose is odd for someone who manages so many of them. My usual answer is *Love In The Time of Cholera*, and although I do love the book, it's an answer I provide mostly to give myself a sheen of literary respectability. I know *100 Years of Solitude* is supposed to be the Marquez masterwork, but I lost track of all the various family members about halfway through and finished it mostly out of a sense of duty.

I've read prestigious prize winners and classical works, but most of them leave me flat and bored. They may display a mastery of language and a massive intellect and a deep understanding of our cultural angst and all that, but by and large they don't really do it for me. Maybe it has something to do with being forced to read so many of them in high school. Even there, it's not cool to admit that half the time you have no idea what the hell Michael Ondaatje or Robertson Davies are talking about.

I got started early. My Dad got me a Classics Illustrated comic book version of *The Time Machine* when I was a kid and I quickly burned through as many more of the series as I could get my hands on: *Treasure Island*, *Dr Jekyll & Mr Hyde*, *The War of the Worlds*, *The Hound of the Baskervilles*, *The Three Musketeers*. I never really made the transition to superhero comics, which I thought were silly. Batman I didn't mind, but Superman was ridiculous. How strong is the guy? Is he just pretending to strain when he picks up a car? Because if a car is a strain, then how in the hell can he pick up a 747 or an aircraft carrier? Is he doing it so that his appearance won't be such an ego bruising event to us lowly humans?

Plus, he has an array of godlike powers but wants to spend his time working as a tabloid reporter and getting cats out of trees? How about stopping the occasional genocide? Power like that would go to your head. I don't care if you are from another planet. If you were more or less invulnerable and strong enough to do whatever the hell you wanted, whenever you wanted to do it, you wouldn't take a job with crappy hours and low pay and spend your down time in an empty ice palace at the North Pole. It's far more likely that you'd put your feet up while an army of human slaves built you the largest pleasure palace in the universe. *That* would be a superhero comic I could read.

Unlike many of my friends from those days, I never became absorbed in science fiction and fantasy Dungeons & Dragons stuff, either. I didn't get around to reading the *Lord of the Rings* until after I saw Peter Jackson's movie adaptations, which I thought did a much better job of telling the story than the books. I know the text is legendary and deeply beloved, but it is also slo-ow. It takes forever to get going. Frodo waits something like five *years* between discovering the ring and leaving the shire. Many characters get little or no introduction, important things happen in flashback or get relegated to the appendices, and the villain never even actually makes an appearance. The real central message isn't about friendship or singsongy environmentalism, but is something that the late wife of William Burroughs could certainly appreciate: never trust a junkie.

Conventional wisdom generally states that the book is better than its adaptation, but LOTR isn't the only example that defies this principle. *The Godfather* is a disaster of a book – the climax of the story deals with Sonny's mistress getting a vagina reduction – but the movie is one of the greatest ever made. I found *Get Shorty* almost impossible to follow on the page, but flies on the screen. *Jaws* is a pulpy mess in which Hooper bones Brody's wife and then gets eaten by a shark that just swims away at the end, but the movie is the very definition of a thriller. *A Clockwork Orange* is a disturbing and groundbreaking film, but the book is unreadable without a syllabus and a servile willingness to indulge the ego of Anthony Burgess.

As I got older, I read Stephen King for horrible descriptions of violent and scary things happening to Northeasterners. I sometimes still do because the guy's a hell of a storyteller, even if that instinct does sometimes cause him to write 800-page bricks that would make better short stories. I flipped furtively through Harold Robbins looking for sex scenes and tried with mixed and fevered success to figure out exactly what, biologically speaking, was going on. I had my naiveté hammered by Harlan Ellison and my worldview shaped by Orwell and Mencken. I travelled the world with the ornery Bill Bryson and dropped gleefully into the seedy underbelly of the sunshine state with the wickedly twisted Carl Hiaasen.

What did I avoid? Anything with a ponderous title was an easy one (like *The Weight of Memory* or *The Postmaster's Declension*). Anything where a tortured young urban professional comes to terms either with sex abuse on the family farm or a single violent act that changed the course of their life forever (which rules out about 95 per cent of Can lit). Any over-privileged and overhyped voice-of-a-generation full of ennui and the need to put out a doorstop explaining that everything is turning to shit. Anything about a dull young woman pursued by supernatural creatures. Anything where a cat solves murders.

Books provided a hidden thrill of the forbidden. Society could keep me out of R-rated movies, but there was nothing to stop me from reading the books that those movies were based on. I started with the usual things that occupy a prepubescent boy (sex and people being masticated by the latest genetically-engineered piece of tax-funded research to escape from the military base on the edge of town), but quickly expanded to just about every subject imaginable. If I wanted to know how the stock market worked or how hurricanes form or why the Palestinians and Israelis didn't get along, there were literally hundreds of books I could read that would explain it to me.

Doling out recommendations is an occupational hazard. I don't have kids, so I don't really know what to recommend for an 8-year-old who is only interested in trucks. Or an 80-year-old who is only interested in stories of feudal Japan and has already read every single Clavell novel five times thank you very much sonny. Or a well-meaning teacher looking for something featuring a strong Latina protagonist challenging bureaucratic authority as a way to introduce a unit on the United Nations.

The staff favourites are a mixed bag. Dante's favourite book is *On The Road*, which he emulated briefly in his late teens by trying to hitchhike to San Francisco. He only made it as far as Windsor before his mother had him arrested and returned to the house on a charge of having stolen her purse (the charges were later dropped). Sebastian likes *Lucky Jim*. Aldous claims to like *Being & Nothingness*, but he really only uses it to disguise the worn copy of the *Hitchhiker's Guide to the Galaxy* I see him reading in the break room. Mina has a special gift edition version of *The Bell Jar* in her backpack. Ebeneezer is always trying to get people to buy *Catch 22*. Willard says he likes *Naked Lunch* but his heart really belongs to a horror series about a vampire bounty hunter named Mad Dog Bludsukka, of which he always grabs the first copy of the latest edition out of the box for himself. Mother Teresa naturally claims the bible, but is equally passionate about *Charlotte's Web*. As far as I know, Lolita only reads angry letters to the editor (which she has also written) and Miroslav has trouble reading a stop sign.

Village Books has a policy that allows staff to sign out a book so long as they return it in sellable condition. It's like the library except we can get new stuff even before it goes on sale. The exception to this was the last Harry Potter book, which came in boxes sealed with a special coloured tape. A publisher's rep threatened to visit the store on the eve of the sale and cut off any future deliveries if any of the seals were broken before midnight. The publisher's rep never showed, but the warning was enough to keep Willard from selling off any advance copies on the black market. Well, that and Dante's promise to attach electrodes to his testicles if he touched a single box.

We used to have a staff recommendations shelf, but every year we lose it to the demands of Christmas stock volume. Last Spring, when the unsold holiday stock was returned, Dante replaced the staff picks with a display cabinet full of tacky gift items like cards, candles, bookmarks and other junk. We all bitched and moaned about it at the beginning, but the damn things sold more dollars per linear foot than anything else in the store. This year it expanded to include e-readers. When I pointed out that we were becoming active participants in hastening our demise, Dante pointed out that our demise didn't need any help from us and we might as well make as much money from it as possible while we could.

Nobody ever aspires to work in retail, even if it is the largest single sector of the North American economy. The pay and the hours are lousy and dealing with the public is like putting up with a houseguest that barfs on the carpet and then complains about the mess. Most of us are here because we are either otherwise unemployable or aspiring towards something better. Dante, for example, has a masters degree in English lit and had just been laid off as a contract professor at U of T when he happened to be standing behind Cynthia Ackerman at the supermarket. He helped her carry her groceries out to her car and she offered him the job practically on the spot.

It's strange to think that, had that not happened, I would not have spent the last three years of my life working here. Sometimes I wonder where I would be right now. Would my life be better, worse, or about the same? For all the complaining I do about it, I do mostly enjoy my job. Mostly. Dropping out of film school propelled me into something of a state of suspended animation: I haven't advanced and I haven't retreated since I've been here, I've just sort of continued to float while I try to figure out what to do next.

Village Books is a comfortable place where I can hide out from the world for a while. Which is exactly what a good book is supposed to be. I suppose the reason I have so much trouble picking a favourite is because I'm in no hurry to come out of hiding.

# -13-

Leah meets me in front of the Prestige where we go to see its annual showing of *The Big Lebowski*. Pete, the owner of the theatre, is a monster fan of the film. This year, he's dressed as the slightly deranged Vietnam vet Walter Sobchak as he sells tickets and works the concession stand. The show always sells out and the place is packed. Waiting in the lobby, I spot four bathrobed Dudes, three purple spandex Jesus Quintanas, a Maude Leboswki in full Wagnerian opera dream sequence mode, a shoeboy Saddam, a Stranger, and three bowling pins.

"I had no idea you liked this movie!" I say to Leah as we find our way to our seats. We are careful not to sit behind the bowling pins as the Prestige is an older theatre and lacks modern stadium-style seats.

"Shut the fuck up, Donny!" she laughs. "I don't like this movie. I looove this movie. My life's ambition is to get a Ralph's card and pay for milk with a cheque."

The Prestige shows the movie at least once a year. The crowd that turns out is hardcore and already well lubricated with Caucasians, but, like the film's laid-back protagonist, is a mostly easygoing and peace-loving bunch. I've never missed a screening since I've been working at the bookstore. I was originally supposed to see this with Sebastian, but the possibility of a date with Leah threw that out the window. Recognizing the gravity of the situation, Sebastian took one for the team and bowed out. It

would have been awkward if he had come along and absolutely
unendurable if he'd brought Mina with him. The last person you want to
see on a first date is someone you once banged in the manager's office,
especially if that person if now dating your best friend. First dates are
tricky, and *The Big Lebowski*, especially when seen with a crowd like this,
is not really a typical first date movie.

Of course, the cynical voice in the back of my head keeps reminding
me, this may not be an actual date. Leah is clearly a big fan of the movie
and wanted to see it and may have just figured I was the least objectionable
candidate to bring along. But we are having dinner at her place later. And
she did just break up with her IT slug fiancé. And it certainly did seem like
a date at the time she asked...

No wonder relationships drive us crazy. You never really know for
sure what's going on, even when they've been going for a while. At the
start, it's downright impossible. It's hard to tell if someone is interested in
you; you just sort of have to assume they are and jump. If there's no water
in the pool when you land, you better be prepared to spend some time in
traction.

Normally, I'm a bag of nerves in situations like these, but Leah's so
relaxed and easygoing that, a few moments of panic aside (like when she
runs into an acquaintance who asks her how the wedding prep is going and
she just shakes her head and says '*don't ask*'), I can almost believe this is
happening.      Having said that, I already decided that I would make no
romantic overtures, sonatas, ditties or jingles whatsoever over the course of
tonight's proceedings. The main reason is that, despite everything I just
said, I might be wrong, and if I'm wrong I'll end up making a total ass of
myself and destroying what the USMC likes to refer to as the operational
effectiveness of future missions. For now, this is just two friends going to
see a movie and then having a bite to eat. I can't allow my expectations to
get ahead of me. If we get back to her apartment and Grover is there in a
'Kiss the Cook' apron pulling a tray of chicken parmigiana out of the oven

and he gives her a big kiss and asks how the movie was, I have to be able to pretend that this was exactly what I expected. Especially if there is a baseball bat or croquet mallet within easy reach.

After the movie, Leah suggests we stop into Falstaff's for a quick pint. The place is packed and we end up standing at the bar, where Mickey pulls her two pints of Scrumpy without even asking.

"Unbelievable," I say as he hands them over. "It took me months of wheedling to get this stuff. And I had to pass a test!"

Mickey shrugs. "Well, you're a right shifty bugger, to be sure. Besides, Bobby an' the lads won, see? So I'm in an accomodatin' mood." He gestures to the TV over his shoulder, where a group of bruised and sweaty men in green and gold uniforms are taking turns holding what looks like a silver cane over their heads. It seems that the Donegal hurling team, whose Gaelic name is both hard to spell and unpronounceable, have just won something of great import, at least to those who are a) from Donegal and b) understand hurling. Since the man who provides me with Scrumpy is both a) and b), I raise my glass and try to look as pleased as possible.

"Well, then, *slainte!*" This is the only word in Gaelic that I know. Well, that and a word that you should never use to refer to a friend's mother in his presence.

Mickey winks at Leah and wanders down to turn the music back up. "The Boys Are Back In Town" by Thin Lizzy. The green-shirted faithful at the end of the bar cheer wildly.

"Drink up!" Leah commands. "The *boeuf bourguignon* will be ready in twenty minutes."

We clink glasses and both take a wooze-inducing gulp.

"Wow! Really?"

"It's my first time making it, so I hope it turns out okay."

"Well, if you're making it, I'm sure it'll be terrific." This is both a shameless compliment and a subtle way of finding out if my nemesis is in fact working away in her kitchen, apron or not.

"Don't be so sure," she warns. "I just basically threw everything in a slow cooker and hoped for the best. I told you I broke up with Grover, right?"

She tacks this last part on like it's something she forgot to include in the recipe. Cremini mushrooms, check. Beef, check. Shallots, check. Fiancé, nope. Although I have just been pushed out of the plane without a parachute, I try to make it seem like I'm confident that I'll find one somewhere on the way down.

"So I heard," I say. Never in my life have I worked so hard to sound so innocuous and never come up quite so short. "How are you doing with that?"

"Urgh. Should have done it a long time ago. I don't know why I didn't. Probably because he was stable and made a lot of money, so there wasn't much pressure on me to go out and get a real job. Plus my parents loved him. Well, my dad did. No surprise. He's almost exactly like my Dad. He used to be an engineer with Nortel, then the company went under and he lost everything. No pension, nothing."

"That's terrible."

"I know, but the irony is, they were always the ones telling me to play it safe. Don't try to act. Just get a job with a share program and drug plan and all the usual corporate junk. Not that there's anything wrong with that, George, but it didn't work out so good for you, so why are you wishing it on me?"

"Are you talking George as in Costanza or is George your father's name?"

"Actually, it's both. Costanza's my nickname for my Dad. I love him dearly, but he's a neurotic pain in the ass. Grover brought him a $500 bottle of scotch when he went in to ask if he could marry me."

"Wow. That's a spicy meatball. He asked your parents first? I didn't think anyone still did that. Who is he? The 17th Earl of Wessex?"

"I know. Like I'm property to be given away. None of them understood why that might make me mad. Of course, my father was so proud you would've thought *he* was marrying the guy. He bragged about it to everybody. Do you know anything about whiskey?"

I shake my head. "Not a damn thing. I can't really stand the stuff. My grandfather, however, used to drink his weight in whiskey every week. I'm sure he'd disown me if he wasn't dead."

"Can I tell you a secret? The only reason I said yes at the time was because I felt guilty about the whiskey. Plus he got me this massive ring. Well, you saw that."

"Yes I did. It was massive. The first time I saw you, I thought you'd won the 2005 Super Bowl."

She takes another drink. "I'm sorry. How on earth did we get talking about this?"

"Don't apologize. I've forgotten too."

"Can we pretend I never brought it up?"

"Brought what up? I was talking about Quintana and O'Brian. Should be pushovers. Also, my rug was stolen."

"Separate incidents!" she laughs. "Guess we can close the file on that one."

We clink glasses and drink some more. I am shocked – shocked! – to see that I have somehow managed to drink almost half my glass. I'm already warm behind the ears and my brain is starting to feel like a kite. It's a good thing neither of us is driving.

"Can I tell you a secret? Well, another one?"

"Of course you can. I'll put it in the vault. And the key…" I hold up my glass "…is exceedingly hard to come by. That means, of course, that you have to agree Mickey, as keymaster, will also hear this revelation by default. But I think he used to work for MI6, so he probably knows everything already."

"You remember the first thing you said to me when we met in the store?"

I feel my face go red. This might not be noticeable, though, because it's probably pretty red already. "Oh yes…I must apologize for that. It just sort of shot out of my mouth before I knew what I was saying. You asked about Mamet and, well, not a lot of attractive women do that, so I was taken by surprise. Not that I agree with his politics or anything. I mean, he's still a hell of a writer and all. But how can you write *The Spanish Prisoner* and then vote for the Tea Party? Or *Glengarry Glen Ross*? It's insane. Plus, you just got hired as a manager, so what I said probably constituted sexual harassment and if you wanted to file a complaint, I wouldn't blame you at a—"

I feel a finger pressed against my lips to get me to stop talking. It's moist from the condensation on the side of the glass and smells slightly of vanilla, which I know is the kind of moisturizer Leah uses to keep her hands from drying out in the store. The store is incredibly dry. A large coffee left sitting without a lid will evaporate in under an hour. Humidity is one of Dante's many obsessions. Mould being an enemy of large volumes of stored paper, after all. Why on earth am I thinking about mould?

"You're babbling."

"I am, aren't I? I tend to do that." Because her finger is still holding my lips shut, this comes out sounding like *I end a oc at*. She takes her finger away, which is extremely unfortunate, as I was rather enjoying its presence. "Sorry. Please continue."

"When you asked, I should have said yes."

No one's supposed to open the door on an airplane at 35,000 feet. It's socially irresponsible. Especially for those who are not firmly strapped down, such as myself.

I smile and somehow manage to stay on my feet. "Well then perhaps I should ask you again."

At which point, she leans forward and we end up kissing. Investigators will never be able to determine how long this lasts because my brain's flight recorder is lost somewhere on the floor of the Pacific, where it will never be recovered. We separate and a great roar of appreciation goes up from the green shirts at the end of the bar. Mickey just rolls his eyes and smiles.

Leah puts her now empty pint glass on the bar. "Ready to go?"

Am I ever. I look at my glass, which is also, somehow, empty. I feel like I have applied for a taxi licence and, due to a bureaucratic error, been assigned to the Ferrari F1 team. "After you, my dear."

We step outside where, on a whim, I decide to save us the six-block walk by hailing a taxi. I love hailing taxis. It gives me such a weird sense of manly authority. There are very few opportunities to look genuinely suave in the modern age, but waving your hand to compel a complete stranger to make a U-turn across four lanes of oncoming traffic just to pick you up has to be one of them. Dropping a credit card on a bill without looking at it is another example, but it doesn't have quite the same public air of *droit de siegneur*.

The two of us pile into the back seat. Leah gives the driver her address and then puts her hand behind my neck and pulls me in so that the two of us can proceed to make out like bandits. I've never made out in the back of a taxi before. It's probably impolite and may even be a violation of some city bylaw, but I must admit that at the moment, neither our driver's feelings nor the legal position of the Corporation of the City of Toronto are high on my list of concerns.

Traffic is light and we reach Leah's apartment in no time. I give Ahmad a twenty dollar bill on a six dollar fare and tell him to keep the change. I have a feeling that the beef stew is going to have to wait.

# -14-

My 12-year-old self would hate me for doing this, but I'm going to skip some details here. The important thing is that the stew burned and we decided to order Thai from the place around the corner.

The apartment is quite fancy: subzero fridge, quartz countertops, heated floors, minimalist black leather furniture. Leah and I are sitting in the dining room, which is almost as large as my entire apartment, munching on pad thai and drinking a bottle of Pouilly-Fuissé that I found on the wine rack. I'm wearing a T shirt and boxers and she's wearing a fluffy white robe tied loosely at the waist.

"Why didn't you tell me you're a writer?" she asks. "I had to find out from Ebeneezer."

I shrug. "I'm not. Well, I don't think of myself as one. People ask me what I do, I tell them I'm a bookstore manager. You know how they say what you do instead of your real job is your real job? It saves explanations."

"What kind of things do you write?"

"The last thing I finished was a novel based loosely – and I mean loosely in the sense that I inserted a religious nut serial killer who didn't exist – on my time in journalism school."

"Can I read it?"

"Sure. It's not Stieg Larsson, but I was mostly happy with the way it turned out."

"Ebby said you came pretty close to getting it published."

"Ebby?"

"Oh come on! He's an old sweetie. He really has the hots for Fermina who runs the coffee shop next door."

"That he does. I don't know that she has any idea."

"Oh she knows," Leah says scornfully. "But she's Spanish. She's waiting for him to be a man and make the first move."

"Maybe we should take him to that new tapas bar down the street and get him some bull testicles for lunch then, because I don't think he has the necessary balls to do it on his own."

Leah arches an eyebrow. "Good thing I didn't follow her lead or you'd probably still be sitting in a dark corner at Falstaff's getting quietly plastered with Sebastian."

"Hey, you were engaged!" I say, feeling compelled to defend myself. "I was trying to do the honourable thing."

"Seriously?"

"Okay, between you and me, I was scheming ways to sabotage the whole enterprise and steal you away for myself. I just wasn't creative enough to come up with something that might actually work."

"You men. You spend nine months waiting to get out and most of the next seventy years plotting to get back in."

"Guilty as charged. Now it's my turn to tell you a secret."

"I'm all ears. Which, by the way, are about the only parts of me that aren't exhausted."

I grin. "Okay, here you go. I am absolutely crazy about you. Have been since literally the first second we met. Haven't been able to get you out of my mind. So put that in your pipe and smoke it, my dear."

She laughs. "Oh yeah? Well I just dumped a prosperous fiancé to be with you. My parents will no doubt disown me. Plus you're a writer, which pretty much guarantees they won't like you, either."

"They don't read?"

"The only thing my father reads is *Golf Digest*. And a worn copy of a magazine called *Anal Babes* that I once found hidden in his sock drawer when they were on a trip to Nassau."

"Eww."

"Like I said, you men are a strange bunch. You're so obsessed with boobs and asses, but then you get them out in the open and what can you really do with them?"

"That's a complicated question to answer. Perhaps after we have some more food, we can delve further into the matter."

She gives me a twisted smile. "I was thinking of giving it some sort of mention at his funeral."

"What? He's dying?"

"No, I mean eventually. '*You can say a lot of things about George Dashwood, but you can't say he didn't appreciate a good rectum.*'"

I laugh so hard that wine comes out of my nose. "I would pay to see that."

"My mother only reads lifestyle magazines and brochures for plastic surgery clinics in Costa Rica. She never had a real job of her own, so she can't really understand why I would want one. Let alone a career in acting."

"Have you always wanted to be an actress?"

"I was loud and kind of obnoxious in school. They didn't know what else to do with me, so they stuck me in drama. I don't know if I'm any good at it, but I sure enjoy it. I was good at poker, too. If Scorsese ever makes a sequel to *Casino* then I'll be ready."

"Nowadays they don't make sequels, they make reboots. Who knows what'll replace those. Apps, probably."

"All of this is my incredibly roundabout way of saying that I knew you were the one for me as soon as I heard your voice. Isn't that kind of insane in a way? I turned around and there you were and something just went click. Something just said this guy is my guy. I've never felt anything like it. Does that terrify you? Are you now going to quietly gather up your clothes and run screaming out into the night?"

"Of course not. I honestly don't even know where the rest of my clothes are. If I run out there like this, I'll freeze to death."

"I would also like to point out that technically we did not sleep together on our first date. Although, if your smoke detector hadn't gone off…"

"Damn that thing. I'm going to take the batteries out of it as soon as I get home."

"Do we need to tell Dante about this? Are we in violation of some human resources edict designed to make sure employees are never happy?"

"I don't think so. Managers aren't supposed to sleep with subordinates, but…"

"You mean like you and Mina?" she snickers.

"Man!" I say, rolling my eyes. "Is there anybody who doesn't know about that?"

"It's kind of weird that she's with Sebastian now. You two are pretty good buds. Hopefully that doesn't screw things up."

"Nah. He seems genuinely smitten. More power to them, I suppose. So long as her husband doesn't show up unexpectedly and go My Lai on them."

"I'm surprised that Dante trusts her with a key, let alone putting her in charge of cash. She doesn't seem entirely stable to me."

"She's not, but I've never seen any irregularities on the tills and she's worked here a long time. You have to remember that, at heart, Dante is a big coward. He just doesn't have the guts to take the key back. He probably thinks it would cause some sort of breakdown. And he might be right about that."

"Do you think his mother is really sick or is she just faking it to get him married off?"

I laugh. "The possibility has occurred to me. Have you ever met Lucretia?"

Leah shakes her head. "I've heard the stories. Based on those, I'm imagining a rhinoceros in a black dress."

"Yeah, that's her. Just add a small silver purse and an Italian accent. It's hard to imagine she'd allow anything as prosaic as a fatal disease to come between her and her mission in life."

"Poor Dante. Maybe I should offer to marry him. That might take the pressure off."

"Only if you're prepared to crank out a couple of grandkids in the process."

"Well, Dante is an attractive man, but I think I would have to draw the line there." She takes a sip of wine. "So you're saying we don't have to keep all of this a secret, then?"

"Probably a moot point. The walls of Falstaff's are loaded with eyes and ears. The news has probably already circled the globe a couple of times by now. And once Mickey's hurling buddies know, it's only a matter of time before the rest of the world finds out, too."

"That's what I figured. Oh hey, did I tell you that Ribika isn't getting charged with anything? I guess it took them too long to do the drug test or whatever, so they just gave her a warning and let her go."

"I bet Taylor Swift's people leaned on the cops to avoid more nasty headlines."

"Oh and Penny told me that Aldous called her up and asked her out."

"Yeah. I walked into the office right after she turned him down."

"I feel sort of bad for him. I mean, he's a nice guy, but he's just so...dirty! You know? The hair and the clothes and those awful sandals that are falling apart. If I saw him out on the street, I'd think he was homeless. Hasn't anyone ever talked to him about it?"

"He asked for my advice. I guess his current look hasn't been the biggest hit with the ladies."

"Oh, and that winter coat he wears! Ugh. He needs to get that dry cleaned. Actually, we should just send Aldous to the dry cleaners and see what they can do with him. He needs to stop smoking that awful pipe, too. His teeth are starting to look like he could play an extra in a western with no touch ups. What did you tell him?"

"Basically to shower and get better clothes. Or at least wash the ones he has more often."

"He's gotta stop wearing that Derrida shirt. It was probably white at some point in history, but it never will be again. I think the damn thing has actually become fused to his body."

I nod. "You'd think he'd get tired of people mistaking it for Albert Einstein, but no. He just uses it as an excuse to launch into an explanation of deconstructivism."

"I've heard him do that," Leah says. "He goes on and on about binary oppositions and the metaphysics of presence, but I don't actually think he knows what the hell he's talking about. I took a first-year philosophy course in university and even I can tell that most of the time he's making it up as he goes along."

"You and Ebby are in total agreement, there. He can't stand Aldous. Naturally, I try to schedule the two of them together on the floor as much as possible. It keeps things sprightly."

"I don't think things need that kind of help. One of these days they'll come to blows. And, despite his bulk, I think Aldous will get his ass kicked."

"Speaking of the staff, I see you were able to reorganize the shelving upstairs without sparking an intifada."

"I went over the numbers with Dante first, so he'd know what I was doing. You know, just in case Mother Teresa decided to try and do an end run around me to get it all put back."

"Dante doesn't mind dirty work so long as somebody else is doing it for him."

"I told her we need more space for holiday stock and that we'll find a permanent home for children's religion in January. If it was up to me, I'd get rid of the section altogether."

"Me, too. I agree with Hitchens that religious indoctrination should be classified as child abuse."

"Good to know," Leah says. "I know a lot of couples who argue about stuff like that."

"Well you're an actress, and since you're no doubt going to become wildly successful, you'll probably have to join the church of scientology as a condition of Screen Actors Guild membership."

"And then you can jump on a couch and tell the whole world that you love me way more than Katie Holmes." She looks down shyly. "Sorry. Little early to bring all that into the discussion."

"Holmes? Yes, that's probably true. I haven't asked your opinion of a single one of her movies. I don't know that I've seen her in anything other than *Batman Begins*. Oh wait. No, she has been in other things. I think I just forgot she was there."

She smiles. "You knob! You know that's not what I meant."

"Are you kidding?" I say, getting up. "I'll do it on this couch right here." I cross the dining room and climb onto the leather couch in the sitting area. "I love this woman!!" I shout, trying to bounce. The stiff leather, however, is not in the least bit spongy and is resisting to my efforts to get airborne. I manage one leap before slipping off and landing butt-first on the hardwood floor with the kind of grace that keeps me out of the Bolshoi. "Wow, this couch really isn't very user-friendly. Maybe I should try the coffee table instead."

Leah laughs. "Get down, dumbass! You're going to fall down and break something."

I climb meekly back down onto the floor, adopting a hurt tone. "Your concern for my well being is most heartening, my lady."

"I meant that you might injure yourself, and I'm not remotely finished with you for the evening." She wags a finger. "C'mere Poindexter."

I hang my head and pad over to her chair, where she stands up and throws her arms around me.

"Thank you for jumping on a couch for me," she says, leaning in for a long kiss.

"Anytime. Thanks for not being a member of a cult."

"Now, it's getting late and I've got an audition and you've gotta open the store tomorrow morning."

I groan. The real world is calling and I want nothing to do with it.

She steps back and loosens her robe, which drops to the floor. "That only leaves us with about seven hours before we need to be somewhere else, and I for one would like to use that time as productively as possible."

I smile and allow myself to be led back to the bed, where it will be necessary to skip a few more details.

# -15-

Despite the hassle of having to get up early, I prefer opening the store in the morning to closing it at night.

I usually arrive about a half an hour before anybody else, so I have the place to myself. I buy a tea at Café Ole and do a quick check to see how bad the damage is from the night before. Generally, the closing staff are able to re-shelve the discards (books people pick up and decide they don't want, sometimes leaving them at cash but mostly on the nearest vaguely horizontal surface) at the end of the night, but during the holiday season it's not unusual to have one or even two carts worth of them still hanging around the next day. I'm surprised to poke my head into receiving and see not a single one. In fact, the store is so neat that it's like no one was ever here.

This is weird enough to make me pause. Mina closed last night. Since she runs cash and takes very little to do with what happens out in the stacks, the mornings after she closes are generally the worst in terms of cleanup. Maybe she was sick again and Dante covered for her. This seems like the most likely explanation, but Dante had already worked the morning. If Mina had dropped out, he would have probably called either Leah or myself to cover the late shift and he didn't do that.

I know from the receipts that the store was a madhouse – we did almost double the sales from the same weekend last year – so it's not a matter of the staff sitting around with nothing else to do. We only have a few weeks to go until Christmas. This is the time that shoppers start to get particularly frenzied as shipping deadlines begin to loom and the availability of desired titles cannot always be guaranteed. I've seen old ladies with walkers bowl small children out of the way to get at the last copy of a certain Maeve Binchy or Ian Rankin. Civility goes out the window in the stacks at this time of year. The aftermath usually leaves the store looking like Baghdad outside the green zone.

So the fact that the store is so neat and orderly is, despite the quiet, extremely disquieting.

Instead of booting up the computers and completing the deposit, which are the two things I would normally do, I make a circuit of the store. I can't seem to shake the feeling that I'm not alone in here, and it gives me the creeps. Maybe Esmerelda is on to something. The upstairs is just as neat as the main floor. The kids books aren't organized in quite the usual way that Mother Teresa does it, but none of them are on the floor and all appear to be in the correct sections. Even all the magazines are put away.

What the hell?

I push open the double doors and walk into the receiving area, which as always, smells like cardboard and Willard's patchouli. Nothing out of the ordinary here. Our returns shelves are piled high with overstock and there isn't much room to move, but there's no sign of any evil presence.

At least, that's what I think until I hear the snoring.

At first I think it's just the heating system, but the vents aren't running in the main store, so why would they be running in here? The noise gets steadily louder as I make my way slowly back past Willard's desk. This is where we store all of Dante's hated promotional items. We used to store the scented candles over here as Ivanka was allergic to them and preferred they sit as far away as possible. We put Willard over here for the same reason. Dante switched to the unscented ones for the next shipment, but we never bothered to find a new spot for the stock.

I move a large box of dancing Santa Clauses aside and that's where I find Sebastian curled up in a sleeping bag under the shelves. Next to him is an empty fast food bag, a six-pack of Heineken (all tapped), his glasses, a dog-eared copy of Swann's Way, and a travel-sized alarm clock that stopped at 3:46am.

"Sebastian?"

His eyes snap open. "Huh? Shit! What time is it?" He sits up sharply and whacks his forehead on the underside of the shelf. Based on his reaction, I'm guessing it's not the first time he's done it.

"How long have you been, uh, bunking in-country?"

He rubs his forehead and crawls out of the sleeping bag. He's wearing a wrinkled white shirt, black slacks and his shoes.

"You sleep with your shoes on?"

He yawns. "Keeps away the rats."

"We have rats?"

"I dunno. Maybe it's just delirium tremens. What time is it?"

I look at my watch. "About quarter to eight. The day staff'll be arriving shortly."

He stretches and rubs his face, which is in need of a shave. "Right, right."

"So your mom threw you out?"

He nods. "Damn alarm clock didn't go off."

"When? How long have you been here?"

"Before I answer, old bean, I'm compelled to ask, am I speaking with my old friend, or with the ship's captain?"

"Come on, Sebastian. It's me. Did you clean up the store after everyone went home last night?"

"I thought I should do something to earn my keep."

"Well, it looks great. It must have taken you hours." Now I'm wondering how I tell Dante that the store isn't haunted without telling him how I know. I'll have to think about that one.

"Old Pious chucked me out a week ago."

"Over Mina? Why didn't you move in with her?"

He glances at my tea. "I'm sorry, but would you mind if..."

I hand it over. "Sure, I haven't touched it."

He takes the tea and drinks almost half of it down in a single gulp. I've been carrying it since I walked into the store and it's not really hot anymore. I was going to throw it in the microwave in the break room, but that will no longer be necessary.

"Mina believes that her husband may be back in town. It's not definite, of course. She thinks she may have seen him out of the corner of her eye a couple of times on the way in or out. Just a feeling that she's being watched."

I know what that feels like, having just spent the last 15 minutes convinced of it. "Why didn't you come to me? I could've put you up."

"Oh nonsense. I couldn't put you out."

"Don't be an idiot. I mean, it's a bit tricky now that Leah will be moving in, but we can at least handle it short term until you figure something else out."

"I absolutely...Wait! What?"

"Yeah." I can't keep the grin off my face and the harder I try, the bigger it gets. "She's only got her place until the end of the month. Her dick ex-fiancé sublet it out from under her."

"She's *moving in*?"

"She is. I'm gonna help her move some of her stuff over tonight after work."

"Wait a minute. Did you say *ex-fiancé*? Holy shit! So, uh, I take it that the dinner and movie date went rather well, then."

"Extremely so. I know, I know, I know. What can I say? I am totally enraptured."

He claps me on the back. "Well, huzzahs to you my man! I'm flabbergasted! My gast is totally flabbered. Now tell me in exhaustive detail exactly how in the hell this happened."

"I can't explain it," I say. "I was crazy about her front the get-go and it seems that the feeling was, amazingly, mutual. We went to see the Dude and Walter–"

"She likes *Lebowski*?"

"Fuckin' A, Donny. She's even been to a Lebowski Fest in LA. She's seen the movie more times than I have. Maybe even more times than you."

"Sweet Jesus on a dragon boat. I hope you've got a ring in your pocket with plans to use it forthwith, because if you don't, I'm going to track this fair maiden down and marry her myself."

"I don't know if she knows anything about Barça, though. We never got into talking about football."

"With all due respect to your beloved Catalans, I wouldn't make it a conditional offer. What happened after the movie?"

"Well, we went to Falstaff's for a pint. And we ended up kissing."

"In Falstaff's?"

"Yeah."

"How could I not have heard about this? I have been truly remiss in checking Mickey's Twitter feed. An unforgivable lapse."

"Then we went back to her place and…talked for a while."

"You rascal. I thought I saw a twinkle in your eye when you rousted me."

I reach into my pocket and get out my keys. "Here, take these. Head back to my apartment and get cleaned up. There's food in the fridge, although stay away from the orange juice – I think it's expired. The date stamp got rubbed off."

He shakes his head. "Thanks, but I'll just go to Mina's. I think she's imagining things."

"How are things going with Mina?"

He sighs. "Oh, you know. It's a bit of a challenge. One day she's fine. She's out and about and chatty as you like. And then the next she can't even get out of bed."

"You're not going to stay there, are you?"

"I might give it the old Belgian endive. The constant suspense will keep me sharp." He snaps his fingers. "On the edge. Where I gotta be."

"Yeah. She's got a great ass. And you got your head all the way up it. This is a lifestyle that may have the latter while depriving you of the former."

"There's that, too."

I put my keys back in my pocket. "Okay, but look. If you think things are getting to weird or whatever, my offer still stands. If I come in to work one day and find out you've been the target of a midnight raid across the Pakistani border, I will be genuinely upset, not pretend upset, like their Inter-Services Intelligence."

"Duly noted, mon frére."

"How did you get in here, anyway? Did Mina give you her key?"

He nods guiltily. "If she was closing, she'd give it to me and I'd sneak out early the next morning before everyone arrived. Or I would have if my alarm clock hadn't fucked me. I suppose the commandant will need to be informed."

"Don't be ridiculous. Dante has enough to think about right now. However, I may need you to dress up like a voodoo priest and perform an exorcism ritual for the benefit of our cleaning lady."

"Well, that seems only fair. Is she expecting full gigolo or can I keep my pants on?"

"I'm not talking metaphorically about whoring you out as punishment. She's stopped coming in at night because she thinks the place is haunted."

"She might be on to something. I heard some weird noises in here after everyone else went home."

"Mina wasn't in here with you too, was she?"

"A gentleman does not dignify such questions with responses."

"I'd really feel much better if you'd just stay at my place. Chalk it up to laziness. I don't want to have to fill out the HR paperwork. Especially not if I have to write 'dismemberment' under the reason for termination."

"That's very kind, but I find it impossible to sleep when people are having sex nearby. It's the same reason I couldn't fall asleep on a bench at the bus station." He yawns and stretches. "I still can't believe she's moving in! She went from fiancée to single to cohabitation in less time than most people take to brew a pot of coffee."

"I know. It's insanely fast. In all probability too fast. At some point, I will probably miss a corner and drive straight into an oil company billboard."

"A what?"

"Or a wall. Whatever they use to keep the F-1 cars from driving into the crowds in Monaco."

"Only if you second guess your instincts. She seems quite solid to me. And if she isn't, then what the hell. You're having fun, right?"

It may be more than fun, but I'm not sure that I'm quite ready to admit that yet. Even to myself. I remind myself that I'm also receiving advice from a man I just caught sleeping on a metal shelf behind a box of Santa-themed wrapping paper.

"Maybe you should ask Dante if you can crash at his place," I suggest. "At least the two of you could commiserate about your mother problems."

"True, but he's far too neat. It would be like *The Odd Couple*, except I would end up killing him."

I know better than to suggest the possibility that his mother might see reason. She once grounded him for a month after she caught him chewing gum during lent. He had given up sugar and it was sugar-free gum, but that wasn't enough. Apparently aspartame, corn syrup and cane extract are all the same when it comes to venial sins.

"Okay," I say. "Well, you know where I am if you spot the heat around the corner."

Sebastian gathers up his sad possessions and bundles them in his sleeping bag, which he tosses over his shoulder like a dead body. As I watch him walk to the door, it occurs to me that, but for a minor tweak here or there, I could be in the same position. If Mina wasn't so crazy and things had worked out or if Leah's ex was trained to kill and inclined to hold a grudge, I myself might be bunking with the candles.

"Wait!" I say. "You should probably go out the back. If the day staff see you on your way out with a sleeping bag over your shoulder, they might wonder what the hell is going on."

"Good point," Sebastian says, wheeling around.

I shut off the alarm and open the back door. It opens out to the receiving entrance, which is a narrow alley that runs the length of the block. Being a small bookstore, we don't get the kind of shipments that would require an 18-wheeler to drop them off. This is good, because there's no way one would fit back here anyway.

Sebastian steps out and almost trips over a black garbage bag that has been placed right behind the door. Our dumpster is on the far side of the alley and although it's not unusual for people to dump things back here, I wonder why anyone would go to the trouble of climbing up eight rickety metal steps to do it right at our door when the ground works just as well. It's strange. So strange, in fact, that I ask Sebastian to wait while I pick up the bag.

It's light. It seems to contain two blocks about the same size and weight as a couple of trade paperbacks. My first thought is to wonder why Willard would throw books in a bag and toss them out when we can just return them. My second is to think that somebody might have lifted them from the store and left them back here to pick up later, thus avoiding the nightly bag check to deter internal shoplifters. It hasn't happened for a long time, but it does happen. There's no one in receiving in the evening, so it's pretty easy to sneak things back here undetected, especially if Dante forgets to lock the back door, which he has been known to do repeatedly.

"What's this?" Sebastian asks. "Someone looking for a five-finger discount you think?"

"Could be," I say, lifting the bag inside and placing it on the floor. I try to untie the knot, but the bag is slightly wet and I quickly give up, deciding to rip it open instead.

"Holy shit!" says Sebastian, peering over my shoulder. "Is that what I think it is?"

What's inside is not a couple of trade paperbacks, although it would, I'm sure, be instantly recognizable to fans of Irvine Welsh or William Burroughs.

# -16-

Leah is in the process of moving my clothes out of my closet and installing her own outfits. Fortunately, the closet is a double, which automatically makes it one of the roomier spaces in the apartment. That means there's almost enough room for her fall and winter ensemble. The summer stuff is still packed up in boxes. She has also occupied the entire bathroom and most of the kitchen. I feel like a Middle Eastern leader in the process of being deposed. If things continue this way, I may have to set up a provisional government in the front hall.

"I can't believe it!" she says. "So you think it was hash?"

As she's saying this, she removes a box containing a small stash of model airplanes and two collectible cases of *Star Wars* figures to make room for her shoe rack. I went through a brief spurt of model making when I was about 13. Over the years the glue has dried out and most of them have shed parts faster than a Chevy in a wrecker's yard. I have a Spitfire fuselage, a Lancaster tail section and the cockpit of what I think was once a Mosquito. I don't know why I don't just throw them out. The same goes for the figurines, which I haven't even looked at for at least ten years. The only advantage to keeping them locked away is that George Lucas can't get in and tinker with them.

"I'm not sure. It wasn't a powder. It was like an actual brick of resin wrapped in plastic. I've never really seen hash before, so I don't know what it looks like."

I'm sitting on the bed watching her reorganize my interior space and reminding myself to remain calm. This is, after all, no longer just my space, but our space, even if my share of it has decreased significantly. Besides, she's moving in, which is pretty damn cool. I've never lived with a woman before. This is unexplored territory. Adjustments will be required. Also on the plus side, she brought along the wine rack, which I noted contains a Brunello, a vintage Amarone and, unless my eyes were deceiving me, a '98 Yquem, a single mouthful of which is worth more than I make in a week.

"Was it dark?"

"Yeah. It looked like a block of congealed coffee."

"It was probably hash."

"How do you know so much about hash?"

"I lived in L.A. for a while," she says absently, as if that explained everything. She pulls out a pair of sneakers I haven't worn in a while and sets them in what I'm starting to suspect is a 'to be thrown out' pile. "So what did the cops say?"

"They asked us a ton of questions about who was in the store and when and blah blah blah."

"Did you lie about Sebastian?"

"Yeah. I told them he came in with me. I'm not sure why. It's not like they're gonna care that he was kicked out of his mom's house. I guess I just wanted to put him as far from the scene of the crime as possible."

"That makes sense. You don't think he knew something about it, do you?"

"No. He was as surprised as I was. Besides, we found them in the alley, not actually in the store. It's a bit dodgy back there. Especially at night. Who knows what goes on. I've found needles, condoms, bullets…you name it."

"Bullets?" she says. "You mean full rounds or just spent casings?"

"Full rounds. Well, Willard found that. He took it home and mounted it on a wooden plaque. Some stupid *'this bullet would have killed me but it was a dud'* sort of thing. He likes to promote the fiction that he was once a gangster. He thinks it'll boost his music career."

"He's in the wrong genre for that."

"Willard's in the wrong genre as a homo sapien."

Leah laughs. "Oh come on! He's not that bad. So what else happened?"

"Well, the whole investigation delayed the opening of the store for about forty-five minutes. I called Dante, who came in to try to smooth things over. I think the cops probably figure some dealer got spooked and dropped it there."

Leah stands back from the closet and tries to figure out where she's going to fit her boots, which are too tall to go on the shoe rack. "Too bad you didn't hold on to it," she says absently. "If you'd sold it, we'd probably have been able to stay in my old apartment."

"You're kidding, right?"

"Mostly. Your closet space is kind of lacking in the space part. If you got busted, though, I promise I would visit every day. Well, you know, at least more than once. Do you have a storage space in the basement where you can put some of this stuff?"

By *this stuff*, she of course means the ever-growing pile of possessions that I have accumulated over my short time on earth. So much of it is pointless junk. It makes one wonder: Why did I buy it in the first place? And why did I hold on to it for so long? It's a universal law that everything gets thrown out eventually. Even us.

"No. The only thing in the basement here is the maintenance guy, Marcus. He used to be a Scientologist, but his parents had him kidnapped and de-programmed. Now he makes handmade greeting cards in his spare time. I'm not sure the de-programming really took, though. His Christmas cards all have volcanoes on them. And his Santas bear more than a passing resemblance to L. Ron Hubbard."

"Are you making that up?"

"Hell no. I bought a bunch of them last year to send out to friends and family. In fact, some of them are probably still in that box you put over there next to the garbage."

Leah ignores this modest provocation. "Well, at least you didn't get arrested."

"One of the cops was the same one who showed up at the restaurant. She's gotta be thinking I'm involved in every drug transaction in the city. I'm surprised they didn't drag me downtown for a strip search. Oh well. At least it wasn't a bomb."

"Who'd want to blow up a bookstore?"

"Not the bookstore. Sebastian. He was in there hiding out from Mina's crazy awol husband."

"And so now he's just moving in with her? Jeez, he's really taking his life in his hands. I don't think I'd be able to sleep with the thought that I might wake up with a knife resting against my jugular and a pair of crazy eyes staring down at me. Or not wake up at all."

"Deep down, Sebastian's one of those guys who thinks he can talk his way out of anything."

"Not easy to do if your vocal chords are no longer connected to your throat."

"I'm trying not to picture that, but I can't seem to do it."

Leah decides to make space for her boots by moving aside the cardboard tubes containing my rolled movie posters, which I suppose I can store under the bed provided I don't end up sleeping under there myself. My Dad collected movie posters for years. He actually worked as an assistant manager in a small theatre in Scotland, where he helped himself to the promotional material before it was tossed in the garbage. When he and my mother downsized to a smaller house after all the kids moved out, he asked me if I wanted any of them before he sold them off. I probably have a couple hundred of them. The nicer ones I'd like to get framed or mounted one day if I ever have a permanent place that's big enough to hang them.

"Sebastian's an interesting guy," Leah says. "He's living his life like he's Richard Burton on the set of *Cleopatra*. He's quite charming, but…"

"He's also something of a cad."

"Yeah!" she says. "That's exactly it. He's like Willoughby in *Sense and Sensibility*. You know. Funny, cute, refined, well-spoken…but at the same time just this completely amoral poon hound. He also drinks too much. I can't believe you let him walk around the store with a hip flask."

I feel obliged to mount some sort of defence. She is, after all, talking about my best friend of the last few years. She is also, however, exactly right.

"Well, he's not a total shit," I say weakly. "He is sticking it out with Mina."

"That girl has problems," Leah says, shaking her head. "I can't believe you were ever with her."

"For about five minutes." I am quite keen to change the subject. "But anyway, you still haven't told me how things went at the audition."

She shrugs. "Oh, you know. It's hard to tell with those things. They tell you you're fantastic, but they say that to everybody."

"What did you have to do? A scene from the commercial or did they let you pull out some Ibsen?"

"No, it's more like an interview. They want to get a look at you to see if you even vaguely resemble your head shot and they want you to talk so they know you don't sound like you've had your larynx replaced and you're talking through a hole in your throat into one of those things. You know, that make you sound like a robot? My grandma was in a home with a guy who had one of those. We used to visit when I was a kid and he scared the hell out of me. He came over and said hello. Maybe he thought since I was a kid that I'd think it was some sort of cool novelty act or something. Like a guy juggling rings in the park. I just started screaming and wouldn't stop. My parents had to leave. I feel bad about it now. Poor guy."

"You were what? Eighteen at the time?"

She gives me a sardonic grin. "Laugh it up, fuzzball. I still have nightmares about it."

"Hey, I'm not judging. I was at a birthday sleepover once in elementary school where we watched *Rabid* and *Alien*. I haven't actually slept since. I just close my eyes and clutch a baseball bat, which might stop Marilyn Chambers but would be useless against a xenomorph."

"Why hasn't there been a movie called *Xenomorph*? It's a good title."

"We could make it. You could play the hot leader of a group of space marines sent in to find out why we've lost contact with the white house after Sarah Palin wins the presidency."

"That would be scary. Genre mash ups are hard, though. And political satire and horror…that would be a tough one to pull off. But it is nice to be described as a hot space marine."

"So they just asked you a few questions and then you were on your way?"

"No. They took some photos and then we did a quick run through on video so they could get a sense of my timing and delivery. They're stretchy sandwich bags, which is actually kind of a cool idea when you think about it. I hold up this bag full of what are supposed to be ripe strawberries but are actually plastic ones and say 'Wow! It holds so much!' and try to look like I think this is the greatest human achievement since the moon landing."

I nod approvingly. "That was really good! Now let's do it again, but this time I want you to squeeze the imaginary bag in a more suggestive manner."

"It's not that kind of commercial. The good thing is that it's a national product launch, so if I get it, the spot would play everywhere."

"Wow! Listen to you. You've got the lingo down and everything."

"I saw my competition," Leah says. "This blonde girl with big fake boobs. She'd obviously had her nose done too. I know she's done a couple of beer commercials. You know, the ones where they try to get you to drink watered down horse piss for a chance to ride on an airplane full of horny sorority girls?"

"I think I have some of that in the fridge right now, actually."

"She had her own makeup and hair person with her. If I wore pants that tight I'd get a yeast infection for sure. And there was this old guy hovering in the background who spent the whole time talking on his cell phone. I don't know if it was her dad or her agent. Probably both. I think they're looking for someone a little more, I don't know, normal or even wholesome-looking. You know, since they're selling food and not panty remover. I can look like a young suburban mom, right? You'd buy me in that?"

"I'd buy whatever you were selling. You could become the face of a new government public sterilization campaign and I'd line up outside one of the clinics. You could sell Soylent Green. I don't know why a company hasn't snapped that name up. Your slogan is a no-brainer: *Soylent Green – It's People!* It sounds so nice and positive and upbeat. Plus everybody already knows it. Who cares if it's indirectly associated with cannibalism? They could present it as the environmentally sustainable choice: *We're taking care of overpopulation and the food crisis at the same time.*"

"Your mind works in some strange ways, hon."

"Well, it's not really my idea. Jonathan Swift had it first. If it doesn't work in a corporate context, we could always translate it to reality TV. Imagine how much more interesting *Survivor* would be if they had to eat the person they voted off. At the end of each episode they could literally just throw them in this giant pot. It would fit the whole tribal motif."

"I know people you could pitch this to. There really is no bottom right now when it comes to TV standards."

"It's a good thing that none of it is going to survive. Imagine what future societies would think if a thousand years from now on some archaeological dig all they found was an episode of some show about former porn stars trying to start their own businesses. The technology won't be there. VHS tapes are gone. Soon DVDs will be gone. Hell, I can't even open a Word document that's more than five years old in the new version of Word. They'll know more about the Egyptians than they will about us."

"Um, how did we get talking about this?"

"You're right. We were talking about your audition. I'm sure you'll get it and not the bimbo. You know why? Because you have class, and that's what counts. Especially when it comes to sandwich bags."

"Are you sure you turned over all that hash to the police?"

"Of course. I wouldn't even know what to do with it, to be honest. Do you smoke it? If so, how? I know you don't inhale it. I'm really in the dark on this one."

"It's probably better that way."

"The only thing I've ever tried is pot. I'm not keen to indulge in any recreational substance likely to lead to a lifetime of body cavity searches at airports."

She gives up on the boots and sits down next to me on the bed. "You sure you're okay with me moving in?"

"Okay? I'm thrilled. You know, the adjusting to the space thing will be tricky, but we'll figure it out. I wish my place was bigger and I didn't realize you had quite as many pairs of shoes as you do, Mrs. Marcos."

"I have friends who make my shoe collection look like something they would take on a camping trip!"

"The fact that you refer to it as 'a collection' is probably the first step in admitting you have a problem."

"Easy for you to say! You have, like, four pairs. You don't have to co-ordinate them with anything. You wear one pair of black Docs to work. You really should get a brown pair to wear with lighter pants. Other than that, you have one pair of running shoes and an old pair of sandals. I don't have *that* many shoes. I used to buy them when I got stressed out. Which is probably why I have the urge to go out and pick up a pair right now."

I put my arm around her shoulders. "Relax. You and your shoes are as welcome as can be. If necessary, I'll move my desk into the parking lot to make room. That way, I can tell everyone that my office is on the street. They'll think I'm a cop or a P.I. or something. From now on, you need to think of this place as yours. Except for the hall closet, of course. Don't open that until I say it's okay. There's a former business associate in there. Well, parts of him. And I need to move him out before the cops start asking questions and poking around."

She laughs and puts her head on my shoulder. "You're a funny guy, Sully. That is why I will kill you last. What say we go to Falstaff's for a pint?"

"A capital idea. Then we can come back here and you can have a nice relaxing bath while I prepare my famous *chicken a la ptomaine*."

"Your what?"

"Actually, it's just *chicken cordon bleu*. I thought it would go nicely with that Vueve Clicquot Grand Dame you brought with you."

"You can cook?"

"I can apply heat to things until they're approximately edible."

"Well, that puts this whole enterprise in a completely new light." She leans over for a kiss. "What say we skip the pint and go straight to the bath?"

Which I think is an even more capital idea.

# -17-

Every year we close up an hour early on a Tuesday night and head to the private upstairs room at Falstaff's for the annual Christmas party. Usually we do this at the end of November, but this year Dante decides we can push it to the second week of December in order to give Leah a chance to settle in.

Tuesday is, admittedly, a lousy night for a party, but it's the slowest night of the week sales-wise and it's better to have staff call in sick or show up slightly hungover on a Wednesday than on a weekend. Nobody really complains. In retail, there's no such thing as a regular workweek, anyway. Many of the staff have other part-time jobs and can count the number of vacation days they get in a year on rabbit ears.

Willard, for example, also works in the kitchen of a Serbian restaurant that was a regular hangout for two men who were recently arrested for war crimes in Belgrade. Sebastian used to work at a movie megaplex off the highway but was fired when management determined that he was the one who had re-programmed the electronic marquee to announce showtimes for "A Very Long Engorgement" and "Drivin' Miss Daisy 2 – Backseat Driver". Ivanka is a personal trainer. Miroslav volunteers as a test subject for drug trials, some of which last as long as two weeks. Lolita works as a greeter in a funeral home.

The party is pretty straightforward. We all show up around 9:30 or so. Mickey has been talking about turning the upstairs into a nightclub for years now, but has never gotten around to it. In between being a brewery and a mansion and briefly a strip club, Falstaff's was also a hotel. The upstairs is a series of rooms that have had many of the connecting walls knocked down, which gives the impression of dining on a construction site. On the flipside, much of the décor and even some of the furniture has been around since the '20s, which provides some refinement amongst the ruin. There's a fireplace, a pool table, a series of banquet-style tables and a never-ending supply of pub grub and drinks. Mickey always goes out of his way to make the space festive by stringing up some green banners. Granted, the banners are for his hurling team, but they do look nice when dangling from the half-timbered ceiling and stone walls. He also pipes up some Christmas music from downstairs. Tonight, it's the Pogues' "If I Should Fall From Grace With God" album on repeat – the rationale being that it contains the greatest Christmas song ever in "Fairytale of New York" and that oughta be damn well good enough so stop yer complainin' ye fookin' gobshite.

Good times are generally had by all. We don't have the kinds of traditions that other workplaces might roll out. There is no secret Santa exchange, for example. People show up, eat, drink, and then stagger home. Both Dante and Mickey are careful to have lots of taxis standing by outside, although that didn't stop Sebastian from commandeering a backhoe from a nearby building site last year and knocking the head off a statue of former premier Mike Harris. He claimed he had no memory of it the next day, but I suspect he knew exactly what he was doing.

We do have a pool tournament, though. Sebastian and I generally wipe the floor with the rest of the staff, but this time it's Leah who walks away undefeated. It's not even close, either. She runs the table three times and when I do get a chance to step up find myself so comprehensively snookered that I end up sewering while attempting a safety. I'm starting to wonder if there's anything this woman isn't good at. Don't get me wrong – I'm not one of those insecure males who expects to throw touchdowns and replace transmissions while his girlfriend shops for cocktail dresses, but I wouldn't mind having at least something I can do that she isn't a pro at.

It's nice to be here as one half of a couple for a change. This party sort of counts as our official coming out, I suppose, and, aside from having my ass handed to me on the baize, I'm enjoying every minute of it.

The opposite of this is Dante, who is also here with a woman. Well, two women if you count his mother. Dante's date is a very nice, extremely mousy woman named Carmelina, who apparently likes to have Lucretia do all of her talking for her. Carmelina used to be married to a roofer named Al who apparently cut one too many corners on materials and fell through his own work into an antique bath tub, where he hit his head on the faucet and died of a massive cerebral haemorrhage. I don't think his body had even been moved before Lucretia started working the phones.

The three of them are sitting at a table in the corner where Lucretia is punctuating the long silences with loud observations in Italian about Dante's manliness and Carmelina's fecundity. It seems that Al, along with being a corner cutter, was also sterile. The rest of the staff is conspicuously avoiding them. Everyone knows about Dante's situation and no one wants to be caught within the gravitational range of a social black hole from which no fun can escape. Anyone else who sits at that table will be stuck there for life or at least the rest of the evening, which will feel just as long.

The other debutante couple of the evening is Sebastian and Mina, who seem to be having fun despite a rocky start. During the tournament, Mina apparently became convinced that Sebastian was flirting with Leah and locked herself in the bathroom for half an hour. Sebastian, who was indeed flirting with Leah, didn't notice until he went to get drinks and Mina wasn't there to receive the hand off of her gin and tonic. The flirting didn't bother me because Leah was only going along to demonstrate to me the extreme limits of Sebastian's caddishness. Meanwhile, Mina had a long talk with

Ivanka in the bathroom and came out willing to give him another chance, convinced that the whole episode was a product of her overheated imagination. Ivanka also managed to talk Mina into signing up for three months' worth of introductory Krav Maga, which, she informs me, is the same form of hand-to-hand combat used by the Israeli Defence Force.

I'm at the bar getting us beers (no Scrumpy up here, alas) when I feel Leah's hand on my back.

"Okay, don't turn around right away."

I freeze, pint glasses in hand. "What?"

She leans in to whisper in my ear. "What the hell, exactly, did you say to Aldous?"

What the hell, exactly, is she talking about? "What?"

"Turn around."

I slowly rotate in place, suddenly conscious of every movement in the same way I might be if I had unwittingly stepped out on stage in front of a live audience. I'm concentrating so heavily on not spilling the pint glasses that I'm not really paying any attention to the party. "What are you..."

Then I see him.

My first thought is to wonder what a Bay Street suit is doing at a party with a bunch of retail wage slaves, but even a first glance is enough to realize that's not it. The suit is at least fifteen years old, bright blue and about two sizes too small for its wearer. It looks like something that was worn for a church confirmation or high school graduation ceremony and then stuffed unceremoniously in the back of the closet to ride out the next ten years' worth of fashion trends in the dark.

The shirt is the colour of stale icing and not buttoned to the top despite the fact that – dear God – it's capped by a spotted red bow tie. The pants stop a couple of inches north of the ankles, which are encased in white socks. The shoes are of the scuffed, steel-toed safety variety favoured by auto mechanics and factory workers.

Then there's the hair. The dreadlocks have been chopped, tamed with more brylcreem than I thought was commercially available, and combed straight back. I can smell the cologne from here. I'm usually no good at identifying individual scents, but there is no mistaking the mallet-like punch of an entire bottle of Polo, even at this distance across a crowded room of competing smells.

"Jesus," I mutter. "He looks like Gordon Gekko."

Leah takes the one of pint glasses out of my hand, which is good as I had momentarily forgotten they were there. "No. He looks like the malformed evil twin of Gordon Gekko that his parents kept chained in the attic."

"He looks like the band leader from a Pocono resort hotel."

"He looks like the manager of a Las Vegas wedding chapel."

"He looks...nothing like himself."

Leah takes my arm and steers me sideways so that I am no longer standing with my jaw hanging open, gaping like a bystander at the scene of an accident. "I repeat: what in the hell advice did you give him?"

I shake my head. "Not that!"

She smiles and shakes her head. "Poor guy. He is trying."

We watch Aldous move through the room as subtly as a rhinoceros at a board meeting. He's trying to make casual conversation, but everyone is too nakedly astonished at his transformation to do much more than gape. A topless woman could jump out of a cake wearing a Henry Kissinger mask and not a single person in this room would pay her any attention. Well, except Sebastian.

"Is that Aldous?"

We turn to see that Dante has joined us at the bar. He has somehow managed to escape his table, although his mother is eyeing him warily, evidently to make sure he doesn't make a break for the door. She must be about the only person in the room not watching the Aldous show.

I nod. "I think so."

"Why is he dressed like a Mexican game show host?"

Leah snickers and looks at me. "That's because *somebody* gave him some advice on fashion and grooming."

Dante looks at me in disbelief. "Seriously?"

The repeated accusation that this is somehow my fault is starting to make me slightly peeved. "That is *not* what I told him to wear. How did you get away from your, uh, date?"

Dante looks uncomfortable. "Ah – I'm getting drinks."

"She seems like a very nice woman. Are you sure your mother didn't have her husband killed?"

"I haven't ruled it out," Dante says, looking uneasy.

"Oh for crying out loud," Leah says, rolling her eyes. "If you don't tell her, Dante, I'm going to."

"No, don't!" Dante says. "Carmelina knows already."

"Say what?"

"I told her after our first fake date," Dante says. "Her husband just died, for God's sake. She's not about to just run out and start up with some other guy. Even if her husband was kind of a shit."

"You mean, aside from being a crappy roofer?"

"Yeah," Dante says. "I guess he drank. Plus he had gambling debts. They're not entirely sure he just fell through the roof, if you know what I mean."

Leah drops her voice. "And she knows you're…"

"Not interested in heterosexual reproduction, yes."

"So why–"

"She's doing it because my mother's sick. Bubby is Carm's godmother."

*Bubby*, I should point out, is short for Beelzebub.

"And now she's making an offer her son can't refuse," I observe. In my head, I can hear the lonely trumpet of Carmine Coppola.

"Carm says she knew I was gay in elementary school, but she never said anything to anybody," Dante says. "Which is good, because I would have gotten the shit kicked out of me on a daily basis. Those nuns didn't fuck around."

"And so how long is she willing to be your beard?" Leah asks.

"She's going back to Italy in January," Dante says. "Then she's going to be travelling around for six months. Apparently Al had a substantial insurance policy and never wanted to go anywhere. Now she has nothing to stop her."

"Jeez," I mutter. "How much do you know about this woman? Do you know where she was when he took his last bath? This is starting to sound like *Double Indemnity*."

"She told Beelzebub she's taking Al back to bury him in the old country."

"Is she really?" Leah asks.

Dante snorts. "Shit, no. Al was born in Windsor. She's having him cremated and then dropping him at the curb with the recycling before she leaves for the airport."

"Oy vey," I mutter. "That's cold. Even for a boozy not-so-handyman on the hook to shylocks."

Whatever Dante is about to say next is interrupted when Aldous appears next to our group like a humpback whale surfacing next to a tour boat. We all make a concerted effort to maintain a neutral expression and breathe through our mouths.

"Good evening, everybody!" he says, sounding like he's greeting the first group of contestants on *Family Feud*.

"Hi Aldous!" I say, and then can't think of a single thing to add. "You're...uh...How are you?"

"Good!" he says. "Really good."

We just stand there and stare at each other for a moment that feels longer and more awkward than watching *In The Cut* with your grandmother. We are saved by Ebeneezer, of all people.

"Swinghammer!" he barks. "I see you've made an effort to make yourself more closely resemble a civilized human."

"Uh, yes," Aldous says, self-consciously tugging at his cuffs, which steadfastly refuse to come any closer to his wrists. "I just thought it was, you know, time for a change, I suppose."

"Commendable," Ebeneezer says, nodding. "You're on the right road, my boy. The destination lies just ahead of you. Persevere!"

Aldous nods blankly. The rest of us breathe a huge sigh of relief. Ebeneezer has managed to say what we were all thinking without making it sound like an insult, which is distinctly out of character. I am surprised to see Ebeneezer here at all. He studiously avoids any invitation to socialize with the employees outside of work and has never come to any of the previous Christmas parties. I notice he keeps looking towards the door, like he's waiting for somebody else to arrive.

"Good to see you, Mr. C!" I say. "You don't always make it out to these little shindigs."

"Indeed," he says, taking a distracted sip of what looks like a Pimm's. I've never seen him drink before, either. Something funny is going on here.

As if sensing my confusion, Leah leans over and whispers in my ear: "I told him I invited Fermina to the party tonight."

Aha! "Did you?"

Leah nods. "She said she would. I'm not sure where she is. Maybe she changed her mind."

I glance over at the door, half expecting Fermina to come strolling in just because I am now aware that she's coming, but the only person over there is Lolita, who has stationed herself there as an unofficial bouncer to remind any non-bookstore employees who come up the stairs that this is a private party and that they can just turn around and go straight back down again thank you. Nobody asked her to do this, of course. I think it's a side effect of all the time she's spent standing just inside the door at the funeral home doing more or less the same thing.

I suddenly remember that I'm holding a beer and, since I can't think of anything to say, it would probably be a good idea to drink from it. I am interrupted by a chirping sound. Leah puts her beer down on the bar and fishes around in her purse to pull out her phone. Her jaw muscles tighten noticeably when she looks at the display.

"Oh boy," she says quietly.

Uh oh, I think. The audition verdict. It has to be. I feel my heart start beating faster.

Leah takes a deep breath and then steps back from the group. "Hello?" she says, trying to sound casual.

I stand there and watch every microscopic change in her expression for any indication. I hate to admit it, but I am mentally steeling myself to help her cope with the inevitable disappointment of not getting it. *That's okay. You'll get the next one. It was only a sandwich bag commercial anyway, right? Who needs that? So they went with the bimbo. We'll never ever buy those particular sandwich bags again, stretchy or not. Bastards.*

"Uh huh." She's nodding. I give her a wide-eyed expression to indicate that I would like some kind of hint one way or the other, but she's not budging, dammit. "Yes."

Aldous is saying something. I have absolutely no idea what it is. I hold up a finger. *Give me a minute, man.*

Leah smiles. "That's fantastic!"

Huh?

"Yeah! Definitely! Okay. Great! Yeah. I'll call you tomorrow!" She hangs up the phone and looks straight at me. "I got it."

"What?" I am honestly not entirely sure I heard what she said. It's not the first time I've failed to hear a big revelation. When I saw *The Return of the Jedi* in theatres and Luke asked Yoda if Vader was really his father and

Yoda said: "Your father he is." I missed it. I had to turn to my Dad to find out what the little green bugger had said. I blame it on the muppet's irritating tendency to put his nouns in front of his verbs.

Leah throws her hands up in the air and screams: "I got it!" She vaults into the air and I catch her, inadvertently dumping half my beer on Aldous's pants in the process. We make up for this by promising to take him out on the weekend and help him buy an entirely new ensemble. At least the beer does something to dampen the power of the cologne, although whether or not it's an improvement is debatable.

Everyone stops by to congratulate Leah on landing the gig. The commercial is going to be shooting next week on a small soundstage in the distillery district. Leah is supposed to be working that day, but I immediately offer to cover for her. I don't even know when I'm working that day. I might end up working a double, but it doesn't matter. I'm so blown away that she got the job that I would agree to just about anything at this point. Even taking Aldous shopping.

The rest of the night is a blur. I drink an undocumented number of beers and radiate goodwill to all mankind. Leah beats me at pool five more times, after which we decide that it's probably a good idea to head home and continue our celebrations in private. Mina's scheduled to open tomorrow, and if she doesn't make it in I have advised Dante that I have absolutely no intention of picking up the phone before noon, so don't even bother. I'm not sure what Dante's response is to this as I'm a little too full of the joys of the season to make it out.

# -18-

As it turns out, I am scheduled to work on the day of Leah's commercial shoot. I'm on to open and she was supposed to be closing. The shoot is tentatively set to run from noon until 4 o'clock, so in theory, she should still be able to get here in time to work her shift.

I've told her not to worry about it. If the shoot does wrap on time, then she can come over whenever she's done and take over. Until then, I will man the fort. Dante can't do it because he's going on a fake date with Carmelina and Mina can't cover because she's taking Sebastian out to play bingo with her mother. Dante says he actually enjoys spending time with Carmelina, who apparently shares his interest in opera. They're going to see *Il Trovatore* at the COC sans Lucretia. Since she already knows his secret, he doesn't have to fake an illness and can simply relax. It's so much fun, in fact, that if he wasn't gay it would be indistinguishable from an actual date.

It's almost 6 p.m. and there's no sign of Leah. I hope she can make it in soon because I haven't really eaten yet and we have that most dreaded of all bookstore events on tonight's calendar: an author reading.

The problem with having a writer come to a bookstore and read from their latest book is that, unless the writer in question is J.K. Rowling, almost nobody else shows up. It doesn't matter how well-publicized the event is (and with our next-to-nonexistent marketing budget, the answer to that one is not very), the whole thing usually plays out like a surprise birthday party for a leper – they show up, often unwillingly, to find out that they are the only one in the room because all of their friends have already died.

I almost always end up feeling bad for the writers in these situations. Especially a new writer out promoting their first book. They're the ones most likely to show up expecting billboards and spotlights and lines out the door. They even expect a couple of reporters to be hanging around waiting for an interview and a burly security guard to keep the throngs in check. When they see that it's just me and some old lady who showed up to get a copy of the book signed for her daughter because she misread the sign and thought it was Danielle Steele instead of Daniel Sterne, a lot of the apple-cheeked swagger goes out of their stride.

More experienced writers are either too successful to come to a place this size or have already been on a tour like this and recognize it for the colossal waste of time that it is for all involved. Writers are not celebrities. You could walk past 99.9 per cent of them on the street without a second glance. They aren't glamorous, either. Kurt Vonnegut once said that most novelists drag themselves around like gutshot bears, and, based on my limited experience, that's pretty accurate. The reason they became writers is because they work best in isolation and not, for example, on stage at Glastonbury in front of a hundred thousand screaming fans.

As I said, I usually end up feeling sorry for the writer in these situations – unless the writer in question is a shit.

I've seen my share of those, as well. One author of a collection of deathly dull stories about the even duller sport of fly fishing once made quite the spectacle of himself by loudly demanding that the entire gift section be cleared of all product to make room for him and the legions of his fans who were certain to mob the place once the event got underway. His book was, after all, a best seller, a minor factoid that we dumbass kids were clearly too illiterate to be aware of despite somehow being employed in a bookstore. And speaking of his book, where the hell was it? We were supposed to have 150 extra copies on hand and he couldn't see a single one. He demanded to speak to the manager immediately.

Because the evening was quite clearly a bust, I took it upon myself to advise him of a few facts:

1) the gift section could not be cleared away because it also happened to be right in front of our cash registers and if, heaven forbid, some hapless sucker did want to buy one of his books, they would thus be prevented from doing so by the presence of the author himself;

2) the event in question was supposed to start 45 minutes ago and would have done so had the author not been late;

3) there were no mobs, nor had there been 45 minutes previously;

4) in order to qualify for best seller status, a book only has to sell 5,000 copies, and his book had only done that because his publisher was counting library sales and promotional giveaways;

5) despite being retail employees, we were neither dumbasses nor illiterate – in fact, one of our staff members had read his book and found no fewer than thirteen paragraphs that had been lifted, without attribution, from *A River Runs Through It*;

6) no one had requested we order an extra 150 copies, but we still had our original shipment of three, which appeared to be three more than were required to meet demand;

7) since his publisher had recently switched to a no returns policy, he was more than welcome to immediately take the remaining three off our hands personally;

8) I was the manager; and

9) he was heartily encouraged to attempt to insert his penis in his own asshole whilst exiting the premises (or words to that effect).

One author of a book that claimed to identify the three questions you would need to be able to answer to get into heaven threw a fit when we didn't have the particular brand of mineral water and dried veggie snacks on hand that her publisher had clearly listed on the event rider. No such rider was received. Another who was out promoting a gastric bypass diet book tried to send Aldous across town to pick up a takeout order of deep-fried cheeseburgers and Mars bars from a "traditional" chip shop called The Cranky Scot. An author of a book on coping with schizophrenia asked if we could turn down the music for his presentation. There was no music playing at the time.

So, needless to say, the prospect of another author trooping into the store only a week before C-Day doesn't exactly fill me with tidings of comfort and joy. I've been on the go since six o'clock this morning. Well, technically, since ten o'clock last night. Leah was so nervous about the shoot today that she couldn't sleep, which meant that I didn't sleep, either. I'm tired, hungry and cranky, which means I'm not in an ideal mood to cater to the whims of another sex-starved, intellectually insecure cave troll.

Fortunately, Julian Bartlett appears to be none of these things. He's a quiet, modest-looking fellow in his late forties who has, I see to my surprise and delight, written a book about the cultural impact of soccer. How this book has escaped my notice, I don't know, but I manage to read the first couple of chapters while cramming in the pop and mixed berry yoghurt that constitutes "lunch" and am transfixed. The writing is sharp but not flashy and manages to capture the almost spiritual thrill that comes with watching the beautiful game played beautifully. We only have ten copies, but I immediately set them up on a small table near the front door and make sure the promotional posters are up where they can be seen.

When he steps in the door a half an hour before the reading is supposed to start, I recognize him immediately from the jacket photo and run over to shake his hand. He's originally from Toronto, but moved to Yorkshire after he graduated, where he got a job covering football for a weekly paper. That lasted for about five years and then he moved back to Canada after he got married. He still does a bit of freelance work here and there, but there isn't as much call for footie coverage on this side of the pond, so he makes ends meet by working in the PR department at an insurance company.

"You're a fan of the game, then?" he asks, when I tell him how much I've enjoyed the first thirty pages of his book.

"Oh yes," I say. "I've been watching the World Cup since I was old enough to sit up. I used to love watching the Brazilian national team, but then they stopped playing like Brazil and started playing like the Netherlands and I lost interest."

He grins. "True. So who do you follow now?"

"Barça."

He nods satisfactorily. "The best team I've ever seen play the game. I met Lionel Messi once."

My jaw drops so hard that I chip a tooth on the floor. I am standing next to a man who once stood next to the greatest football player on the planet. "Holy shit! What'd he say?"

"Not much. It was at a press conference. He's a pretty quiet guy."

When Messi first started playing for Barcelona, he was so quiet that his teammates nicknamed him *el mudo* – the mute. Since he started showing a superhuman talent for scoring goals, he picked up a new nickname: *la pulga atomica*, or the atomic flea. He's not a big guy, but he's fast enough to shoot past defenders like they aren't even there and the ball doesn't leave his foot until it hits the back of the net. He doesn't dive and he's not a preening showboat like Cristiano Ronaldo (although level-headedness is probably a lot to ask from anyone coached by an eye-gouging nutjob like José Murinho).

I think the word genius is wildly overused, but this is one case where I am happy to apply it. Einstein may have been able to figure out the relationship between energy and matter, but I doubt he'd be able to do much on the receiving end of a perfect curling pass from Xavi Hernandez in the 18 yard box. You want to see a genius in action? YouTube the words "Messi", "Awesome" and "Goal". You'll get about 400,000 results.

The funny thing is, if I was walking in the Plaza de Cataluña in Barcelona and bumped into him, I haven't the faintest idea what I'd say. And that's not just because I don't speak much Spanish. Does the greatest footballer on the planet (arguably, ever) need to be told that he's the greatest by some random foreigner who will probably screw up the pronunciation of a key noun and call him the greatest upholsterer instead? After all, it's not like he's walking around with *my* name on the back of *his* shirt.

Much to my relief, there are actually about a dozen people waiting for the reading to get started. I hang out near the back to listen in. We sell out the ten copies we have and I immediately order 15 more. I ask the author to sign the copy I have sitting in the office (which I also buy, using my staff discount), which makes it the only signed edition that I have in my collection. He tells me he's doing an interview on the CBC morning radio show the next day, which will hopefully draw a little more attention and get him out of insurance writing purgatory. Football is starting, slowly and painfully, to become a bigger deal at the professional level in North America, but I still think archaeologists will be picking over our bones before TFC finally figures out how to stop embarrassing themselves on the pitch.

We're just shaking hands to cap off what has been a successful evening for both of us when things take a sudden and rapid turn for disaster.

# -19-

Piecing events together after the fact, it's pretty obvious to me now that I should have realised the situation was not salvageable as soon as I saw the gun.

It turned out that Mina's husband was not a special forces black ops soldier stationed in Afghanistan, although he had worked as a peacekeeper in Rwanda years ago when he enlisted straight out of high school. I guess he saw some pretty horrendous things and was given a psychological discharge shortly after the end of his first tour of duty. He made it through six months of training as a tool-and-die maker before he dropped out and went to work part-time in a meat packing plant. He went through quite a few jobs in the space of a few short years, during which time he also became seriously attached to alcohol and oxycodone. He also married Mina, whom he met in the waiting room of their mutual shrink.

I know all of this because the police filled me in on some of the details when I was taken to the hospital after I was shot.

Apparently, the whole thing happened in about eight seconds, but to me it seemed like half an hour. I remember that I was walking Julian Bartlett to the door after his reading when a man, later identified as former Master Corporal Nicholas Bovary, yanked open the door and charged inside, knocking over a university student (later identified as 22-year-old Peter Brzinski) who was on his way out the door with a stolen copy of

*FHM* magazine hidden under his jacket. For obvious reasons, no charges were filed against the student even though he later admitted to stealing the magazine. The cover, incidentally, featured a Venezuelan pop singer named Booti, who was dressed only in a python .

I remember saying something along the lines of "Whoa!" and holding up my hands to indicate that there was no need to make such a dramatic entrance. My first thought was that he was just another crazy Christmas shopper keen to get his hands on something before it sold out. When I got a better look at his bare feet, stained track pants and torn T shirt, I thought he was a homeless guy looking for a place to sit out of the cold and flip through a newspaper. We don't get as many of them as they do at the library, but we do get them. As long as they don't hassle anyone and they don't stink too badly, we usually leave them alone.

Then I saw the gun.

I have no idea what kind of gun it was. Despite a lifetime of going to action movies, I don't know a damn thing about weapons. All I know is that it was a handgun. There was no mistaking the shape of the black tube protruding from his right hand as casually as a museum security guard's walkie-talkie. I had been on my way to help the guy he had knocked down, but as soon as I saw that, I stopped in my tracks.

The first thought that went through my head was: Shit, I'm going to have to stay late tonight.

Some people handle extreme stress overload quite well. I'm not one of them. My brain tends to abandon my body like supporters fleeing a political candidate who is caught fucking a goat on national television. The thinking part of my mind simply shuts down and waits for everything to be over. Two cars smashed into each other in an intersection right in front of me once and I just stood there on the corner while other people ran out to make sure there were no injuries and called the police on their cell phones.

The crazy guy looked around. His head was a ball of black stubble. His eyes were surprisingly clear under thick, bushy eyebrows. He had some sort of shield-shaped tattoo on his neck just above the left collarbone, which I remember thinking was a weird place for a tattoo.

"Where's Mina?" he asked. His voice was higher and more nasal than I would expect from a crazy gunman.

Aha, I thought. That explained puzzle piece number one. *Mina's husband*. In a strange way, it was almost a relief to come face-to-face with the guy. In my head, I had imagined some crazy-ass, massive, battle-scarred Sgt. Rock with grenade launchers in both hands. This guy was shorter and skinnier than me and only carrying a semi-automatic. Based on his appearance, though, he certainly seemed to have the crazy-ass part down cold.

"She's not in tonight," I said, surprised at how flat and even disinterested my voice sounded. The words seemed to be coming not from me but out of an overhead speaker. I could feel the air crackle.

He pointed the gun at me. Anyone who tells you that humans are incapable of understanding the concept of infinity is wrong. Dead wrong.

"Are you Sebastian?"

I shook my head. It was the first thing I was able to make my muscles do since I had spotted the gun, and it required more effort than a solo assault on Everest without oxygen.

"No, I'm not."

He spun around, swinging the gun as he did. Somebody up at cash gasped and dropped to the floor in a crouch. An old lady in line dropped a paperback box set of Harry Potter books, which landed flat on their side with a smack.

"Where is he?" he asked, walking along the cash line and peeking down between the stacks. There was still space from where I'd cleared away some gift items from the reading and he could see straight to the back of the store.

"He's not in tonight either," I said. My throat was so dry that the words came out sounding like a bad Clint Eastwood imitation.

"I don't believe you," he said, walking over to the magazine racks. Ivanka was standing there next to the cart she was using to collect discards. He tried to push her out of the way to get a look down the aisle. In a single lightning move, she grabbed his hand – the one holding the gun – twisted it at an incredibly improbable angle, and spun his arm up behind his back.

I heard two very distinct pops. The first was the sound of his thumb breaking as it was compressed against the trigger guard. The second was the sound of the gun going off. That was all it was – a pop. Not that much different from a cherry bomb or those stupid cap guns I used to play with when I was a kid. No giant blam or boom or even a bang. Just a stupid, inane little pop. It didn't even have the percussive force of a balloon. It sounded ridiculous. I'm pretty sure I even laughed.

Everyone in the store screamed and ducked at almost the same time as Ivanka grabbed the gunman by the neck and pushed him face-first to the floor with enough force to break his nose, which started to gush blood on the tile.

I felt a burning hot pain in both legs simultaneously and fell down, letting out a small and decidedly un-masculine screech as I went. I had been shot! Twice! How was that possible?

Ivanka yanked the gun out of the prone and apparently unconscious nutbar's hand and put it on the bottom shelf of her cart. She then grabbed a roll of tape off the top shelf and bound his hands and legs together in a flash, trussing him up as efficiently as a turkey. People started clapping. Someone cheered.

I sat up and looked down at my legs. Police would later determine that the bullet had ricocheted off two bookcases and the cash desk before passing almost precisely between my legs, grazing the inner thighs at a distance of approximately six and a half inches below the groin. These details were published in the subsequent page four news story ("Hero Employee Stops Bookstore Shooter") that generated some extremely tasteless jokes about my reproductive system on certain morning drivetime radio shows the next day.

The wounds weren't serious and didn't even require stitches, but they did burn like hell. Apparently the bullet was so hot that it cauterized as it went, so I didn't bleed as much as I might had the same wounds been caused by a knife. This didn't really matter much – I'd still need to get a new pair of pants courtesy of the paramedics who cut them off as they were bundling me on to the stretcher. Fortunately, this was before the TV crews arrived.

I managed to reach Dante during the first intermission ("I've been shot! I need you to cover my closing shift!"), but Leah's cell phone was turned off and for some reason her mailbox was not accepting new messages.

*Where the fuck is she?* I wondered as we made our way through traffic to the hospital. They had decided not to use the lights and siren because my condition was not life threatening, but I was still a gunshot victim and couldn't be expected to make my way there myself. It occurred to me that I was covering her shift – that she should have been there instead of me – and a cold finger went down my spine. Anything could have happened. What if he had come in shooting? What if Ivanka hadn't acted when she did? It could have been a massacre.

At that point, the monitor next to me started flashing and beeping and the next thing I remember was waking up in the hospital. The doctor told me I had passed out due to shock and they were going to keep me in overnight for observation. I didn't argue. Normally, I hate hospitals, but this time I actually found all the quiet orderliness quite soothing. They put dressings on my legs and gave me painkillers. I swallowed two (one for each leg) and tried to read a year-old *National Geographic* article about barbary apes, but my brain just couldn't focus on their plight.

I wasn't allowed to use my cell phone, so all I could do was sit. Fortunately, I didn't have to sit for very long before the police showed up and asked a few thousand questions. They told me that former Corporal Bovary had been enrolled in a local inpatient drug counselling program up until three days ago, at which point he disappeared. His absence was noted, but the authorities were not notified because his attendance was not mandated by any court order and he was not considered a threat to himself or others.

I suggested that this aspect of his diagnosis should probably be reconsidered in light of the hole he nearly put in my scrotum. They aren't sure how he got his hands on the gun because it's not registered, but it probably wouldn't have been all that difficult.

I told them as much as I could remember and that Ivanka should immediately be nominated for every citizenship and bravery award available. They wrote everything down and told me that I'll probably need to come in and give a formal statement when I'm able. I should also be prepared to testify when and if the crown decides to bring charges, although this is up in the air pending a psychological evaluation of the suspect.

This is not exactly what I'd like to hear. What I'd like to hear is that he's been locked in a metal box which will be sent into space and dropped in a bottomless crevasse on one of Jupiter's more remote moons, not that he may be discharged by some underpaid and overworked Dr. Phil wannabe who went into psychology after flunking out of taxidermy school.

After the cops leave, I am overcome with exhaustion and don't so much fall asleep as throw myself at it. When I wake up a few hours later, Leah is lying on the bed next to me, snoring quietly. She looks so cute and amusing that any residual bitterness about not being able to get a hold of her after I was shot (fuck me – *I was shot!*) evaporates. I just lie there and watch her for a few minutes. Her jaw is hanging open at an odd angle and she's drooling slightly on the pillow.

She opens her eyes, takes a moment to focus, and then throws her arms around me and starts to cry. She says a lot of silly things, like thinking that

I was dead and wishing that she'd been there in my place and so on before I finally get her to calm down.

"I got back to the store and there were cop cars everywhere!" she says. "I asked what happened and they told me some crazy guy showed up with a gun and shot one of the managers! I freaked out! Seriously, I lost it. I thought you were dead. But then Dante showed up and told me he'd talked to you and you were okay and on your way to the hospital. When I got here, they wouldn't let me in because the cops were in talking to you. And then when they finally did let me in, you were asleep."

"I think it's the painkillers. Although I did pass out in the ambulance on the way here. They told me it was shock."

She puts a hand on my forehead. "Are you okay? Does it hurt?"

"I'm fine. I've had worse scratches from falling off my bike. They told me I was lucky. An inch or two either way and it could have gone right through the femoral artery. I would have exsanguinated – which is just a lovely word, by the way – all over the floor in front of cash. Would have taken about five minutes. Esmerelda would have had a helluva time cleaning it up in time to open the store tomorrow."

"Can I see it?"

"Be warned: I'm not wearing anything else under this robe. When they heard it was a gunshot wound, I guess they got a little overexcited in emerg and cut everything off when I came in. They probably even cut off my socks."

She moves the blankets off and lifts up the robe to look at the dressings, which strike me as a little excessive, considering that both wounds could probably be covered with a couple of band-aids.

She whistles. "Wow. An inch or two higher up and we wouldn't have to worry about birth control."

"Don't remind me. At least the scars won't be visible. Unless I'm wearing a speedo."

"Promise me you'll never do that. As attractive as a man may be, there is no pressing social need for the world to know the exact location of his cock and balls at all times."

"Well, the whole world probably knows where mine are by now."

"It was on the late news, but they didn't use any names. Except for the guy they arrested. I'm guessing that was Mina's husband?"

I nod and tell her the entire story from start to finish. Her eyes widen when I tell her about how Ivanka disarmed and neutralized the guy.

"Holy shit! I think I'll be signing up for some of her self-defence classes myself! Don't worry, by the way. I called your parents and told them you were okay."

"Thanks. I forgot about that."

"Your father has such a cute accent! I'm surprised that you don't have one."

"I do, but it only comes out around other Scots, which is rarely. I long ago learned how to blend in amongst you flat-voiced, well modulated Canadians with your perfect news anchor pronunciations. I tried to call you but your phone was off."

She sighs. "I'm sorry! I had to turn it off for the shoot and then I forgot to turn it back on."

"How did the shoot go?"

"Great! Better than great, actually. I was gonna tell you, but then all this happened…"

"Tell me what?"

"Well, the director on the shoot is friends with this guy Jeremy, who's an agent who works with the casting director for a couple of shows on CBC that shoot up here. Anyway, Jeremy just happened to be at the shoot and saw me and said he thinks I'd be perfect for a three-episode guest spot they're gonna be shooting early next year. You know *Royal Target*?"

"Isn't that the show about the RCMP detail assigned to guard the prime minister?"

"That's the one! They're doing a three-arc episode thing next month about a shellshocked Afghan vet who tries to kill the PM just before the election."

"Jesus. That's a little close to the bone, if you'll pardon the pun."

She laughs. "I know! Well, now I've got experience with it, right? Anyway, I'd be playing the sister of the vet who tries to help them track him down before it's too late. It'd be a really huge break for me if I got it."

"Wow, that's awesome."

"I know! The shoot wrapped pretty much on time and then Jeremy invited us all out to dinner. That was where he explained it to me."

I think I've counted the name Jeremy more times in the last few sentences than I like, but force myself to keep my suspicions in check. My suspicion is, naturally, that he's only pretending to dangle this acting opportunity in front of Leah because he wants to get into her pants, but I can't say this out loud because I will be implying that she has no acting talent and people will only ever be interested in her for her body, which is not true. Granted, I've never seen her act and so am not really in any kind of position to judge, but it doesn't matter because my impartiality is out the window where Leah is concerned.

"Uh huh."

"The best part is I haven't even told you what the best part is."

"What's the best part?"

"Jeremy also knows the guy who's going to be doing some of the casting for the new Tarantino movie, and if the show thing works out, he might be able to get me in. Well, for an audition at least."

"Holy shit." I am genuinely impressed. Tarantino may have an ego the size of all outdoors, but he is also the real deal. So long as he doesn't sustain a brain injury and do something stupid, like a Transformers sequel, they'll be talking about him in the same breath as Lean, Hitchcock and Kubrick in ten years. If Leah got in on something like that, it would be more than just a gig. It could, potentially, be part of cinematic history.

"I know what you're thinking," she says, narrowing her eyes.

"What am I thinking?"

"You're thinking that he's only telling me all this because he wants to fuck me."

"No," I say. "I think you're an incredibly talented actress who deserves everything you've got coming to you. The fact that he might also want to fuck you is just a function of the fact that you are an attractive woman and he happens to be male."

"Don't forget," she says. "I've been doing this for a while. I'm not exactly little red riding hood. I checked this guy out. The stuff he says he's done, he has actually done."

"I'm not arguing with you," I say. "I think it's awesome. If you got it, that would be incredible. Even to just try out for it is incredible."

"I'm glad you agree," she says, leaning over to kiss me. "Now, say something Scottish."

"What?"

"You almost had your manly parts blown off," she says, starting to unbutton her blouse. "I think it's probably a good idea that we make sure they still work before you're discharged."

"But what if the nurse walks in?" I ask halfheartedly, casting a wary eye towards the door. "I have no idea how often they're checking on me."

"Then we'll tell her that we're conducting a study," Leah says, wriggling out of her jeans and tossing her panties on the floor. "The ability of gunshot victims to maintain erections for long enough to generate multiple orgasms in their actress girlfriends."

"I bet the Lancet would have more readers if they published a study like that," I point out as she climbs on top of me. "But they'd probably reject it for having too small a sample group."

"Your heart rate is going up," she observes, unbuckling her bra and tossing it over the monitor.

"This may be my best hospital stay ever."

"I thought you were going to say something Scottish."

My mind is totally blank. "Uhhh…Drumnadrochit."

"More."

"Tam O'Shanter."

"That's a hat, you silly fucker."

"Sean Connery. Edinburgh. Bagpipes. Robert Burns. Haggis."

"Are you sure you're Scottish?"

"I'm just saying all of these things to get into your pants."

"Well you're there, so I think you can stop saying them now."

"Okay."

Fortunately, the nurse doesn't come in to check on me again for a couple of hours.

# -20-

Christmas is, especially when compared with the lead up, a quiet affair. Leah and I put up a small plastic tree the night before and then curl up on the couch to watch poor Ralphie almost shoot his eye out in *A Christmas Story*. We make hot chocolate with brandy and gorge ourselves on churros, which I picked up at Café Ole just before it closed early for the holiday. Oddly, Fermina didn't pump me for information about the shooting or any other store gossip, which is uncharacteristic.

The next morning, we sleep in, make ourselves mimosas and exchange gifts. I'm actually pretty jazzed about my picks: I got her a necklace that she pointed out a couple of weeks ago because she thought it was nice, a Walter Sobchak action figure, a deluxe set of her favourite bath oil, and a gift certificate for a full spa treatment at a new place on Yonge Street that was a big hit with the TIFF crowd. The credit card is going to be in a bit of discomfort after this, but I think it's better to overshoot a little with these things.

The big present, however, is still tucked at the back of my top drawer because I haven't exactly decided when to give it to her and Christmas morning doesn't seem like the right time. I'm going to have to give this some serious thought.

She buys me a box set of all the championship matches from FC Barcelona's 2008-09 season –the year they won everything. I am dumbstruck.

"How did you know?" I ask, looking with awe at approximately 15 hours of football viewing wonder.

She laughs. "Are you kidding? You've done a pretty good job of hiding your football obsession up to now, but I live here too. You treat that number 10 jersey like it's the Hope diamond. I've seen you hand washing it in the sink. I also know that Dante usually sets up the schedule so you're not working during their home games."

"Well, I guess now you know everything about me."

She takes a sip of her mimosa. "Whew! I better take it easy on these things. I'm starting to feel lightheaded already. We should eat something."

I fry up a big breakfast of bacon, scrambled eggs, toast and gourmet coffee. Leah brought over one of those fancy hot drink machines that makes everything using barcoded plastic containers that you drop in. I think that it was technically included as part of the lease on the old place, so it's one more reason to thank Grover for being such a dick. If he wants it, he's going to have to pry it from my warm, cappuccino-stained fingers. I don't like regular coffee, but I am settling quite nicely into my new role as a latte-slurping elitist.

There are no family entanglements for either of us. Her parents are in San Francisco and mine are in Scotland. My parents offered to cancel their trip in light of my recent shooting, but I told them not to worry. Both wounds have already healed and they didn't buy cancellation insurance, so there was no point in them losing a few thousand dollars over what amounts to a couple of paper cuts.

I think they were glad to go, although they probably would have stayed had I asked them to. My Dad's brother recently broke his foot after he staggered drunkenly out of a pub and mistook a cinderblock for a soccer ball, so a lot of their visit will probably involve him sitting in front of the

TV with his foot elevated while they fetch items for him from the fridge and stubbornly insist that it's no trouble, no trouble at all.

After breakfast, Leah hops in the bath to try out her new oils and emerges half an hour later smelling heavenly. This gives me ideas, but she insists that we have a busy day ahead and pushes me into the shower. After I emerge, we head out the door to catch a matinee of *It's A Wonderful Life* at the Prestige. I know it's a classic, but I've never been a big fan of that one. I always found the whole alternate universe thing a little contrived and the ending overly sentimental. And would passing the hat really cover a run on the bank? But Leah loves it, so I keep my opinions to myself.

When we get home, we start making dinner. A turkey is a bit much for two people, so we're doing a duck in a red wine sauce with sweet potatoes and green beans. The sauce needs quite a bit of wine, so for that I've bought a cheap tetra pack of Australian shiraz. The dinner requires something a little bit more special, so for that I uncork a 2005 Opus One.

"So what is it exactly that makes this a five hundred dollar bottle of wine?" Leah asks, sipping it as she stirs some garlic and onions.

"I'm not sure," I say honestly. "Robert Parker must have said he likes it. Imagine what the movies would be like if there were only two critics and you could charge a higher admission price if at least one of them gave it a thumbs up. That's the wine industry. It's all about prestige and perception. Take the year after *Sideways* was released, for example. The main character pisses all over merlot and cab franc and raves about pinot. Next year, merlot prices tank and pinot prices double. But what's his prize bottle of Cheval Blanc? It's a blend of merlot and cab franc."

"So he's supposed to be a wine snob, but he gets everything wrong."

I take a mouthful of the Opus One and try to swirl it around, but I'm as much in the dark as she is. I like wine but have what a sommelier might diplomatically refer to as an unrefined palate. If blindfolded, I probably couldn't tell the difference between *Bâtard-Montrachet* and Baby Duck.

"Well, sort of. Cab franc really is pretty terrible by itself, but it does work nicely when blended. Merlot isn't bad, it's just that a lot of cheap wineries pour chemical essence of oak into it to try to make it taste like it came from Burgundy and not from some muddy field behind an old tannery in Ohio."

She rolls her eyes. "So if I came home with a bottle of Red Rocket, you'd throw me out on the street?"

"That's where you're supposed to drink Red Rocket. It says so right on the label: *For gutter consumption only.*"

We finish dinner and then spread out on the living room floor to play some Trivial Pursuit, which we agree to end in a draw after accumulating five pie pieces each. We're too stuffed, tired and tipsy (three bottles divided between two people is a not insignificant amount, even if a large portion of one of them went into duck gravy, where the alcohol supposedly boils off during reduction) to function at our mental peaks, so we agree to call it a night.

Before we know where we are, it's New Year's Eve. Mickey always closes Falstaff's for a private party, tickets for which must be purchased at least a month in advance. Leah and I arrive just after nine to find Sebastian and Mina tucked into a back booth. Sebastian buys us both a Scrumpy and apologizes for the hundredth time for my taking a bullet on his behalf.

"I owe this man my life!" he says, slurring slightly. Based on his level of inebriation, I calculate that they've probably been here for about an hour. "Or at the very least, my nuts. If you are ever in need of an organ or testicle, you come to me first."

"I'll keep that in mind," I promise. I almost say that I can't take it because I don't know where it's been, but that wouldn't be the best thing to say with Mina sitting there.

"How's your husband doing?" Leah asks Mina.

"He's back on his medication, so I think he's doing okay," Mina says, doing her best to avoid looking at me. If my communications with Mina became strained when she started dating Sebastian, they got positively polar after her husband shot me. Aside from the communicating that we have to do at work about scheduling, deposits and the like, the two of us have been doing our best to pretend the other doesn't exist. That's just fine with me, as her constant lamenting of how the system failed her nutso husband was starting to get on my nerves. "They won't let me in to see him until he gets a psychiatric evaluation, but there's quite a backlog. It'll probably be a while."

The longer the better, I think. I don't want this man to be released from prison until my grandkids are old enough to teach their kids to drive hovercars.

"Is it just us?" I ask, looking around.

Sebastian nods. "Carmelina's leaving for Italy tomorrow, so Dante's taking her to some gallery party. Aldous got invited to some university dorm party–"

"By who?" I ask. "Not a woman?"

"Not sure," Sebastian says. "But I think he's hoping to meet one there and try out his new look. It's all philosophy students, so I suppose they can all get together in a big group and complain about alienation. Willard's working his personal taxi service again."

Every year, Willard borrows the 1988 El Dorado belonging to his girlfriend's father and shows up outside bars after midnight offering to drive people home for varying amounts of money. A surprising number of people take him up on it considering he isn't actually licensed to drive and has only a passing understanding of the rules of the road. Last year, so he claimed, the star of a real estate reality TV show was so hammered that she tried setting off fireworks through the sunroof. This might have worked had the sunroof not been closed at the time she lit the fuse. Apparently, a roman candle makes quite a lot of noise and smoke if you set it off in a contained space. Willard had to spend all the money he made that night getting the car cleaned before he took it back. The incident also burned off most of the hair on the back of his head, which didn't actually make much difference in terms of his appearance.

In the corner, a traditional Gaelic thrash band called The Big Fat Bollocks are rocking through a version of "Danny Boy" that, were he still alive, would kill Bing Crosby stone dead. Mickey is running around like a madman, keeping everyone stocked with plates of deep fried food and beverages. New Year's is the one night of the year that anyone can order Scrumpy without prior approval. Since it's a private party, though, most of the people here are already in the club. I'm here, but for the first time at a Falstaff's Year Ender, feel completely detached from my surroundings.

Sebastian keeps talking, but I'm not really listening to him, either. My mind is totally occupied with what I have planned for later. I check my inside jacket pocket compulsively to make sure what I put in it at the start of the night is still there. My stomach is lurching around like punch drunk boxer and my pint glass keeps slipping because my hands absolutely will not stop sweating. I keep going over the details again and again in the vain hope that it will calm me down when what it's actually doing is the opposite. I only manage to drink about half of my pint and barely touch any of the food. After a while, Leah notices something is up.

"Are you okay?" she asks, leaning over to whisper in my ear. "You look like you're coming down with something."

I look at my watch. It's not even eleven. Fuck it.

"Come with me," I say, standing up and grabbing my jacket.

Leah looks curious. She still has almost a full pint left and just started in to a large plate of calamari, but seems to understand something out of the ordinary is going on. "Can you keep an eye on my food for a sec?" she asks Mina. Sebastian is by now too far gone to do much more than sit up, and he's having difficulty even with that.

Mina nods, looking concerned. She evidently doesn't want to be stuck here with a date who is in line to enter catatonia. "Are you leaving?"

"Just for a minute," I say, helping Leah into her coat.

"What's this about?" she asks me when we get out on the street. The air is cold and her breath trails up over her head like smoke. "Where are we going?"

"To commit a minor B&E," I say, taking her by the arm and leading her down the street. The short walk to the bookstore goes by in a blur. My mind is on autopilot as I open the front door and deactivate the alarm. By now, she knows something is up and is looking at me with the kind of wary amusement you would direct at a street performer who singles you out to assist with his act.

I turn on the lights and lead her back to the drama section.

"This," I say, slurring slightly due to nervousness, "is where we first met."

"Yes," she nods. I can see that her wariness is starting to be replaced by something bigger. I hope it's not panic. If it's panic, I'm a dead man.

"Do you remember the first thing you said?"

She thinks for a second. "I asked where the Mamet was. Wait, no! I asked if this was all the Mamet we had."

"Correct," I say. "You were looking for *Speed the Plow* or *Sexual Perversity in Chicago*."

"Right."

I reach into my inside jacket pocket and hand her a copy of *Three Plays* by Mamet. It includes the two she was looking for plus *American Buffalo*. It was the only one I could find that was still available. It took two nerve-wracking weeks to arrive from a small publisher in New York after I special ordered it.

She laughs and looks at the book. "Well thank you! It's nice to be in a place that really goes the extra mile for its customers. Even opening up specially after hours on a holiday."

"Now," I say, taking a deep breath. "Do you remember the first thing I said to you?"

She freezes. I honestly think she may have thought that I brought her all the way here on New Year's Eve just to hand her a copy of a hard to find BACKE. She takes a moment before she answers. "Ye-es."

"And what was that?"

She just stands there for a moment looking stunned. Then she looks like she's about to cry. I have a horrible feeling that I may be about to make a huge mistake, but there's no backing out of it now. The boat is heading down the ramp to the water. If it continues straight to the bottom, then I am going down with the ship.

"You asked me to marry you."

I reach into my pocket and remove item number two, which cost considerably more than item number one. I think it's safe to say that two months' worth of my salary is probably less than Grover made in two days. I decide on the spur of the moment to get down on one knee. I had originally told myself that I wouldn't do this because it would seem clichéd and corny. Plus, I am no longer looking her in the eye but staring at her hips.

She takes the small blue box out of my hand and opens it up. Inside is a simple white gold ring with a diamond only slightly larger than a fruit fly. I'm a little self-conscious about its lack of ostentatiousness, but it's all that I could afford.

"Oh my God," she says, taking it out of the box and looking at it. "It's beautiful!"

I'm still on one knee and my heart is hammering in my chest hard enough to break a rib. I can't take the tension any longer.

"So whaddya say?"

She sniffs loudly as tears start leaking out the corner of her eyes, then lets out a surprisingly loud whoop. She yanks me to my feet so hard that we almost fall backwards and pulls me into a violent kiss. Her cheeks are wet and now mine are too. Am I crying? The truth is I have no idea what I'm doing.

Somewhere in the middle of it all, she says yes and slides the ring on her finger. It's a little loose, but the jeweller said they would resize it for free once they could measure Leah's finger with something more accurate than my vague estimations ("Not as big as mine. Or maybe bigger. You know…I'm not sure.").

I lead her to the staff room, where I stashed a bottle of champagne and a couple of glasses earlier in the day. A purist will tell you not to pop champagne because it lets all the gas out too fast, but right now the purists can keep their opinions to themselves. I send the cork flying across the fiction section and bubbles spurt out all over the carpet. It's a good thing Esmerelda is back on the job.

"What would you have done with this if I'd said no?" Leah asks, taking her glass.

"Drank it myself, of course," I say. "And then probably eaten the bottle. Cheers."

"It's a little early probably, but happy new year," Leah says as we clink glasses.

"A little early?" I say, feeling a tiny stab of apprehension. Did she only say yes because I put her on the spot? "You mean a little early to propose? I know that we've only been dating for a couple of months, but–"

"No! A little early for new year, you doofus!" she says, laughing. "It's probably only, like, eleven thirty. Like I said before, I knew I wanted to marry you almost as soon as I saw you. What a relief! I thought you were acting so weird all night because you wanted to break up or something."

"Seriously?"

"I dunno. I thought maybe my moving in was too much. You hardly said a word to me all night. I was worried."

"Sorry! I was just trying to run through everything in my head so I didn't screw it up. I had originally planned to do it on the stroke of midnight – I even timed out the walk from Falstaff's – but in the end my nerves just couldn't take it."

"You timed out the walk?"

I smile sheepishly. "I did. I tried it a couple of ways. One if you were wearing your black fuck-me boots with the big heels and another with the flats."

"You didn't actually wear the boots, did you?"

"I got some funny looks, believe me. People probably thought I was an off-the-clock drag queen. It was the middle of the day, after all."

"I know you're kidding because you'd never get your feet into my boots in a million years. I hope."

"Yes, I'm kidding. I had to use my artistic imagination. I don't know if you've ever noticed, but you're something of an erratic walker."

"Say what now?"

"You weave a lot," I say, getting up to offer an imitation between the stacks. "You like to take your time and check things out. Whereas I tend to program a destination into my head and shoot towards it like a sidewinder missile."

"You sayin' I'm poky?"

"No, I ain't sayin' that. I'm sayin' you like to take your time. There's a difference."

"So which shoes were faster? The fuck-mes or the flats?"

"I think the fuck-mes were a couple of minutes faster than the flats. The heel-toe motion just sort of propels you forward. It's like stepping out of starter blocks with every step."

"Well then, it's a good thing I wore the fuck-me boots. Otherwise we might still be outside and you could've lost your nerve."

"No way, baby," I say in my best John Wayne voice. "Once a man's been shot at, it takes a lot to rattle his nerves."

"That's not why you're doing this, is it? Because you almost died and now you're thinking: *Shit! I need to get married before another whacko with better aim comes along and blows off my junk?*"

"That's exactly it," I say. "I need to get you all good and knocked up while I've got the chance. If I don't pass the family monkey fingers on to the next generation, my father will never forgive me."

"Well don't get too far ahead of yourself," she says, wagging a non-monkey finger. "It'd be kinda hard for me to play a revenge-driven, mercenary-for-hire kickass assassin chick if I'm eight months pregnant."

"Maybe it would add additional depth to the character. Although it would make it more difficult to fire from a prone position. That's the way I was taught in cadets."

"You were in cadets?"

"Somebody has to keep this country safe in the event it's invaded by an army of paper bullseye targets. That somebody won't be me, though. The only target I hit actually belonged to LAC Wainwright, who was two spots over to my right. He was pissed. All of his shots were inside the first ring. In light of my obvious skills, I was recruited for a top secret program tasked with peeling potatoes and dropping them into hot water."

She laughs and takes a gulp of her champagne. "Oh, what have I done? I'm engaged to a crazy man."

"Hey, that's true, isn't it? I'm a fiancé now. I'm going to have to get used to calling you that." I mime an introduction with enough pomp for a visiting head of state. "*And may I introduce you to my fiancée? The brilliant and famous Lady Leah Dashwood?*"

"Just brilliant and famous?" she says, pretending to be hurt. "Not super hot?"

"The super hotness is self-evident. Besides, I don't think you're allowed to describe someone as super hot when introducing them to the king of Sweden at a Nobel Prize awards dinner."

"And who's winning the Nobel Prize in this scenario of yours?"

"Well you are, obviously. For super hotness. That's why I wouldn't have to point it out when introducing you. You have to admit that it would seem just a little self-serving. *And may I introduce you to Lady Leah*

*Dashwood, this year's recipient of the Nobel Prize for super hotness. Isn't she super hot?* It would really seem like you were grasping for additional praise when none was necessary."

She puts down her champagne. "C'mere."

I do a stumbling imitation of my fuck-me boots heel-to-toe walk. She pulls me into her arms and we kiss.

"I love you," she says. "You're a goofball."

"And I love you," I say. "Even if you are a desperately insecure superhot Nobel laureate."

The sounds of car horns erupting and cheers float in from outside.

"Happy new year," she says. "Looks like your timing wasn't so bad after all."

"And to you," I say. "So what would you like to do? Do you wanna finish off our champagne and head back to Falstaff's?"

She thinks about it for a moment. "Nah. Let them enjoy their party. Tonight is just for us. Now that you've made an honest woman of me, I think we should go home and spend some time getting into our new roles as future wife and husband."

"New roles? Is that where you say you're too tired for any funny business because you have to get up early tomorrow for a rehearsal and by the way I forgot to take out the garbage?"

"You know, one of these days, you're going to get too cute for your own good and talk yourself right out of getting laid."

"I swear I was just kidding."

We finish our champagne and head back out onto the street, which is alive with light and life and noise. Our feet don't even touch the ground.

# -21-

New year's day is where it is because of a papal bull signed on February 24th, 1582 by Gregory the 13th. It replaced the Julian calendar with the Gregorian one we use now by fine tuning the time between the solstices. Considering that the universe isn't sentient and thus doesn't care how we measure our time here, I'm forced to ask myself the same question that ol' Greg probably did: how much difference does a new year really make?

Like the rest of the stars and planets, I am, relatively speaking, in the same place. I still live in a small but comfortable apartment and am working a passable but mostly crappy retail job with lousy hours. I still have no car. The last car I had was a ten-year-old Hyundai Accent that, like many seniors, was starting to leave important things behind, such as bearings, sections of the exhaust and any semblance of dignity.

I developed a sneaking suspicion that it was trying to kill me when I found out there was a hole in the floor that was allowing noxious gases to enter the passenger compartment. This suspicion was later confirmed when it blew a tie rod on the DVP. Had I been going any faster than walking speed, I would probably have flipped right over the guardrail and landed within suicide range of the Bloor viaduct. A tow truck guy was there within five minutes and I gave him twenty bucks to tow the whole thing to the nearest scrap yard.

Let's see, what else? The possibility of getting published had just gone kaboom, so professionally speaking, I was back to the blocks. Rumours were flying that the store was going to close. I spent most of my spare time with my coworkers at Falstaff's or the Prestige, drinking and whiling away what little time and money I had to spare. I wasn't making much forward progress.

Now a year later, many of those things haven't changed. I'm still in the same place, but everything is different.

I have to admit that it was a lot of fun to call my parents in Stirling and tell them that their oldest son was now engaged to a woman they had never met and spoken to only once. My mother, bless her, took the news quite well, even going so far as to say that Leah had sounded quite nice when she called to tell them that their first born had been shot by a mentally deranged army vet.

My father didn't know what to make of the news. He married my mother when he was 19 and she was 17. Back then, getting married was just something you agreed to do after ten dates. The next step was to move into a tiny room in your parents' house and endure five or so years of simmering acrimony before saving up enough money to get a council house and have a kid. Since I was that kid, I've always been grateful that I was the end product but never had any interest in starting out the same way.

Leah's parents had a similar reaction. Her mother seems to have long ago resigned herself to the fact that her daughter is going to do whatever the hell she likes no matter what anybody says and welcomed me to the family with exhausted good humour, the kind that not-so-subtly hints that the listener better know what he has just gotten himself into. Her father was more circumspect, if not standoffish. I think he actually liked Grover and didn't appreciate that his daughter had kicked a fellow titan of industry, a real go-getter, so casually aside for another slacker wannabe *artist* type.

The anxiety generated by listening to his thinly-veiled hostility was tempered by the secret knowledge that this voice belonged to a man who spent his spare time looking at women who bent over and pulled their butt cheeks apart for a photographer. I was tempted to ask him if Grover has asked for the whiskey back, but decided that dowry jokes were not the best way to ingratiate myself with my future father-in-law. Leah says he's a pain in the ass but she loves him, so he must have some redeeming qualities.

News of our engagement took a surprisingly long time to spread through the store. People were used to seeing Leah with an engagement ring and just either forgot she was no longer with Grover or assumed she was still wearing it to keep customers from hitting on her at work. It was only when Lolita submitted one of her many memos to management, this one suggesting that employees should not be allowed to wear jewellery on the job, that it came up.

Lolita has submitted so many suggestion memos over the years that Dante started keeping them in a file, which he breaks out and reads for fun whenever he feels particularly stressed. Her past suggestions have included: forcing all new hires to take elocution lessons; requiring all cashiers to wear white cotton gloves (overtop of rubber gloves); requiring all employees to wash their clothes by hand using hypoallergenic lye extract; requiring all employees to wear hairnets; requiring all coins to be placed in cash drawers tails-side up (she refuses to pick up any coin where the head is facing up and will often open a new roll if there isn't a qualifying piece of change in there, even if it means the drawer overflows); and, my personal favourite, her suggestion that the books be reorganized so that they'd be shelved by the author's star sign instead of alphabetically by their last name.

Her request that all jewellery be removed was argued based on her belief that metal and rocks contained too many narrow cracks and crevices where bacteria could hide that could not be reached by simple washing. Obviously, the continued presence of rings and necklaces and earrings on the premises was just a ticking time bomb of employee sick days waiting to go off.

Lolita often bases her recommendations on the premise that their adoption will reduce sick days. This doesn't provide much reinforcement considering that it's coming from a woman who takes more sick days in a year than almost all other employees combined. In fact, it tends to work against her because most of the rest of the staff are strongly in favour of any proposal that will keep her out of the store for more time than she's in it.

"You believe this?" Dante says, handing me the memo. It's the second week of January and the two of us are dug in like infantrymen in front of the computers in the manager's office running the reports that will identify the massive quantities of overstock we can now begin sending back to the publishers. This will be almost my sole professional occupation for the next two months. "What if I've got a piece of jewellery where it's not visible? Think she'd want me to remove that too?"

I try not to think about where Dante may have metal attached to his anatomy, but I see his point. "Well, she did already request we set up one of those full body scanners at the front door. You know, like the ones they have at airports that provide a picture of what you look like without clothes. She even offered to train on how to run it. I think I actually voted in favour of that one. Well, in certain cases. But at a couple million each, it would probably take a few thousand years to recoup the cost."

Dante shakes his head and drops the memo into Lolita's suggestion file, which is as thick as a screenplay and more entertaining than most. "God, it's not like we've got a staff full of Elizabeth Taylors or anything like that. People don't show up at work like it's the red carpet at the Oscars, for crying out loud. The biggest thing is probably that giant topaz wedding ring that Mother Teresa wears, and she probably couldn't get that off if she tried. She has those big sausage fingers. They'd have to take the digit off and try to reattach it later. I'm sure Leah's fiancé wouldn't appreciate it if she had to take hers off, either."

"No," I say. "I sure wouldn't."

"Yeah, like–" Dante stops. "Wait. What?"

"Dante, did you seriously not know that Leah and I were together?"

Dante looks confused. "I thought she was with that I.T. guy."

"Nope. They broke up a long time ago. Well, a while ago." I'm not surprised that Dante doesn't know about this. For one, we didn't tell him. Two, he's been so pre-occupied with his own romantic distractions of late that he wouldn't notice anything short of an orgy in the lifestyles section. Third, being the general manager, he's generally out of the loop on the key gossip.

I can see him slowly putting it together in his head. "So…"

"Keep going, Columbus. You're almost there."

"Wait a minute. Are you joking or are you seriously…*engaged*? As in, to be married?"

"Is there another way to be engaged?"

Dante just stares for a minute. "When did this happen?"

"New year's. We were gonna tell people, but then we thought it might be more fun to try and keep it under wraps and see how long we could go before something slipped out." Which, I realize, it just did.

Dante bounces up out of his chair and bounds across the room to shake my hand. "Well, shit! Congratulations! You set a date, yet? Can I tell anyone else?"

"Thanks!" It's actually a relief to have another person aside from my distant family who knows about it. This lessens the Twilight Zone possibility that I will wake up all alone in my bed tomorrow morning and realize the whole thing was just a sadistic fever dream. "We haven't set a date or anything. Leah's been pretty busy with her acting jobs."

Has she ever. Since New year's, Jeremy (who is now her agent, incidentally) has set her up with auditions for two TV shows and three more commercials. This puts me in a difficult position because I have to cover her shifts when these sessions conflict with her work schedule. I can't ask Mina to do it because she's tied up with her husband's pre-trial mess and is only marginally stable at the best of times. And I can hardly pressure Dante to cover the shifts or hire another manager. For one thing, it would take him at least a year, and for another, it would give him the impression that Leah isn't taking the job seriously and should be canned. Not that I think Dante would ever do that, but neither Leah nor myself can really afford to lose our jobs at the moment.

"Oh that's right," Dante says. "How did the sandwich bag thing go?"

"Good. They told her it'll be on the air in a few weeks."

"Well, this is a big deal! We should all go out for a drink!"

"We'd love to," I say. "We can't do it this weekend, but how about one night next week?"

Saturday, Leah has planned a feat of matchmaking in the form of a dinner to which we have invited both Ebeneezer and Fermina. When I say "we", of course, I mean Leah. She invited them both separately and neither knows that the other is coming. It's an ambush double date, and I am trying to steel myself for what could be the most uncomfortable dinner ever.

I tried to argue that it wasn't our place to interfere, but Leah was having none of it.

"Oh come on," she said. "They've been going on like this for years. If somebody doesn't do something soon, they're just going to be miserable until they die."

"But they're old and set in their ways," I protested.

"They may be old, but they're not dead yet. Ebby's got a lot more spark in him than you give him credit for."

"He does?" I have never thought of Ebeneezer as a man with spark, a quality I mostly associate with plucky teenagers in bad made-for-TV movies starring Steve Guttenberg.

"If he was 30 years younger, he might have swept me off my feet and carried me off before you got around to it, mister man."

"But—"

"But what? Live a little, Poindexter. It'll be fun!"

This isn't the only improvement project Leah has thrown herself into lately. She has also taken it upon herself to help remodel Aldous into something more closely resembling a babe magnet. Or at least a non-babe repeller. The two of them went out on her day off yesterday to acquire him a new wardrobe. They stopped at a salon where the stylist was able to do something with his hair, and then went on to pick up new shoes, cologne, a watch that doesn't have a plastic band, a wallet that isn't made of canvas and doesn't attach by a long chain to his belt loop, and a new shaving kit.

After that, she brought him back to our apartment, where we had a practice dinner party. She pretended to be his date, punctuating the courses with constructive advice about what girls pay attention to and giving him little tips to keep him on track.

I have to admit that the transformation was a lot more successful than his first rebranding experiment. Not that my opinion mattered. In light of my role in that fiasco, I was told in no uncertain terms to keep my ideas to myself this time around.

For his part, Aldous has thrown himself into his reinvention with a drive I didn't think he had. He hangs on Leah's every word and treats her like a big sister who actually talks to him. It made for an odd dinner, though. I was given the role of waiter (one I played more sullenly than any bistro server in the world) and instructed to eat my dinner in the kitchen so as not to throw off the pseudo boy-girl dynamic. Leah treated it like an acting workshop and didn't want anything to mess with her Stanislavski method-like preparations.

"Now Aldous, sweetie," Leah would say, a forkful of Caesar salad poised for consumption, "I don't know if you're aware of this, but you have a tendency to scratch your balls a lot. In future, if you find things getting super itchy between the bars, it's best to excuse yourself and head to the bathroom to get it out of your system. Talc might be a good idea, too. Now why don't you ask me a few more questions about my job? And remember to lean forward so it really looks like you're listening."

By the end of the night, Aldous was actually starting to resemble a normal, functioning, socially adept single man on the make, and I felt a small pang of regret. Although everything she's doing will certainly help to make sure that his batting average will start to climb out of negative territory in the future, I couldn't help but feel sad to see the old Aldous disappearing under this bright new sheen.

"I know what you mean," Leah said after he left. "But he's gotta grow up. He's a sweet kid, but if we don't do something, he's going to end up drinking poisoned Kool Aid on a compound somewhere in West Texas because some blonde hippie chick flashed her boobs at him. Or trying to fly a stolen Cessna into the side of the parliamentary peace tower because a bunch of frustrated jihadis promised him virgins. No sex for that long fucks with the old noggin wiring."

"How old were you?" I asked, mostly out of reflex.

"Fourteen. I got tired of constantly being pressured for blow jobs and thought I might at least get something out of it."

"And shortly thereafter the bishop transferred him to another diocese?"

"Har har. Very funny, Carlin. How old were you?"

"On the advice of counsel, I decline to answer."

"Oh come on. Was it me?" she tittered. "Oh wait, no. It couldn't have been. Was it Mina? Did she make a man out of you?"

"No. I think I was 19 at the time."

"You think? You must have been pretty drunk, boyo."

"I appreciate what you're trying to do for Aldous. I just hope he's still Aldous when you're done."

"I'm not out to re-program the boy. He's taking a girl to a movie tomorrow. I've told him I expect a full report."

"Really?"

"Her name's Simone. She's a French exchange student. He met her at that philosophical New Year's Eve thing. They're going to see a revival screening of *The Seventh Seal* at the Prestige."

"Well, that sounds like something the old Aldous would do. French, eh?"

"I know," she said. "Our little boy's jumping in at the deep end. Oh, it's so hard to watch them go off on their own."

"So who's next? Are you going to try to sort out Dante's problems with his mother?"

That was when she told me about her plans for Ebeneezer and Fermina. Commendable though they are, these little schemes are cutting in on the precious little time we've been able to spend together lately just ourselves. I have no desire to see an improvement in the love life of Aldous Swinghammer coincide directly with a downgrade in my own.

Before I can deal with any of that, however, I have a more pressing employee concern to deal with: I have to go and get Sebastian out of jail.

# -22-

Sebastian looks like hell – even worse than the time I caught him sleeping under a shelf in receiving. I meet him at the courthouse, where his mother has posted his bail, and the two of us head to a coffee shop a couple of blocks away.

The list of charges is impressive: attempted theft over a thousand dollars, operating a motor vehicle while having a blood alcohol level of more than .05, trespassing, public intoxication, destruction of private property, assault, resisting arrest, and assaulting a police officer.

"I have no memory of the last one," Sebastian says. "I think they just tacked it on. Maybe I took a swing at one of them, I don't know. Fascist goons."

The last few days have not been kind. Shortly after New year's, Mina told him that she wanted to try and work things out with her estranged husband and asked him to move out. Sebastian says that he saw this coming, but I'm not sure that he did. He spent a few nights sleeping on the floors and couches of old university friends and loose acquaintances before going on a three-day bender, during which time he doesn't remember sleeping anywhere.

After being refused service at three different bars because he was clearly intoxicated, he threw something of a fit in bar number four when they asked him to leave, knocking an entire rack of wine glasses to the floor and smashing a half-empty bottle of Stoli on a nearby pool table. They called the cops, but Sebastian somehow evaded the bouncer and ran out the back door.

Unfortunately, he'd left his jacket behind. Since his wallet was still in the jacket, it was pretty easy for police to determine who was responsible for the damage. Being the middle of January, it was also pretty cold out on the street. Sebastian walked for a while, completely disoriented, and eventually found his way on to a residential side street.

That was where a TTC mechanic getting ready to leave for the night shift had left his car running in the driveway to warm it up. Sebastian saw the car, climbed in on the driver's side, and almost immediately fell asleep. The next thing he remembers is waking up in the drunk tank.

Since Sebastian was intoxicated behind the wheel of someone else's vehicle with the engine running, I guess it was fairly straightforward to charge him with the DUI. The attempted grand theft auto part seems like a stretch to me, but I don't know much about the workings of the legal system. Maybe if he'd climbed in on the passenger side, they wouldn't have been able to charge with either one, especially since he was passed out at the time the cops showed up. The assault charges are based on his pushing the bartender out of the way and the fact that he probably wasn't all that enthusiastic about being woken up and pulled out of the car by the cops.

Of course, at this point, all of that is academic. If he gets dinged on all counts, he could be looking at something like 15 years.

"It'll never come to that," I say, trying to sound positive. "You've got no previous record. Most of the serious charges'll probably get dropped. They're just stacking the indictment to give the prosecution a better bargaining position when it comes time to plea bargain." Jesus, listen to me. I've seen way too many episodes of *Law & Order*. This isn't TV, though. This is my best friend looking at actual jail time.

"My mother posted the bail," Sebastian says, drawing out the words like a blade across his throat. "Ten thousand bucks."

"Wow. Well, at least she did. If not, you'd probably still be in stir. I don't have quite that much sitting around in my account. Not since the whole Madoff debacle, anyway."

My weak joke raises not even a flicker of a smile. "The bail conditions stipulate that I have to live with her. I can't drink. I'm not allowed to leave the house except for work and court-approved appointments, like going to see a lawyer or to the doctor to have my prostate poked."

"You have a prostate problem?"

"Not yet," he says. "But I'm sure there'll be no shortage of amateur proctologists in the prison showers."

"Do you have a lawyer yet?"

Sebastian sniffs at his coffee and swirls it around in the cup. "My mother hired one. Some Bay Street shyster. I was thinking of just going with the public defender or legal aid or whatever the hell it is."

"Are you sure you want to do that?" I ask. "A real lawyer would probably be able to get a lot of it knocked down. You might not even have to go to trial or have a record when it's all said and done. Hell, they might even settle for letting you repay the bar for the cost of the Stoli and a new table cover. From what I've heard about legal aid, it's a bunch of overworked kids who just passed the bar exam and are clocking time until they can get real jobs. You go that route, you might actually end up going to jail."

"You don't understand," Sebastian says. "I'm in jail either way. If I let my mother take control of this, she'll own me forever. It'll be worse than jail. At least in jail, there's a chance for parole."

"There's also the criminal record."

Sebastian's mother was the one who called me and asked me to pick him up at the courthouse. She thought if she showed up there in person, Sebastian might not want to leave his cell. She sounded so genuinely concerned and even remorseful about the way things had unfolded since she'd kicked Sebastian out of the house that I'm actually finding it hard not to argue her position on this one. Plus I don't want to see Sebastian getting sodomized in the shower for the next five years out of stubborn spite.

She dropped her car off at the store and then took a taxi home. It's a Lexus SUV and, not having been behind the wheel of anything in some time, I found it a little intimidating to steer it through the streets at rush hour. It actually knows how to park itself, which is good because I never would have been able to squeeze into that spot in front of the courthouse without leaving tire tracks on the other two cars.

Sebastian groans and looks out the window. "Maybe you're right. How are things with Leah?"

"Good," I say. How on earth do I bring up the fact that we're engaged? It's impossible to introduce your own good news in the middle of somebody else's disaster without seeming like a narcissistic asshole. It's like jumping up in the middle of a funeral to announce that you just won the lottery. The thing is, now that the word is out, he's bound to find out from somebody else and then he'll be pissed that I didn't tell him. Oh well. Nothing to do but just say it.

"We got engaged."

His eyebrows arch and a little colour actually floods into his pasty cheeks. "No shit?"

"On the level. Remember when we left Falstaff's just before midnight at the Year Ender?" Oh crap. He probably doesn't. He was pretty much topsoil by the time we left. "I asked her then."

"And she said yes?"

"Yes, surprisingly."

"Well, huzzahs, my friend!" He gets up and the two of us hug awkwardly in the aisle before sitting back down. "A bachelor party will no doubt be a violation of my bail conditions, but I can't think of a better reason to throw one. You set a date?"

"Not yet. We're thinking maybe in the spring or the summer. Things have just been so crazy lately that we haven't had time to really talk about it. You however, will be my best man. If you want the job." And if he's not in jail.

"Fuckin' A, bubba. I'll see to it that you disappear three days prior to the ceremony and wake up on the roof of a convent in Honduras surrounded by naked postulants."

"Leah might prefer it if we just played paintball or went to dinner or something, but I'll leave it to your discretion."

"I haven't seen much of you good lady around the store," Sebastian says. "So I didn't even notice that she was wearing a ring again. You, on the other hand, seem to be running the place almost single-handed."

"Leah's got a new agent and he's setting up a lot of auditions for her on commercials and TV shows and what have you. Some of them are pretty last minute, so I've been filling in for her quite a bit."

"You look almost as tired as I do. And I probably look like the recently-unearthed corpse of Medgar Evers."

"So Mina's gone back to her batshit psycho killer jailbird husband," I say, keen to change the subject. "When did she drop that little nugget in your lap?"

Sebastian rubs his face. "A few days after Falstaff's. She said she'd talked to him on the phone a few times and felt guilty. Didn't want to abandon him in his time of strife and all that."

"That's bullshit," I say with more venom than I intend. "She had no problem doing it before."

"She said she didn't necessarily want to break up, just that it was going to take time for her to get everything figured out."

Yeah, I think, if what she means by time is 25 to life. At least, that's how long I hope her husband is kept out of circulation. "And how do you feel about that?"

"You know, I'm okay with it," Sebastian mutters. "She was so much, well, *work*. All the different medications and the sleeping all the time and the black moods. Not to mention the constant gut-rotting apprehension that her husband might pop up out of a rice paddy at any second and put a cap in my sorry ass."

"Well, it wasn't your sorry ass, it was mine. At least you don't have to worry about that anymore. Unless of course some bleeding heart shrink cuts him loose on the grounds that his mommy and daddy let him surf too much porn as a teenager. Or not enough."

One of the side effects of being shot is an uncomfortable tilt to the right of the political spectrum on certain things. I hope it's temporary. When I saw the PM on TV the other day talking about building a whole raft of maximum security prisons and introducing mandatory minimum sentences and three strikes-type laws, I was surprised to find myself nodding my head and thinking: *Yeah! Right on!* I have to get this out of my system. The end result of that type of thinking is a nation of trigger-happy idiots where the richest one per cent live in walled compounds into which the remaining 99 spend their time trying to break and enter. It's no way to build a lasting, sustainable society, but I have to admit that the idea of living in a walled compound with barbed wire and armed guards did hold a certain appeal for a while after I was released from hospital.

"I mean, I had a hard time with it at first, but now I mostly just feel relieved. About that, anyway. Apropos of nothing, how is it possible to become obsessed with a person you can't stand?"

"I think it happens all the time."

"She would tell these endless stories about her therapy sessions. Did you know she was convinced that her shrink was trying to have her committed? She never did any laundry or cleaned, so the place was always a mess. I tried doing it once, but most of the clothes stacked up on the floor weren't even hers. I think they'd been sitting there since the previous tenant. As far as cooking went, she could just about handle Mr. Noodles. And her poetry! Did she ever read you any of her poetry?"

I nod sympathetically. "I was subjected to a stanza or two."

"Ye gods! Worse than Paula Nancy Millstone Jennings of Sussex! She decided to read some of it to me one night in bed. It was like…listening to an endless stream of recorded 911 calls. There was just something just so hideously *wrong* about it that it made me feel physically ill."

"Did she do the one about the avocado?"

"No."

"Consider yourself lucky."

He sighs and bangs his forehead on the table. "The thing is, if she called right now and asked me to come back, I would."

Except that the court wouldn't let you, I think. "Everybody says that. Give it a few days."

"How are things going with your cohabitation?"

"Great." I don't say that I'm growing increasingly suspicious of the real motives of this Jeremy character and starting to feel a little worn out from work and frustrated about the fact that Leah and I rarely see each other. It's there, sure, but it doesn't loom large in my consciousness because the time we do spend together more than makes up for it. Things will get better. I hope.

"Yeah, really good. Did you want another coffee?"

"No thanks," he says. "It's probably time to play the penitent man and crawl back to the Vatican. You know she wants me to go back to university full time?"

I shrug. "That might not be a bad idea. You're not too far from getting your degree, are you?"

"She was talking about me going to teacher's college. Can you picture me as a teacher?"

Not with a criminal record, I think, but once again hold my tongue. "I remember you talked about that when you first started working at the store."

"Or law school. She just wants me to get some sort of post grad. '*A bachelor's degree has one use and that's toilet paper*', she says. And I don't even have that, so what does that make me? The shit? That is pretty much how I feel at the moment, so I suppose it makes sense."

"Listen, man, don't let her talk you into doing anything you don't want to do."

He gets up out of the booth and tosses his cup in the garbage. "But I don't know what it is that I do want to do. I thought I'd get into acting or something, but it just never seemed to happen and now it's like it's too late to start. What am I supposed to do?"

I get up and follow him to the door. I notice that his shoes are untied and wonder if they took his laces to keep him from hanging himself. Do they really do that in jail or just in the movies? I'm beginning to wonder if I should remove them as a precaution. I've never heard Sebastian talk this way before and it's unnerving.

"I don't know," I say, buttoning my jacket against the wind. "Do you really want to be an actor? Or was it just something you flirted with because it seemed easy and glamorous?"

I can't remember Sebastian ever going out to an audition or getting involved in community theatre. His principal involvement with acting to date seems to involve going to a lot of movies. Being engaged to an actor, I'm starting to get a feel for just how much work is involved, and it's more than sitting on a barstool with your boobs hanging out waiting for the ghost of Irving Thalberg to walk by. Leah spends hours preparing for her auditions, even if they don't last longer than five minutes once she's in the door – and most don't – but that doesn't stop her from going out on the next one.

Sebastian, however, has never struck me as the workhorse type. He's not a striver. He's more like the third generation of a robber baron dynasty: content to lounge by the pool with a cocktail or flit about the world with a pile of steamer trunks accumulating ex-wives and a coterie of socialites whilst dear old papa tries to keep the empire from being sold to the Mongols. All he's lacking is the money and the steamer trunks. And I suppose, the Mongols.

He waves the question away. "Ah fuck it, dude. Let's go bowling."

This is Sebastian code for: *let's go drinking*. Ninety-five per cent of the time, I accede to this suggestion. Driving him home from jail after being busted for DUI and grand theft and assault, however, magically falls in to that rare five per cent of the time when I don't think it's a good idea.

"Well, if by bowling you mean to your mother's house, then by all means let's go," I say, trying to sound jocular and mildly authoritative at the same time. It's how I handle Sebastian whenever I need him to do anything at work. It is, after all, no fun telling your friends what to do all the time. People tend to resent it.

Sebastian steps through the door, wrinkling his face against the chill wind. An old lady sitting at a corner table gives him a dirty look for leaving the door open for too long, but says nothing.

He sighs. "All right. I guess the war is over. Time to suck it up and sign the treaty."

By the time we get back to the car, there's a ticket on the windshield because the meter expired five minutes ago. I insist on paying it, but Sebastian snatches it out of my hand with something close to a smile.

"Forget it," he says. "In fact, really step on it on the way back. Maybe we can accumulate a few more of these."

# -23-

It's Saturday afternoon and I'm in the kitchen trying to convert ingredients and instructions into something resembling the glossy photos in the autumn edition of *Food & Drink* magazine.

Leah got a last-minute callback to audition for the guest star spot on *Royal Target*. This is her third one. Jeremy, which is a name I can barely hear without grimacing let alone say, claims there is absolutely no doubt they're going to give her the part. He says they're just going through the motions because one of the lesser executive producers is a friend of a friend of the hairstylist of one of the other girls up for the role. Or something. Leah claims to have her emotions under control, but then, the engineers at Chernobyl also claimed everything was under control right up until they blew a radioactive hole in the troposphere. She was vibrating at such a high frequency before she left that she practically microwaved everything she touched.

She has promised that she will absolutely not, under any circumstances, be back any later than 6:30. Ebeneezer and Fermina are scheduled to arrive at seven, which means that the bulk of the cooking duties have now fallen on the shoulders of yours truly.

Now, I'm not the kind of jock Neanderthal who has never cracked a cookbook in his life or only watches a particular cooking show because the host is a hot Italian woman with big boobs (although I have seen that show). I do have a few signature dishes that I developed over the years to make sure that I didn't have to subsist on a diet of frozen entrees and pub food. I can make a decent, although meat-centric, pizza. I have experimented, with varying levels of success, with chicken parmagiana and pad thai. I can make an approximation of meat loaf. The problem with my repertoire, however, is that it doesn't include any of the dishes on tonight's menu.

Because Fermina is Spanish and Ebeneezer is from England, Leah decided that the meal should be a melding of their respective culinary heritages. That means we're starting with *pa amb tomàquet*, which is like a Catalan version of bruschetta with grated tomatoes. This will be followed by a variant of *paella* that uses diced, broiled potatoes instead of rice. Dessert will be *spotted dick*, the actual recipe for which was hard to find because the first few hundred search results contained nothing but pictures of herpes victims and Brett Favre.

I don't know how to make any of them. My only contribution was to select the wine. I picked a simple, off-the-shelf Bordeaux on the grounds that France is geographically between Spain and England and thus represents exactly the kind of meeting in the middle that Leah is so keen to create between our two guests.

Unfortunately, I drank half that bottle while reading the recipes and trying to calm my nerves, so I had to go out and get another. That leaves just over an hour until Leah is supposed to be back.

I decide to start with the *paella* since the potatoes have to first be boiled and then baked, which will take almost an hour by itself. The recipe advises that *paella* "can appear daunting to prepare". No shit, I think. The list of ingredients is massive: chicken, mussels, sausage, pepper, garlic, saffron, shrimp, parsley, onion, wine…well, at least I've got plenty of the last one.

I take a hearty swig and start to work measuring things out. I decide on the fly to ditch the potatoes and stick with the rice, which is easier.

Considering that the executive chef has run out the door right before the Michelin guide reviewers arrive, I think this grants me, as sous chef, the right to let my newfound authority go right to my mildly swirling head.

Since I will need the wine for the recipe and my wits about me to avoid setting myself or the apartment on fire, I pop the cork back in the bottle and switch to beer. In no time, I have pots bubbling and pans sizzling. The list of ingredients is long, but the prep is actually pretty simple. Timing is everything. I forget to pour off some of the excess oil when cooking the chorizo and add the garlic too soon, but am perfectly willing to forgive myself for both errors. No matter how much of a backend I make of this, it's my first time making it. Plus I'm going to be stuck eating it too, so if it's terrible, I'll suffer just as much as everyone else.

Besides, I think there's a distinct possibility that I'm not screwing it up: the kitchen is actually starting to smell pretty good and I haven't burned anything yet, including myself.

I'm just transferring everything to the large pan to go in the oven when the door opens and Leah walks in. Her movements are robotic and her expression masklike. *Uh oh.*

"Hey babe," I say, buoyed by my success in the kitchen. And probably the wine. "How'd it go?"

Leah sits down and pours herself a glass of wine. She swirls it contemplatively for a moment and then shakes her head and pushes it away. She takes a deep breath and looks up at me. I'm so convinced that she's about to start bawling that I sprint forward and put a consoling hand on her shoulder. There, there, I think. You'll have plenty of auditions. I can't say this yet, though. I have to wait until she tells me that she didn't get it.

"I got it."

The two of us just sit there blinking at each other for a moment. I want to explode like I did when she got the commercial, but somehow the vibe just isn't right.

"You did?"

"I have absolutely no idea how to process it," she says. "I went in and read the scene for what had to be the thousandth time. When I was done, the director took me aside and told me the part was mine if I wanted it."

"And…you said?"

"I think I said yes. I mean, I'm pretty sure I did. Jeremy was just over the moon, of course."

"You don't seem like you are."

"It's just…I've never done anything this big before. What if I suck?"

I let out a sigh of relief. I was thinking she had turned it down. Or that she just found out she had some terminal disease or something. "That's what you're worried about?"

She nods. Tears seem to explode from her eyes and she even starts hyperventilating. "It's just…I've been working…for this for…so long that…if I finally get in there…and I can't do it…"

"Where do you get these crazy ideas?" I ask, pulling her into a hug. "You're going to be great! You can do this."

Her face is muffled against my shirt, which soaks through almost immediately. Crap. I picked this shirt out especially for the dinner and now I'm going to have to change. Oh well.

"But…"

"But nothing. You've got this shot in your bag. It's like golf. There's absolutely no reason to feel nervous when standing over the ball at the first tee. You know why?"

"No."

"Because your body knows how to hit the shot. Your body has hit the shot a thousand times before. It knows what it's doing. Worrying about it won't help. Worry is interest paid in advance on a debt that never comes due. It's the enemy, so just forget about it and do what you know how to do."

I got this advice once when I won a free golf lesson at a college frosh week event. The pro in question was a dishevelled fat guy who was extremely disappointed that I wasn't an excitable 18-year-old coed in a tight tank top and shorts, but gamely went through the motions of trying to help me improve my swing nonetheless. My drives did get marginally better, but it was the advice that stuck.

"Where did you hear that?" Leah sniffs.

"Just something a wise man once said." A wise man who put away three double bourbons before 10 a.m., wore a mustard-stained shirt with the Hooters logo stitched over the pocket and bore an uncanny resemblance to John Daly. Was it John Daly? To this day I wonder.

She lifts her head up and wipes her eyes. "I like that. But what happens if I slice the ball through a window?"

"So you take a mulligan. It's TV. You're not on stage. It's not like they're gonna run out of tape."

When Leah got the audition, we sat down and watched a few episodes of *Royal Target* to get an idea of what the show was like. It's actually not as terrible as I thought it was going to be. Canadian TV has come a long way since *Mosquito Lake*. I wouldn't go so far as to say it's good, but at least they manage to go for more than fifteen minutes without a doughnut joke or an appearance by one of the Dale sisters.

"Yeah, I guess that's true," she says, calming down.

"So can I officially say congratulations now?"

"Thanks," she says, smiling. "I hope you don't mind, but I invited Jeremy to dinner, too."

My grin becomes a rictus. Is it possible to add even more tension to what is shaping up to be the most awkward dinner in history? "You did?"

"Relax. He's got something else on, so he probably won't be able to make it. But he said he might stop in later."

OK, so he might not actually show up. I decide to set that possibility to one side for now.

"It smells great in here," Leah says, looking towards the kitchen. "Looks like you've turned into quite the Gordon Ramsay."

"Ugh. Without the screaming and aborted football career. So when do you start shooting?"

"In a couple of weeks. Right now it's three episodes, but it might be four. What time is it? I should call Dante and tell him that I'm quitting."

This takes me by surprise. So much so that I try to sit down and almost miss the chair. "You're what?"

"I have to," she says, digging into her purse to find her phone. "It's three weeks of shooting. Maybe four. Full days plus some night shoots. I can't just ask for a month of vacation."

"But..."

"Don't worry about the money," she says. "I'm not getting paid a fortune, but it's still more than I'd make at the bookstore in almost a year. If anything, we can start looking for a bigger place."

My head is spinning. I actually have to grab the sides of the chair to keep myself from falling off. She only just started! How can she be quitting already? I haven't even shown her how to run the returns reports yet.

She speaks on the phone for a second before hanging up. "Dante's already gone for the day. I'll tell him tomorrow."

"Are you sure you have to quit?" I say. "I mean, maybe...I dunno...maybe I could..."

"Don't be silly," she says. "You can't cover all my shifts for a month. Dante needs to hire somebody else. He should have done that a long time ago anyway. You guys need more than four people. You don't even really have four considering Mina is hardly there even when she is."

*You guys.* She's already referring to the store in the past tense. Like she cut the brake lines on our car and slipped up when being interviewed by the cops. *I don't know how it could have happened – they were such a nice group of people. I mean 'are'. Are a nice group of people.*

She takes her jacket off and drops it on the couch. "So where are we at? It looks like the *paella*'s ready to go in the oven." She looks over and notices I haven't gotten up from the chair. "Hey, are you okay?"

"I'm okay," I say. "I just can't believe you're leaving."

She comes over and crouches down next to me. "Hey, I'm quitting the store, not us! You look like I just told you we were breaking up or something."

She's right. It's ridiculous. I have no idea why the thought of Leah quitting Village Books makes me sad, but it does. It's not the fact that Dante will take another six months to get around to hiring a new zone manager (although he will). It's deeper than that. But for the life of me, I have no idea what it is.

"You're right," I say, forcing myself up out of the chair. "We should be celebrating! I believe there's one champagne left on the rack. It isn't chilled, though. Do you want me to put it in the fridge?"

"If you don't pop that sucker this minute, I'm going to wrestle you to the ground and open it with my teeth."

"Actually, that sounds delightful."

"Save it for later, Romeo," she says, heading to the sink to wash her hands. "Do you want to grate the tomatoes or start the spotted dick?"

"Are you still talking about sex?"

She rolls her eyes and shakes her head. "You're incorrigible. You are not corrigible."

I get a couple of flutes out of the cupboard and start working on the cork. The champagne, I notice, is a Cristal. I twist the cork out and it foams up all over my hands and puddles on the floor. I manage to fill two glasses and hand one over to Leah.

"Here's to the world's premiere thespian on the eve of her debut as the sister of a homicidal lunatic," I say, holding up my glass. "I'm sure it's just the first of many great roles to come."

We clink glasses. "Thanks for talking me off the ledge," she says, taking a small sip. "I couldn't do this without you. You worked all those extra shifts so I could go to the auditions. You helped me with my scenes – even though some of your line readings were a little…well, let's just say you made some interesting choices."

"I told you I can't act my way out of a paper bag. That's not bragging; it's a fact. I was supposed to play a paper bag in the fifth grade school play and I almost suffocated. It was about going to the grocery store. They had to carry me off the stage. The romaine and the cereal were quite traumatized by the whole thing. I'm a method guy. I really got inside the mind of the bag. Unfortunately, I wasn't able to get out again without assistance."

She laughs. "Well, thank you. Now, are you ready to cook?"

"Are you–"

"No. But I promise that after everyone goes home, we can take a nice long bath and you can grate the tomatoes – or whatever you want to call it – as much as you like."

I immediately agree, but not entirely for libidinous reasons. I need to eat. I've had a little too much to drink already and the champagne is really going to my head. If I don't eat soon, I am going to pass out in the shrimp. That may make dinner easier for me, but it would be distinctly awkward for everyone else.

"Okay," I say. "Do you want me to do the bread so you can get your hands on the *spotted dick*? I was reading up on it and it looks kinda hard."

"Are you going to be like this all night? I will have sex with you right now if it'll help you get this out of your system."

"Sorry. Couldn't resist. But you had to know what you were signing up for when you selected that particular dessert."

"Can you promise no more double entendres or other penis-related references while our guests are here?"

"I can promise that I'll do my best. But sometimes even when you get the wave off, it's hard not to swing at a pitch right over the fat part of the plate."

"You know, for a guy who doesn't watch baseball, you're pretty good with the references, so here's another one: any more dick jokes while Ebeneezer and Fermina are here and your bat will not be coming anywhere near home plate this evening."

"That's not really a reference; it's more of a threat."

"Take it for what you will, my dear," she says, pecking me on the cheek. She gives me a saucy smile. "Now why don't you start on the tomatoes so I can get this dick in the oven?"

# -24-

Of course, Ebeneezer figures out what we're planning before he has even taken off his jacket.

All it takes is one glance at the table, which is obviously set for four, and a sniff of the *paella* cooking away in the oven for him to guess, correctly, that he is being set up. It takes him less than five seconds. He greets me, steps inside, notices the table, sniffs the air, and his eyes narrow. I can tell that he is considering a tactical retreat, but there is no way for him to do that this late in the game without appearing rude, and that is one luxury he would never allow himself – at least not in front of Leah.

Fermina hasn't arrived yet. It's precisely seven o'clock. I know this because my watch reads 7:04 and I happen to know my watch is four minutes fast.

"Very kind of you to invite me," he says, handing me a woollen coat that is almost as old as he is. I've never held his jacket before and it's surprisingly heavy. No wonder he never looks cold in the winter. I remark on its heft.

"A gift from my dear wife," he says. "She bought it from a small shop in Charing Cross Road in London. A family-owned establishment. All clothing handmade on the premises. Been there for two hundred years. Naturally, it was recently replaced by an adult video emporium, which also sells what I believe they refer to these days as marital aids."

I have no response for this. Thankfully, Leah appears and Ebeneezer's countenance brightens considerably.

"Ah, my dear!" he says, bending theatrically to kiss her on the hand. "So kind of you to invite me. Whatever you are cooking smells delectable!"

"Thank you!" Leah says, blushing slightly. "Don't credit me, though. This guy did most of the cooking."

"Truly?" Ebeneezer says, arching an eyebrow my way. "Then he is a man of many hidden talents."

I grin stupidly. Hidden? Was I just insulted? Dammit. I shouldn't have had so much wine while I was cooking. You need to stay sharp when dealing with a guy like this.

"Actually," I say, keen to divert attention away from myself. "There's a second purpose to tonight's dinner. Leah just got a part on a TV show!"

Ebeneezer's face positively lights up. "Indeed! That is fantastic news! Heartiest congratulations!" He kisses her hand again. "Without question, you are as talented as you are beautiful."

Leah just giggles and blushes an even deeper shade of red. Women are putty in this man's hands. I could learn a thing or two from this guy.

His gaze shifts suddenly back to me. "If that is only the secondary purpose, then what, pray tell, was the primary reason for this evening's degustitary rapprochement?"

I continue to grin stupidly. This will be, I fear, my default expression for the evening. My only chance will be to either sober up in the next five minutes or drink a whole lot more. "Er..."

"Just a simple dinner with friends," Leah says. "Please, do come in."

Ebeneezer leaves me squirming on the spot and follows Leah into the apartment. I realize that I'm still holding his jacket and quickly hang it up in the closet. It's too heavy for the wire hangers and I have to shift one of Leah's jackets off a heavy duty plastic one to avoid having the jacket land in a pile on the floor. I actually consider checking the pockets to see if he has, like Virginia Woolf, stuffed them full of rocks. No fabric weighs this much! If he spotted me, however, there would be no socially acceptable way to explain myself. *Yes, er, I was just checking the lining to ensure that you didn't stumble into a river and die.* Not a convincing cover story.

Leah hands Ebeneezer a glass of red wine. He tilts it, sniffs, and then tries a tiny sample that he swirls around in his mouth for a good 30 seconds. I'm so convinced that he's about to spit it out that I start looking for a pot or a bowl into which he can expectorate. Much to my relief, he just swallows and regards the glass thoughtfully.

"Very nice," he says. "A Côtes du Rhone? 2008?"

I revert once again to my default expression. I had no idea that the guy even drank, let alone that he knew anything about wine. "Yes! How did you know?"

"My niece is a sommelier," he says. "That and I read the label of the bottle sitting on the table."

Leah lets out a snort of laughter, which Ebeneezer clearly finds delightful.

"So tell me more about your new role, my dear," he says, eyes twinkling. "Is it drama? Comedy?" He leans forward and drops his voice to a husky whisper. "Romance?"

"More of a thriller, really," Leah says. "I'll be doing a three- or four-episode spot on a show called *Royal Target*."

"Ah! I know the show!" Ebeneezer says, stabbing the air enthusiastically with a finger.

Huh? Five minutes ago, I would have confidently bet my savings account that this man did not own a radio, let alone a TV. If at some point during tonight's dinner he reaches into his pocket and pulls out an iPhone, I am going to soil my trousers.

"If I am not mistaken, you'll be working with Callum Guthrie," he says. "Who, if memory serves, played a very commendable Coriolanus at Stratford two years ago."

"That's right!" Leah says. "He plays the head of the security detail – the one who has to try and keep his telepathic abilities a secret."

"Of course," Ebeneezer nods. "Who could forget last season's finale, when he had to plant evidence in the home of a man he knew to be guilty in order to avert a national catastrophe?"

"Fortunately, he was able to get inside the minds of the review board or he'd have been thrown out of the unit for good," Leah says. "We watched those episodes when I was getting ready for the audition."

"Highly unethical on his part, but it makes for compelling viewing," Ebeneezer observes. "So of what will your role comprise?"

"My character's name is Cassandra Templeton," Leah says. "She's the sister of a mentally disturbed Afghan war vet who escapes from a high security military prison with plans to shoot the PM on Canada Day."

"Fascinating." Ebeneezer glances at me. "Particularly in light of recent events."

I shift uncomfortably. "Fortunately, my wounds were entirely superficial."

"Thanks in no small part to the superb work of young Ivanka," Ebeneezer says. "If not for her swift and decisive action, we may all have come out of the evening considerably worse off. I understand her self-defence classes are now completely booked for the next two years. She told me the other day that she's looking into expanding into her own space."

Ebeneezer takes another sip of his wine and looks around the apartment appraisingly. "So tell me, my dear Leah, does this new role mean we will see less of you at the store for a while?"

Leah pops open the stove door to both check on the *paella* and avoid meeting his gaze. "Actually, it means I won't be there at all. It's almost a months' worth of rehearsal and shooting, so I'll be quitting the store. I tried to call Dante to let him know earlier, but he was already gone. I'll have to tell him tomorrow."

Ebeneezer looks so stricken that he almost drops his glass. "No! Surely he would give you the time off! I know his mother well. I have no doubt she could convince him to come to some sort of accommodation."

Leah smiles sadly. "It's not just that. I'm getting so many auditions for so many other jobs and a lot of them come up at the last minute. It's not fair to expect other people to cover for me all the time." She shoots me a guilty look as she says this. I want to tell her that I will gladly cover for her, but the truth is that I'm getting more than a little burned out. If I have to work one more double shift, the next one to run into the store with a gun might be me.

Ebeneezer opens his mouth to object and stops himself. "Ah…well. The store will miss you greatly. But I'm sure we're all buoyed in watching you move on to the brighter and bolder horizons that are certainly your due."

Leah sniffs and wipes away a tear. "Thank you."

Ebeneezer raises his glass. "Now, now! No sadness. Tonight is a night to celebrate your triumph! To Leah and all her future glories!"

He raises his glass. Leah picks up her champagne glass (which I notice is still almost full – did she refill when I wasn't looking?) and does the same. I don't actually have one and am forced to awkwardly raise an imaginary wine glass to be part of the moment. Fortunately, I am saved by a knock at the door. I rush to answer it and find Fermina on the other side wearing a bright red coat and hat.     "Hola," she says, stepping inside and handing me her purse, which is large enough to store hockey equipment. "Good evening. Sorry I am late."

"Not at all," I mumble as she quickly piles her jacket and hat on my shoulders and straightens her dress, which I notice is the same colour of orange as a prison jumpsuit. No one has ever accused her of subtlety.

"Ebby!" she smiles, simultaneously shooting Leah an accusing look. "I think our young friends are up to something, yes?"

Leah hands her a glass of wine and assumes an innocent expression. "Just a pleasant evening with friends, Fermina."

Fermina sniffs the air and glances at the table. "Ah, *paella*! And *pa amb tomàquet*! You make my favourite dishes, so I forgive you your scheming!"

Leah blushes. "You may want to reserve judgement until the dessert comes out. I'm not sure I mixed it quite right."

Fermina takes the glass and swings her gaze around the apartment like a radar dish, taking in everything for future cataloguing and study. "I almost did not think I would make it," she says. "These legal things, they take so long."

"Legal things?" I ask, trying to sound innocuous. Having had so much exposure to the justice system of late, I am starting to feel like I could take the bar exam tomorrow.

"Yes," she says. "But now everything is final, so I can tell you."

The rest of us look confused. This is the pattern when drawing information out of Fermina. She drops discrete little nuggets of information and expects you to keep bending down to pick them up. It's the conversational equivalent of following a trail of bread crumbs.

"Tell us what?" I prompt.

She takes another long sip of wine. She loves to draw out tense moments like this. It's a good thing she doesn't hand out awards. The audience would kill her.

"I plan to do this for years. Today, I finally do it!"

Uh oh. I have a horrible feeling that I know what she's about to say. She's beaming like a high school kid who just caught her home room teacher smoking pot in the boiler room.

"Fermina, did you sell the café?"

The words are out of my mouth before I can stop myself. Fermina shoots me a dirty look. She dislikes being scooped on big announcements. In her mind, it's like a dockworker grabbing the champagne bottle out of the queen's hands and smashing it against the side of the ship himself. After watching hundreds of launches, though, your patience would probably wear out because sometimes the old bag just takes too damn long.

She recovers quickly, her smile dropping for only an instant. "I sell the café!" she says as dramatically as if I hadn't spoken.

I glance at poor Ebeneezer, whose mouth is hanging open like a dead polar bear's. First Leah and now Fermina. He has been resoundingly kicked hard in both nuts.

Leah and I look at each other. Neither of us is entirely sure how to react. Fermina is clearly as over the moon with this news as Ebeneezer is under it.

"Wow," Leah says cautiously. "Uh, when did you do that?"

"They approach me before Christmas," Fermina says.

"Who did?" I ask. "Not the Umex guys?"

"*Si*," Fermina nods. "They double their offer again. This is enough for me to buy small house and café I have my eye on back home for some time. Plus have money left over. All is final today."

"So…" I am being careful not to get ahead of her too quickly or she will refuse to speak to me for the rest of the night even though she is in my apartment. "You're moving back to Spain?"

"*Si!*" Fermina says. "No longer will I have to freeze through another one of your terrible winters."

It doesn't matter how long Fermina has been in this country, she still refuses to take ownership of any of the less-pleasant aspects of being here. It's always *your* weather. *Your* 401. *Your* hospital wait times. *Your* Don Cherry. She's like a parent who takes credit for a child's good behaviour and blames all tantrums and defects on her spouse.

Leah is looking at me like she expects me to do something. What does she expect me to do? Change the subject? To what? The shaky future of the euro? The fact that almost every Toronto sports franchise is in last place? The benefits of breastfeeding over bottle? Ebeneezer looks like a man who just caught the eye of Medusa on his evening walk, but changing the subject now would be more difficult than moving his statue off the sidewalk.

"Well, isn't that something," I say. If I were a superhero, my name would be Banalman. "When are you going?"

"I close the café next month," she says. "And then I return home shortly after that."

"Wow, that's fast," Leah says.

"Yes, but is time. I will miss many people, but I cannot wait to get home and see my family again. My new place will be on top of a small hill that overlooks the sea. My sister is short walk away. She will help me to get it ready."

Dammit, I wish I was holding a glass of wine right now. "You sound like you've got everything worked out."

Fermina sighs contentedly and takes another look around the apartment. "*Si*. The Umexes were very keen to buy. They say they have closed deal to buy entire block."

Wait, what?

"They said what?" I ask. "Did you say they bought the entire block?"

"This is what they say," Fermina says. "They say café and bookstore were last holdouts and now they have deals for both. I don't know if bookstore deal is closed yet, but they say they have deal in place for both places."

I have not heard a peep about the Umex buyout since Dante last mentioned it, which was shortly after Leah was hired. If Dante has been keeping this from everybody, I am going to brutally kill him until he is dead. And then I'm going to get really nasty.

"Are you sure?" Leah says. "Because we haven't heard anything about that."

"This is just what they tell me," Fermina says, smiling like a toddler that has just dropped a fox into a bin full of baby rabbits. "Perhaps they have exaggerate."

I walk over to the table and pour myself a large glass of wine. It is, I think, going to be the first of many.

# -25-

Leah and I decide to head into the store the following morning to find out what's going on. Neither of us is working, but this is the kind of thing best handled in person as opposed to over the phone.

We find Dante in receiving, where he is helping Willard process a large return of diet books that were recently recalled by the publisher when it was revealed that the author was not in fact the nutritional consultant to the Australian Olympic team but in fact a former Salomon Brothers bond trader with thirteen convictions for fraud.

Publishing has seen many of these types of scandals over the last few years. The last big one was a book written by a guy who claimed to be one of the trapped Chilean miners but who was in fact a lieutenant in the Cuban army who had been on safari in Africa at the time of the events he claimed to depict firsthand. A few news organizations worked themselves up into a froth over it for a day or two, but nobody really cared. I think reality TV has completely eroded the public's expectation of veracity in these matters. The irony was that his book was better written than some of the ones that came from actual sources.

Dante finishes dealing with Willard and waves us into the manager's office. It's a Sunday morning and the store is not exactly a hive of activity. Miroslav is shelving the latest batch of *Black Lace* romances with his bandaged hand and Lolita, having traded with Ivanka for the morning shift, is upstairs reading *The Paper Bag Princess* to three terrified preschoolers as part of scheduled storytime. It's not the story that's scaring them, of course. Lolita apparently came within a half-mile of one of the thirteen thousand things she is allergic to yesterday and now her right eye is swollen up like a veiny tennis ball. She looks like she's in monster makeup from a 50s horror movie. Or, I should say, more like she's in monster makeup from a 50s horror movie than usual.

"I heard about this a couple of days ago," Dante says, sitting down. "Sorry I didn't tell you about it, but my mother went into hospital at about the same time."

My anger is immediately jerked out from under me. I came in prepared to do some actual yelling, but I can't be mad at the guy when his mother is sick. Well, maybe I can, but I'm going to have to save it for later.

"Oh my God, Dante!" Leah says. "Is she all right?"

Dante shrugs. "They think it's just the flu. But with the kind of cancer she's got, it seems that her immune system is weaker and she's a lot more vulnerable to simple infections. Plus she has a harder time fighting them off. They're keeping her in for at least a week. Maybe longer."

"Is there anything we can do?" I ask, although I have no idea what that might be. I hope he doesn't ask me to take over his shift. I drank rather a lot of wine last night and am not exactly feeling at 100 per cent this morning. The rest of the dinner was a predictably stilted affair. Fermina spent most of the time talking about her plans for Spain. Ebeneezer recovered himself to the point where he was able to speak in complete sentences, but his *savoire faire* was dented beyond repair. Jeremy, mercifully, did not put in an appearance, but did call Leah to apologize and hint that he was working on something even bigger for her than the TV show, although he wouldn't say what it was.

"I don't think so," Dante says. "I talked to Lucy last night. She wants me to keep her in the loop. If mama doesn't get any better, then she might have to cut her Africa trip short."

This is the first time I've heard Dante refer to his mother as *mama*, and I have to say, it's a little discomfiting. I'm much more comfortable with Beelzebub. *Mama* makes him sound like a scared four-year-old. Although, I guess, right now, that's kind of what he is. Dante has never been without his mother hanging over his shoulder. As much as he complains about her, I don't think he'd know what to do with himself if she wasn't there.

"Jeez, well, I hope she's feeling better soon." This is a stupid thing to say. People don't tend to feel better soon when they have terminal cancer. But what else can you say in a situation like that?

"Anyway," Dante says. "What's happened is that Cynthia Ackerman slipped on her way out of the shower and hit her head. Right now, she's in a coma and they don't know if she's going to come out of it. What with Marty stuck in 1976, the kids have stepped in to run the business. The sale to Umex is set to go through unless Cynthia wakes up in the next 30 days."

"How did you find out about it?" Leah asks.

"I got a message from some property development company I'd never heard of," Dante says. "They wanted access to do a complete structural inspection. Plumbing, electrical, everything. I thought it was a joke, so I just ignored it. Less than an hour later, I got a call from Maude telling me that she had taken over running the company and to give Umex everything they ask for. I asked what happened. She gave me a quick synopsis and then hung up before I could even ask how her mother was doing."

"That sounds like Maude," I observe. "She's a nasty piece of work."

Maude has, as far as I'm aware, visited the store only once. It was shortly after I had started as a full-time manager. Cynthia came in (something she used to do quite often before her hip surgery) with Maude and Walter in tow. Maude spent the entire visit texting on her cell phone and looked up only once to remark that she thought the place was a dumpy hole in the wall and her parents should get rid of it as soon as possible. Walter, meanwhile, walked out with three Playstation hacking guides and an illustrated *Kama Sutra*, none of which he paid for.

"So that's kind of where we're at," Dante says. "For now, I guess, we just keep going like normal and see what happens. There's not a lot else we can do."

"We have to tell the staff," I say. "Fermina's not exactly keeping this a secret. If they hear it from someone else first, we're going to have a mass freak-out on our hands."

Dante rubs his face. He looks more tired than I have ever seen him. "Yeah, you're right. We should have an emergency staff meeting or something."

"I'll organize it," I say. "We can have it tonight right after we close. Maybe sooner. Sundays are usually pretty dead." I cringe. Shit. Poor choice of words. "We can close a bit early and let everyone know what's going on."

"I have to be at the hospital tonight," Dante says. "Can you guys handle it?"

Leah and I exchange a look. Dante really should be here for this. He's the store manager. If getting up in front of everyone to tell them that they might shortly be out of work is anyone's job, it's his. In his current emotional state, however, he's probably not the best one for the task.

"Of course," I say. "I'll get on the phone and start calling the ones who aren't here." I look at Leah expectantly. *But first…*

Leah sighs and sits forward. "Uh, Dante, I know this probably isn't the best time to deliver this particular bit of news, but I'm going to be leaving."

Dante frowns. "Leaving? As in…quitting?"

Leah squeezes her hands between her knees and nods. "Yeah. I got another job. It's TV. The shoot'll probably last a month and it's not like you can just give me three or four weeks off. Plus I've got other things coming up all the time. It's just not fair to everyone else."

"A TV job?" Dante says, too exhausted to sound enthusiastic. "When do you start?"

"Next week," Leah says. "So I'll be out of here by Friday."

Dante sits back and puffs out his cheeks. "Wow. That's two in one day."

"Two?" I say. "Who else is quitting?"

"Ivanka," Dante says. "She's starting up her own fitness and self-defence training studio for women. I guess she got a lot of interest after that whole thing with Mina's husband. They interviewed her on practically every news show in town. Studio interviews, too, not just the on-the-street stuff."

I suspect part of the reason for this, aside from her obvious bravery and technical competence, is the fact that Ivanka looks like a supermodel. The *Sun* put her on the front page with the headline "Drop Deadly Gorgeous!" I understand that she turned down an offer to be the Sunshine Girl, amongst many other bikini-centric opportunities. I'm sure there will be no shortage of photographers when she collects her citizen's bravery medal at city hall next month.

"It's too bad," Dante continues. "I was thinking of giving her a key. Now we need to think of somebody else. But who?"

"That's a tough one," I agree.

Ebeneezer is the most responsible person who works here, but he only works part time and he's getting a bit old to hump in here at seven in the morning. Plus he'd be way too cranky to deal with customer complaints and personnel issues. Sebastian is probably next in line in terms of experience, but trusting a key to a man up on so many criminal charges might not seem like the most prudent choice. I wouldn't trust Willard with the key to a Scooby Doo mystery, let alone the store. Lolita would see it as the first step in the establishment of a Fourth Reich. Mother Teresa refuses to work Sundays. Miroslav would probably swallow it. Christ, the pickings are slim.

"What about Aldous?" Leah suggests. "He's always looking for more hours and he's a bright kid. I think he could handle it."

Dante and I look at each other. A month ago, I would have balked at this suggestion. Right now, however, I am forced to admit that it's not the dumbest idea I have ever heard. And, sad to say, he might be our only real option.

"That might work," Dante says. "Do you think you can train him in time?"

"Sure," Leah says. "He picks things up quick."

I smile at this. Leah has already transformed almost every other aspect of Aldous's existence. Why not his employment prospects as well?

"Okay, let's do it," Dante says. "I mean, assuming he wants it. It might not be for very long, anyway."

"Are we quite sure that Cynthia slipped in the tub?" I ask. "I mean, that it was an accident? Doesn't Walter live in the basement? He has a pretty nasty gaming habit and no other source of income. Where was he during all this? She's not diabetic, is she? Do Walter and Maude have Alan Dershowitz on retainer?"

"I wouldn't try to sell the movie rights just yet," Dante says. "Conspiracy theories aside, we have to be ready for the possibility that the store will be closing at the end of next month."

"Ready how?" I ask. "Aside from telling the staff, I mean."

"Well, we've got all that stock out there that we'd have to return," Dante says. "What we can't return, we'll have to mark down and sell off."

"No, no, no!" I say, cutting him off. "Fuck that. Maude and Walter want to sell the store right out from under us – under their own parents, the rightful fucking owners, in fact – then that's fine. I'm not gonna paint the walls and stage the furniture and serve them tea and cookies while they do it."

Dante looks confused. "Huh?"

"Sorry, that's on me," Leah says. "I like to watch real estate reality shows on HGTV to unwind. He gets his Barça games. I watch lifestyle porn. That's the trade off."

"I thought you liked watching Barça games," I say.

"I do," Leah says. "Just maybe not quite as much as you do. You get pretty loud when they score. I don't think you even realize how into it you are. You're normally such a quiet guy."

"Sometimes you get pretty rowdy during *Property Virgins* and *Home To Flip*," I point out.

"Some of those people have totally unrealistic expectations about what they're gonna get in a first place!" Leah protests. "Seriously! There are two of you. Why do you need 5,000 square feet in Rosedale with granite countertops and four bathrooms and stainless steel appliances and heated floors? Who do these people think they are? It just makes me mad."

"I can tell," Dante says.

"Sorry," I say. "Internal discussion. Anyway, my point is, if those two devil spawn want to sell the place, there's no reason we should make the job any easier for them. It's all I can do to stop myself from going out there and slapping 90 per cent off stickers on everything. Hell, let's just give the stock away for free. Let those two greedy buggers cover it out of the proceeds."

"I don't disagree with you," Dante says. "But a few things to keep in mind. One, we might not actually close, so we can't start giving stuff away just yet. Two, Maude is a soulless Bay Street lawyer who would have no problem suing all of us into old age if we did something like that. Three, a lot of the stuff we carry comes from small publishers. Umex would probably just tell them to get lost and they'd be out the money for all that stock. They don't have the money to sue and it wouldn't be worth their while to try. They'd just get caught in the middle. No reason for them to get screwed, too."

"You're a good man, Dante," I say. "And what you say makes sense. Very sad, depressing sense. That's why you can have no part in what's about to happen."

Dante grins. "Just promise me you won't break out the mattresses until the time comes, Santino."

Leah looks confused. "What are you guys talking about? Are you talking about *The Godfather*? Is that what all this secret code talk is?"

I take the spare key out of the drawer and hold it up. "I'll go give this to Swinghammer. We need good people. Responsible people. People who aren't gonna get carried away. I mean, we're not murderers, no matter what this bookseller says."

"I believe in America," Dante says. "America has made-a my fortune. And I run-a my bookstore in the American fashion."

Dante and I break out laughing. It starts small and builds up to the point where we're both out of breath and tears are pouring down our cheeks. It feels like we haven't laughed like this in a long time. When I first started, Dante and I used to sit back here and riff on movies and books all the time. It wasn't always classic stuff, but we've always had the ability to make the other one laugh. Lately it seems like we've just been too busy or had too many other things to think about. It's nice to recapture some of that, even if it is tinged with the realization that it might not be for much longer.

Leah rolls her eyes. "Jesus. Look at you two. No matter how hard I try, I will never understand the male brain."

"Hey, me either," Dante says, finally starting to get himself under control. "And I have one."

There's a knock at the door and Miroslav pokes his head in. "What happen in here? Lots of noise. It sound like when my cousin show me how to insert *kypau* into chicken."

This is too much even for Leah. She may never understand the male cortex, but no one will ever know what goes on inside of Miroslav's, and that includes its owner. The three of us start laughing and don't stop for a long time.

## -26-

Everyone is able to make it to the staff meeting except for Sebastian, who has to go to a lab to provide a urine sample to prove he isn't drinking or imbibing any other proscribed substances. It's part of his bail conditions and they are not flexible about the scheduling of his appointments.

"Jesus!" he says when I tell him what's going on. "If the store closes, I'll never be able to leave the house! Aside from having my precious bodily fluids periodically drained, it's the only time I'm allowed out. I need to interact! I'm not in the habit of denying women my essence, Mandrake. Sneaking out at night is devilishly difficult, especially when my mother keeps changing the code on the security system without telling me."

"I don't doubt it." I wonder absently if the cops have tapped his phone. It's a ridiculous idea, of course, but since the G20, Toronto has felt a little more like East Berlin than it used to. I never thought I'd see mass detention centres set up in public parks for anything short of a hockey riot.

"What are the odds that the old broad will pull through, do you think? Are we talking routine knock on the head or full-on Von Bulow?"

"I honestly don't know," I say. "Dante's going by the hospital to visit both Cynthia and his mother tonight, so maybe he'll have more information tomorrow."

"Perhaps we should consider contingency plans," Sebastian says, his voice cagy. "You know, in the event that Cynthia doesn't rise to the occasion in time."

"What are you talking about?"

"Well, what if young Maude were to accidentally impale herself on a ken-do staff during a corporate retreat? Or Walter was to electrocute himself whilst playing video games in the bathtub?"

"I'm sorry, Sebastian, I'm having trouble hearing you. Furthermore, I would like to repeat that last statement for any law enforcement officials who may be listening."

"Don't be such a knock-kneed Shadyac. Sometimes drastic situations require manly responses."

Shadyac, I should mention, refers to the director of such cinematic excretions as *Patch Adams*, *The Nutty Professor* and *Bruce Almighty*. To be referred to as a "Shadyac" is to be called, in our private lexicon, a cowardly, pandering, PG-13 level wuss.

"Shadyac? Fuck you, Shitmaker! I'm the one who got shot while you were out boning another guy's wife."

Shitmaker, incidentally, is our nickname for Joel Schumacher.

"Are you still talking about that? Man, it happened like a month ago. You'd think you were the first man in history to be shot by a jealous psychotic husband. Are you sure you've still got both balls?"

"Goodbye, Sebastian."

"Wait! Do you think you'd be willing to submit a notarized schedule that states I'm working next Saturday from five 'til say, two in the morning? No, make it three. Call it inventory or something like that. I just met this pre-med student online who'd like me to come over and help her with gross anatomy and I am most keen to grasp her innuendoes."

"Once again, I have no idea what you just said, but I'll see what I can do."

"You're a gentleman of means. Now I must dash. The fellow I purchase all my urine from will be here any minute. I have to transfer it into a colostomy bag that I strap to my ankle and squeeze at the right moment to give the impression of veracity. These buggers walk right into the room with you, but usually don't pay too much attention when one whips out the sword of Damocles, if you follow my meaning."

"I certainly do not."

"Apparently, they also test athletes right before and after major sporting competitions. What kind of an occupation is that? You spend your life walking into depressing little white rooms watching other people pee?"

"I'm sure your source for black market urine probably grew up dreaming of bigger things, too."

"Speaking of which, there's the door. Ciao!"

We close the store half an hour early and the staff assembles in the storytime area on the second floor. It's a little discombobulating to deliver such grim news surrounded by wooden train sets and talking turtles, but it's the only space large enough to accommodate everyone. It doesn't exactly come as a surprise since we've all been living under the cloud of this possibility for the last couple of years. They take the news about as well as can be expected.

"Shit, man, I hope she doesn't kak," Willard observes. "If this place closes, where am I gonna get my discount on Mad Dog Bloodsukka?"

"I knew I could count on you to see the big picture, Willard," I observe.

"If this mendacious sale does go through," Ebeneezer asks, "how long do you expect the store will remain open? We do, after all, have quite a lot of books that will need to be returned to their publishers."

"That's a good question," Leah says. "At this point, we don't know. Dante has told us to proceed with business as usual for now. We're not going to be returning anything more than we normally would to get the store back down to the usual post-holiday inventory levels."

"How can this Maude bitch even do it?" Willard asks, earning a dirty look from Mother Teresa which he ignores. "She doesn't even own the place!"

There is a general murmuring of agreement at this, along with a few muted calls for the junior Ackerman to be pilloried, guillotined or run out of town on a greased electrified rail.

"Actually," I say, raising my voice slightly to suppress the din. "We were wondering the same thing. Dante did some digging and it turns out that Maude has the legal authority to sell the store anytime she likes. There's a clause in the articles of incorporation that automatically cedes all control to Maude should Cynthia or Marty ever become incapable of running the business themselves. Since Marty is already incapacitated, that happened as soon as Cynthia hit her head and didn't wake up. The 30-day delay is coming from Umex. I think they're trying to create enough of a buffer to avoid any legal blowback should Cynthia wake up and decide she disagrees with her daughter's decision. They're also probably trying to avoid any bad publicity that would make them look like a bunch of vultures who swoop in before the body's cold."

"Screw that," Willard says. "I say we call the papers. Those fuckers are trying to steal our store!"

This is greeted with a few cheers and a lot of head nodding.

"Loathe as I am to agree with my partially scalped fellow employee," Ebeneezer says, "but a surge of negative public opinion may be exactly the thing needed to scupper this underhanded and sordid little arrangement."

Leah and I look at each other. This was a point that we spent a great deal of time debating with Dante, with the two of us arguing passionately in favour and Dante just as strongly against. Both Leah and I thought that the only way to sabotage the deal, short of Cynthia waking up, was to generate enough bad publicity to embarrass Umex into backing out. Dante argued equally hard that any publicity would also cause a great deal of embarrassment to Cynthia and Marty, who would be mortified to see the inner workings of their family splashed across the business pages.

"But Cynthia's in a coma and Marty only gets upset if he gets chicken instead of ribs!" I said. "Neither of them are exactly in the picture right now."

"It's not just that," Dante said. "If Maude gets any hint that somebody from the store talked to the press, she'll shut us down tomorrow. I guarantee it. She won't care if it torpedoes the Umex deal. She'll close the store and turn it into a hair salon or whatever strikes her fancy. Everyone will lose their job."

"Tomorrow or a month from now, what difference does it make?" Leah asked. "We shouldn't just let her get away with this! The store shouldn't go down without a fight."

Dante shook his head. "We need to wait. I don't want to contact the press unless we have absolutely no other option."

"But if we wait, then it'll be too late!" I said. Dante's general lack of a spine is irritating at the best of times, and even Dickens would recognize that these are not the best of times. "The deal will be done and we'll be screwed."

But Dante would not budge. I think he feels a great deal of loyalty towards Cynthia because she gave him his first sort-of real job. In many ways, she's like the mother he would have preferred. Considering that both his real mother and work mother were in the hospital at the same time, I didn't want to argue the point too vehemently, but it took all the restraint I could muster. Dante is the reason that people like Mussolini and Maude come to power.

But I digress.

"Dante has advised that he doesn't want any employees of the store to contact the media," I say, trying not to gnash my teeth. "Remember, Maude is currently in charge and probably wouldn't take kindly to being called a, quote, bottom-feeding, backstabbing saprophyte, end quote, in the paper."

"Can I quote you on that?" Aldous asks, grinning.

"Not officially."

"What's a saprophyte?" Willard asks. "Some sort of lesbian thing?"

"Any other questions?"

Lolita raises a hand. "Do you know if Iterations is accepting applications yet for the new store? Do you have a contact we could forward them to?"

This earns her numerous dirty looks and even a few boos, which she studiously ignores. It's no secret that, since she started, Lolita has applied for every managing position that has come up, including mine and Leah's. The fact that Dante has consistently hired from the outside is a message she has stubbornly refused to receive.

"I haven't the faintest idea," I say, not trying too hard to keep the scorn out of my voice. After a question like that, I can't think of a better time to bring out the second piece of news. I really ought to leave it to Leah, but opportunities to smack down Lolita are few and far between. "I should also let you know that Leah is going to be leaving us at the end of the week. Aldous will be starting tomorrow as an acting manager."

Aldous smiles and tries not to look too pleased with himself. Things are really starting to turn around in Swinghammer town. Aside from the new look and the promotion, he told Leah that things went well enough on his first date with the French exchange student that they are actually going out again. A second date is a rare commodity in his back catalogue.

There are several confused and even hurt looks from the others. I can tell they're wondering why one of their favourite managers (oh, who am I kidding? – she *is* their favourite manager) is abandoning them in their time of direst need. The question has even crossed my own mind once or twice.

"Why?" asks Mother Teresa, looking shocked.

"Yeah!" says Willard. "You can't leave us now!"

"I know and I'm sorry," Leah says. "But something's come up that's going to take all of my time and I can't turn it down. I'm really going to miss all you guys, though. And I promise I won't abandon you. Whatever I can do to help keep the store open, I will."

"But what is it?" asks Ivanka.

"Did you get another acting job?" Aldous pipes up. We told him that Leah was leaving, but not why.

"Is it in the new Batman movie?" Willard asks. "I heard they're gonna be shooting that in town. Are you gonna be the new Catwoman?"

"Ladies and gentlemen, please," Ebeneezer says, raising his voice over the growing mob. "We must not pester young Miss Dashwood with jabber. Her reasons for leaving are entirely her own and none of our affair. If she wishes to leave, then it is our lot to accept her decision, no matter how distressing it may prove."

Leah smiles and gives a small nod of thanks, but I keep watching Ebeneezer. Something is going on there. It's the first thing I mention once Leah and I are ensconced at our usual table at Falstaff's a half hour later. I'm having a large Scrumpy with the house burger. Leah says she has a mild tension headache and has settled for a club sandwich and a water.

"He wasn't talking about you," I say, gobbling my fries. "Well, partly he was. But mostly I think he was talking about Fermina."

"You think so?" says Leah. She seems oddly distracted. Usually she's far more attuned to other people's emotional states than I am, so the fact that I appear to have noticed something she missed is weird.

"Are you kidding? It's obvious. He's just gonna let her go."

Leah sighs. "Well, you know. Maybe he should."

I can't believe my ears. "What?"

"Well, she seems pretty determined to leave. And can you picture him living in a small village in Spain?"

"But..." I don't even know where to start. Up until practically five minutes ago, I was arguing from the other side of the fence. What the hell is going on? "But you spent all that time and energy trying to get them together! The dinner! The grated tomatoes! The fish stew that I overcooked!"

"Yeah, and it didn't work," she says. "Maybe we should just accept it and move on."

Something is clearly bothering her. Is it having to tell everyone that she's leaving? Wait, I did that. Is she mad at me for jumping in and stealing her thunder? She has barely touched her food.

"Are you okay?" I ask. "You seem distinctly out of sorts."

"I'm fine. No, wait. Look…well…there is something I should probably mention."

More alarms. Oh shit. What could it be? I feel like I just remembered to turn the radar on in time to catch a squadron of Heinkels about to drop their bomb loads on London and it's too late to warn the civilian population to take cover. I take a deep swallow of Scrumpy.

"Okay."

She shakes her head. "Christ, on top of everything else." She says this in a whisper, clearly meant to indicate that she is talking to herself. Now I am deeply worried. I put the glass down on the table so I don't drop it.

"What?"

She takes a deep breath. "Okay. Remember when I joked in the hospital that if the bullet had been any higher, we wouldn't have had to worry about birth control?"

"Yeah!" Pleasant memory. Oh, wait. Boing. "Oh."

"Exactly."

"How long, uh, have you known?"

She looks down at her plate. "Since yesterday. I took one of the tests and it came up positive, but it was only sort of positive, you know? I mean, you could kinda see that it was a plus sign, but not by much. It looked more negative than positive, really. So I went to the walk-in clinic. The lab called to confirm the result right before I went in for the final audition."

"Holy shit! Not exactly the best timing."

"Who knows. I mean, maybe it helped. I'm supposed to be playing somebody who's coming apart at the seams. The truth is, I barely remember what happened between when I got the call and when I got home and had my mini-breakdown."

Ah, so that's what it was really about. She did a good job of covering up. No wonder she got the part.

"Why didn't you tell me?" I ask, scooping her hand into mine.

"Well, you know we had that stupid dinner and then Fermina blabbed that the store was closing and everything seemed to be going to hell. God, I even had champagne! What was I thinking? I'm a terrible person!"

"You're not a terrible person. You're a kickass person. You're just under a lot of stress."

She takes a few deep breaths and manages to get herself under control. "I think we can both agree that this isn't a great time for me to be pregnant. I mean, I'm starting this job and you're about to lose yours and who knows what'll happen after that."

"'Who knows what'll happen'?" I say. "What d'you mean?" It's a sentence that sounds overtly threatening in the same way that a naked man walking up your driveway with a rifle is threatening. Is she suggesting that we…egad…break up? How can you suddenly go from munching sweet potato fries to the end of the civilized world as you know it?

"With my career," she says. "I mean, things are just starting to take off. I can't just suddenly drop out for a year."

"So what do you want to do? I'm not running off anywhere. I mean, I have to check that my passport is still valid and then I'll be on the first flight to Bolivia, but in the meantime I'm here with you all the way."

"God, we were so stupid," she says, shaking her head. "All that unprotected sex. What on earth made me think that I wouldn't get pregnant?"

"Don't blame yourself. The videos you watched in Grade 8 health were probably just as bad as the ones I saw. They didn't show anything.

Two stick figures would be standing next to each other. Sperm would come out of one and sail all the way across the screen into a uterus diagram on the other side. No intercourse, no erections, nothing. Until I was about 15, I thought those no-see-ums you swat at in summer were renegade sperm that got lost on the trip to the fallopian tubes. They gave the impression that women could be spontaneously impregnated when standing forty feet away on a subway platform. Religion made a lot less sense when I found out how things really worked. You know, in terms of the immaculate conception."

"I can't do anything about it until after the shoot is over," she says. "The schedule is just too tight. Thanks to the commercial and the show, I can get on the actor's union medical plan. I think you can get on there too once we're married."

"Just a random question, but your father doesn't own any firearms, does he?"

She smiles for the first time in ages. "No. Old George went to one of those places in Vegas where you can shoot an AK-47 last year. He took the safety off before they told him to and shot himself in the foot. I don't think you need to worry."

"And let's be honest, what are the odds of two completely different people trying to shoot me in the nuts in the same year?"

"You?" she says. "Probably one in five."

"Thanks, babe."

"Hey, I thought about it myself when I saw that little plus sign, believe me. But it is only partly your fault, you horny little bastard."

"So what do you want to do?"

"I'll go to a clinic as soon as the shoot is done. Are you okay with that?"

I get the distinct impression that it doesn't really matter whether I am or not. This decision has already been made. And it's not entirely – or at all – mine to make. Still, it's one thing to deal with it in the abstract and quite another to consider the possibility that there are, technically, three of us at the table. It's not quite the difference between reading about a shooting in the paper and actually being the one shot, but it's not far off. My bystanding days are over.

"I am okay with that."

"Are you sure?" Leah asks. "We never really talked about kids. I'd like to have them...it's just...now's not a good time."

"I understand." Now doesn't seem to be a good time for anyone.

# -27-

Leah's last day at the store is an emotional one. She was hoping to finish her morning shift and sneak out the door, but the rest of the staff won't have it. Mother Teresa bakes a cake designed to look like a film reel, with "Good Luck!" written across the front, and everyone who can manage it gathers in the break room to see her off.

The rest of the staff chip in and buy a replica Oscar with a plaque that reads: "Best Performance By An Actress In A Management Role". After hours of stalwartly holding it together, she breaks down and begins to sob uncontrollably when it's time to say goodbye.

"There there, my dear," Ebeneezer says, allowing himself to be pulled into a hug. "Shed no tears for us. We shall endure, as always, in whatever form endurance takes."

Willard is less eloquent.

"If you really are the new catwoman, I want you to steal a piece of the batmobile. Like a mirror or something. That fuckin' thing's cool."

Aldous in particular is taking her departure very hard. He's spent the last five days following her around like a puppy that knows it's going to be driven out into the country and abandoned in the woods. Leah and I have spent the entire week going over procedures with him. Tomorrow will be his first attempt at opening the store on his own. I am fully expecting a phone call tomorrow morning at seven thirty from the security company to advise that someone has broken into the store because he has forgotten to deactivate the alarm.

"Don't worry, Aldous," Leah says, wiping her cheeks. "We're going to stay in touch. I can't wait to meet Simone."

"They're showing *Berlin Alexanderplatz* as an all-day marathon screening at the Prestige next weekend," Aldous says. "Simone's very excited about it. I'm sure she'd love it if you came along with us."

Leah smiles. "That's very considerate, but my shooting schedule's going to be pretty demanding. Don't worry, though. We'll work something out."

I breathe a mental sigh of relief. Fifteen and a half hours of Fassbender is a bit much to take, especially when accompanied by fifteen and a half hours of Swinghammer commentary. Aldous is one of those people who cannot shut up during a movie. He doesn't yell at the screen or anything like that, but if an idea enters his head, he will lean over and whisper it to whoever is unfortunate enough to be sitting next to him. I know this because I once had to listen to him expound at length about what he called "the negation of the self" during the chase through the subconscious sequence in *Eternal Sunshine of the Spotless Mind.*

Listening to him drone on made me think that someone should invent a slightly milder form of pepper spray that can be used to ward off social intrusions. Not enough to blind the perpetrator, perhaps, but enough to make them shut the fuck up and watch the damn movie.

After she says the last of her goodbyes, we head back to the apartment for a quick shower and change of clothes before heading to Enrico's for dinner.

"So how does it feel?" I ask once we're ensconced in my favourite table near the fireplace.

"Pretty good," she says, letting out a big sigh. "Scary, too. But it's an excited kind of scary. I'll miss those guys."

"Not Lolita so much. Or Mother Teresa."

"Mother Teresa and I got along pretty well, all things considered. She's like a crazy relative. You just have to know what topics of conversation to avoid and you'll be fine. But yeah, Lolita is a socially retarded nutcase. Now that I am no longer her manager, I can say that out loud."

"Hell, I still am her manager and I've said far worse."

"And how long do you plan to stay that way?" Leah asks.

"What do you mean?"

"I mean, even if the store doesn't close down, you need to start thinking about what you want to do next."

Uh oh. This is coming out of the blue. I thought tonight would be a relatively relaxed chance for us to reminisce about the fun times we had at the store while avoiding the pregnant elephant in the room, the fate of which has already been discussed and decided. I didn't suspect that the spotlight was going to be spun around on me. I begin mentally recalling troops from weekend furloughs to shore up my abandoned defences.

"Do next?"

"I feel kind of guilty, actually," Leah says. "There I was spending all that time trying to help Ebby and Aldous. I never realized that the one I should have been helping was you."

"I need help?"

"Not like them, no. But I read your book, you know. It's good. Have you sent it to anybody since that last publisher couldn't do it?"

"You read it?" I'm surprised. I don't recall ever seeing her crack it open.

"I needed something to occupy my mind with on those nights I couldn't sleep because I had an audition the next day. Especially since I'd already gone through whatever scene I was working on a million times. You were snoring."

"I snore?"

She smiles. "Only when you lie flat on your back. If I give you the elbow, you usually roll over on your side."

"Sorry about that. I had no idea."

"It's not like you can help it. But don't change the subject."

"Well, I'm glad it didn't put you to sleep. Or did it?"

The waiter comes and asks if we're ready to order. I get the *chicken parmigiana* and Leah orders *veal scaloppini*. She's still avoiding alcohol, so I order a single glass of the reserve Chianti while she settles for a mineral water.

"No," she says. "I actually stayed up late to finish it the other night because I wanted to know how it ended. You even left it open for a sequel, I see. That was smart."

I'm glad she seems to have genuinely liked it. Asking friends to read something you've written can be awkward in the extreme. The only opinions that are worth anything are the honest ones, but sometimes an excess of honesty can be the end of a friendship. I always tell people to be merciless, but few of them are willing to risk it.

"Thanks," I say. "It wasn't intentional. I just liked the characters and thought it might be fun to write more about them."

"So now you've got this thing to sell. What's your plan to sell it?"

I shrug. "I don't know. I hate the whole marketing side of things. I'm also terrible at it."

She takes a sip of her water. "Well, suck it up, boyo. You think I enjoy trooping all over the place for auditions? I hate them. They're terrible. You go in competing with a thousand other people for ten seconds of airtime and mostly you don't even know you don't have a chance in hell because you're a redhead or you don't weigh a hundred pounds or the director's already picked his girlfriend and is only going through the motions for the producer. Selling yourself is always difficult. You have to start with the belief that you've got something worth selling, which is not as easy as it sounds."

No wonder so many performers crack up, I think. You have to have a unique combination of insecurity and ego to make it work. Insecurity creates the need to be lavished with attention and ego makes you believe you deserve it. If the combination tilts even slightly out of balance, you can end up with a personal assistant covered in panda guts.

I've never seen any evidence of that with Leah, though. Yes, she's more emotional than me (the last time I cried was when Barça won the Champion's League trophy), but she's also more grounded and practical. Or maybe I just haven't known her long enough to see her Norma Desmond side come out yet.

As a side note, however, if I should ever be found floating face down in a swimming pool, I would like a full coroner's inquest into the event.

"Wow," I say. "I didn't know you hated them that much."

"They're terrible because they're so personal. Sorry, you're too short. Sorry, too tall. Sorry, your face doesn't have the angular quality we're looking for–"

"What!" I stand up from my chair. "Point me in the direction of the nematode responsible for these words and I will turn his face into a cubist masterpiece!"

"Sit down!" she says, looking around embarrassed. "My point is you can't take it personally. You shrug it off and move on to the next one."

I sit down. "Thanks for the pep talk, coach. Now what do you suggest?"

"Start going after the agents and publishers again. You got their attention before, you can do it again. If not, you could always turn it into a screenplay. I know people who know people."

"Like Jeremy?"

"I know you don't like him, which is funny because you've never even met the guy. The thing is, he's exactly the kind of person you need. He can make things happen. He doesn't sit on his ass and wait for people to come to him."

This is starting to feel more like an attack than I was prepared for and I find myself getting defensive. "Am I sitting on my ass?" I look down at my chair. "I mean, yes, right now I am. I do that in restaurants because I dislike eating standing up, but–"

"Don't be a smartass. You know what I mean."

My wine arrives and I take a sip. I can tell that the bottle has been open for several hours – possibly even a couple of days – and it's a little stale. "Hang on a sec. Are we fighting?"

Leah holds up her hands in mock surrender. "No. You've been fantastic over the last few weeks. You know, covering my shifts at work and taking care of stuff around the apartment and putting up with my rehearsals and general craziness."

"Thanks." I put my wine glass down and consider saying something to the waiter, but decide against it. I like this place. I don't want to develop a reputation as a guy who complains. So the wine is a little flat. At least it's not corked. That is something I couldn't ignore.

"I'm just saying that I don't want to see you stall out, that's all."

I tap my finger on the stem of the glass. It's not genuine crystal, so it makes a dull gong instead of a satisfying and resonant ding. "Do you think I've stalled out?"

Why am I arguing with her on this point? I know I've stalled out. I'm arguing because she's hitting my contrarian joint with her little hammer and I'm flexing involuntarily.

"How long do you think you'd keep working for Village Books if it doesn't close down? Another year? Two? Ten? Do you feel like you've accomplished something in the last three years that would make another ten years of it worthwhile?"

"Jesus, that's a little harsh."

"Sorry," she says, rubbing her forehead. "I didn't mean for it to come out sounding like that."

"Okay. Why don't you try it again with the slightly less soul-destr oying version?"

She lets out a groan of frustration. "Gahh! I wish I could have a glass of wine right now."

"Why aren't you having one?" I ask. "Under the circumstances..."

She takes a deep breath and stares at the tablecloth. "I would, but...I haven't...entirely...made up my mind about certain things yet."

I don't know what to say to this, so I just have another gulp of my blunt Chianti. "Uhhhh..."

"You know what? Can we leave that whole...issue...to one side for now?"

"Sure."

"What I'm saying, or trying to say, and obviously doing a terrible job, is that I really love you and I don't want to see you toiling away in a place like Village Books for the rest of your life. You're better than that. Way better than that. I don't care what you do so long as you care about what you do. I don't care if you become a famous writer or a famous...I don't know...auto mechanic. Whatever. Doesn't matter. I just don't want you to turn into one of those sad middle-aged guys who looks back on his life and thinks: *Shit, what a waste of time*. Does that make any sense?"

I smile. "It makes perfect sense. That really is a much nicer version. In fact, it might be the nicest thing anyone's ever said to me."

I move the candle aside so we don't burn ourselves and we kiss across the table. No sooner do we disengage than the food arrives. The waiter asks if we have everything we need and I decide now is as good a time as any to take the initiative.

"Actually, this Chianti is quite flat. Has the bottle been open for a while?"

The waiter apologizes profusely and whisks my glass away to bring me another. Leah gives me an appraising look.

"Well, I can see my little pep talk had some of the intended effect."

"Hey, it's just a glass of wine, but I might as well get my money's worth. Of course, I'm sure he's probably in the back room spitting in it as we speak. Or worse."

She looks around the room wistfully. "This is gonna be our last chance to do something like this for a while. Starting tomorrow, things are going to be pretty crazy for me. I have to be down there for hair and makeup at six. Shooting runs for pretty much twelve hours. I'll be so exhausted when I get home that I won't have time to do much more than collapse into bed."

"Any chance I can come down and visit you on the set?"

"I don't see why not. Let me talk to the director or first AD tomorrow and figure out the best time."

"Maybe when I drop you off or pick you up. But then I wouldn't get the chance to see you in action."

"Mmmm," she says, taking a bite of her dinner. "You don't have to. I actually get my own union driver for the duration of the shoot."

"A real live teamster?" I look suitably impressed. "Somebody who might actually know where Jimmy Hoffa is buried?"

"Her name is Millicent and I think she's about 18 years old," Leah says. "So odds are she's never even heard of James Riddle Hoffa."

"Millicent isn't really a teamster name. Do you think she'd mind if I call her Rocky? Or Knuckles?"

"She might not, but I would," Leah says. "Not that it matters. She's only allowed to drive production staff, so you'll have to get to and from the studio on your own. Something to do with insurance."

"Will you at least ask if she knows the name of the guy on the grassy knoll? Mickey is convinced that it was Tito Puente."

Leah just rolls her eyes and shakes her head. In the meantime, my replacement glass of Chianti arrives.

"Better?" Leah asks.

I sip. "Better."

# -28-

It doesn't take long for word to leak out that the store is closing. I'm not sure who the source of the leak is, but it could have been anyone. Despite what Dante thinks, there really is no way to keep something like this quiet and keep the store running normally.

The first giveaway is at the special orders desk. Customers can't prepay for anything that might take more than a few weeks to come in because the store might not be open when their delivery finally arrives. This means Dante has had to put a moratorium on all special orders. It's impossible to do something like that without raising some eyebrows, particularly amongst our most ardent group of long-term customers (the ones who order through us instead of going through an online source) and questions get asked. Answers are provided in hushed voices. Outrage gains volume.

Dante should have realized that there was no way he was ever going to be able to keep a lid on this, but with his mother still in hospital and not doing very well, he's not as focused on our predicament as he normally would be. Lucretia developed bacterial pneumonia a couple of days ago. That was followed by a dangerous drop in blood pressure and then a staph infection. She's been running a fever of 102 and has been on and off a respirator for the last 48 hours. The cancer is spreading aggressively, but she's far too weak for chemotherapy. The doctors say it may be a matter of hours, not days. Dante is a mess.

With Leah gone, Mina prepping for her husband's pretrial hearing and Aldous in training, I'm left trying to hold everything together. It's not a role I feel supremely qualified for.

It's been three days since Leah started work on the TV show. She's up at five every morning and out the door by six, when her driver shows up out front in a shiny blue Camry (no limo, alas). I got up the first morning to make her breakfast, but she told me not to worry because the craft department puts out a huge spread for the cast. I gave her a kiss good luck and watched her head out the door with the strange feeling that I was never going to see her again.

I did, but not much. She got home at nine that night, exhausted but happy. The cast and crew were very nice, she said. The only exception was Callum Guthrie, who spent all of his down time in his trailer and yelled at a couple of grips who were moving equipment while he was trying to "meditate in the bathroom," which is set code for his habit of stripping naked, drinking an entire case of Red Bull and playing an online Japanese multiplayer game called *Ninja Hokkaido Entrails Explosion*. A scheduling problem meant that the next day's work would be a night shoot, so she was off all day and left to start at five, which was right before I got home.

Today she's off in the morning and starts work at noon. She said she probably wouldn't be back until after ten, maybe later.

The apartment is so quiet that it's almost like being single again. Last night I was so badly in need of something to take my mind off things that I went to see *The Royal Tenenbaums* at the Prestige. It's my favourite movie and I have it on DVD, but I needed an excuse to get out of the house. Sebastian said he was going to try and sneak out to see it with me, but his mother came home unexpectedly from an out-of-town board meeting and he couldn't escape.

On top of that, Leah said that her role has been expanded slightly. I guess she made quite the positive impression on the director and now it looks like she might be there for four weeks instead of three. I tried my best to sound excited about this, but my heart wasn't really in it. I'm a shambling husk of a man after three days, so there's no telling what's going to be left of me after three weeks, let alone a month. Fortunately, I think she was too tired to notice.

The first phone call from a newspaper comes in at ten on Wednesday morning. Mother Teresa takes the call out on the floor and doesn't know what to do with it, so she puts them on hold and comes to find me in the manager's office, where I'm in the middle of finishing up the last of Ivanka's HR paperwork. Thursday is her last day. We need somebody else who can take over magazines. It's a complicated department involving a lot of manual paperwork dealing with predetermined sell-through rates and a Byzantine returns process. Dante thinks we should give it to Sebastian in the short term, but that will leave me one short on the floor. The only other person with any experience in the department is Willard, but he's up to the tip of his green hair in returns. We really need to do some hiring, but there isn't much point until the fate of the store is decided.

The reporter is remarkably well-informed. She knows about Cynthia's coma, Marty's dementia, Maude's little end-run and Umex's 30-day condition on the deal. Umex has not been very popular in the media of late since it turns out they own a waste disposal facility in Honduras that pumps toxic sludge directly into a nearby river. Leukemia rates in the town three miles downstream are 400 per cent higher than the general population, but the company is denying any knowledge or responsibility.

"Would you care to comment on the potential sale?" she asks.

I open my mouth and then slam it shut again. Having trained as a journalist, I know enough to think before I speak to one. Words, especially angry ones, have a tendency to look a lot worse in print, particularly when presented as a 48-point pull quote on the front page. I'm torn between two instincts. My loyalty to Dante and the store tells me to shut up. The angry young man who hates wearing blue and brown and working for the clampdown is screaming at me to open up with both barrels. The paper's only loyalty is to the story, and this one is a made-to-measure David and Goliath job with soap opera overtones. With Umex already in the news, it's guaranteed to go above the fold.

If I say what I'm really thinking then Maude will fire me for sure and Dante will be down two managers in almost as many days. If I don't say what I'm thinking, then my head is going to explode. The easiest thing to do would be to hang up the phone and pretend the call never came in, but that won't be the end of it. More calls will come. This is just the beginning.

So what do I do?

Fuck it. What Maude is doing is wrong. Her parents spent their lives building up this business and now she's swooping in like some hellish valkyrie to sell it all out from under them at the first opportunity. Despite what Dante says, I don't think Cynthia would want us to just stand back and let it happen.

I take a deep breath. "You appreciate that you would have to quote me anonymously?" There's no point in saying *off the record*. Everything I say can be quoted. I just don't want my name attached to it. Yet.

"Are you afraid you'd lose your job if you spoke about it?"

*You're fucking-A right I'd lose my job*, I think, but that's only part of it. I have selfish reasons, as well. If my words were directly or indirectly responsible for imploding the deal, that would make Umex extremely unhappy. Umex owns a lot of bookstores (215 at last count). No publisher is terribly keen to sign an author who can't get distributed in 75 per cent of a national market.

"Are we agreed?" I say.

"You're the one who was shot, right?" she asks.

"Okay, I'm hanging up now."

"No wait!" she says. "I'll list you as 'a manager who asked not to have his name printed'. Does that satisfy you?"

She sounds like she's all of 18 years old. Having worked as an intern, I know what it's like to be handed stories like this. That doesn't mean, however, that I am remotely sympathetic.

"No. We're not exactly Microsoft. We don't have a thousand managers. You quote me as an unnamed employee."

A sigh. Like *I'm* being an uncooperative pain in the ass. I toy with the idea of telling her that we record all incoming calls for security and training purposes, but she'll know that's bullshit. Even if she doesn't call me on it, what would be the point? "Fine. So what do you think of the sale?"

I take a moment to think about exactly how I'm going to phrase this. What I am about to say is, sadly, going to be more widely read and distributed than any of the things I've spent hours cobbling together in front a of computer screen. Words may be deleted and re-arranged to make it sound more punchy. I need to get it exactly right.

"I think if Maude Ackerman wishes to sell the store that her parents have spent their lives building only moments after assuming control, then that is entirely her legal prerogative."

"Huh." This isn't entirely the answer she was looking for. She's looking for another angry serf raging impotently at greedy corporate America. I know that's what I'd be looking for if I were in her shoes. "But doesn't it make you mad?"

"Why should it make me mad? I'm not the legal owner. The legal owner is in a coma and unavailable for comment."

She's not giving up that easy. "But what about Umex? Do you think they just want the location for their next Iterations?"

"I'm not on their board, so I have no idea what their plans are," I say. "Perhaps they'll open another waste treatment facility like the one near Yoro."

"Are you serious?"

"If they started pumping toxic waste right out onto Bloor street instead of into a river seven thousand miles away, people might pay more attention, don't you think?"

She switches tack. "Village Books has been there for over 30 years. Do you think this marks the end of an era?"

"Maybe it's the start of a new one. People seem to like uniformity. If they build another Iterations here, I'm sure it'll look exactly the same as the one in Vancouver or Montreal or Islamabad. Isn't that really the ultimate aim? To turn the whole world on to free market democracy by converting every last square inch of living space into Disneyland?"

"Is that what you think is happening?"

"Who am I to say? But if you can think of any significant difference between capitalism and feudalism, I'd love to hear it. It's like Lenin said: you look for the person who will benefit. And we're still fucking peasants as far as I can see."

And, with nothing else to say, I lean forward and hang up.

"Well spoken, my boy."

I spin in my seat and am surprised to see that Ebeneezer has managed to sneak into the office without my realizing it. I shake my head. I lost my cool and am genuinely annoyed with myself. But also exhilarated. "I shouldn't have done it."

"Nonsense. You may be tilting at windmills, but it makes the cause no less just."

"Leah told me I should get off my ass and become more of a master of my own destiny. I may have just done a masterful job of getting us all fired. As soon as Maude reads that, I'm sure she'll come storming straight down here and throw us all out on to the street."

"Do you think there is any possible appeal to the younger Ackerman's reason or decency that would alter that outcome?"

I laugh.

"Precisely. I have known Maude since she was ten years old. Even then she was of a singularly acquisitive and self-interested bent. Her brother did not share her ravenous instincts and was relegated to the cellar, where he softened his mind with electronic distractions and his form with processed food."

It's true. The last time Walter set foot in the store, he had trouble getting through the front door. He comes here instead of getting his game guides online because he has to pay for them online. Dante long ago worked out an arrangement with Cynthia to keep track of what he takes and reimburse the till. I doubt that Maude or Iterations will be quite so tolerant.

"Ah well," I say. "I suppose it doesn't matter. So one more bookstore closes down. We're not the first. We won't be the last."

Ebeneezer purses his lips like he's about to say something, then reconsiders and changes the topic.

"And how is our young Miss Dashwood enjoying her time on the set of *Royal Target*?"

"Quite a lot, I think. I've probably only seen her for a combined ten minutes over the last three days, so it's hard to tell."

Ebeneezer nods sympathetically. "My wife, Viola, was a member of a local theatre company for many years," he says. "She gained a certain amount of renown. In fact, her performance of Nora in *A Doll's House* was once singled out for praise by the drama critic of the *Star*."

I raise my eyebrows as much in surprise as a desire to seem impressed. This is the first time I have ever heard Ebeneezer talk about his wife. In fact, until now, I didn't even know her name.

"Wow," I say. "Did she do a lot of work on stage or television?"

"Well, television work wasn't as common back then, of course. But the stage productions did keep her extremely busy. And when she wasn't on stage, she was preparing to be. She was offered a film role. Not a starring one, naturally, but promising. I believe she was going to be playing the wife of a fellow who steals a great deal of money from an insurance company or some such thing. It was during the physical exam, which, ironically enough, I understand they do for insurance purposes, that they found the tumour."

"God, I'm sorry."

"I missed many of her performances. I confess that in my younger days I believed performing to be something of a frivolous occupation. I regret that now more than anything."

"I've never seen Leah perform," I say. "I've seen her rehearse, you know, at home. For her auditions and stuff. But it's not the same thing. She had to drop out of the theatre group when she got the TV job. Although her agent did call to say that her commercial is supposed to start airing on the weekend."

Ebeneezer looks around the office, which is a mess of returns reports, resumes, paperwork and Dante's quick-reference printouts from WebMD. He reaches out and picks up an old advanced reading copy of *Barney's Version*. Publishers used to send these out to boost awareness of upcoming titles. They're compiled from galley proofs, often printed with spelling and formatting mistakes intact. Few publishers bother to send them out anymore because it's much cheaper and easier to send out an electronic version. Or do nothing.

"I have spent much of my life dealing with stories," Ebeneezer says. "Both teaching them and selling them. At times, I can succumb to the belief that my life has become intertwined with them. But life is not a story. It's not some vulgar mystery to be solved or a happy-ever-after romance or some fantasy adventure involving fairies and monsters in high castles."

"It certainly isn't genre fiction," I agree. "Unless you start the day with Kenneth Graham and then get off at the wrong subway stop and wander into Philip K. Dick. Or, God forbid, Clive Barker."

"Stories are dangerous," he says. "They can turn us into lifelong spectators. We spend all of our time looking for fictions. They trick us into relinquishing responsibility for our own narrative."

What the hell is he talking about? He's staring off into space. Miles away. Does he regret working here? Or spending all those years as a teacher? Or just missing a few performances of *The Cherry Orchard*? I have no idea.

"Well, as long as I'm opening my mouth without thought to the consequences, would you like my opinion on the matter?" I ask.

He returns from the netherworld of his thoughts. "Hmmm? Oh, indeed."

"Go get her."

His cheeks flush and he looks totally flummoxed. "What? Er, I..uh–"

And with nothing more to say, I get up and make my exit.

# -29-

After work, I head straight over to Falstaff's. Mickey is sitting behind the bar playing with his new iPad. I assume he's using it to watch the Donegal Salach Liathroid Ciceals, but he is in fact reading the newspaper.

"Well if it isn't deep throat hisself!" he says as I sit down at the bar and order a pint of Scrumpy.

"What are you talking about?"

He tries spinning the tablet around so that I can read the screen, but the screen stubbornly re-orients itself, so I'm forced to pick it up to see what it says: *Umex Swoops To Swallow Competition.*

Oh shit.

I scan the article quickly. My comments appear in paragraph nine. Jesus, did I really say all that? Umex and Maude had no comment. A few people described as "longtime customers" describe Umex as "vultures" and their conduct as "so far beneath contempt it's fossilized." Interestingly, two other unnamed employees are quoted. One calls the sale "a total (expletive deleted) screw job" (probably Willard) and the other refers to Umex as "an opportunistic collection of unprincipled carpetbaggers" (either Sebastian or Ebeneezer).

Oh well. So much for containment.

Mickey hands me the Scrumpy. "That's on the house."

"Uh, for what?"

Mickey waves dismissively. "We Irish have been standin' up to the fookin' man since the dawn of time. Tonight, boyo, you are an honorary Irishman."

I take a sip. "Thanks, Mickey. It's a good thing you're giving this to me for free. I probably won't be able to afford it much longer."

"We have a sayin' where I come from," he says. "It's better to get yer ass kicked in a fight than bit by a gorilla runnin' the other way."

"They have gorillas where you're from?"

"Truly I am a citizen of the world," he says. "Over here, I believe you call 'em Englishmen. Where is yer good lady this eve?"

"She's in the distillery district shooting a show called *Royal Target*."

His eyes widen. "Is that about some plot to kill the queen?"

"No, the prime minister. You know, now that you mention it, the title is kind of weird."

"Ah, and there I was gettin' all excited. She's a fine lass, ye know. Leah, not the queen. The queen can shove a polo mallet far enough up her arse to bugger Prince Philip with the handle."

"I know. I'm a lucky man." Who doesn't see her very much.

"She was in here just last night an' all."

What? "What?"

"Yeah," he says, taking the iPad back so he can continue reading. "With some blond fella in a suit. They were sittin' at tha' table in the corner there."

What the hell? Who could that be? Jeremy? I've never met him and have no idea what he looks like. What I do know is that she was supposed to be working on a night shoot yesterday. If she was in here, then she most certainly was not working on a night shoot.

"When?"

Mickey thinks for a moment. "Ah let's see. Woulda been just before we closed, sure."

Falstaff's usually closes at two, but on slow nights it often closes at one. "Did you close early last night?"

Mickey shakes his head. "Nah. We were open later'n usual, tell the truth. The boys were playin' Limerick."

"Huh." Calm, calm, calm, calm.

"She just had a water. He ordered some daft martini nobody'd ever heard of. I gave 'im an Englishman's Tits."

An Englishman's Tits is a sherry and water with a beetroot cube and two olives. It's what Mickey serves to anyone who tries to order a drink that is not listed on the menu. Although I've never had one, I can vouch for the fact that they are as horrible as they sound. Sebastian once drank fourteen of them in a row and spent the rest of the evening barfing in my toilet. The only thing worse is an Englishman's Balls, and you don't want to know what goes in that. Mickey says he's saving it for the day Dermot Gleeson sets foot in the place.

"Any idea what they were talking about?" I say, trying to sound nonchalant.

"Nah," Mickey says. "We were watchin' the game, see? They didn't stay long."

Leah made no mention of going out for drinks at two in the morning with a blond guy in a suit. I can't bear to bring myself to ask Mickey any more questions. It's too embarrassing. What to do? Fuck! First the store and now this?

I reach into my pocket and pull out my cell phone. Leah specifically told me not to call her while she's working. Nothing is more disruptive or embarrassing for an actor on set than if their phone goes off in the middle of a take and she sometimes forgets to turn it off. Is this worth breaking the phone rule? I have a flip phone, so it's not like I can claim to have pocket dialled her by accident. *Oh, and while I have you on the line, who was the blond guy you were out with last night?*

I flip it open. The battery is dead. Of course. Despite the fact that I never use the damn thing, the battery is dead. I never use it, so I never charge it. Therefore, I never use it. I think the last time I used it was on the night Mina's crazy husband shot me. Have I charged it since then? Evidently not. To be honest, I don't even think I know where the charger is.

I stuff the phone back in my pocket. Okay. Deep breath. Is everything Leah and I have managed to create over the last few months really so fragile that a few innocuous words from a saloon owner can trash it? Think it through. If she was...arrgh...*cheating*...would she really do it in a place where we both go all the time and everyone on staff knows her? That would be pretty stupid, and Leah is certainly not stupid.

But she did dump Grover pretty fast, didn't she? That might indicate that she doesn't feel too rough about tossing guys aside when she's through with them. And we did just have a sort of fight about the fact that her acting career was taking off and my career was going nowhere. Who is this guy? Some hotshot director or actor or something? Who wears a suit to a pub? Mickey was suspicious enough that he served the guy the second crappiest drink in the house. That should say something right there.

But wait. She's pregnant. And she's thinking about keeping it. She wouldn't go running out with some other guy in that situation, now would she?

No sooner have I laid this trump card down on my argument than another little voice pipes up from the back row.

*Yeah, unless it's not yours.*

Okay, we have just blown all circuits. This gives me time not to think while I run into the basement, throw the master and wait for the lights to start coming back on.

This is ridiculous. I do not believe that Leah is cheating on me. Isn't. Wouldn't. No way. Uh uh. I will simply wait until she comes home tonight and then sort of slip it casually into conversation. *'Oh yeah, Mickey said you stopped by Falstaff's last night with some guy in a suit?'* Then I'll see what she says. I am positive that there is a logical, rational explanation. So rational, in fact, that we'll laugh about how silly it was for me to be suspicious in the first place.

I may doubt many things – myself, my ability to drive standard, that TFC will ever make the playoffs – but I don't doubt Leah. I flat out refuse. I am not going to be that guy.

Convinced, at least for now, I sit up a little straighter and take another sip of my cider. Someone taps me on the shoulder and I turn around to see Dante.

"Maude called me."

"Hi Dante. What'd she say? Or do I need to ask? Should I bring the gasoline and you bring the matches?"

Dante sits down and motions to Mickey, who draws him a Dead Joe's Cask Ale. "I told her I had no idea who had talked to the media. She demanded I find out and fire them. She said if I didn't find them, then she'd fire me."

"Nice. I think I have my key here in my pocket."

"I told her to go to hell," he says, smiling.

"Good for you. How's your mom?"

"Better. She's off the ventilator and her temperature's back to normal. They might move her out of the ICU tomorrow."

"Well that's good news. What brings you in here? Just needed a break?"

Dante takes a long drag of his ale. "I wish. I'm supposed to be meeting some woman."

"You're kidding!" I say. "The woman's in the ICU and she's still setting you up on dates?"

"You don't understand," Dante says. His eyes are hollow and his skin looks like wet cardboard. He is not exactly the charming and lively picture of vivaciousness one might expect from a person going out on a blind date.

"She believes she's on her deathbed. She very well may be. It is her dying wish that she see me settled down before she goes."

There's irony in this. For all these years, Dante has been using horrible, life-threatening illnesses as an excuse to get out of dates and now his mother is using the same thing to checkmate him into one. It is not an irony that I think he needs to have pointed out, however. At least, not at the moment.

"So who is it this time?"

He sighs. "Some woman named Jan. She's a history prof at York or something. Some daughter of friend of a friend of my aunt Constanzia."

"And you decided not to fake *lupine porphyria* to get out of it this time?" This was always my favourite of Dante's many excuses. I once called in sick with it and Dante never said a word. *Sorry, I can't come into work as I have just turned into an extremely feral and hairy wolfman.*

"No. She might not have a lot of time left. If I can give her even five minutes of happiness before she goes, then mission accomplished."

I think Dante may see Lucretia live long enough for him to regret that sentiment, but there's no point in trying to talk him out of it. Time for a topic change.

"So you're saying I'm not fired, then?"

Dante smiles. "I knew the main quote was you. I told you to keep a lid on it, but I knew it would get out sooner or later."

"The other quotes probably came from Willard and I think either Sebastian or possibly Ebeneezer. I didn't do any TV or radio. Kinda hard to stay anonymous when your face is plastered on a giant news feed in Yonge-Dundas square. And that voice alteration technique they use is so lame. Everyone sounds like ED-209 from *Robocop*."

"That thing was pretty badass," Dante observes. "I don't think it would worry too much about being recognized by its employer."

"True."

"I stopped in to see Cynthia, too," Dante says. "No change. Doctors say she could stay exactly like that for the next twenty years or she could wake up tomorrow. I'll tell you one thing, though. No sooner had I sat down next to the bed than she opened her eyes."

"I've heard that coma patients sometimes do that."

"Well I had no idea," Dante says. "I nearly shit my pants! I jumped outta the goddamn chair so fast I practically went into orbit!"

I laugh. "Be careful you don't injure yourself, boss. We don't need any more staff in comas than we already got. Managers are dropping faster than RIM share prices around here."

"My cousin said he made a fortune short-selling his shares in that. I've never understood how you can make money on something when its value goes down."

"You borrow the stock and sell it when it's high," I explain. "Then you buy it back three months later for less and pocket the difference. Of course, if the price goes up in that time, you're fucked. It's what the villain was trying to do in *Casino Royale*."

Dante shrugs to indicate that he still doesn't get it. "Anyway, I yelled so loud that half the staff ran in. It was like they called one of those code blues like they do on TV. It was a tad embarrassing, let me tell you."

"I can imagine."

Dante takes another chug of his beer. "It's tough enough visiting somebody in the hospital, but when they're not conscious, it's even worse. You know, you just sort of sit there and look at monitors and equipment and wonder what the hell is going on. That was what it was like when I went to see my mother. Then one of the nurses comes in and tells me I should talk to her. Says she might be able to hear me and it might help her feel a little more comfortable, so I figure what the hell. I felt a little stupid at the beginning, especially with somebody else there. But after a while it wasn't so bad.

"So then when I got in to see Cynthia it was the same situation, right? I figure okay, same deal. I'll tell her what's going on with the store and the article that just appeared in the paper. Well, I'm in the process of explaining this – and keep in mind, her head is turned so that she's looking right at me – when her eyes open up. I pretty much had a total cardiac arrest. It just freaked me right the hell out."

"It'd be like the scene in that Stephen King short story where the kid's in the house with his dead grandmother and she comes to life and tries to take possession of his body," I say. "I think it was some sort of voodoo thing. I can't remember if he ever explains why the kid's in the house alone with a dead body. Who does that? But anyway, the kid calls his aunt – who's like a white magic priestess or something – and she tells him this incantation he needs to say to send the old woman back, but he keeps mispronouncing the words and she's getting closer and–"

"Stop!" Dante says. "You're giving me the willies and I'm already edgy enough. Does the kid say the right words?"

"No. He fucks it up and the old lady gets him. The kid wakes up the next day, but he's not really the kid anymore, if you know what I mean."

Dante shivers. "Yeesh. Why did I even ask?"

"That's not even one of his best!" I say. "Did I ever tell you the plot of *The Boogeyman*? There's this guy going to see a psychiatrist–"

"Enough!" Dante says. "I'd like to be able to get to sleep tonight without barricading the door and swallowing a handful of pills."

"Sorry. I forgot horror isn't really your thing. You prefer those doorstop historical fictionalizations of real people and stories about cave women screwing Neanderthals."

"Say what you will about them. At least they don't have any demon psychiatrist zombie grandmothers in them."

"And how is that a selling point?"

The two of us are interrupted by a third voice from behind. "Ahem. Excuse me, I don't wish to interrupt, but I believe you're Dante, aren't you?"

We turn in our chairs to see a short, skinny blond man in a blue dress shirt and brown slacks standing behind us with an expectantly optimistic look on his face. He appears to be in his late 20s to early 30s. He has green horn rimmed glasses and a short beard.

"I am," Dante says. "Can I help you?"

"I'm Jann Devries," the man says, holding out his hand. "Connie told me you would be meeting me here."

Dante just blinks. "Sorry?"

"Sorry," the man says, taking a step back. "Are you Dante Andolini?"

Dante nods vacantly. "Sorry...who..."

"I'm Jann," the man says, tapping his chest. "Uh, Connie Tomassini's daughter Julie said you'd be meeting me here?"

I can see the realization go off in Dante's head like a bomb. The problem is that it also destroys the part of his brain that he does his thinking with.

"Uhh..."

"I'm sorry, is this a bad time?" The man glances at me, evidently thinking that Dante may have been waiting so long that he already made a connection.

"Not at all," I say, sticking out my hand and introducing myself. "I work with Dante."

"Nice to meet you," says Jann. "I heard on the news that your store might be closing."

"Only if the forces of evil have their way."

"Well, I don't want to interrupt–"

"Probably better that you did," I say. "I don't think it's legal to plot to destroy the headquarters of a major multinational holding company, even if they deserve it."

Jann smiles weakly, evidently unsure if I am entirely kidding. "Heh. Yeah, right. Probably not. Well, look, I'm, uh, right over there…" he points to a table in the back corner "…so whenever you're ready…"

I look at Dante. His eyes are still somewhat glassy, but at least he seems to know where he is. "Oh I think we were done talking for now, right, Dante?"

Dante nods. "What? Right! Yes. Uh, why don't we..?"

Dante gets up and follows Jann over to the other side of the bar, almost forgetting to take his beer with him. Mickey ambles over after they leave, shaking his head in disbelief.

"Never thought I'd see the day," he says. "Miracle of miracles."

I don't believe in them, but I have to agree. It seems that Lucretia has finally seen the light before the one at the end of the tunnel.

# -30-

It isn't until the end of Leah's third week of shooting that I'm able to come down and watch them working on a scene. Having studied film and watched thousands of them, I like to think I've got a pretty good idea of what goes into a shoot, but it's the first time I've ever been on a real set and my first impression is that it's smaller and tackier than I imagined.

No wonder these things cost so much. There must be at least 200 people milling around on the soundstage, most of whom don't actually appear to be doing much of anything. Everything is built solely based on how it will look on camera, which is kind of like stepping into a house designed for a nearsighted one-eyed man. The walls are all plywood which has been painted to look alternately like stone, brick and stucco.

Huge backdrops hang from the rafters. I can see one that looks like night, one day, one rolling countryside, one of city skyscrapers, and one that looks like Whoville. The latter apparently belongs to a kids' show called *Neener's World*, which shot here up until the show was cancelled a few years ago. I guess they're hanging on to the backdrop in case Neener returns or *Royal Target* decides to do an LSD-themed episode, neither of which seems likely.

I have to stare at my feet as I walk because it's not terribly well lit on the part of the set the camera doesn't see and there are wires snaking all over the place. Either I stare at my feet and bump into people or watch where I'm going and trip over a wire that is probably attached to a three million dollar lighting rig more powerful than the sun, which will then crash to the ground and smash.

They are in the middle of shooting a scene where RCMP agents run down an alley after the suspect only to have him escape by tossing a grenade under a nearby car and blowing it up. The car will be blown up on a secured outdoor set tomorrow afternoon, which sucks because I was hoping to see a real fake movie explosion up close. Movie explosions always involve fireballs. I think this is because fireballs are visible (and surprisingly outrunnable, at least by A-list stars) in a way that concussive blasts of air and shrapnel are not.

Leah is in makeup. Being a guest star, she doesn't have a trailer of her own per se, but has to share a trailer with whoever else happens to be a featured guest star this week. I guess that's what you get with Canadian TV. On a spectacle scale, it's not exactly Michael Bay.

I'm trying to be inconspicuous as I watch the lighting crew set up some sort of flash effect designed to simulate the car blowing up. The director of photography is a skinny guy with stubbly short black hair who is wearing cargo shorts that appear to have approximately 1,000 pockets, each one of which has some sort of light meter, cable, tool, filter, or scrim roll sticking out of it.

It's easy to tell the crew apart from the actors because the actors don't look like they've been wearing the same clothes for the last three months. Most of the men have scraggy beards and the women large bags under their eyes. The life of a film & TV technician in Canada is not all peaches and gravy. When the work comes, which is rarely now that California is getting antsy about so-called runaway productions, it can be an intense, two- or three-month, around-the-clock grind followed by eight months of unemployment. Most end up packing it in to work other jobs or relocating down south. Of all the people I went to film school with, only one is still working in the business, provided you're willing to consider stuffing envelopes for Netflix part of the business.

Leah is supposed to accompany the RCMP detail down the alley only to be wounded in the blast (a broken arm and a small scrape on her cheek). The fact that she is injured is one of the keys to her brother's eventual capture. I know this because I read the script, a copy of which Leah brings home with her every night. It really does have different coloured pages for all the revisions, of which there have been a lot. I don't know how she keeps track of them. Most are minor dialogue tweaks, but in her second episode, they changed her from single to a married woman with two kids. The two kids, aged 8 and 6, were then included in a scene that had to be shot *the next day*. It's madness.

"Hey, you must be Leah's boyfriend!"

I turn to see a tall blond guy with a ridiculous spiky haircut and expensive-looking suit walking towards me effortlessly over the hazard-ridden floor. He's drinking a coffee with one hand and checking his phone with the other, all while paying absolutely no attention to where he's going. I'm having trouble just standing here and I have nothing in my hands.

This, of course, is Jeremy. He's the one Leah was sitting with that night at Falstaff's. Apparently, there was a delay in setting up for a nearby location shoot and the two of them stopped in to talk about some casting opportunity he's working on for her south of the border. Leah wouldn't elaborate on what it was, so it must be pretty big. I think it must be the Tarantino thing, but she's not saying a word. Which is odd, because she's not usually the superstitious type.

"Fiancé, actually."

He shakes my hand. Where the hell did his phone go? "Fiancé, right." I'd like to say that he's wearing too much cologne, but he's actually wearing just the right amount. He didn't miss any spots with his razor when he shaved this morning, like I did. His watch is the same one that gets lots of product placement in Bond movies. Bastard. I hate him.

"What d'you think of our little shoot?" he asks.

I'm not sure what to make of it now. If he describes it as 'little', I can hardly say it's impressive, can I? "Uh…"

"Leah's not gonna be doing stuff like this for very long," he says dismissively. The phone, I notice, has re-appeared, and he's typing away on it with his thumb as he talks. "She's got a real quality. Real star quality. We've got some big things lining up. This time next year they'll be talking about her in two, two-plus terms. Year after that, she'll be right up there in the fives."

Two? Two-plus? Five? What the hell is this guy talking about? Two…million? That doesn't seem possible. I feel like I'm talking to a Moroccan cab driver.

"So you work in a bookstore or something?"

I've never heard anyone talk so fast. How many coffees has he had? Is that a fake English accent I detect? Dammit, I wish I'd worn nicer clothes. "Uh, yes. That's correct."

"And Leah says you write. Any scripts?"

"No. Just a novel."

"Ha!" he laughs. "People still read those?"

Yes, you smarmy prick, they do. "Actually–"

He holds up a finger and raises the phone to his ear. I didn't hear it ring. "Jeremy Smithwhite."

Smithwhite? What the hell kind of a last name is that? It must be made up. This guy is a big phoney. His real last name is probably Assbutt or Ballclench or Cockstuff. And that is a fake English accent, I'm sure of it. This guy is about as British as Robert Downey Jr.

"Hello Juliet!" he practically shouts. "How is the world's loveliest and most talented casting director this afternoon? Did you get the file?"

One of the assistant lighting directors yells out that they're going to be testing the flash effect. A PA comes by and reminds us not to look directly at it. Jeremy disappears to have his meaningful conversation with Juliet elsewhere. There's a countdown and then a big flash that I forget not to look directly at. Apparently, it doesn't go exactly the way they want and they get back to work setting it up differently, which means that 98 of the 100 people I can see go back to standing around.

Jesus. William Goldman was right. Movie sets are bo-oring. I've seen baseball games that were more exciting than this. It blows my mind that Middle Americans call soccer boring when their national pastime is something as static as baseball. I don't think you should be allowed to classify anything as a sport if the players spend half the time sitting on their asses and the other half standing around waiting for something to happen. If you edited the average baseball game down to just the action, it would probably run about 35 seconds, which is probably roughly the same amount of screen time they'll get out of today's shoot.

"Hey babe!"

I turn around to see Leah made up for her upcoming scene and almost don't recognize her, partly because I'm still blind from the big flash.

"You're blonde!"

She looks up at her hair sheepishly. "Yeah. I was supposed to keep my original hair colour, but the director decided that blonde provided better contrast during the night scenes or something. This is a wig."

I can't really tell that it's a wig, but then my experience of wigs is limited to the one my uncle George wore after his divorce, when he went from being a sad bald man with a comb-over to a sad bald man with a marmot corpse on his head.

I lean in for a kiss and she pushes me back. "Sorry, hon. No smooching. They'd have to re-do my makeup."

"Okay. Wow! You look so glamorous! Is this the scene where you break your arm?"

"Yep. The after makeup is not quite as nice. One of the other officers gets killed, so I'm covered in a lot of fake blood. Urrggh! I hate that stuff!"

"One of them gets killed? That wasn't in the draft I read last night."

"No, they just changed it this morning. They think it'll goose the ratings a bit."

"Who's spraying you with his innards?"

"Joanne. She plays Officer Tessa Dominikos. I guess she's being a hardass about her contract renegotiation for next season, so the producers are just writing her out. She's pissed! So pissed that she's refusing to do the scene. One of the stuntguys is doing it in her place and they're re-blocking it so they shoot her from behind. If you see her coming, I recommend going the other way. Fast."

"Good to know." Some business. Not only do they fire you, they blow you up when you're not even there. "Did you say they're replacing her with a guy?"

Leah nods. "Our only stuntwoman is off with appendicitis. They'll fix it in post."

Fix it in post. That seems to be the industry answer to everything these days. Shame they can't apply that logic to giving me back the two hours of my life I lost watching Adam Sandler's last movie (in my defence, it was not my pick). "You just missed Jeremy. He was here a second ago."

"So you finally met!" she says. "Now you know I'm not making him up."

I just smile. If she made up a guy like that, I wouldn't believe her. "He was talking to some woman named Juliet. He sounded very excited."

Leah's expression changes immediately. It's a look that makes me feel like I just stepped into a room full of iron chef contestants with a 13-episode contract dangling from a tiny chain around my neck.

"Juliet! What did he say? Where did he go?"

"Uh, I'm not sure. Something about asking if she got the file he sent or something? I take it that this is about that thing you won't tell me about?"

Leah's head spins in every direction, but the elusive Jeremy is no longer in sight. "Damn!"

Another announcement goes out to advise that they're going to re-test the flash again. This time, everything seems to go according to plan and I remember not to look. The assistant director announces that they're finally ready to shoot.

"Okay, I gotta run," Leah says, blowing me a kiss. "I'll see you later!"

"Break a leg!" I say. "Or an arm, as the case may be."

I stick around to watch them shoot the scene. I'm too far away to be able to really see very much. I can see Leah and three people dressed as undercover RCMP officers (one of whom is a man wearing a woman's suit and wig, I assume to replace the departing Joanne) run into the fake alley set. Somebody yells, there's the now familiar flash, and everybody falls down. Then they do it three more times. Leah still has six more scenes to shoot and I have to get to the store because I'm scheduled to close tonight, so I say goodbye and head out the door.

Yesterday was the last day Café Olé was open and the windows are dark. I stopped in for my last hit of churros yesterday at noon, but they had already run out and weren't making any more. Tonight, Fermina flies back to Spain to open her new café in her hometown. Ebeneezer has said nothing since our little chat in the office and has been more anti-social than usual, preferring to sort the returns alone in the back and avoid almost all contact with staff and customers. This is the way he has dealt with Fermina's temporary absences in the past and I have no intention of messing with his coping strategy. The store might only be open for a few more days anyway, after which point his love life will no longer be one of my professional concerns.

When I arrive, Aldous is up at cash dealing with a customer issue. A pudgy guy in a vintage Leafs jersey is demanding fifty per cent off a computer book because the cover is slightly dented. Our standard markdown for damages is ten per cent. In extreme cases, we might go to twenty, but fifty is not going to happen, even if the book is radioactive.

Since the word got out that the store might be closing, two different kinds of customers have come out of the woodwork: the concerned community types looking to try and keep us open and the vultures looking to scoop a few deals off our soon-to-be carcass. This guy is clearly the latter. If he gets his fifty per cent, the book will be up on eBay five minutes later.

I leave Aldous to it and head back to the manager's office, where Sebastian is sitting with his feet up, slurping coke through a straw and flipping through the latest issue of GQ.

"Hey man! How was the shoot?"

I take off my jacket and throw it over the back of my usual chair. "Not too exciting. A lot of standing around. What are you doing here? Isn't Ebeneezer supposed to be closing tonight?"

"Didn't show up for his shift," Sebastian says. "Aldous called me. Always looking for an excuse to get out of the house, I am. Home? Home to what? A porter's uniform outside a restaurant and six penny tips from belching civilians for closing cab doors on their blousy women? Bugger that, brother Dravot."

"Didn't show up for his shift?" I say. "Ebeneezer has never missed a shift in his life. What—"

Wait a minute...could it be?

Aldous opens the door and steps inside. "Yeesh."

"Hey Aldous," I say. "You get rid of the cheapo Maple Laughs fan?"

Aldous nods. "That guy's been in before. I think he's the one damaging the books. We should ban him from the store."

"No argument from me. Next time he tries it, take his picture and post it next to cash."

The phone rings. Sebastian picks it up. "Peachy Carnahan's Palace of Carnal Exploration. Peachy speaking." His face reddens slightly. "Oh, hi Dante. Yeah, he's here. Hang on a sec." He leans over and hands me the phone.

"Hey Dante."

Dante sounds out of breath. "I need you to get over here right now."

"Over where? What's going on?"

"I'm at the hospital," he says. "Cynthia woke up. She wants to speak to us. Bring Aldous with you."

# -31-

Officially, Cynthia is only allowed one visitor at a time, but Cynthia is not the kind of person who allows anyone to tell her how many visitors she can have at a time.

Dante, Aldous, Mina and myself are crowded around her hospital bed for what is the first real manager's meeting we've had in months. Sebastian is temporarily in charge of the store until I get back. This was Dante's idea. Technically, I think it's a violation of Sebastian's bail conditions, as he is supposed to be in a "supervised" environment at all times. This would seem to preclude him from being the one doing the supervising, but what the hell do I care? Spending any time around Cynthia can leave you with the distinct impression that having spent your life in general observance of the rules of civil conduct has been a giant waste of time.

When the nurse tells us that there are too many of us in the room and that three of us will have to leave, Cynthia informs her that this is a critical board meeting that absolutely cannot happen over the phone and if the hospital staff interfere in any way shape or form, she will sue their sorry bureaucratic asses into a very large and uncomfortable legal hole in the ground.

"Plus, that male nurse kept groping my tits when I was unconscious," she says. "I was comatose, but I could still feel and hear everything that was going on in here. Wanna hit the headlines, Miss Nightingale? We'll do it in grand fashion!"

The nurse, who evidently prefers Cynthia in her unconscious state, grumbles something under her breath and leaves.

"Did they really grope you?" Dante asks.

"Probably," Cynthia mutters. "I've seen what happens to seniors in places like this. Not me. The sooner I'm outta here, the better."

"How long before that happens?" I ask.

Cynthia blows a raspberry through pursed lips. "Soon. This dipshit doctor wants to keep me around for a couple of weeks for *observation*. The only thing he's going to *observe* is me wheeling my ass out the front door right pronto."

"Is there anything we can do?" asks Aldous.

"That's very sweet of you to ask, sonny," she says, taking a sip from a clear plastic cup full of what looks suspiciously like margarita mix. "What's your name, anyway?"

"Aldous. Aldous Swinghammer."

Slurp. "Didn't you usedta look different?"

Aldous adjusts his collar and pats his hair nervously. "Uh, yes. I used to have longer hair."

"Right!" Cynthia barks. "You were that damn hippie kid! With the sandals. Always wore that fuck-ugly Derrida shirt. Smelled like a damn New Delhi dump. Well I must say you look a hell of a lot better. If I were 40 years younger without the bum hip, I'd ride your rocket all the way to Union station."

Aldous's face goes beet red. "Uh…thanks."

"You're a manager? What happened to that young actress chickie?"

"She had to quit," I say. "She got a job on a TV show."

"No shit?" Cynthia leans forward. "Anything good? Like CSI or the one with that skinny fucker used to be on *Blackadder*? Plays a doctor?"

"It's called *Royal Target*. It's on CBC."

Cynthia frowns. "I've seen that. Parts, anyway. No offense, but it's about as entertaining as a dog shitting on my lawn. Still, she's talented. I'm sure she'll get better gigs. You're boffin' her, right?"

I'm slightly more acclimatized to Cynthia's personality than Aldous and long ago learned not to take anything she says personally. She may seem crass, but she's also one of the smartest and most observant people I've ever met. She thinks life is too short to do anything other than speak her mind. Some people call this approach "radical honesty." Cynthia, naturally, has another name for it.

"We're engaged."

"Mazeltov," Cynthia turns to Mina. "Mina, how're you doin'? They finally got you on the right pills?"

Mina nods her head, looking terrified. "Uh, I think so."

"Speak up, sweet cheeks. I can barely hear you over the roar of these damn machines."

"Yes!" Mina shouts.

"And how's that batshit Manchurian Candidate husband of yours? Still in jail?"

Mina nods.

"Well, no offence, dear, but I hope he stays there for the rest of his goddamn days," Cynthia says. "Strolls into my store with a gun and shoots one of my best managers in the nuts–"

"Actually, it wasn't the nuts," I say. "But it wasn't far off."

"Just as well. You don't want Olivia deHavilland there leavin' ya for a guy who can still point north on the compass. That girl – Vanna or Olivia or whatever the hell her name is – the one who stopped him…"

"Ivanka," Dante says. "She left to start her own training centre."

"Shit, we're just losin' all our best people!" Cynthia complains. "Ah well, no surprise I guess. Speaking of which: to business."

Everyone in the room takes a deep breath while Cynthia slurps the remainder of her drink.

"As of one hour ago, my darling bitch of a daughter's plan to sell my own goddamn store out from under my formerly unconscious ass is officially dead."

This is greeted with an audible sigh of relief from the assembled.

"I'm sure she'll fight it," Cynthia continues. "Come up with some shit about how I'm still not in my right mind or whatever. Well, she can go fellate a French firefighter in frogtown as far as I'm concerned. She's not really my daughter anyway. She's adopted. Doesn't know it, though. I've been saving that one for the right time."

Dante and I exchange a glance. He has often told me that the Ackerman family dynamic is a twisted one and the less I know about it, the better. He is right. The more I find out, the more I feel like Jack Nicholson at the end of *Chinatown*. In the words of the immortal Spinal Tap lead guitarist Nigel Tufnel, there are certain mysteries best left unsolved.

"What about Walter?" Aldous asks. "Is he adopted, too?"

"Unfortunately no," Cynthia mutters. "That sorry lump of Nintendo shit is all mine. He has been a great disappointment to us. Marty had such hopes for the boy. Wanted him to take over the bookstore when he got older. Tried to give him a job. Remember that, Dante?"

Dante nods wearily. Walter's infamous 22 minutes on the job are the stuff of much speculation. The only people who know the details of his short career at Village Books are Dante and Ebeneezer, and nether of them are talking. One rumour has Walter being caught in the erotica section with *The Story of O* in one hand and his other hand nowhere to be seen. In another, he deletes the main inventory program off the office computer to make room for an online game from Japan called (and I'm translating here) *The Warrior of the Twelve Crotches*. The truth, should it ever come out, is probably much worse.

"All he wants to do is sit in the basement blowing shit up and whackin' off all over my bamboo interlock," Cynthia continues. "Well, he ain't doin' it on my dime any more. I don't care what he does. He can join the Peace Corps and sell butterfly nets and rubbers in Africa. Attracting bugs and blowing jizz is about all he's got any talent for anyway. Maude I'm not worried about. She's a conniving, backstabbing, mercenary little dyke, but at least she's got a brain in her head. More like me than her brother ever was."

Maude's a lesbian? Sometimes it's hard to tell if Cynthia is serious or if she's just talking. Is this something I want to ask about? No, it is not.

"The bookstore," Cynthia says, recapturing my attention. "The bookstore was Marty's thing. He loved that damn place. Quit his job. We got a small business loan and threw everything we had into it. Why? All because he read *Catcher in the Rye* when he was a kid and decided that ideas like that needed a place to live. A place where little kids could come in and always find Charlie Bucket and Charlotte's Web and Harry Potter and even all that stupid Twilight bullshit waiting for them. Never understood that series myself. What's with this one pouty little broad that every vampire and werewolf for a hundred miles wants to bone her? Meh. Not my thing.

"Anyway, after he had his stroke, I kept the place going. I'd put so much into it by then that there was no way I was just gonna walk away. And there was no way in hell I was gonna sell out to those greedy Umex bastards. Dante told me what you said in the papers," she says, looking at me. "Couldn'ta said it better myself. Good way to prove your nuts didn't get shot off after all. Cui bono? Liked that."

"Thanks."

She sighs. Her lungs sound raspy and ragged. "But the fact of the matter is, like the old black cops keeps sayin', I am getting too old for this shit."

"Old black cop?" Aldous says. "You mean, like, Danny Glover from the Lethal Weapon movies?"

"Thanks for the clarification there, Ebert," Cynthia mutters, looking pointedly at Aldous's gut. "Until I need another one, I'll ask you to stick your two thumbs up someplace I can't see 'em."

Aldous shifts his weight and looks at his feet. Since his makeover, he has actually lost a few pounds and done a better job of picking clothes that don't accentuate his paunchiness, so reminders of his weight are especially painful.

"C'mon Cynthia," Dante says. "That's not necessary."

"Apologies," Cynthia says, waving a hand. "I ain't exactly at my best. Anyway, like I was sayin'. It's time for me to step down and move somewhere nice while I'm still young enough to pop a few pool boys."

Mina raises her hand. "Uh, so you *are* going to sell the store?"

"That's right, sugarpop. But not to those toxic corporate maggots. Not as long as my name's still on the deed, anyway."

We all look at each other. I wasn't aware that there were any other buyers for the property in the running.

"Well, if not Umex, then who?" asks Dante.

Cynthia grins and shakes the icy slush at the bottom of her drink. "You."

Dante is more than momentarily confused. "Me?"

"The offer is open to all of you. What I'm proposing is that I sell Village Books – the building and the business – to the staff. You'll have to secure financing, of course, but I can help you with that. I can also make the payment terms extremely flexible. This is a big thing, so I don't expect you to answer right now. In fact, I'm not going to listen to anything you say right now. But I will need an answer by the end of the week."

This is not what any of us were expecting. What we were expecting was that she'd say the deal was kaput and everything was going to continue running along in a traditional business-as-usual fashion.

"Now I need all of you to clear out," she says, pulling a cell phone out of the bag on her nightstand. "I need to call to my daughter and I'm going to use a few words that shouldn't be uttered in polite company."

Where did she get a phone? Surely she isn't allowed to use one in here. Not that such things are of great concern to Cynthia. We all mumble vague encouragements and then shuffle out into the hall.

"Did she just say she wants us to buy the store?" Aldous says after the door closes behind him. "I mean, she really said that, right? I wasn't hearing things?"

"She did really say it," I agree.

"I can't buy a bookstore!" Mina bleats. "I'm still trying to figure out how to pay for a lawyer and a third party psychiatric evaluation for Nick!"

"Look, I don't think we should talk about any of this right now," Dante says, taking charge with uncharacteristic firmness. "Not now and certainly not here. Let's all head off and think about it and then I'll arrange a meeting later in the week to talk it over."

Aldous and Mina nod and head off in different directions. I hang back.

"Did you have any idea she was going to do that?" I ask. I'm still a bit shellshocked and need to talk it over with someone else in a position to appreciate how crazy it is. Dante however, appears distracted and barely aware of my presence.

"Huh?" he says, his eyes staring vaguely off into space. "Yeah. I mean no. Sorry. Look, I've got to get going. I'll talk to you tomorrow."

I watch him go and wonder absently if I should follow along behind to make sure he doesn't step off the curb right in front of a bus, but I should be getting back to the store. When I walk through the front door, Sebastian is standing in his usual spot behind cash.

"So what happened?" he asks, looking up from the latest issue of *Variety*. "Are we still Bedford Falls or should I put up the Pottersville signs?"

The store is quiet. There are a couple of people browsing in fiction and a mom with two girls upstairs in kids' books, but that's it. *'Round About Midnight* is playing quietly on the speakers. It is, in almost every measurable respect, a perfectly ordinary Sunday night.

I wander past the cash desk and stand staring mindlessly at the gift section, which is currently stocked with the last of the Christmas leftovers, all marked down by 75 per cent. After a moment, I realize that this was where I was standing when I was shot and quickly move back to cash.

"Hey man," Sebastian says nervously. "I hate to say this, but you're spooking the horses. What's happening?"

"Sorry," I mutter. "The good news is we're not being sold to Umex."

"All right!" he says, marking an invisible scoreboard. "Sebastian one, man zero. I take it from the way you phrased it that there is also some sort of bad news?"

"She wants to sell the store to us."

Sebastian looks momentarily confused. "What? You and me?"

"And everyone else. She wants to sell the store to the employees."

His temporary confusion becomes more permanent. "What? All of us? How does that work?"

"I don't entirely know."

"Perhaps her tumble in the shower has dislodged something of a cranial nature," Sebastian speculates. "Did they run a CAT scan while she was in there? Or an MRI?"

"She seemed compus mentis," I say. "But with Cynthia sometimes it's hard to tell. Any sign of Ebeneezer?"

"Not a dicky bird, guv'nor," Sebastian says. "I even tried calling his house like you asked. No answer."

I head into the manager's office to check the schedule. The last time Ebeneezer worked was three nights ago. Mina was closing that night. There's no point in asking her if he seemed out of sorts. Anyone who can spend any significant time around her husband has already had their barometer for crazy dangerously recalibrated. He isn't scheduled to work again until next week. I think I did that because I knew Fermina was leaving, which would put him in an even bigger funk than usual.

So…

Either he has run off to the airport after finally being overcome with a surge of last-minute romantic idealism.

Or…

He is lying dead on his living room floor.

I am giving serious consideration to throwing my coat back on and walking over to Ebeneezer's house to stare in through the windows (he lives only 20 minutes away and walks to work in all weather) when the phone rings. I grab it.

"Village Books."

"Good evening, my boy."

"Ebeneezer?" His voice sounds tinny and far away.

"Sorry to do this at the last moment, but I felt that I should notify you that I do not believe I will be in for my shift tonight."

"Where are you?" I can hear a lot of crowd noise in the background.

"Amsterdam," he says. "I am standing in front of a large board that is failing to communicate – in three languages I might add – precisely where I am supposed to be in fifteen minute's time in order to make my connector flight."

"Connector flight? Ebeneezer–"

"Ah! There it is. G22. And I am at…A15. Oh, son of a bitch."

"Ebeneezer…"

"Sorry, my boy. I must run. Literally. Give my regards to Miss Dashwood!"

And with a click, he is gone.

# -32-

The news that the Umex deal is off turns the store into something of a cause célèbre amongst the anti-corporate, Occupy and organic crowd, and over the next week, we see a lot more combat pants, piercings and home dye jobs than usually appear in this part of town. Somebody with an arty bent modifies the Umex logo slightly to make it look like a stick figure being crucified on a large letter U. and in no time spray-painted versions begin popping up on signposts and crude hand-drawn versions appear on denim jackets.

Most of the mainstream media drops the story after Cynthia wakes up, but we get a lot of play in alternative weeklies and online 'zines, many of which I must confess I've never heard of before. All of them want detailed accounts of how a small bookstore gave the finger to the big, evil, toxic waste-spewing multinational conglomerate and somehow didn't come away with said finger bitten off at the elbow.

None of them have any idea that the fate of the store is still very much up in the air. None of us have said a word about Cynthia's offer since the hospital visit. Anytime I try to raise the subject with Dante, he suddenly finds some pressing reason to leave the room. There have been a couple of times where I have actually considered throwing myself at his ankles and bringing him down like a wide receiver. After a while, I just give up.

Our meeting with Cynthia is tomorrow and I have no idea what's going to happen. I don't mind working here, but I don't really have any interest in buying an ownership stake in the place. I don't think Mina or Aldous have any ambitions in that direction, either. If Village Books closes down, they could just as easily get cashier or sales jobs in a million other places. The only one who might jump at the opportunity is Dante, but he's refusing to stand still for long enough for me to get any answers out of him.

Tired of chasing Dante around the store, I grab a cart out of receiving and head out onto the floor to begin pulling returns out of the biography section, where both Newt Gingrich and Justin Bieber's numbered days are finally up. There's something oddly satisfying about stacking these two side by side, boxing them up and sending them back to be returned to the pulp from whence they came. It's a reminder that their place in our cultural firmament is only transitory, and no matter how much they may annoy the crap out of us with their refusal to go away, today they are both BACKE and the choice is out of their hands.

No sooner have I finished than I become aware someone is standing behind me. Customers adopt many strategies to signal that they need help in a bookstore. Some walk up and ask for it. Some sidle up and stand there silently until you notice them. Some stand in front of a shelf making confused grunts. Some yell. Some snap their fingers. One actually used her cell phone to call the store and ask if there was anyone available to come into the fiction section and help her locate something in the Gs.

I stand up and am surprised to find myself staring at Julian Bartlett. The last time I saw him, he was talking to a cop while I was being carried out of the store on a stretcher.

"Ah!" he says. "I was hoping you'd be working today. I was just on my way by and thought I'd stop in."

"Hello again!" I say as we shake hands. "We just got in the latest shipment of your book. I was just about to put it out."

"Actually, I'm here to talk to you about your book."

"My book?" What the hell is he talking about?

"Yes," he says, noticing my confusion. "Did you not know that Ebeneezer had passed it along to me?"

"Ebeneezer?" My confusion deepens.

"Yes. He was my high school English teacher. Most kids were terrified of him, but he always encouraged me to write and so we got along quite well. I ran into him again on the night of the uh, reading. The one that was interrupted by that fellow with the gun."

"Right." I do remember the evening in question.

"How are you doing, by the way? I trust there were no permanent injuries? Some of the radio stations–"

"They got a bit carried away. I'm fine, thanks for asking."

"Excellent. Well, Ebeneezer told me that you're a writer as well. Insisted that I read your book. Dragged me back to his house so that he could give me his copy. Well, I just finished reading it last week. I would have done it sooner, but I had a few other author events to do outside the city."

I nod as if I have any idea what he's talking about.

"Terrific stuff," he says. "Now it's not something that my publisher would be interested in. They strictly handle non-fiction stuff, specifically sports and business books. But – if you don't mind – I've given it to my agent, Tom Prufrock."

Is he talking about what I think he's talking about?

"He's given it a read and is pretty confident that it's something he thinks he can place. Now, I've been trying to get a hold of Ebeneezer to get your contact information, but he doesn't seem to be answering his phone."

"I think he's stepped out of the country for a moment," I say, wondering if he made his connector flight or if he's still wandering around at Schipol looking for his departure gate. It is, after all, a big airport.

"Well, that would explain it," he says. "Did he go on vacation?"

"I'm not sure I'd call it that," I say. "It's a bit of a long story."

"Well, anyway, Tom would like to get a hold of you and as I had no way of doing that, I thought I'd stop in and see if you were working. I hope you're okay with that. I didn't know that he hadn't mentioned it."

Am I okay with that? Is he kidding?

"Oh yes, I'm okay with that!" I say, grabbing his hand and shaking it. "Thanks!" I give him my phone number and email address. He gives me his agent's card, which I examine like a prized relic before tucking into my shirt pocket. He tells me that he'll pass my contact info along to his agent, who will be in touch shortly.

The rest of the afternoon passes in a blur. Today is Leah's last day of shooting on *Royal Target* and I can't wait to get back and tell her the news. She thinks I've stalled out and I'm not going anywhere? Ha!

When I get back to the apartment, however, it immediately becomes apparent that I'm not the only one going places. Leah is rushing around talking on her cell phone and tossing items in a large open suitcase on the bed.

"Hey," I say, wondering what I have walked in on. "What's up? Is the FBI about to break down the door at any minute or something?"

"Hey babe!" she says, giving me a quick peck on the cheek and hanging up the phone. "You are NOT going to believe this!"

Believe what? I remind myself not to panic. "Oh, I don't know. I'm the credulous type. Try me."

She throws a hair dryer in her suitcase and takes a deep breath. "Okay, remember Jeremy said he was working on a big thing?"

"Sure do." Stay upbeat, I think. Perhaps this is not what it looks like.

"Well it turns out he got me a small role in the next Woody Allen movie. He's really good friends with the casting director. He sent her a tape of some of the scenes they'd cut together from *Royal Target* plus the commercial. It was nothing big. I had, like two words. I was supposed to be playing a manager in a bookstore, ironically. But then the most amazing thing happened!"

Dare I ask? "What happened?"

"Scarlett Johannson came down with hepatitis! I don't know how it happened. Her publicist is calling it the flu, so don't say anything. Anyway, I guess Woody saw the footage of me and liked it enough that he's considering offering the part to me instead! I have to go down there to meet with him tomorrow and if I get it, we start shooting on Monday! I mean, can you believe it? This is the greatest break I have ever gotten in my entire life!"

I am stunned. This puts my own news firmly into the anticlimax category. "Wow! That is...amazing. You're actually going to meet Woody Allen?"

"I know!" she says. "Woody Allen! Woody *Fucking* Allen! I mean, *Hannah & Her Sisters* is one of the reasons I wanted to be an actor. And now I might actually be an actor in one of his movies? I mean, to say nothing of what this might do for my career! No more sandwich bag commercials, that's for sure!"

She runs into the bathroom, pulls open the cabinet and starts tearing at it the way a lion might tear at a wildebeest.

"I haven't seen the script yet. It's an ensemble piece, I know that. So I wouldn't be, like, the star by any stretch of the imagination."

"Who else is in it?" I ask, having to shout over her slamming and grabbing.

"I'm not a hundred per cent on that," she says. "But I think one of the names is Matt Damon. Oh, and Paul Giamatti. Maybe Helen Mirren. I'm so nervous that I already barfed twice!"

"Wow. Yeah, that would probably do it to me, too."

She comes out of the bathroom carrying a stack of tubes and jars, which she pitches into the suitcase. "I have to be at the airport in ten minutes. I had to skip out on the after-party for the show. That's no big deal. Most people don't go anyway 'cause Callum Guthrie usually drinks too much and grinds his crotch against women's asses. He says he's just joking, but one of the makeup girls told me he grabbed her hand and stuffed it down the front of his jeans. She left nail marks in his nuts. How was your day?"

"Um, you know. It was good. I think I got an agent."

"An agent? How?"

I explain my meeting with Julian Bartlett and show her the card, which she barely has time to glance at before running off in search of her carry-on bag.

"Oh my God, hon! That's fantastic! Have you seen that little zip-up toiletries bag anywhere? The green one? I swear I put it in the drawer and now I can't find it."

I locate the bag in the drawer she just checked and hand it over. "How long will you be gone?"

She pulls open the closet, doesn't see anything she likes, and goes to the dresser instead, where she pulls out a couple pairs of pants and a small pile of shirts.

"Uh, well, that depends," she says. "If I get it, then, uh, three months."

"Three months!"

She goes back to the closet and grabs a large sweater. "The whole thing is shooting in New York. Well, with a couple of quickie location shoots in Florida."

"Three months?"

She comes into the living room and sits down on my lap, putting her arms around my neck. "I know that's a long time. But, you know, this is kind of going to be what my life is like from now on. It's not going to be a nine-to-five, home at the end of the day sort of deal. It'll be, you know, three months in New York and then six months in Los Angeles and then two weeks in Paris and a month in, I don't know, Budapest or somewhere."

A car honks its horn out on the street. She jumps up out of my lap and runs to the window. "Oh shit! My cab is here!"

I carry her suitcase down the stairs while she stuffs her passport, a few makeup items and a pack of gum into her carry-on bag.

"Christ, I hope I remembered everything," she says as the cabbie, a short man with grey hair and a sweater bearing the Italian flag, loads her suitcase into the trunk.

"I think you managed to fit half the apartment into that suitcase," I say, watching the cabbie struggle to get it over the edge of the trunk. "I wouldn't be surprised if I go back upstairs and find the bed and TV missing."

"I'll call you as soon as I get there," she says as we kiss goodbye. "Let me know what happens with this agent guy, okay?"

"Will do. Good luck!"

She pulls open the door and jumps inside, almost forgetting her carry-on bag. "Love you!"

"Love you too," I say, blowing a kiss in the frigid air as the taxi pulls away. I watch it make its way down the slushy street until it's out of sight, heading for some unseen point on the horizon.

# -33-

Sebastian advises me to sneak around to the side door so that the six-pack I am carrying won't be found and confiscated by the commandant, who is busy working on some sort of teacher evaluation report in the office upstairs.

"Ah, lifeblood!" he says, taking one of the beers and popping it open. "Come on down into my lair."

His lair is a small computer room in the basement where he is supposed to be taking the online correspondence courses he needs to finish his degree but is instead using to stream online movies and troll through dating sites. The computer is conveniently located right next to the cold room, where he has stashed an entire case of beer and three bottles of vintage champagne in a plastic tub that is normally used to hold camping supplies. He stores his black market urine somewhere in there as well.

"It's not much, but it'll do," he says of the space. "Want anything to eat?"

"No thanks." I have no appetite whatsoever. "How are things going with your case?"

Sebastian takes a seat on an old armchair and pushes it back into full recline. "Can't complain. In fact, things are looking decidedly up. The officer who arrested me is being investigated on corruption charges. It seems that he has a hard time keeping his pecker pocketed when making prostitution arrests and one enterprising young lass even has video footage."

"So what does that mean? Are they going to toss the charges?"

"That's the ideal outcome," Sebastian says. "The sun hasn't quite risen over the Donleavy estate yet, but the sky is getting lighter."

"You went with the lawyer your mother got?"

He nods. "Where one's liberty is at stake, I thought it wise to spare no expense."

"Particularly when you're not the one doing the sparing."

He raises his bottle. "Cheers!"

I raise my bottle and take a swallow. I suppose it was naïve to assume that anything as insignificant as being arrested for multiple indictable offences would be enough to slow Sebastian down. If anything, it may have sped him up.

He lets out a burp. "So your good lady has left you, then."

"That's right." I kicked around the apartment for a couple of hours after Leah left, but in the end I just had to get out of there, so I called Sebastian and he invited me over.

"Still, it's for Woody Allen. No offence, old bean, but I'd probably leave you for Woody Allen, too."

"Thanks Sebastian," I say sardonically. "I knew I came here for a reason."

"Oh, cheer up!" he says. "It's only for three months, right?"

I take a deep chug. Should I get drunk? If not now, then when? Sebastian has an entire case in the next room. It would be civically irresponsible for me to let him drink the whole thing himself. In fact, I should drink as much of it as possible. For his own good, of course.

"Until the next job," I say. "She said it herself. She's not in a nine-to-five sort of gig. It'll be three months in New York and then four months in L.A. and five months in Rome and a year on the moon shooting Michael Bay's new vampire movie–"

"Is Michael Bay actually shooting a vampire movie on the moon?"

"No, but it sounded plausible, didn't it?"

"The dark side of the moon would be the perfect place for vampires," Sebastian muses. "Aside from the total absence of victims, of course. And the fact that it's two hundred degrees below zero, give or take. But they probably wouldn't care about that. Cold-blooded bastards."

"We should write it. I'm sure we could find a way around those problems."

"Vampires have never interested me much," Sebastian says. "Aside from the Freudian implications: you know, the ritualistic penetration of young maidens and the blood and so forth. I think girls like it because, for once, they're the ones leaking fluid on the men. No wonder it appeals to the puritan mindset. You have sex and you'll turn into the undead! Although, I suppose that's a fairly accurate description of my parents before they divorced."

"I never thought of it that way."

"But you knew that was what you were getting into when you got engaged, didn't you?"

"What, the undead?"

"No," he scoffs. "Her rather eccentric schedule."

I groan. "I thought I did…but…you know, she was still working at the store. I knew she wanted to be an actress, but the truth is, I just never…"

"…thought that she was going to succeed?"

I try not to look too guilty. "Something like that."

Sebastian sits back and takes another swig of beer. "Well, from where I'm sitting, I think you're looking at this all wrong."

"How so?"

"Allow me to illustrate a case study in perspective," Sebastian says. "I am currently a prisoner in my own basement whilst awaiting trial after being arrested by a man who solicits blow jobs from crack-addicted 16-year-olds. Now, my situation is not entirely uncomfortable. I have the necessities and have been able to avail myself of the black market to provide a few of the luxuries."

"Yes."

"You, on the other hand, are a man at liberty who is currently engaged to a beautiful and talented young woman who is, by all accounts, soon to become the next Hollywood It Girl."

"She's also pregnant."

Sebastian spits his beer out over the chair and then rushes to clean it up using Lysol and paper towels. His mother does come down here on occasion and he can't afford to leave visible traces or smells of his extra-legal activities. "She's what?"

Sebastian is the first person I've told about this. I don't know if Leah has told her agent, so it's possible that he's the only other one who knows. We didn't tell our parents because Leah hadn't decided whether or not she was going to keep it.

"Knocked up. With child. In confinement. I don't know. However you want to say it."

Sebastian finishes cleaning the armchair and then sniffs it to make sure there are no suspicious traces. He has also gotten beer on his shirt, which he immediately tosses into the laundry before pulling on a new one.

"Well congratulations are in order," he says. "Or are they?"

"I don't know. She initially said she didn't want to keep it, then she wasn't so sure. But now that she might have this big acting job…"

"Good Lord," Sebastian says. "No wonder you haven't been laughing at any of my premature ejaculation jokes of late."

I'm about to say something when I'm interrupted by four quiet taps on the basement window. Sebastian jumps to his feet.

"Excuse me a mo, old chap. That's my, er, connection, if you will. I'll be right back."

He turns and runs up the stairs. I hear him open the side door, then a hurried exchange in muffled voices. This is followed by two sets of footsteps coming back down the stairs. I perk up in my chair. I'm curious about the kind of person who sells urine to bail violators. Sebastian steps back into the room a moment later followed by a familiar face.

"Willard!"

Willard looks terrible. What I at first think are bags under his eyes are in fact bruises. On closer inspection, I see a band aid on his chin and a tear in his leather jacket that has been patched with silver duct tape.

"Willard is your black market connection?" I say, looking at Sebastian.

Sebastian shrugs like it should be obvious. Which, I suppose, it is. After a moment's thought, I'm not really as surprised as I think I am.

"It seems that our friend Willard may be in some trouble," Sebastian says.

I look more closely at Willard's injuries, which appear to be a few days old. He was supposed to work yesterday, but called in sick. The manager side of me kicks in.

"Willard, what happened? Are you okay?"

Willard takes a deep breath and shakes his head. Seeing my half-empty beer sitting on the table, he grabs and empties it in a single gulp.

"That was my beer," I observe weakly. "But I guess I was done with it."

"I'm in trouble, man," Willard says, rubbing his hands together nervously. "A lot of trouble."

I look at Sebastian, but he appears to be just as much in the dark as I am.

"Willard," I say. "Why don't you have a seat and explain the situation?"

Willard, however, cannot stop pacing. "Sorry to bug you guys here, but I don't know what else to do."

Watching him pace is making me nervous. "What's the problem? I'm sure we can figure something out." Of course, I'm not sure of anything of the kind, but this is the kind of thing you say to a person in this situation. Whatever Willard's problem is, I'm pretty sure we're not going to be able to do a damn thing.

"I need money," Willard says. "I thought I could get it together on my own, but that didn't work out."

"Okay," I say. "How much?"

He grits his teeth. "Twenty five thousand."

Sebastian and I look at each other. "Willard, what in the hell do you need twenty five thousand dollars for?" I ask.

Willard rubs his mostly bald head and peers skittishly through the basement window to make sure there's no one out there watching him. "Okay, look. The other place I work. The restaurant."

"The Serbian place?" I venture.

"Right. Well, there's this guy who comes in there from time to time. After a while, we sort of struck up this business arrangement."

"Uh huh." This is sounding worse by the minute.

"He had access to certain, uh…stuff…that he would bring in and I would, you know, sell for him."

I suddenly feel like I no longer want to be part of this conversation, but there's no leaving the room now. "What stuff, Willard? I take it you're talking about drugs?"

Willard nods. "Nothing huge. You know, not like huge amounts or anything. Not containerloads. Sometimes heroin, sometimes hash or cocaine or whatever. Just, you know, whatever came in that month. The idea was that I'd leave the receiving door unlocked and one of his guys would leave it back there for me to find in the morning. I'm always the first one in. The problem was, that night I guess I forgot to unlock the door, so he musta just left it outside."

Sebastian and I look at each other, both of us flashing back to the morning I caught him sleeping under the shelf. The morning we found the garbage bag that was not full of shoplifted books.

"So that was your brick of hash or heroin or whatever that was that we found behind the receiving room door that morning?" I don't phrase this as a question.

Willard nods.

"Jesus, Willard!" I say. "You're dealing drugs out the back door of the store?"

"No," Willard whines. "Well, a couple of times, maybe. It was mostly just a place to handle deliveries. He didn't want to do that stuff outta the restaurant since one of the owners got busted."

"So now you have to come up with twenty-five thousand dollars or what?" I ask. I'm finding it hard to come up with any sympathy for a guy who has been breaking the law for who knows how long right under my own nose. Under my direct supervision, in fact. "They break your legs? They take you out fishing on Lake Ontario and use you for bait?"

"And why are you coming to us?" Sebastian says. "I can't speak for my counterpart here, but I don't exactly happen to have a quarter cino stuffed in an envelope under the mattress."

"I dunno," Willard says. "I figured your mom has money, right? You were talking about all the cash she dropped on that Bay Street guy you've got representing you."

"Hiring a lawyer is one thing," Sebastian says. "She might have a different outlook if I were to ask her to recompense for twenty-five thousand dollars' worth of lost drug revenues."

"What about you?" Willard asks, looking at me. "Leah just got that big acting job, right?"

I laugh in his face. It actually feels good to do this. "Are you kidding? You're dealing drugs outta the back of the store – which we found and handed over to the cops, incidentally – and you expect *me* to give you the money to cover them?"

"Well, you found them!" Willard whines. "Technically it's your fault that all this is happening!"

I can't believe this guy. I'm so mad that I have to suppress the urge to pick up the beer bottle he just drained and hit him with it. "Are you kidding?"

"Who is this guy?" Sebastian asks. "Who were you doing this for?"

"He's just a guy," Willard says dismissively. "I think he's Ukranian. Maybe Estonian. He drops the stuff off at the beginning of the month. I sell it and get him the money by the end. Well, it's almost the end of the month. He was outta the country. He didn't know the shipment got *intercepted*." He uses this word like an expletive, looking at me as he says it. "He thinks I'm just holding out on him."

"Willard, why on earth are you selling drugs?" I ask. "You have two jobs! Was that really the only way to make extra money?"

"You don't understand!" Willard says, throwing his hands up. "Janine lost her job at the massage place after it got shut down by the cops. We needed the money to cover her tuition for the legal secretary course. She's almost done. And Raven needed all this stuff for preschool, which costs a fortune! There's only so many hours in the day, man!"

"The Black Rose was shut down?" Sebastian says, sounding disappointed.

"I guess they sent in some undercover cop who found out they were doing tugs for twenty-five and blows for fifty," Willard says, evidently more bothered by the fact that the place was busted than the fact that the mother of his child may have been involved in these activities. It is starting to occur to me that I have seriously misjudged this guy. I had always assumed that Willard was a slightly dopey but well-intentioned character, his delusions of rock stardom tempered by his responsibilities to his family. It now seems like his desire to meet those responsibilities has gotten the better of him. Or something has. He's still dopey, but he sure as hell isn't well-intentioned.

"That's too bad," Sebastian says. "It was a quality establishment."

"You *went* there?" I ask, looking at him in disbelief.

"Certainly," Sebastian says, looking nostalgic. "Sometimes the stress of the job requires a gentleman to blow off steam, as it were. Yvette was my favourite. She would whistle Edith Piaf songs. *Je ne regrette rien.*"

"She's working out of her house now," Willard says. "I can tell you where she lives–"

"Look, Willard," I say, doing my best to head off this interchange. "I don't think you're going to find anyone who can just hand you twenty-five thousand dollars in cash, so I think your only option is going to be to be to walk away and if necessary, go to the cops. Oh, and by the way, you're fired."

"Fired?"

"You just admitted to dealing drugs out of the store!"

"But I admitted to it, didn't I?"

"Like that's supposed to make everything okay?" I say. "What, you think you're two years old and I just caught you dropping jewellery down the toilet? It doesn't work that way. You're lucky I'm not calling the cops to repeat this."

"But I can't go to the cops!" Willard says. "This guy's serious bad news! He's like, international! He told me if I didn't pay up that he'd burn the place down!"

"Wait," I say. "What place?"

Willard looks at me like I'm an idiot. "Where else? The bookstore!"

There's a long pause during which none of us say anything.

"Sebastian," I say. "Please go upstairs and tell your mother that we're going to need to borrow her car again."

# -34-

We can see the flames from four blocks away.

Police cars have blocked the street off at each intersection, forcing us to abandon Sebastian's mother's car and walk the rest of the way. We can only get to within about fifty yards, where the fire department has set up barricades to keep the curious crowds back. People are actually climbing up on benches, cars and bus shelters to see what's going on. We walk back and climb up onto the bed of an empty pickup truck for a better view.

It's hard to say how long the fire has been burning. Flames are still shooting out of the upstairs windows of the bookstore. Two ladders have been extended to pour water down on the roof, where a giant column of smoke is disappearing into the night sky. The fire appears to have spread to the empty Café Ole on one side and the investment planning place on the other. The front window of the café has been smashed and firefighters are running in and out, possibly to make sure that there's no one still inside the apartments on the second floor.

The heat is incredible. Even fifty yards away, I can feel it. Every now and then, there's a crack and a boom and I get a blast of it not entirely unlike what you might experience when opening an oven to check on a thanksgiving turkey. The whole street is bathed in an overpowering orange light feebly interrupted at intervals by the red and blue flicker of the strobes atop the emergency services vehicles.

Having to roar over the wind generated by the fire, I ask one of the other bystanders how long the place has been burning. He just shrugs and yells something back that I can't quite make out. I think he says he only got there five minutes ago himself and has no idea.

The owner of the truck shows up and screams at us to get the hell off the back of her vehicle. We climb down and move several yards further down the street, where the heat isn't as bad and there's no crowd to block the view.

I count three separate TV news trucks set up on the periphery, each one with a crew set up to get the story. I check my watch. It's just after midnight. My only concern at the moment is that there was no one in the store when the fire started. Who was closing? Aldous. It was a weeknight. It probably wouldn't have taken him very long to get everyone out. The only one who might still be in there is Esmerelda. Did the fire department check to see if the bookstore was empty? I have no idea, but I have to find out.

I run back up to the perimeter and find one of the firefighters talking on a walkie talkie next to one of the trucks. He's too far away to notice me, so I climb over the metal barricade and grab him by the arm. I explain who I am and ask if they checked to make sure the store was empty. He tells me they did one sweep of the ground floor, but weren't able to check upstairs because they were worried that the roof was about to give way.

No sooner does he say this than there's a huge booming crash. A shower of sparks and debris shoots hundreds of feet up into the air and rains down on the street in what looks like slow motion. I feel something shoot past my head and look down to see a flaming copy of the Hollander translation of *Purgatorio* that must have just missed me by inches. The firefighter yells at me to get back behind the barricade and then starts barking commands into his walkie talkie.

I run back down the street at a crouch, like an infantryman dodging enemy fire, and find Sebastian standing more or less where I left him. Willard, I notice, has skedaddled.

"Jesus!" Sebastian says. "Somebody just said the roof collapsed or something! Did you see it?"

I shake my head. "No. But I think I did just see my life flash before my eyes. Where's Willard?"

"I think he thought you were going to talk to the cops and took off. Last I saw, he was heading down Bathurst in the general direction of the Mexican border."

"That asshole. I can't believe he was selling drugs out of the store."

"Ironically, it was probably our most profitable product line," Sebastian observes. "At least now we know where he got the money to buy all those vintage Superman comics and toys. How does it look up there?"

"Not good," I say. "They told me they checked the main floor, but not upstairs. From the sound of it, there no longer *is* an upstairs."

"I was just talking to a guy who lives in one of the apartments over there," Sebastian says, pointing. "He said he first saw the smoke about half an hour ago and called 911. The fire trucks only got here about fifteen minutes before we did."

A familiar figure emerges from the smoky darkness and wanders towards us.

"Aldous!" I shout, waving him over. He's followed by an extremely thin girl with short blonde hair that he introduces as Simone.

"'Allo," she says, shaking our hands with unusual formality.

"What happened?" I ask. "Did everyone get out okay?"

"Everyone got out fine," Aldous says. "I closed the store just like any other night. We were at Falstaff's when we heard the sirens. We came out to see where they were going and saw the sky looked strangely brighter in this direction, so we walked over to see what was going on."

"Well, now you know," Sebastian says flatly.

Aldous holds his hands up in disbelief. "What happened? Do they know yet? Is it faulty wiring or something?"

Sebastian and I exchange a look. Is this really the time to explain that the store was burned to the ground by an angry Ukrainian (or possibly Estonian) small-time mobster in retaliation for twenty-five thousand dollars of heroin (or possibly hash) that did not find its way to our former head of receiving for distribution? Is there ever going to be a time to explain that? To anyone?

Before either of us can answer, a car pulls up behind us and Dante gets out, followed by the man I recognize as Jann, his most recent blind date. I fill him in quickly with what details I was able to get from the fire chief on the walkie talkie.

"It's okay," Dante says. "I called Esmerelda. She didn't go in tonight because she threw out her back."

This, at least, is a partial relief. If Esmerelda wasn't in the place when it went up, then chances are nobody else was, either.

"We were just at Doug's gallery showing," Dante says. "Somebody told me it was on the news that the store was on fire. Holy shit."

All of us just stand there and watch silently as the flames shoot up into the sky illuminating the bright white flashes of thousands of loose pieces of paper propelled into the sky by the updraft. It looks like a snowstorm in reverse. It's horrible and beautiful at the same time – like watching a baby being born.

Aldous looks at it wistfully. "Damn. I was going to buy the place, too."

Everyone looks at him in disbelief.

"You were what?" I say.

"It's true," he says. "My trust fund had just been released. My family is quite rich, you know."

This is too much for me to accept. "Aldous, if you're rich, then why were you toiling for slave wages at a low-rent bookstore located in not the best part of town? Why weren't you, you know, living like Brett Easton Ellis in some New York loft with a string of supermodels on speed dial?"

He shudders. "I hate the family business. I don't understand investment banking. Plus I only just got the money a few months ago. I didn't know what I was going to do with it. To be honest, I was just thinking about giving it away to charity."

"Did I mention that I was thinking of starting up a charity organization?" Sebastian interjects. "The Sebastian Donleavy Foundation for the Promotion of the Imbibification of Quality Fermented Beverages? It's not registered, but I can personally guarantee that every dollar donated goes right to our front line mission."

Aldous grins. "I don't know about an endowment, but we can certainly set you up with a one-time donation in the form of a beer."

Sebastian bows. "We gratefully accept all bequeathments, regardless of their size. Although, that said, a case of Veuve or Dom wouldn't go amiss, either."

"Aldous," I say, "are you seriously sitting on millions of dollars that you now don't know what to do with?"

Aldous nods. "Well, not millions. I'm not sure how much is in there exactly. A million and a half or something. I was going to use it to buy the store, but now I'm not sure. I'm almost done my treatise. Maybe I'll start my own publishing company just for philosophical works."

"Well, at least one of us was interested in buying the place," Dante says, leaning out to watch as another fire truck races up and the cop cars pull out of the way to let it through.

"Wow, Dante," I say. "I thought you were the only one who would."

"Nope," he says. "I think I've had my fill of retail. Jann helped get me an associate professor's job at York starting in September. I was going to be quitting in April so that the two of us could do some travelling in Europe first. I just couldn't figure out how I was going to break the news to Cynthia."

So that's why he's been so quiet over the last few days. It seems that Dante has spent more time than most trying to avoid delivering unpleasant news to domineering women.

"Speaking of Cynthia," I say. "I take it that none of us has yet apprised her of this er, situation?"

"I called her," Aldous says.

Once again, I'm surprised. "You did?"

He nods. "I originally called her a couple of days ago to let her know I was interested in her offer to buy the place."

"You told her the place was on fire?" Dante asks.

Aldous nods.

"How did she sound?" Sebastian asks.

"Not too bad," Aldous says. "She said it was one less thing to worry about. Now she's just going to take the insurance money and move to Port au Prince."

"Well I'm glad she's happy," Sebastian says. "I, however, am now without gainful employment and am therefore legally confined to the house. And I have also lost a valuable source of contraband urine."

"Quoi?" says Simone, looking mystified. "Deed you just say zat you buy ze urine?"

"Indeed," Sebastian says. "And a reliable source is more difficult to locate than one might expect. Those most willing to sell are generally least likely to provide a clean, quality product. Perhaps I shall post a notice on the board at my mother's school. I'm sure she has terrified those girls into abstinence from all intoxicants and other social indiscretions. It's probably as pure as the virgin Mary's tears."

"Just remember, Sebastian," I say, "if you ever need a character witness at your trial, do not call on me. I know too much."

"That's all right," Sebastian says. "Perhaps I'll finally start up that witness-for-hire business we talked about. I'm sure our friend Willard would jump at the chance if the Estonians don't find him first."

"The who?" asks Dante.

I consider whether or not to tell Dante how the store came to be on fire. Maybe I will at some point, but this doesn't seem like the right time. It's a strange thing to watch the place you've spent most of the last three years go up in smoke. Part of me is sad, part of me is relieved, and part of me just can't believe it's happening.

I feel like I have opened my front door and stepped out into outer space. Tomorrow I was supposed to get up at 6:30, shower, dress, and eat some sort of breakfast. There's nothing of a breakfast nature to eat in the apartment, so normally I would stop at Café Olé, which I can't do because it's closed (and currently on fire). Then I would open the store, do the deposit, power up the computers and finish working on the last of the returns, a large skid of which is currently sitting in receiving awaiting a 9 a.m. pickup that will now never come.

Now I'm not going to be able to do any of those things. What on earth am I going to do with myself? I feel completely untethered from all of the things that used to keep me in place. It's a little terrifying.

"Well," Dante says after a while. "I don't think there's a hell of a lot more we can do here. I suggest we go to Falstaff's. The first round is on me."

"Yes!" Sebastian says, pumping his first in the air. For him, free drinks are always a source of excitement, no matter the circumstances. I wonder if he has enough urine stockpiled to cover himself until he can locate another source. "Hey Aldous, you guys need a ride?"

"Sure," Aldous says, putting an arm around Simone, who doesn't seem to mind. "We walked over and it's pretty cold. Well, when you're not standing next to the store anyway."

They all begin moving back to their cars. I hang back.

"Gentlemen," I say. "I'd just like to say that it's been a pleasure and an honour working with you. Please give my regards to Mickey. I'm sure I'll see you all again sometime. But right now, there's somewhere else I've got to be."

Sebastian walks back over and shakes my hand. "Best of luck, brother Dravot. Remember, it's detriments like us that built this bloody empire. Give my regards to your good lady."

"Hats on, Peachy," I say. "If you do need a good witness, I know a fellah who can supply them at very reasonable rates."

Dante comes over and we shake hands. I ask him how his mother is doing.

"Not well," he says. "The irony is that we're getting along better now than we ever did. Jann and I went to visit her last night. She says she's determined to last until the wedding."

"You're getting married?" I ask, surprised.

"We haven't planned anything, but it's my mother," he says, shrugging his shoulders. "She has sworn on her deathbed that she's going to see me married before she dies. If it's not to a woman, then she's willing to settle for the next best thing. Lucy went to visit the other night and she didn't throw her out of the room, so I guess that's progress."

Aldous and I shake hands and he pulls me into a slightly awkward semi-embrace. He smells like cologne and smoke.

"Thanks," he says. "And thank Leah, too. If it wasn't for you guys, I would have never met Simone. Or at least she would never have agreed to go out with me."

"Oui," Simone says, pecking me on the cheek. "Merci beaucoup."

"Will do," I say. "Send me a copy of your treatise when it's finished."

"It's actually a video piece," Aldous says. "Simone has been helping me edit it. Once it's done, I'm going to upload it to YouTube one chapter at a time."

"What's it called?"

"I'm calling it *Scarlett Johansson Naked – An Epistemology*."

"Well, I'm sure you'll get a lot of hits."

With a final wave, I step off the curb and start walking. The world behind me is just smoke and ashes and I think I've spent enough time watching it burn.

And so…

It's been over a year since Village Books burned to the ground. The fire marshal pegged the blaze as suspicious and started a full investigation. The investigation determined that not only was the fire deliberately set, it was set by somebody who wasn't terribly good at arson. Had the building not been full of flammable material, it might have survived the blaze.

At that point, the police became involved and were able to determine that the fire was not set by Willard's Ukranian (or Estonian) drug connection. The person who actually carried three canisters of gasoline (purchased using a credit card only three blocks away) in through the receiving door using a copy of the master key was none other than Walter Ackerman, Cynthia's pudgy gamer son and shoplifter-in-chief. Subsequent inquiries revealed that young Walter carried out said task on the orders of his sister, Maude, who had taken out a sizable insurance policy on the property in her own name while her mother was in a coma, presumably as a backup in the event that the sale to Umex fell through.

Not a complete idiot, Walter pleaded guilty to a lesser accessory charge in exchange for testifying against his sister, who is facing disbarment, a raft of criminal charges, and a sizable civil suit filed by her mother. I don't imagine that conversations around the Ackerman family dinner table will be any less strained in the coming months. Except for Marty, of course, as long as he gets his ribs.

Despite her words to the contrary, Cynthia sold the bookstore site to Umex. Three weeks after the sale was finalized however, the company filed for bankruptcy. Apparently, most of their foreign infrastucture projects – power plants in India, movie theatres in China, a geothermal station on the Balearic Islands – existed solely on paper. One of the only things that did actually exist was their waste treatment facility in Honduras, the lawsuits brought against which were instrumental in tipping the company over the edge and into the financial abyss.

While executives fled into the hills with their offshore account numbers hidden in small laser ampules in their backs, the court sold off the company's traceable resources to pay its many creditors. One of the smaller purchases was made by the scion of a distinguished family of Swiss industrialists, whose plans to turn the space into a multimedia company/think tank/gallery puzzled just about everyone who bothered to ask.

After the store burned down, I walked home, packed a suitcase, and flew to New York. One thing I will say for Manhattan is that it's almost impossible to get lost. If the numbers are increasing, you're going north. If they're dropping, you're going south. If you hit water, you've gone too far east or west. If they're just letters, you're in Alphabet City and should probably turn around, as it's not the best part of town.

Wanting to surprise Leah, I called the casting agency and pretended to be Jeremy's assistant. I told them I was setting up a photo shoot with Entertainment Weekly and needed to know when and where I would be able to track Leah down after her meeting with the legendary Woody. Amazingly, this worked. That's how I came to be standing on West 57th Street holding a bouquet of blue roses when she emerged from the Brooklyn Diner on a snowy Thursday afternoon.

We got married the next day. Jeremy's actual assistant was able to help us with the details and Jeremy himself acted as one of our witnesses. The other was – yes, I'm going to name drop – Matt Damon, who had met Leah at the casting meeting and personally encouraged the Woodster to hire her on for the role, which he did.

Matt is a hell of a nice guy. One night after shooting, we found a bar in Greenwich that serves Scrumpy Jack and got loudly pissed in the corner with Paul Giamatti, who insisted we learn all the words to the Pogues' *Turkish Song of the Damned* before we left. I remember most of the first two run-throughs, but after that, things are a bit fuzzy.

We spent the next three months in New York, where I bravely learned to ride the subway and even took it all the way into the Bronx once because I got on an express train by mistake. The production paid for the cost of an apartment on the upper east side near a great produce market, where Leah would regularly send me to purchase obscure food items and I would routinely come back with something that was close to but not exactly what she had asked for (I didn't know, for example, that there was a difference between celeriac and celery).

Once production wrapped, we went on a honeymoon that took us to London, Paris, Rome and Barcelona, where I was able to watch my beloved Barça hammer Real Madrid 5-0 in person at the Camp Nou. We also stopped by the newly opened Café Fermina in the village of Luceno del Sol, where I can highly recommend the paella even if the service is a little on the crotchety side.

After that, we returned to Toronto, where Leah squeezed in a role in a Ridley Scott science fiction action movie playing the hot leader of a group of kickass space marines before taking time off to give birth to our daughter, Charlotte.

Being a dad is the biggest adjustment I've ever had to make. My days of being a selfish, come-and-go-whenever-I-want sort of guy who sleeps until noon after getting pissed with movie stars are done, at least for now. Charlotte's needs are simple. She wakes up about every three hours or so requiring a diaper change and a bottle, the contents of which she occasionally regurgitates with surprising force. She has her mom's red hair and my blue eyes, so it makes sense that she would also inherit my tendency to puke after drinking too much. It's probably a recessive trait.

I've been taking most of the night feeds to take the pressure off Leah, who is working eight hours a day with a personal trainer to lose the baby weight in order to be ready to start shooting a historical drama with Clint Eastwood in London this summer.

I know. It's surreal. Jeremy warned that when things start to take off, they do it so fast that things seem to happen in future tense, so you'll suddenly find yourself working with icons before your last project has even opened. Matt Damon isn't so far apart in age from us, so that wasn't as difficult as meeting the big man. I remember sitting in his surprisingly small and spartan office on the Warner lot and watching him bounce my daughter on his knee while he explained to my wife why he thought she needed to be in his movie and thinking: "Holy fucking shit! I am sitting in a room with Clint Eastwood! Gahhhhh!"

Charlotte was evidently feeling the same way, because she barfed on his leg. Fortunately, he didn't take it personally and Leah still got the role.

I've managed to keep in touch with most of the old gang. Dante's mother lived long enough to see her son get married, even though she couldn't attend the actual ceremony. After her death, Dante and Jann took her ashes to Sicily where, in accordance with her wishes, they were scattered in her sister's swimming pool. Needless to say, the two of them did not get along. Dante is now teaching a course called "The Poetry of Protest" and no longer spends most of his days looking for diseases on WebMD. He and Jann have started the process to adopt a baby from Ethiopia. Dante asked if I would be willing to write a character reference letter for him to submit with the application, which I was more than happy to do.

Most of the serious charges against Sebastian were dropped. He pleaded guilty on the lesser counts of trespassing, destruction of property and public intoxication, and was sentenced to 140 hours of community service. He was originally supposed to serve this out by reading to old people at a senior's home, but was asked to leave by the activities co-ordinator after he inserted one too many nonexistent and racy passages into Lucy Maude Montgomery and Len Deighton novels. Many of the residents of the Sleepy Valley Lifestyle Community were extremely sorry to see him go and made repeated requests that he be reinstated.

He finally finished his degree and recently accepted a job teaching English to 14- to 18-year-old girls at a juvenile detention centre in Bangkok. It's a rare thing that anyone lands their dream job right out of school. In five years, I fully expect him to be living in a walled compound deep in the jungle with at least 12 wives and a growing population of suspiciously light-skinned children.

Mina's husband was determined not psychologically competent to stand trial and remanded to a psych ward where, I hope, he will stay for some time to come. Mina got a job working for the Toronto Public Library and self-published a volume of her own poetry called "Running Through Sunflowers On The Sun", which included her ode to the avocado and did not go into a second printing. She still visits her husband every day and is optimistic that he will improve.

Willard dropped off the grid for a while and resurfaced as a hip hop/metal artist named Fatal D. The video for his song "MonkeyFukka" became a minor internet sensation and raised the ire of PETA by appearing to show a woman having sex with a gorilla. Willard was able to demonstrate that the gorilla was in fact him in a suit. The woman was identified as Yvette Desormaux, a former employee of the Black Rose gentlemen's salon and spa. The notoriety generated sufficient interest to launch a minor North American tour, which came to an ignominious end at New York's JFK airport when Willard was caught trying to sneak through security with an albino boa constrictor in his hand luggage. Customs officials were not swayed by his argument that he had no idea how it got there. The snake was impounded and Willard was unceremoniously returned to Toronto on the next available flight.

Mother Teresa sold all of her possessions and moved to a compound northeast of Algonquin Park after being advised by the head of her church that the rapture was going to take place at the dawn of the vernal equinox. After residents of a nearby town raised concerns about unidentified weapons being sighted within the encampment, it was raided by the RCMP, who found no weapons, just a crowd of 220 men, women and children who all testified that their leader had been taken up by "celestial lights."

The celestial lights were in fact the navigation lights on the Boeing CH47D Chinook helicopter the leader used to catch a ride to a nearby airport, where he caught the first in a series of connector flights to Venezuela. Like all true believers, Mother Teresa is still convinced that he will return one day and deliver unto her the two-storey semi-detached condo unit (or cash equivalent) she donated to help the church with its financial needs in the life to come. She is currently working as a receptionist for a paediatric dentist until this comes to pass.

Lolita also fulfilled a long-frustrated dream and got a job as a management trainee at Iterations. That lasted until the company was sold off as part of the Umex bankruptcy and her store was converted into a big box pet supply centre. She stayed on as assistant manager of exotics until a mass scorpion breakout forced the store to be shut down by the ministry of consumer affairs. By the time it re-opened, her probationary term had expired and her employment contract was not renewed. She still works regular greeting shifts at the Carlton Brothers Funeral Home, where she is regularly mistaken for the deceased.

Miroslav decided to supplement the income lost as a result of the closure of Village Books by volunteering for more elaborate drug trials. The bizarre side effects that resulted from his testing of an experimental human growth hormone were published in the August edition of the Lancet. The Portugese researcher who first identified the condition gave it a name that translates roughly as "cannon ball testes", but it is known more colloquially as Mirsolav's Disorder. Miroslav has taken advantage of his limited notoriety by choosing to star in several Croatian-financed adult films, where he has adopted the name Mighty Elephantballs.

Ivanka opened her own fitness centre and released two very successful fitness and self-defence DVDs. The last I heard, she was in talks with Nike to develop her own brand of "Defiant Woman" workout and protective gear. When she received her bravery award at city hall, a frisky city councillor surreptitiously patted her ass and received three broken fingers for his trouble. His threats of a lawsuit quickly petered out after no fewer than five people came forward with cell phone pictures of his clumsy attempt, one of which graced the front page of the Sun under the headline: "Coun. Gregory Grab-Ass!" It is widely assumed that he will not be running for re-election.

Like almost all available space in the city, the former Village Books site was bought and turned into condominiums. The bottom two floors have been set aside for commercial operations. Aldous bought a small chunk of space on the second floor, roughly where kids' books used to be, to create the Swinghammer Centre, which is a combination art gallery, bookstore, "think space" and café. Today is the grand opening and, since we're temporarily back in town, Aldous asked if we could stop in to say hello and see what it's about.

The Woody Allen movie opened a week ago and Leah's getting a lot of positive buzz about her role – even Oscar buzz, which she is doing her best to ignore. Now that she's becoming more well-known, it's getting harder and harder for her to move around without being recognized. Jeremy told her that things are only going to get crazier, so she better start adapting to it. I haven't seen paparazzi hiding in the bushes trying to snap pictures of us yet, but I am starting to get more paranoid about going out, particularly with Charlotte. I guess barfing on Dirty Harry comes with a price.

Fortunately, there are no cameras around for the opening. The place is flashier and more high-tech than I was expecting. The walls are lined with monitors displaying all ten volumes of *Scarlett Johansson Naked – An Epistemology* at once. It doesn't seem to be so much of a philosophical statement as it does a video installation piece, the point of which is, I admit, lost on me. There are no pictures of the *Lost in Translation* star in the altogether that I can see, just a lot of shots of men in bowler hats while a voice, which sounds like Simone's, mutters unintelligibly in the background.

The café section has a long light table where customers can use its touch screen functionality to page through newspapers, update their profiles, watch concerts and play video games while they drink their coffee. The bookstore section offers a small selection of philosophical titles available in hard copies and e-reader versions. Behind that is the gallery, which features a series of installation works that, to my untrained eye, look like birth control devices fashioned by some primitive Amazonian tribe. The price tag on the nearest one is $2,500. I hope he isn't expecting us to buy any of these things.

"You made it!" Aldous shouts as we walk in. He looks an entire order of magnitude slicker than the last time I saw him. In the past year, he has gone from grimy deadhead to someone who could pass for an interior design consultant in Chelsea. He's wearing a sparkly black shirt with the sleeves rolled up just below the elbows and a wide collar. His hair is longer and styled in a boisterous, floppy part. He even has some designer stubble.

"Egad," I whisper to Leah as Aldous makes his way over. "Dr. Frankenstein, meet your creation."

She gives me a dismissive glance and then throws her arms around Aldous. I am prevented from doing likewise owing to the fact that I am carrying our baby daughter in a Snugli. For the moment, she's asleep and drooling contentedly over my number 10 Barça jersey. Leah asked me to wear something different, but this really is the perfect fabric when it comes to drool, sweat, puke and other unexpected expectorations.

"The place looks great!" Leah says, looking around.

"It does," I agree. "Although it's strange to think that the spot where we got engaged is now an establishment providing designer herbal enemas to upper middle class white women."

"You mean *Lavage*?" Aldous says, pointing down at the floor to indicate the store directly beneath us. "Actually, they do them for men, too. The Perrier and rosemary supercleanse is just–"

"Thanks, Aldous," I say. "You really don't need to say any more."

"It's so strange to think that kid's books used to be right over there," Leah says, pointing to the gallery area. "I spent so much time reorganizing all of it and now it's like it was never even here."

There's a note of sadness in her voice. I can tell she's thinking about impermanence and the fleeting nature of things and mortality. I give her shoulder a squeeze. "Hey, if the dinosaurs could be here right now, I'm sure that, after the carnivorous ones ate most of us, they'd be looking around wondering what in the hell happened to their cretaceous forest."

"Thanks, dear," she says. "You always know exactly what to say to make me feel better."

"Are we the only ones?" I ask. "From the store, I mean?"

Aldous nods. "Mina said she'd come, but you know. Dante's in Palermo. Sebastian's in Thailand. I think Willard's still in jail. Something to do with operating a mobile bawdy house. I'm not too clear on the details. He called me at three in the morning to ask if I could post bail for him and some girl named Yvette. Said he also needed five hundred bucks to get a 1998 El Dorado out of impound. Simone answered the phone."

I laugh, relieved that I never gave Willard my new cell number. "What did she say?"

"Said he had the wrong number and hung up," Aldous says, grinning. "Let's see, who else? Ivanka has some charity mixed martial arts event or something. She's fighting three guys at a time to raise money for breast cancer."

"So when did you decide to switch from philosophy to art?" Leah asks, looking at the video wall.

"I haven't, really," Aldous says. "The Epistemology is racking up a lot of views on YouTube. I'm hoping to parlay some of that into some government and private sector contracting opportunities to create new, thinking spaces. Imagine a building that actually absorbs, projects and displays the moods and ideas of the people inside it."

"Hmmm," I say. "I think that would make BMO Field the saddest place on earth. Well, after the Air Canada Centre. What kind of images do you think they'd project in a place like *Lavage*?"

"Please excuse my husband," Leah says. "He's been doing a lot of the night feeds and I'm afraid his brains are more addled than usual."

We don't stay too long. There really isn't that much to look at and we have to carefully plan our excursions around Charlotte's feeding schedule. It's an unseasonably warm April day, with temperatures in the mid-twenties. In a couple of weeks, we'll be packing everything up and moving to the grey skies of London, so I want to enjoy as much sunshine as I can while we're here.

We wander past my old apartment. According to the buzzer, it's now occupied by someone named Chong, but it still looks the same from the outside. From there, we head over to Falstaff's for something to eat. After all the changes made to my old workplace, I'm pleased to see that my favourite pub is still the same, although the clientele is a little different. As more condos go up, so have the numbers of well-heeled yuppies, at the expense of the students and nostalgic ex-pats. I remark on this to Leah as we take a seat at one of the booths.

"Hey, that's us now, too," she says. "We're not exactly poor students any more."

It's true. Leah isn't making astronomical sums of money yet, but she's still making more money for four months of work than I ever envisioned having in one place at the same time. I can't complain, either. James Prufrock (the agent that Julian Bartlett recommended) managed to get a publisher to pick up my book, which is supposed to come out in September. Jeremy then sold the option on the film rights for more money than I would have made if I worked at Village Books for the rest of my life. I no longer dislike Jeremy as much as I used to. I even got to write the first draft of the screenplay, which was promptly rewritten by David Mamet and twelve other people. I plan to start work on the sequel as soon as Charlotte starts sleeping through the night.

"You know," I say as we settle in. "You never told me why you changed your mind about keeping the baby."

"It was a no-brainer," Leah says, settling Charlotte comfortably into the crook of her arm as I get a bottle ready. "I'm a feminist and staunchly pro-choice and all that, but what it boiled down to was that a movie or a TV show or a commercial just wasn't a good enough reason. I mean, isn't she better than any movie you've ever seen in your life?"

I look closely at my daughter, who has an oddly pensive look on her face. Is that how she's going to look at me in 16 years when I ask her where she thinks she's going dressed like that? "Yes. She really does tie the room together."

Mickey comes by to take our order and coo over Charlotte, whom he compares favourably with the most attractive women in the Donegal Ladies' Auxiliary, whatever that is.

"Unfortunately, there isn't a drop o' Scrumpy to be had in the place," he says.

"What?" I ask, even now sensitive to the possibility of some perceived Scrumpy violation. "Really?" Did we just sit in the wrong section? Is it because we're yuppies now? Because we have a baby? Whatever it is, I'll fix it.

"I talked to the distributor this mornin'," Mickey says. "He told me some fellah named Matt Damon ordered the last five kegs in the country. Won't be able to get any fer at least a month. Who the hell's Matt Damon?"

It's probably not necessary to mention that Mickey doesn't go to many movies. The last thing he saw in a theatre was an old Kevin Spacey film called *Hurly Burly*, which he went to entirely on the basis of a misunderstanding.

"What did you guys get up to the night you went out drinking with Giamatti?" Leah asks. "I had to get up early to shoot the next morning and you came breezing into the apartment at four a.m. singing what sounded like the Notre Dame Fight Song."

"I would love to answer your question, my dear, but am precluded from doing so by the fact that my recall of these events is nebulous at best."

Leah gives me a suspicious look. "As a writer, you should know that's not really the right context for the word *nebulous*."

"Shhh! Charlotte doesn't need to hear that I was plastered. She needs to be able to look up to me as a responsible parental role model."

"A responsible parental role model who fell into bed fully clothed, mumbled something unintelligible about making a sequel to *Annie Hall*, groped my left boob, and then promptly passed out."

"Are you sure it was me? It may have been Giamatti. None of us could really remember our addresses."

Mickey takes our order for a couple of Dead Joe's Cask Ales and heads back to the bar.

"Don't worry," Leah says. "I'm sure there'll be plenty of places you can get Scrumpy in London."

"I wouldn't be so sure. Sounds like that bastard Damon's trying to corner the world market. This is a seriously destabilising move. We need to communicate that all options are on the table at this point. I don't think diplomacy will do it."

Charlotte rubs her eyes and starts making noises. "Somebody's waking up!" Leah says, bouncing her gently. "You got that bottle ready?"

I pass over the bottle, which my daughter begins sucking down with lightning speed. As this can often be a prelude to barfing, I check the diaper bag to make sure we're well stocked with towels and wipes.

"So were you sorry to see that the bookstore was gone?" Leah asks, angling Charlotte slightly upwards to slow her intake slightly. "You went there almost every day for all those years and now it's just...not there anymore. Are there even any photos of it anywhere?"

"There were some photos in the paper, but those were just outside shots of the building. There are probably others. It was there for over 30 years, which isn't a bad run." I think that's probably longer than the Swinghammer gallery will last, but who knows?

"Yeah, but aside from a few photos and the memories of the people who worked there, it's almost like the place never existed, you know?" Leah says, shivering. "I think that's one of the reasons I wanted to be an actress, especially in TV and movies. Just so that, even when I'm gone, there'll be proof that I was here. I won't just pass through this big net of existence without even being noticed."

"It's funny," I say. "That was one of Aldous's theories. He said that the prime motivator for all human action was the paralyzing fear that seven billion people have no idea you exist."

"I think he's got something there," Leah says. "What did you think of the, uh, gallery?"

"I don't know. I hope they make a go of it. He certainly has the money to keep it running. For a while, anyway. I'm not sure exactly what he means by transforming public spaces, but he has certainly transformed himself."

A young couple wander in and start looking around for a place to sit. I see the woman, who appears to be in her mid-twenties, do a double-take as soon as she spots Leah. She then elbows her date in the ribs and gestures in a way that she thinks we won't notice. His eyes also lock on Leah. He shakes his head and mumbles something, then pretends to keep looking for a table. His date is evidently having none of it. She nods her head and obviously tells him to look again, which he does.

Uh oh, I think. Here we go. I had forgotten that the Woody movie was playing at the Prestige down the street. The matinee probably just finished and I'd be willing to bet cash money that these two just came from there and are now arguing about whether or not the woman sitting in the booth feeding the baby is the same one they saw up on the screen only ten minutes ago. The woman, predictably, is the one who makes the approach.

"Hi," she says tremulously. "I hate to bother you, but we were just at the movies and, uh, are you Leah Dashwood? You are, aren't you?"

Leah nods and smiles. This has happened several times before and she has been unfailingly polite every time.

"Oh my God! I can't believe it's you!" the woman says, pulling her date forward. "We just saw the movie and now here you are! It's just…wow!"

She laughs awkwardly. Mickey arrives with our pints and gives the two of them a scowl that the woman is oblivious to.

"Did you enjoy the movie?" Leah asks.

"We loved it!" the woman gushes. "Oh my God! You were so incredible in it! And Paul Giamatti was so funny. And Matt Damon played such a heel! He doesn't usually do that!"

The last name registers with Mickey, who stops on his way back to the bar. "Who the fook is Matt Damon?"

The woman notices Charlotte for the first time. "Oh my God! You have a baby? I had no idea!"

Does this woman start every sentence with anything besides 'Oh my God!'? And why would she expect to have any idea that we have a baby? It's not like we forgot to include her in the birth announcement. I want this woman to go away now.

The woman reaches into her pocket and pulls out a cell phone. "I know you're super-busy, but would you mind if we got a photograph? Otherwise none of my friends will ever believe me!"

"Certainly," Leah says. Charlotte has finished feeding and she hands her to me. The woman hands her cell phone to her boyfriend and moves into the booth to sit next to Leah. For once, I would like to put my daughter's projectile vomiting talents to good use, but there's no way to hit this woman without catching Leah in the crossfire.

The first picture snapped by the boyfriend is ruled out by the woman because she's making "a weird face" and so a re-shoot is required. This apparently goes to her satisfaction and the two of them begin their retreat.

"Oh my God!" she says. "Thank you so much! Your baby is super-cute, by the way!"

"Thank you," Leah says.

"Are you in Toronto shooting another movie, or...?"

"No," Leah says. "Just visiting some friends."

"Hey, well, we're going to a party at my friend Lanie's place in Cabbagetown later. You guys should totally come if you can make it! She saw the movie before I did and thought you were just totally awesome! She was the one who told me to see it!"

"Thanks," Leah says, still smiling. "But we have to get home to put this little girl to bed."

"Oh, of course! Right! Well it was nice to meet you! I'm Jasmine and this is my boyfriend, Ryan, by the way."

"Nice to meet you, Jasmine and Ryan."

Jasmine lets out a little squeal, presumably because she just heard a movie star say her name and finally – finally – the two of them make their way to a table on the other side of the bar.

"Oh my God!" I say under my breath once the two of them are out of earshot. "My name is Jasmine and my friend Lanie told me that I'm, like, the most annoying celebrity stalker in, like, the whole world!"

"As long as she buys a ticket for my next movie, it was worth it," Leah says. "If I treated her like dirt, the word would get out so fast that half the world would know about it before you even finished your beer."

I throw a towel over my shoulder and start trying to get a burp out of our daughter. The best technique for this is to bounce her up and down slowly while drumming gently on her back with my fingers. If I bounce or drum too hard, she'll barf. If I don't bounce or drum quite hard enough, she'll wait until she lies down again and barf through her nose, which she will not enjoy any more than the next person (me). It's a delicate balance.

I've only been working for a moment when she burps and farts loudly at the same time. Leah and I look at each other and laugh.

"Wow, Charlotte!" she says. "Nice commentary. Oh my God, why couldn't you have done that two minutes ago?"

"It was indeed," I say. "Breaking wind at both ends simultaneous! Brother Carnahan would be right proud."

Leah takes a sip of her own drink. "You sure you're ready for this? Like Jeremy said, it's only gonna get crazier from here on out. Living out of suitcases. Travelling all the time. People recognizing me on the street. Privacy out the window. It's not exactly what people talk about when they talk about a normal life. It will involve a lot more people like Jasmine and Ryan and Lanie. Not to mention paparazzi. Guys who will call you a cunt on the street in front of your daughter just to get a picture of you with an angry face."

"I don't care about Jasmine or Ryan or Lanie. Them I can handle. What I can't handle is not being around you or Charlotte. As long as I have you two, then sign me up. I don't care if we're shooting a Michael Bay movie on the moon."

"Ugh," Leah says. "I think I'd rather do something where I'm not supposed to just stand in front of a slow-motion American flag in a halter top and Daisy Dukes for three hours, thanks."

Charlotte begins smacking her lips together in a way that often indicates she's still hungry. Leah starts putting together another bottle while I try to entertain her with funny faces. To date, my daughter has not found any of my funny faces to be funny. Since the food is evidently not coming as fast as she would like it, she starts to howl.

"I'm working as fast as I can, sweetie!" Leah says, mixing the formula together. "Can you do something to amuse her other than make scary faces?"

"Scary?" I say, feigning offence.

"Just try and keep her calm."

"I thought it was the stated policy of this administration that we did not negotiate with terrorists."

"Well, your hardline stance does not appear to be weakening your daughter's resolve."

Leah manages to mix the formula and gives the bottle a shake before handing it over. Charlotte immediately goes quiet and gets to work draining it as quickly as the first one.

"I'm not surprised she's hungry," Leah says. "She didn't eat as much as usual before her nap."

I look up to see Mickey making his way over to Jasmine and Ryan's table with a couple of familiar but rarely served drinks on his tray. He gives me a wink as he goes by.

"What's Mickey doing?" Leah asks. "What kind of a drink is that? Jeremy got one of those once when we were in here. It was terrible."

"It's an Englishman's Tits," I say, smiling. "I'll explain later."

THE END

# About The Author

Craig McLay was born in Scotland and asked to leave shortly thereafter. He currently lives in Guelph, where he spends most of his time trying to prevent his sons from changing gears while he is driving. This is his first book. Reach him at his Facebook author page (www.facebook.com/cmvillagebooks).

# Also By The Author

Deadline

www.ingramcontent.com/pod-product-compliance
Lightning Source LLC
Chambersburg PA
CBHW010830250626
47157CB00010B/3235